Devil's Salvation
Book Four of the Chosen Chronicles

Sirena Robinson

Supposed Crimes LLC • Matthews, North Carolina

Published in the United States.

ISBN: 978-1-938108-63-1

www.supposedcrimes.com

This book is typeset in Goudy Old Style, licensed by Ascender Corporation.

Devil's Salvation

Sirena Robinson

Other Books by Sirena Robinson

The Chosen Chronicles

Devil's Dilemma
Devil's Despair
Devil's Redemption

Coming Soon

Nephilim Rising
Nephil's Destruction
Nephil's Destiny

PROLOUGE

"What happens next?" Amaya bounced excitedly in her bed as Gabriel finished the story. "Does Gage become a human? Do Alaria and Gabriel end up together or does she end up with Braxton?"

Gabriel looked out at the lightening sky. "I've kept you up all night, child. You should get some sleep while you can."

Amaya shook her head. "I'm not tired. Tell me the next part. The third task, where they have to cast out the demons. I want to know if they succeed or fail." She bounced out of the bed and paced the room dramatically. "I also want to know whether the Gabriel in the story is you."

Gabriel smiled. "You told me when I got here that you thought it was another Angel with my name."

"I've been thinking. What're the odds of there being two Angels with the same name? I'd think God would want to avoid the confusion." She looked at him pointedly. "If it is you, that was a really crappy thing that you did to Alaria. She didn't deserve it."

He shook his head sadly. "No, she did not." He sighed. "You're ready for the next part, aren't you?"

Amaya smiled brightly. "That's what I've been trying to tell you! I've been hearing these stories all my life, and only now have you started telling me new ones. I want to know the ending, Uncle Gabe. I want to know what happens."

Gabriel nodded. "Okay. You already know that the third task is the hardest, and you know from the last story that Lucifer is trying to find a way to burst out of Hell. In order for them to succeed at casting out demons, they have to collect the wings from the original Archangels and perform the ritual before Lucifer escaped."

"How could Lucifer break out?"

"Garrick had been working on a way since they pried open the gates. There is another door to Hell, the one Father Dooley was looking for, that was only ever used to put Lucifer there. He can only come out through the door he was put in through. If the Devils find that door and manage to open it, Lucifer could come out."

"I thought that the second task sealed the doors shut for good."

"It's complicated." Gabriel smiled. "There are three doors. The main Gates, which Aradia sealed shut when she killed Garrick. The back-door, which is what Alaria opened in order to allow Greer to enter Hell. That door is kind of like a one way. Only souls that do not belong in Hell could leave, and only humans have the power to open it, though it could potentially be used to put demons back through one by one. Because of that, it remains open, but only if the proper ritual is performed. The third is the hole God crammed Lucifer down. It can only ever be used for him, and it was created by God, not by the Angels. That door is unaffected by the tasks because God did not anticipate that Lucifer would ever be able to break free or that he would become a factor in the third task."

Amaya squinted her eyes. "God doesn't make much sense."

"Sometimes it seems that way, doesn't it?" Gabriel crossed the room and stared out the window. "You have to understand that the Choosing was supposed to end it. When that failed, God washed his hands of the situation. He offered little to no guidance, and He was not directly involved in the tasks. The Angels did much research and consultations with God in order to determine what was necessary. Most of it involved magic, which is one thing Angels do not like. Most never touch magic, and those that do find it distasteful. It is mans' way to manipulate what God created, and Angels do not like the implications of that. It was magic that erected the temporary wall, magic that closed the Gate permanently, magic that opened it in the first place, and it is magic that will both attempt to cast out all the demons and free Lucifer."

"It sounds like God doesn't have much to do with it."

"He didn't, at least not directly. He assigned His Angels to it and then left it to them to figure out a way to correct the issues."

Amaya sat down at her desk. "I kinda get that part. It's going to be like the other stories, isn't it? Where it makes more sense as you tell it?"

Gabriel chuckled. "Yes. It will make more sense as I tell it."

"Would you tell me what happens to Braxton and Alaria?"

"You'll find out during the story." He ruffled her hair and looked toward the door. "It sounds as if your parents are home."

Amaya yawned. "I still want to hear the story. Promise that you'll still tell it?"

Gabriel stared at the door, a worried look in his eyes. "I'm afraid the story will have to wait until another time." He grimaced when the door opened and Amaya's parents walked in.

Her mother was a tall woman with long black hair. She offered a tight smiled to Gabriel and went straight to Amaya, gathering her daughter close in a hug. Amaya's father stood near the door, his long legs crossed in front of him. He was a tall man with a rangy build and muscles that strained the seams of his t-shirt. He had dirty blonde hair tinged with silver and a two-day stubble on his jaw.

"Has your Uncle Gabe been keeping you up telling stories again?"

Amaya smiled sheepishly at her mother. "We lost track of time. I like Uncle Gabe's stories."

Her father chuckled. "I know you do. Normally you're asleep before we get home. What story were you hearing, sweetheart?"

Gabriel closed his eyes with a pained expression on his face. Amaya looked at him quizzically before turning back to her parents. "He just finished telling me about Aradia and Gage and Garrick. He was getting ready to tell me about Alaria and her baby and the third task." She looked between her parents as they stared at one another, sensing the worry but unsure as to the cause. "What's the matter?"

Her mother sighed deeply and looked at Gabriel. "We asked you not to tell her these stories. We wanted to be the ones to tell her."

Gabriel looked recalcitrant. "I know, and I'm sorry, but I wanted to be involved with it. She deserves to know."

Amaya looked between them. "What's going on? What did he do wrong? What don't you want me to know?" She looked to her father. "Daddy?"

"It's okay, Amaya. Nothing's wrong." He wrapped his arm around her shoulder and looked at Gabriel. "I think we can handle it from here."

"I want him to stay and finish the story!" She looked at her mother, angry, confused tears welling in her eyes. "Why can't I hear the story?"

"Come here."

Amaya crossed the room and climbed into the chair with her mother, sitting on the woman's lap. "You're scaring me. Why can't he tell me the story?"

"Amaya, your mother and I have tried very hard to protect you and your sisters. There are reasons we haven't told you who we are or what we do. Finley knows more because she's older. We had this talk with her about a year ago. We planned to talk to you when you turned thirteen, and we'll talk to Eden and Donovan when they're thirteen. The stories your Uncle have been telling you aren't stories. They're about us, and our friends, who you've never met. We wanted to protect you from this as long as we could."

Amaya blinked back tears. "Which ones are you?"

Her mother's voice was soft and gentle. "What story were you about to get, Amaya?"

"Alaria and Braxton?"

She smiled and pressed her cheek to her daughter's. "Well, seeing as how that's our story, I think we should be the ones to tell it. Don't you think, Brax?"

Braxton nodded and left the room briefly to fetch another chair. He looked at Gabriel with thinly veiled hate. "I think we've got this, Gabriel."

Gabriel nodded. "I'll make sure the other kids get off to school."

Alaria offered a smile as he left the room before looking down at Amaya. "Where did he leave off? With Garrick being killed?"

Amaya nodded. "You're really Alaria? And you're really Braxton?"

Alaria chuckled. "We're Mom and Dad to you. Do you want the story or not?"

"Yes!"

Braxton laughed. "Okay. Tell it, Alaria."

Alaria leaned back in the chair and closed her eyes. "If I remember right, things were calm for a few weeks, but by the time mid-July came around, we were all getting antsy to get things done. It started when Braxton had a dream...."

Braxton knew the moment he opened his eyes that he was on the dream plane. Everything looked like it was covered in a sepia lens—slightly dull and off color. He looked around the room and his chest constricted. He stood in the room he and Griffin had shared in the Choosing Place.

Griffin was on the bed, lying on her stomach and flipping through a book. She looked up and grinned, and Braxton immediately recognized the scene. It wasn't a dream but a memory replaying.

"Hey. I was wondering if you were coming up to bed."

The words came from his mouth without a thought. "I took Sam home with instructions not to come back. It's not safe for her here anymore."

Griffin chuckled and rolled onto her side. "It's not exactly safe for any of us, Brax." She climbed to her feet and grabbed his hands with hers. "Let's get some sleep. You don't come up here nearly enough. I miss having you at night."

He lowered his head and brushed his cheek against her hair, savoring the feel of the silky strands and the subtle scent of her shampoo. "There's a lot of work to get done."

"Nothing more to be done today." She tugged his hands. "You need some sleep. You've barely stopped since the wedding."

Braxton looked down at the shining gold rings on their fingers and smiled. "We're in the home stretch. If we can just keep them out a little longer, we'll have made it."

Griffin pressed her finger to his lips. "I feel good tonight, Brax. Better than I have in a long time. Whatever Gabriel did to make me healthier is working. I don't want to talk about the Choosing. It's coming whether we talk about it or not. Tonight, I want to lay down with you and just talk about anything else. Can we do that?"

The hope shining in her eyes was more than he could bear. He nodded and shucked off his shirt and pants. "We can do that." He slipped between the sheets and tucked her against his side, relishing the feel of her body against his. "What do you want to talk about?"

Griffin stretched to turn off the light. "If you could be anywhere in the world right this second, where would it be?"

Braxton pressed a kiss to her head. "I would take you to my favorite beach in Spain. We'd lay on the beach and drink cocktails and watch the sunset." He ran his hand down the side of her body. "You'd be topless, obviously."

She laughed and squirmed. "Obviously."

"Your turn. Where would you be?"

"I would want to go to Jamaica and live in one of those huts out on the dock with a glass floor to look down at the fish."

Braxton smiled. "Done. We'll leave tomorrow."

Griffin's face mirrored his smile. "I'll pack our bags." She leaned up and kissed him gently. "I love you."

"I love you, too."

She sobered and stared up at the ceiling. "I want things to be different."

"Me too, baby, me too."

As quickly as it had started, the scene changed, and he was following Griffin up the stairs and into the same room. He recognized her clothing as what she'd been wearing the night before the Choosing. Their last night together.

Griffin led him into her room with a determined step. She stood in front of him and unbuttoned his shirt, sliding it off his shoulders. When she spoke, her voice jarred him out of his trance and into the memory.

"Take off your shoes."

His body moving without active participation from him, Braxton bent to obey her, kicking off his boots and pulling off the socks. His throat clogged with emotion as he looked into her face for what he knew was going to be one of the last times. Once he straightened, she undid his belt, then unbuttoned and unzipped his jeans, sending them to the floor as well. Silently, he stepped out of them. Her hand slid down his arm, and she twined her fingers with his.

"Come lie down with me."

Still silent, Braxton followed her to the bed and slid under the covers with her. He lay flat on his back, one arm curled underneath his head, the other stretched out to pillow hers. She curled into his side, laying her head in the crook of his shoulder and wrapping one arm around his waist. After several minutes of silence, Braxton cleared his throat. The words came quickly, and from memory, the scene as clear as if he had just lived it.

"I don't know what to say here, Griffin. I don't know if I should say anything."

"I don't think there are any rules. No instruction manual." She propped her head up on her hand. "No one has ever done this before. We're just playing it by ear."

"What do you want to do?"

Griffin laughed. "Travel the world, have babies, and grow old. Seeing as I'm going to die tomorrow, I'll settle for spending the night with my husband."

Absentmindedly, he ran his fingers through her hair. "This all feels so surreal. Like we're going to get through tomorrow and someone is going to tell us that it's all been a joke."

"It's not a joke, Brax." She laid her hand on his face. "This is our last night. This is my last night."

"How are you so calm? When I think about it, I want to punch something, yell–do something! You just talk about it like you're discussing whether or not to go to the grocery store tomorrow."

"I've made peace with it." She stared up at the ceiling. "All of this, it's like a dream. It's like I'm watching it happen to myself through some sort of a camera lens, like a movie. I know it's real, that I'm actually going to die tomorrow, and I'm not sure if it's some sort of feature built into this whole thing or if it's just me, but I'm not scared, at least not right now. Tomorrow is the day I do what I was born to do, and I think my soul knows that. I've been careening toward this since my first breath, since my first heartbeat."

Braxton pressed a kiss to her forehead. "I don't want to let you go."

"You have to. We both know you would find it in you to stab me yourself if you thought I wouldn't do it."

He chose not to respond, partially because it was true but mostly because he was ashamed it was. The words had more of a punch than they had the first time she had uttered them. Grief rose within him, and it became hard to finish out the memory. "I wish we could make tonight special for you, or tomorrow. But with everything going on—"

"I know." She laid her finger over his mouth to shush him. "You don't have to apologize. We're being attacked. Warriors have given their lives to get me here. I'm not about to jeopardize that, to make it worth nothing so that we can have a candlelit dinner. The odds of any of them making it out of here alive tomorrow are slim to none. I will not let that be for nothing."

He gathered her close, relishing the feel of her hair against his face, the feel of her skin under his hands. "I will never forget you." He kissed her fervently. "I will always love you. You've shown me what love is this past year. I didn't want to feel it—tried not to—but every time I looked at you, I fell deeper. You are the strongest, kindest, most amazing person that I have ever had the honor of meeting. I want you to know, if you never have known anything else that this world is a better place because of your life, and I am a better man because of you."

"I want you to be happy, Braxton. Being with me, that is so selfless. It's helped me get through this, and I honestly don't know if I'd have the strength to do this without you here. But me letting this happen? That was selfish. I know that it's no good for you, and I've let it happen anyway because I wanted it and because I love you. I want you to know that it's okay to move on—that it's okay to be happy." She braced her forehead against his, tears slipping down her cheeks. "I need you to promise me something."

"Anything."

"Don't waste a second of your life mourning me."

Guilt and grief rose in his chest, and he choked on the words. "Griffin—"

"No. Don't argue. Promise me. I want you to have the life that you deserve, that we should have gotten to have. I want you to find someone and marry her, and have lots of babies, and coach softball, and intimidate poor, unsuspecting teenage boys who come to take your daughter on a date. I want you to walk her down the aisle, and hold your grandchildren. I want you to grow old with someone special next to you, holding your hand. I want you to watch your grandchildren grow up, and I want you to die an old man, at home in his bed, with a good woman next to you. I want you to get everything I won't. You have to promise me, to swear on all that is good and holy, that you will not let this be the end for you." She framed his face with her hands. "I need that, Braxton. I need to know that you'll be okay. That you'll move on. I need you to promise me."

His heart shattering into a thousand pieces, tears trying to force their way out of him, Braxton nodded. His voice was harsh and strained as he spoke. "I promise."

The scene changed a third time, and he was standing in a field. In front of him, her gown swirling around her legs, was Graciela. Braxton shook his head to clear it and forced himself to focus on the witch.

"Why did you bring me here?"

"Because this is something you needed to see." She touched his arm gently. "I am just an intermediary, Braxton. From time to time, I am called upon to make things possible. I have dominion over the dream plane, and God allows me to remain here in exchange for answering when the Angels call. What you will soon be asked to do is going to bring up the memories of the Choosing and of Griffin. You will need to return to the place where she died. It is necessary. In order to do so, and to maintain your abilities to handle what will be asked of you, I have been asked to take certain steps to help you."

Curious despite himself, Braxton crossed his arms. "What steps?"

"In certain circumstances, it is possible to bring a soul out of Heaven. God is all powerful, and nothing is outside of His power. You have grieved too long. It is time for you to find closure."

"Just how do you think you're going to do that? Cast a spell on me?"

The voice that sounded from behind him was one he hadn't ever thought he would hear again. Griffin's voice floated through the air, clear and strong. "You made me a promise, Braxton. You haven't kept it."

Braxton turned slowly and found himself looking at Griffin. Her hair was shiny and thick, her body filled out in the same way it had been the first time he'd met her. Her eyes sparkled with life, and she offered him a gentle smile. He looked at Graciela, a mixture of hope and disbelief in his eyes.

"Is this real? I mean, I know it's a dream, but is she really here?"

Graciela nodded. "She's really here. As I said, there are times when it becomes clear the best thing for all is to have a soul brought temporarily from Heaven to the dream plane in order to accomplish a particular task." She touched Braxton's hand. "I'll leave the two of you alone."

Braxton ran his hand through his hair and stared at Griffin. He took in everything about her, from the touch of color in her cheeks to the trim white suit and heeled boots. It was the most polished he had ever seen her look.

"It's almost like Gabriel hand-picked the outfit."

Griffin laughed. "He did. I don't have a closet full of clothes." She started to reach out for his hand, then changed her mind and withdrew it. "I know this is weird. Until a few minutes ago, I had no memories of you or what happened. Heaven is everything you could ever dream it could be. I've been happy." She cocked her head to the side. "How long has it been?"

"Nineteen months."

"A year and a half?" She laughed, the sound music to Braxton's ears. "You're still this much of a mess after that long? What happened, Brax?"

He sighed and looked down. "I was okay. Not great, but okay. Then Lucifer made a play, and there was a warlock who was able to pry open Hell again and let all the demons out. It was like you died for nothing."

Griffin shook her head. "I didn't die for nothing. I died because God picked me. Do you really think if we had known what was going on they would have let me out of it?" When he didn't answer, she shook her head. "They wouldn't have. I was going to die no matter what we did and no matter what happened. You knew that when you met me, when you took me to bed, when you married me, and the day I died. You knew the score, Braxton. We both did."

"That doesn't make it any easier." He plowed his hands through his hair and paced. "I don't know what to do here. I've dreamed of this a hundred times since you died, and now that it's happening, I don't know what the fuck to do."

"Me, either." She laughed nervously. "Fill me in on the last year. How are your parents? Did Sam have the baby?"

Braxton's face fell. He stared at her blankly. "You don't know."

Griffin looked at him with a questioning look. "Know what?"

"They're all dead. Sam and my parents. Gabriel stashed the baby for safekeeping until we're done with all of this. They were killed by Devils."

She wrapped her arms around him in a tight hug. "I'm so sorry." She brushed tears from her eyes and stood back. "What about Father Dooley and Alaria? Gage?"

"They're all fine. Gage found a wonderful woman. There's a chance he could earn his humanity back, and they're hoping he does. Father Dooley is doing some research on the third task we have to do. He's good."

"What about Alaria?" She looked at him curiously. "Is she around?"

"She's pregnant. Gabriel knocked her up. Due in February."

Griffin's eyes widened, and she stared at him in amazement. "Wow. Is that allowed?"

"I don't even pretend to understand that. It's way too complicated for me." He sat down against a tree and leaned against the trunk. "Why did they send you here, Griffin? It wasn't to make small talk."

She sat next to him and leaned her head against his shoulder. "Gabriel didn't fill me in completely. What I know is that he feels he's hurt you and that me being here will make it better. There was a mention of some parts of the Choosing coming into play with what you have to do, but I have no idea what that means. He didn't tell me." She sighed. "I can tell you're sad. I don't want you to keep doing this to yourself. You promised me that you wouldn't grieve me. I want you to forget I ever existed. I want you to move on and be happy. More than anything, I want you to have the life we wanted."

Braxton stared down at the top of her head. "I'm confused."

"About what?" Griffin sat up. "What is it that confuses you?"

"I don't know how to feel about any of this."

"Braxton, you've now grieved me for twice as long as we knew one another. I loved you and you loved me, but I'm dead, and that's not going to change. I'm at peace. I'm in Heaven, and I'm happy. I want you to be happy, too." She placed her hands on his face. "It's time to forgive yourself and let me go." She kissed him gently and leaned her head against his. "I don't have much more time. You need to move on from this. I'm not coming back, and you're not dead. You don't need to keep doing this to yourself."

"I almost slept with Alaria."

The words were out before he could recall them, and they took Griffin by surprise. She sat back on her haunches and stared at him, blinking rapidly. "Until I came here, I had no clue if I died yesterday or a thousand years ago. I'm trying to feel mad about that, or sad, or anything I should feel because I was your wife and I wanted to spend my life with you." She smiled and kissed him again. "I'm glad you did. I want you to move on, and now that you've told me, I can really say that and know I mean it, because it doesn't upset me."

"I wanted to hate her for what she did to you."

Griffin laughed. "She did what she had to do, and when it counted, she was there for us, risking her life. I liked Alaria, at least at the end." She stood. "I have to go now, but I want you to promise me you are going to forgive yourself and move on. I want you to promise me, and I want you to mean it. Whether it's Alaria or someone else, I want you to be happy." She tilted her head. "Have you had sex since I died?"

Braxton couldn't help the spurt of laughter that burst from him. "No. You were the last."

Griffin grinned, and he was struck by how beautiful she was. He took in every inch of her, knowing it was a gift he'd been given in getting to see her again. She shook her head and grabbed both his hands in hers.

"If you love me, you'll get over this. I don't want you to grieve. We didn't have any control over what happened to me. You can control what happens to you." She smiled sadly. "Don't waste your life because I got mine taken away. You get to live, Braxton. I want you to get every ounce of life out of the time you have. For me."

She was gone before Braxton could so much as open his mouth to speak.

Chapter Two

Braxton was jerked from sleep by a pounding on his bedroom door. Gage's voice came through the wood. "Wake up. Angel invasion."

Braxton groaned and rolled out of bed. He stumbled in the dark, yanking on pants and a wife beater over his boxers. He yanked open the door and blinked against the bright light. He saw Greer and Damon heading down the stairs, her hair mussed from sleep and him dressed only in shorts. Aradia came down the steps from Gage's chambers, wearing one of his shirts and her own jeans.

"Did you wake Alaria up?"

Gage turned. "Yeah. The morning sickness is back. She said she'd be down when she was done throwing up."

"Has Greer helped her?"

"Not yet this morning. Alaria won't let anyone in until she's done."

"What the hell are the Angels doing here at—" he looked at his watch. "—four-forty-three in the morning?"

"The fuck if I know." The vampire yawned. "All I can tell you is that I was sound asleep and then there was a bright light and Gabriel was standing in my bedroom, telling me I needed to assemble the troops and meet him and Michael in the kitchen."

Greer's voice carried up the stairs. "Coffee's on!"

Alaria emerged from her room, scraping her hair back from her face and into a ponytail. Her face was pale and drawn and there were black smudges beneath her eyes. She spared a quick look at each of the men before starting down the stairs. To her chagrin, she had to hold onto the railing as she climbed down and her knees shook by the end. She went straight to the coffee pot, pouring a cup and drinking deeply.

Gabriel looked at her with concern. "From my knowledge of human gestation, I believe caffeine is something that should be avoided during pregnancy." He gestured to the coffee. "That liquid is quite high in it."

Alaria glared at him over the rim of the cup. "Fuck you." She smacked the empty mug down on the counter and sat next to Aradia. "I don't need pregnancy advice from the son of a bitch that did the knocking up."

"Traditionally, prospective fathers do get an opinion in the manner in which their child grows." Gabriel perched across from her.

"You're a sperm donor. Big difference, asshole."

Gabriel opened his mouth to retort, but Michael cut him off. "Now is not the time for petty verbal sparring." He looked at Gabriel sternly. "I warned you that their moods would be less than accommodating by coming here during their sleep cycles."

Gage took a gulp of his blood and cleared his throat. "Why don't we all call a truce and the two of you can tell the rest of us why the hell you're here before five in the morning?"

"We have come to instruct you in the third and final task." Gabriel looked around the room. "As you know, you must carve the remnants of the wings from the backs of the original fallen Archangels." He met Braxton's gaze and held it. "What you do not know is how you must accomplish that."

Michael laid one hand on Braxton's back. "In order to succeed, you must take them to the place where the Choosing occurred and use the knife with which Griffin took her own life."

Braxton felt like his whole world upended. He struggled to breathe, and his vision blackened as he fought his way through his first panic attack. It felt like his whole chest constricted. Air stagnated in his lungs, unable to move in or out. His fingers bit into the granite of the countertop and he sagged onto one of the stools, unable to hold himself up. Fighting to breathe, he closed his eyes and fought the need to vomit as wave after wave of nausea rolled over him.

When he surfaced, all eyes were on him, expressions of concern mirrored in all the faces he saw. Uncomfortable, he lurched out of his seat and busied himself with pouring another cup of coffee and putting on another pot to brew.

When he spoke, his voice was ragged. "Why? Why there? Why with that knife? Just why?"

"Because Griffin's blood is powerful. It is the purest blood, other than Jesus' himself, that could possibly be used. In her Choice, she cleansed herself of all remnants of sin and became pure. To do these rituals where her blood still remains will give it extra power." Gabriel sighed deeply. "I know it will be hard for you, and for that I'm sorry. There is no way around it."

Gage held up his hand to draw attention to himself. "What do we do after we get the wings? It can't possibly be as simple as that."

Michael chuckled. "Your optimism is uncalled for, Gage. There is nothing simple about the task in front of you. You must find the Devils, capture them, and literally carve the roots of their wings from their backs. It will not be easily accomplished. However, you are correct. That is but the first step of three. After you have the wings of the five Devils, you must find the hatch through which Lucifer was brought and summon him there in order to take his."

Alaria slammed her cup against the counter for the second time. "You're telling us that we have to break the chains and call Lucifer onto Earth? How the fucking hell are we supposed to keep him from melting us all and being free from Hell?"

Michael's expression was sober. "It's a risk I wish we did not have to take, but I am not the designer of the tasks, merely the messenger telling you of them. You will need to make the place as secure as possible and lay traps and wards over every inch of it, both Angel and Devil, since Lucifer was the most powerful of either. However, there is a significant chance that you could fail."

Alaria laughed. "Significant? It's a fucking foregone conclusion!"

Gabriel stood abruptly, his chair scraping against the tile and smacking into the sink as it toppled over. He gripped the granite counter hard enough that he broke off a piece in both places he had held it. When he spoke, his voice was dark and angry.

"I have cut you more slack than I would have ever done for any other person. This is your job, Alaria. It is one of the reasons you were made human, and it is the reason you were chosen as a vessel for that child. You should be on bended knee kissing my feet for what I have done for you. Instead, you second guess at every turn, you reduce yourself to petty verbal barbs, and you attempt to undermine our authority to give you tasks. You're human now. You're one of the insignificant beings we used to watch. It is our role to instruct, and yours to sit down, shut up and do the fuck as you're told!"

Everyone sat in shocked silence at the outburst. Gabriel tossed the two pieces of granite to the floor and stared at Alaria, his eyes hot. Slowly and deliberately, she climbed to her feet and walked around the island. Greer leaned over to Braxton and pressed her lips to his ear.

"Don't you think we should do something?"

Braxton shook his head. "Nope. She'd eat him and us for breakfast if we interfere. Alaria's a big girl, she can handle herself."

Alaria's steps were measured and slow. She stopped directly in front of Gabriel and crossed her arms over her chest. She took several deep breaths before speaking, and when she did, her voice was little more than a whisper.

"You were supposed to be the one person we could trust. Your job isn't to give orders, it is to guide and lead. Instead, you've left us to fend for ourselves, and you act as if we should be grateful when you pop in to give us some kernel of wisdom." She took a deep breath and lifted her gaze to meet his. "We have succeeded in spite of you, Gabriel, not because of you. I loved you, and I believe you loved me, but we've both let those feelings affect our decisions too much." She looked sad for a moment. "I think from now on it would be better for everyone if you let Michael handle this part of the tasks."

Gabriel opened and closed his mouth several times. Finally, he dipped his head. "If that is what you wish, it can be arranged." He glared down at her. "I hope you don't ever expect to go back to the way things were. If you do this, Alaria, if you send me away, I won't come back. Not to you or to any of them. I'll fight for this cause if that is required, but I will not be here to help with anything else. I hope you understand what you're doing."

"I don't do things I don't understand. I'll accept the consequences if there are any. I think this is best for everyone."

Gabriel looked past Alaria to the other five. "Do the rest of you feel the same?"

No one spoke for several seconds. After ten more, Gage spoke. "We're a team, Gabe. It's how we all feel."

"Fine." Gabriel looked around, angry and hurt. "Don't expect me to come running when you call."

Michael chose not to speak until Gabriel had disappeared. When he did, his voice was sad and solemn. "I understand the choice you made, and in some ways, I agree with it." He turned to Alaria. "I know what is happening is scary and unfamiliar and that you are angry. You have every right to be. I hope you believe me when I tell you that Gabriel did not believe he had a choice in what he did. We were told you were to be the vessel, and if Gabriel was unable to impregnate you, God would find an Angel who was willing. It is likely that if Gabriel had refused, you would have been forced. He was trying to spare you a worse fate than this, regardless of how it may feel."

Alaria sat back down and folded her hands. "The problem is that he didn't even give me a chance to make the decision. If he'd have come and talked to me about it before he did what he did, things might be different now."

Michael smiled gently. "Would you have agreed to let him impregnate you?"

"No."

"Then there was no point in talking to you." He laid his hand on hers gently. "I know you're angry, and you have every right to be, but you must also understand Gabriel has never been like you or me. He lives to obey. You lived despite obeying. Gabriel could not turn down a direct request from God. Not for you, not for me, not for himself. It's not the way he was made. I hope one day you can forgive him for that."

Braxton cleared his throat. "Let's get back to the more important task at hand. How is it that we're supposed to get ahold of the Devils?"

"I'm not going to lie and tell you it's going to be simple. The truth is that it's likely going to be extraordinarily difficult. The Devils are in hiding, and are not likely to come out on their own. I'm going to try and ascertain where they are, and as soon as I have that information, I will come and tell you. Until then, you should use all available resources you have in order to figure out where they are." Michael cleared his throat. "As I was not there and Gabriel is not here, do any of you know what became of the knife with which Griffin killed herself?"

Alaria thought back. "The last I saw of it, it was laying on the floor in the chapel at the monastery. I don't think any of us picked it up before Gabriel took us back to Philly. We had no clue we were ever going to need it."

Braxton shrugged. "I didn't pick it up. Gage?"

Gage shook his head. "Why would I?"

Michael chuckled softly. "None of us had any inclination it would ever be needed again. I will take one of you to get the knife so you will have it." He looked amongst the six. "Which of you will accompany me?"

Braxton's chair scraped the tile as he stood. "I'll go. It's only right that it's me."

Alaria looked between Braxton and Michael. "I'll go with you. I don't think you need to do this alone. It's going to be hard."

Michael lifted his shoulders. "Go put shoes on and gather a weapon or two just in case. To the best of my knowledge, there has been no activity at the Choosing Place from either side in this since the battle, but it is best to always be careful when doing things such as this. The good thing is that I do not believe the Devils know that the Choosing Place and the knife are necessary. We must do our best to make sure they do not find out."

Gage grimaced. "I'll order some paint and get it ready. We're obviously going to have a painting party to put all the wards back up that Garrick broke through when they sieged." He rose. "I'll order a new fucking countertop while I'm at it. Ten thousand dollar Italian marble and he cracks it like it's a twig." The vampire continued to mutter under his breath about the counter as he left the room.

Alaria and Braxton ascended the steps together, entering their respective rooms. Alaria shoved her feet into sneakers and went down the hall and into Braxton's bedroom. She perched on the edge of the bed and listened to him moving around in the bathroom for several seconds before speaking.

"I can go alone if it's too much for you."

He stuck his head out. "I'm going to have to get used to it one way or the other. Obviously this isn't a one-time thing, and better for me to go back there when I don't have five other people waiting for me to crack." He yanked on a t-shirt. "I'll be fine."

"If you're not, I understand. It'll be hard for me to go back there, too. A lot happened in that building, for both of us."

He bent to lace his boots. "I know. I think it's time we both just let go of it." He sighed. "Graciela brought Griffin to me in a dream last night." He shook his head and smiled. "She scolded me for still grieving her, and when she says it, it just sounds so stupid. She's been gone twice as long as I knew her, and while it might be as clear as yesterday to me, she has no clue how long it's been. I told her we almost slept together."

Alaria's eyebrows nearly met her hairline. "What did she say to that?"

"She thinks it's a good thing and she likes you and would like for us both to be happy. She told me she didn't remember anything about us, only that she's happy and content and had no idea if it had been a day or a millennia since she died." He looked sad. "I believe her, Alaria. Somehow, knowing that she really is still up there and she's got some sort of a life, even if it's one I can't see, makes it easier to deal with the fact that she's gone."

Alaria reached out and squeezed his hand. "Don't be too optimistic about your recovery yet. We'll talk about it after you have to stand where she died and deal with all of those memories." She stood. "Let's get this over with."

As they walked back down the hall and passed the door to her room, Braxton laid his hand on her back. "I am glad you moved out of the basement and up here with the rest of us."

She lifted her shoulder in a shrug. "After the fight with Gabe when I tortured Abalam and how that started to spin out of control, I didn't want to stay where he and I had been together. It brought back too many memories and it made things too hard on me."

"You don't have to explain escaping memories to me." He laughed ruefully as they went back down the stairs where Michael waited at the bottom. "Ready for this?"

She nodded. "As I'll ever be."

Michael smiled grimly. "Then let's get this done and over with, shall we?"

THE ONLY difference between the day of the Choosing and the day they went back was the absence of the bodies.

The first thing Braxton noticed was the smell. Even nineteen months later, the smell of battle hung in the air. He inhaled the scent of gunpowder and sulfur and wrinkled his nose. Next to him, Alaria had turned an interesting shade of green and covered her mouth with her hand. Michael was solemn beside them.

There was dried blood on the stone walls, and debris littered the floor. In some places, bits of bone poked out of the piles of wood and stone, left over from those who had been incinerated during the battle and had had no fleshy parts to cart off and burn.

For the first time, Braxton wondered who had taken care of dealing with the leftover remains from the day of the Choosing.

As if reading his thoughts, Michael cleared his throat. "Gage took care of the clean-up. There's a mass grave out back where they burned the bodies and covered up the remains. He didn't think you'd be able to deal with the logistics at the time."

Braxton swallowed a wave of nausea and managed a tight smile. "Remind me to thank him later."

They moved through the monastery in solemn silence. As Braxton muscled open the door leading from the pantry to the tunnel and then into the chapel, he watched a mental replay of the day of the battle.

There were still piles of rubble where Azazel had slung Braxton into the pews and a pile of wood pieces where he had lain, half-conscious, as the clock had ticked down to zero. He remembered the exact spot where Alaria had taken on Azazel in those final moments, risking her own life and buying them just enough time to get to midnight.

In the middle of the room was a large brown stain on the gray concrete, and Braxton's stomach twisted as he saw it. Griffin's blood—every drop of it—had made that stain and instead of holding her as she died, he'd been unconscious in a corner and had missed the entire thing. He'd missed his opportunity to say goodbye.

The knife lay two feet from the middle of the stain, still in the same place it had landed as it fell from Griffin's fingers and clattered to the floor. Alaria bent and retrieved it, wrapping it in a piece of cloth and tucking it into her waistband. When Michael spoke, his voice shattered the silence and echoed throughout the empty room.

"I know it's difficult for you to be here. I wish there was a way I could spare you this, but to my knowledge there is no other blood powerful enough—save that of Jesus himself—to work the magic you will need in order to accomplish this." He looked at Alaria with sympathy. "I'm sorry for what you must go through, but your wing roots, too, must be carved out."

Alaria shook her head. "Aradia has ways to make it painless, I'm sure, and Greer can heal me as soon as it's done."

"Aradia is not allowed to take the pain. It is through the pain that the spell works and the magic is woven to connect the roots to one another. You must experience the same as the others, Alaria. You must feel what they feel."

"Then Aradia can just numb them all." Braxton shook his head. "There's no way we're going to torture her like that."

Michael lifted his brows curiously. "Did you not beat and stab Greer when it was necessary? Did you not accompany Aradia to where she may have died because it had to be done?"

"This is different."

The Angel shook his head. "The only difference is in your head and heart. You care for Alaria differently than you did for Greer. It makes you want to protect her, and I understand that, but it does not change what must be done."

Braxton growled. "It has nothing to do with my feelings and everything to do with the fact that she's got a baby inside her. I don't know much, but I do know that a lot of stress or pain can cause a miscarriage, and the last thing I want is for fucking Gabriel to come and rape her again just because God told him to."

Alaria cleared her throat, amused. "No offense, boys, but I make my own decisions, and I don't need input from the peanut gallery. I appreciate the gesture, really, but we all know I'm going to do this whether or not either of you thinks it's a good idea. I don't need anyone to tell me what to do, and I don't appreciate being talked about like I'm either not here or am so stupid I can't comprehend the enormity of what is being asked." She shook her head adamantly. "I'm going to have to let one of you carve wing stumps out of my back. I'm going to have to feel every slice and every second. It will hurt, and I will scream, and we can only pray I pass out before it gets too terribly bad, but nothing is going to change."

Michael looked around the room. "There's a lot of work that will need to be done to this place in order to make it fit for what we need to do. We'll need to make it defensible, and I'll see what I can do about putting up the Angelic protections as well as the wards you will paint. It would also hold more power if you could paint the wards in blood that has been blessed."

Braxton nodded slowly. "Gage can get us all the blood we need. Does it have to be human?"

"That would be best, yes." The Angel shifted his wings. "I don't have any desire to watch this play out. You know as well as I that the odds of this succeeding are substantially slimmer than the odds of you succeeding in the other two tasks. To hail Lucifer from Hell is going to be a fearsome task in and of itself. To attempt to hold him here and carve the roots from him while keeping him from blasting his way out is a task that is too difficult to comprehend. I don't envy you this."

Alaria laughed. "I don't want it. I'd be happy to pass it off on to some other unsuspecting soul and let them risk their lives over and over again."

Braxton cleared his throat. "Back to the first topic of conversation. What can we do to make sure that what we have to do to Alaria doesn't hurt the baby?"

Michael smiled. "The child is blessed by God. Nothing anyone can do to her is going to affect that child. It will be fine."

"Still, I think she should probably see an OB and have an ultrasound after we're done."

"I can handle myself, Braxton. Yes, I'll see the doctor after it's all over. It'd make me feel better anyway. At least that way I can make sure the damn thing doesn't have horns and a tail."

Michael snorted. "It is not the Antichrist you carry, Alaria. Your child will look like a normal human."

"It's the fact that you said 'look like' instead of 'will be' that worries me." She touched the handle of the knife gingerly. "Let's get back so Gage can start tossing his money around getting this place back to order and we can get painting. We need to get this show on the road as fast as possible."

Gage lifted his eyebrows and chuckled. "You need fifteen gallons of human blood?"

"Michael says it'll make the protections around the Choosing Place stronger if they're painted with blood instead of paint." Alaria looked at Braxton ruefully. "Sure would've been nice if they'd have told us the first time around. You and I painted every inch of that monastery."

Braxton shrugged. "I wish they'd have told us a lot of things, but that's all relative now." He folded his hands and leaned across the island. "We need to get a cleanup crew in there to make it habitable. I'm not saying we have to stay there, but we sure as hell have to go back and forth a lot, and odds are that we're going to have an overnight occasionally. We need to be comfortable when we're there, and we'll need to put guards on it around the clock. That'll make it safer for everyone."

Gage nodded. "I'll make arrangements with some people I know in the region to make sure everything is underway. Honestly, even with my contacts, it'll take a few days to get that much blood without raising some eyebrows. I don't necessarily mind being noticed since I have the money to make it go away, but I also don't think we should do things we know are going to get us attention."

Alaria picked up her cup of coffee and sipped. "I agree completely. I think we have some time to play with, both because the Devils are in hiding and because we need to be thorough. This isn't a sprint—it's a marathon, and we need to pace ourselves. We're going to have to get each of the Devils individually, take them to the Choosing Place, do what needs to be done, and send them back to Hell so they can't warn the others what's going on. Even doing it that way, I think we need to move on more than one at a time if we can."

Greer shook her head. "I don't think that's a good idea. I'm with you on everything up until that, but we have no idea what we could be walking into. They have to know we're coming for them eventually, and you know word has likely gotten out that Garrick and Javal are dead. If we split up, we're opening ourselves up to being killed a lot easier. It's harder for them to fend off six of us than it is two or three. We have to pace ourselves and take the time we need. Technically, we have forty-eight years and some odd months before the time runs out that God gave us. Realistically, Alaria is about eleven weeks pregnant. We'll have about thirteen weeks or so before she's really showing, and about twenty weeks before she's too big to do what we need her to do. That's four and a half months. We can take the time to do this right."

Damon gestured to Alaria. "You know them better than anyone. Do you have an idea of which order we should go after them?"

Alaria considered the question carefully. "That's a hard question. They're all tough. However, some are smart, others are predictable, and some are crazy. If I were the one making the call, I'd go for Lilith first, and not just because I hate the psycho bitch. It's because she's actually, literally crazy. She's unpredictable and hard to take down. She thrives on challenges, and she thinks there's no one bigger or badder than she is. She's the one most likely to come after us."

Gage poured himself a mug of blood and stuck it in the microwave. "Then she's the one we go after. I would have said Abalam and Abaddon, but that's just me. I think they're the ones we're going to find together. Abaddon has been working for Abalam so long and they know each other so well that I think it's likely he's caring for Abalam."

Aradia's eyebrows drew together. "How did Abalam get out anyway? I thought he was in Angelic custody after Alaria tortured him before I was here."

Alaria scowled. "He was. They busted him out a few days after Greer went down to Hell. Once they knew he was missing, it didn't take them long to find him and get him out." She looked around the island. "That's the other thing. While I don't think they're going to be staying in close contact with one another, I do think they're going to have some system by which they communicate. If one goes too long without checking in, they'll figure out that something's wrong, and they'll scramble. They'll also likely all have lackeys—demons—to do their bidding, so when we go in, we have to make sure nothing makes it out alive. If one does, they'll all go into hiding, and that is the last thing we need. For some of them, especially Beelzebub, we need to get to him before he knows what's going on or we might not ever find him."

Gage chuckled and opened the door of the microwave to remove the steaming cup of blood. "No one can hide from me. If he's on planet Earth, I can find him." He sipped, swished the thick liquid in his mouth while he gave their situation some thought, and swallowed. "I think we go for Beelzebub last. The more panicked he is and the more he knows we're coming, the stupider he'll get. Lilith is a crazy bitch, Azazel will be waiting for the fight because the son of a bitch is so cocky he thinks he can't lose, Abaddon and Abalam won't separate, and Beelzebub is most vulnerable when he doesn't have the others to manipulate. If we use their weaknesses against them, we'll have our best chance at succeeding."

The phone ringing startled them all. Braxton strode to the counter and picked up the handset, pushing the 'talk' button and pressing it to his ear. "Hello?"

"Brax?"

"Yeah. Who's this?"

"It's Father Dooley. How are you guys?"

Braxton smiled into the telephone. "We're all alive, which is as good as it gets. What's the password so I know you're really you?"

"Cantaloupe."

"Good enough for me. What's going on?"

Dooley coughed. "I've been working on those papers that you sent me. I think you should come down here and look at what I've found. I'd tell you over the phone, but we both know that isn't secure, and I doubt these guys will let me get on the next flight to Scotland."

Braxton chuckled. "No, they definitely won't do that. Have you found what you were looking for, or is it something else?"

"I think it's what we were looking for, but I don't want to say too much on the phone. This is more complicated than we knew it was, Brax. When do you think you can be here?"

Braxton looked at Gage, who held up one finger as he spoke into the phone. "One week, give or take. It's quite a haul to get to you."

"It certainly is." Dooley laughed softly. "I'll see you in a few days then."

"Sure thing. Stay safe, Brad."

Braxton hung up the phone and looked at the others. Gage pulled his cell phone out of his pocket, scrolling through his contact before selecting one. He held the phone to his ear and waited until someone on the other line answered.

"Hello? This is Gage Windsor. I need to rush order another private jet." He walked out of the kitchen and toward the office, his voice carrying back. "Yes, I know I just had one delivered last week. That was because my first one crashed into the ocean. I am telling you I need a second jet, and I need it in three days." He opened the door to his office and stepped inside, leaving it open. "No, I don't care how expensive it is."

Alaria shook her head and giggled. "He has more money than God, I swear."

Aradia smiled softly. "He makes good use of his fortunes. Without it, we would not be able to do this." She yawned. "It is getting late, and it has been a long day. I think we should all get some rest. Obviously that is going to be in short supply for the next weeks. We'd might as well stock up on it while we can."

ALARIA LOOKED around the sanctuary warily, her heart pounding in her chest. The room had been cleaned, all of the debris removed, and the walls covered in protection symbols. In the middle of the room were four chains—two anchored to the ceiling and two to the floor. Shackles gleamed, shiny and new, at the end of each chain. Silver glimmered along the edges of the Devil's traps painted on the floor.

Gage's voice broke through her thoughts. "Do you think you can hold still for us to do this, or would you prefer to be chained?"

Alaria rolled her shoulders. "I think you oughta chain me up." She peeled off her shirt and looked around. "For whatever reason it makes me feel funny that everyone is going to be ogling my tits. I've never had that feeling before."

Greer chuckled. "No one is going to ogle, but from what Michael showed me, the roots of the wings are directly attached to your shoulder blades and we have to run the length of them to get the whole thing out. A bra gets in the way." She looked sympathetic. "If you want, I can send the men away and I'll handle this. Aradia can help."

Alaria shook her head. "Just don't stare." She sighed. "I've never been self-conscious in my life, and now I pick a fine time to be worried about how I look."

Braxton rubbed her shoulders briskly. "It's a mental thing. Your brain focuses on something it can control to take the edge off of what it can't." He crossed the room to the chains and unlocked the shackles. "Ready to get this show on the road?"

Alaria nodded hesitantly and strode to the chains, her gait much more confident than she felt. She stood still while Braxton clamped the shackles on her hands and feet and tested the chains, her arms suspended above her head so that she couldn't lash out. and her feet anchored to the floor and spread wide enough that she could not kick.

"We might have to adjust for different heights, but this is good for me." She looked around. "Who's going to slice me open?"

When no one stepped forward, Damon sighed. "I'll do it." He picked up the knife Griffin had used and turned it over in his hand. "I don't want to do this—I hope you know that." He looked at Greer. "You be ready as soon as I am done with this. I don't want her in pain for a second longer than it takes to do this."

Greer nodded. "I'm ready to heal her. Don't worry about that."

Gage looked at his watch. "Let's get this done."

Alaria gritted her teeth. "Make it fast, Mackenzie. No practice cuts. Cut straight and deep."

Damon gripped the handle of the blade and plunged it into her back, slicing through skin and muscle until he felt the resistance of bone. He cut downward, opening up an incision eight inches long right next to Alaria's left shoulder blade.

The moment the knife cut into her, tears sprang to Alaria's eyes. Her knees threatened to give out, and she choked back a scream with nothing more than ironclad will. Blood ran freely down her back, soaking into her jeans and staining the denim red. Every nerve in her back fired as pain rippled through her body. Sweat beaded on her forehead and she clamped her mouth shut to stop herself from crying out with agony. Her muscles strained as she struggled against the binds, her body bucking and writhing, and she bit into her tongue until she tasted the metallic tang of blood.

Damon used his fingers to spread the incision wider to allow him to look. Pale skin gave way to red and purple muscle, the long cords and fibers that covered her skeleton. He scraped the muscle away from the bone with the knife and used a rag to sop up some blood. The sound of the blade hitting bone echoed through the room—a sharp noise like nails on a chalkboard that made them all cringe and Alaria howl. Damon took a half-step back and stared when he saw the glimmering silver of the wing root.

The root delicate and long, reaching from one end of her shoulder blade to the other. It was bright silver, a half-inch thick and shimmered in the light from the lamp Damon was using to see what he was doing.

"How do I get it out?"

Gage pushed off the wall and peered into the wound. He reached over and snagged a clamp from the tray. "I suggest pulling. Here, let me."

When Gage reached in with the clamp and attached it to the root, Alaria screamed, her head falling back and her knees giving out. Her shoulders popped and burned from bearing all of her weight, and her eyes rolled back in her head from the pain. Fire spread through her body until it felt as if she were burning alive. She sobbed and begged, her words a jumbled mass of incoherent pleas for them to stop. His heart clenching in his chest, but knowing he had no choice, Gage jerked the clamp and ripped the root from her bone.

Alaria's wail was a keening cry that echoed through the room. Tears ran freely down her face, mingling with the blood she spat and dripping from her chin in a pink, frothy mess. Sweat poured from her, soaking her hair and skin, and the blood from her back ran down to her knees.

Damon looked around nervously. "I need her back up to do the other side."

Alaria shook her head. "I can't. I can't do it." She sobbed piteously. "The pain—God—I can't do it."

Braxton crossed the room and bent, wrapping his arms around Alaria and pulling her to her feet. He locked one arm around her waist and held her on her feet, using the other hand to grip her chin and turn her face toward his.

"You can do this. You *are* doing this. We're halfway done." He stroked his hand over her cheek. "You scream, yell, whatever you need to do. Bite if you need to. I'll hold you up. I've got you. Just lean on me and let me hold you up."

Damon looked at Braxton questioningly, and the other man nodded sharply. Damon dug the blade into the other side of her back and opened up another incision. Alaria shrieked and sagged against Braxton, her whole weight pressing against him. When Damon gripped the other root with the clamp and ripped it from her, she gasped in a strangled breath and screamed from both pain and loss as she felt the last remnants of her Angelic days were ripped from her.

Greer pressed her hands to Alaria the moment Damon was done. The skin and bone healed and formed over quickly. Unlike any other wound Greer had healed, Alaria was left with two silver scars running down her back. Alaria still couldn't regain her balance after the healing and sagged against Braxton, her breaths coming in deep, heaving gasps.

Braxton reached out and snagged the towel Aradia held, wrapping it around Alaria to cover her upper body and lifting her into his arms. She trembled, her entire body shaking from the trauma.

"What do we do with the roots?" Greer spoke up from where she stood in front of the tray, studying the two silver rods.

Gage lifted a lockbox. "We keep them as safe as we can until we have them all."

A rustling sound echoed throughout the room and Michael appeared. "I'll keep them for you. There has been a place in Heaven prepared for them."

Gage held up his hands. "Be our guest. That's one less fucking thing we have to deal with." He handed Michael the box. "We wanted to get this done and over with to give her some time to heal before we go after the others. Father Dooley thinks he has some information that will help, so Braxton and Alaria are leaving tomorrow afternoon to head toward Colombia. They'll be gone for a few days while we're trying to hunt down the location of the other five. Ideally, we'll move on the first one within the next ten days."

Michael nodded. "That timeline is acceptable. I don't want to push you to do more than you are ready to. I have been looking into where they may be, but they have left no trail for me to follow. I fear without Godly interference, you may have to resort to purely human means to find them."

Gage nodded. "I'll find them. I have no doubt about that." He looked at Braxton and then down at his watch. "I suggest you take her to get cleaned up. We barely have enough time to get her to town before her OBGYN appointment. I reserved a slot with the only American doctor around the Vatican, so you won't want to miss the appointment."

Michael lifted one hand. "I'll transport them to save on time." He looked at Braxton. "Do you need help getting her cleaned up?"

Braxton shook his head. "I can handle it." He shifted Alaria's weight in his arms and stooped to pick up the small duffel bag with her change of clothes in it. He carried her out of the chapel and into the full bath on the main floor of the monastery.

Alaria was still shaking when he placed her on her feet. She held onto the sink for balance and leaned against it heavily but remained upright. Braxton reached in and turned on the water. The pipes creaked and groaned out of protest and the water that spurted from the faucet was orange for the first ten seconds, but it grew hot and clean.

"Do you need help?"

Alaria shook her head. "I can manage." She looked around ruefully. "This is where I brought Griffin to clean her up after the Familiars attacked us." She sighed deeply and shucked off her jeans. "This is hitting way too close to home, Brax. Everywhere I look there are memories." She coughed and rubbed her throat, sore from the screaming.

Braxton nodded solemnly. "You don't need to tell me about it. I'm right there with you." He held her hand to help her balance as she climbed into the shower and pulled the curtain shut. "I'll wait right outside in case you need me." He paused at the door. "This is going to be hardest on us. You know that, right?"

Alaria poked her head out. "We've been careening toward this since the Choosing, maybe even before. It was never going to be easy, and it was never going to be right. It was just always going to be."

Braxton ran his hands over his face. "I think that's what makes it the hardest. I didn't have much of a choice with Griffin. You and Gabriel had to happen. You and I are choosing this when we both know we shouldn't."

Alaria disappeared back into the shower. "We deserve that choice, Braxton. We've paid our dues. We've both done everything they've asked and everything they've demanded. We deserve to make some choices on our own."

The waiting room at the clinic was sparse and clean. There were several chairs and a pair of couches. Water and coffee sat on a cart in the corner, and the receptionist was bright and bubbly. She greeted them in Italian and then switched to English when both Alaria and Braxton looked at her blankly.

"Sorry. We don't get a lot of Americans in here. You must be Mr. Windsor's sister. Is that right?"

Alaria nodded. "Gage made the appointment for me, yes."

"Great." She handed Alaria and Braxton both guest passes. "Mr. Windsor preregistered everything, so you're all signed in. If you'll go to that door, I'll buzz you in and meet you on the other side. We're all ready for you in the back."

Braxton chuckled and shook his head as they crossed the waiting room. "That man can buy anything, I swear to God." He paused at the door. "Do you want me to wait here for you? Or I could try and get Gabriel. Maybe this is something the two of you should do together."

Alaria glared at him. "Gabe has no right to be here." She hesitated. "I don't really want to do this alone. Do you mind?"

"Not at all." He walked with her through the door and stood patiently as the nurse took Alaria's vital signs.

Alaria stepped on the scale barefoot, then stood to let them measure her. She sat silently while they took her blood pressure and temperature and checked her glucose levels. Her abdomen was measured, and she was given a cup and pointed to a bathroom.

Emerging two minutes later, she glared at Braxton, who was trying not to laugh at the sight of her with the cup of urine in one hand as she emerged. "Not a word."

He waited until the nurse had taken the cup and placed it on her desk. "Wouldn't dare."

The nurse smiled and led them into one of the exam rooms, gesturing to the table. "You'll need to undress from the waist down and sit on the table. There's a sheet on the table to cover yourself with. Push the button on the wall when you're done and the ultrasound technician will be in shortly. We'll run the analysis on the urine specimen to check your hormones, and then you'll see Dr. Barnes briefly before you leave."

Braxton turned his back to give her some privacy while she undressed and settled on the table. She wrapped the sheet around her waist and climbed onto the exam station, tucking the cloth around her knees and making sure it completely covered her ass. She crossed her ankles and folded her hands in her lap.

"You can turn around."

Braxton turned and dropped into the one chair in the room. "I don't have to be here. I can wait outside."

Alaria lifted her eyebrows. "Do you want to wait in the waiting room?"

"I don't want to make you uncomfortable. This seems like a very personal, intimate thing, and I kinda feel like it's not really my place to be here. I know you and Gabriel are at odds, but it's his baby. It feels like he should be here."

"I don't want him here." She clasped and unclasped her fingers in her lap. "Brax, I know this is complicated and hard, and I know that it's a horrible place for you to be in. You're standing here, and I'm getting ready to have an ultrasound because I'm knocked up with an Angel's baby. This is something so crazy not even a soap opera would tackle it, and I understand if you don't want to be here. But Gabriel is not going to take your place if you're not. I don't want to influence your decision, and I'm not asking you to stand by me or hold me up or whatever. I'm strong enough to do it by myself, and I don't want you to feel any pressure or like I'm trying to maneuver you. I'm not. This is your choice. If you want to stay, then stay. If you don't, go, and I'll do it alone. Either way, Gabe is not coming in this room, and he is not taking the place next to me." She looked at him steadily. "I loved him. A part of me still does and always will, but he and I were over before we started. We were over before he got me pregnant, and we are always going to be over. I hope we can eventually get to the point that we can tolerate being in the same room, but right now, I don't want him anywhere near me."

The door opened and a woman wearing pink scrubs walked in before Braxton could formulate an answer. She smiled brightly at them both and went directly to the ultrasound machine.

"I'm Marci, and I'm going to be your technician today." She pulled on gloves and flicked a switch on the machine. "Have you had an ultrasound before?"

Alaria shook her head. "No."

The woman looked at the chart and nodded. "Your chart lists January thirty-first as your due date. That would make you eleven weeks and three days along. That should be far enough to do a transabdominal ultrasound instead of the more invasive transcervical one." She picked up a bottle and shook it. "Lie back for me, and I'm going to lower the sheet a bit. The conducting gel is warm, so it won't be too uncomfortable." She smiled brightly at Braxton as she adjusted the sheet on Alaria's body and flipped off the light. "Dad, if you want to come stand over here, that way you can hold Mom's hand while we take a look." She patted Alaria's knee. "Is this your first child?"

Alaria nodded. "It's my first." She looked at Braxton, a silent plea in her eyes.

Braxton looked slightly panicked and more than a little torn. He shifted from foot to foot, unable to decide what to do. His fingers twitched and he clenched and unclenched his hands several times, his mind racing from what the nurse had said. Alaria's unspoken request hung in the air and he nodded slightly, crossing the room to stand by her head.

She reached out and took his hand in hers. "What are you looking for?"

Marci squirted blue gel onto Alaria's stomach and rolled the ultrasound wand around her abdomen. "We're checking for development. I'll look for blood flow, normal limb and brain formation, heart rate, that sort of thing. I'll take some measurements to make sure that the baby is the right size for gestation and make sure that the heartbeat is good and strong. If everything looks good, the doctor will take a quick look at the pictures, do an exam, we'll take some blood, and you'll be on your way."

Marci turned the screen so that both Alaria and Braxton could see the gray fuzz. She rolled the wand across Alaria's stomach and fiddled with some knobs on the machine. Slowly, the picture came into focus and the blob turned into barely discernible body parts.

"Here we have the little arms and legs." Marci pointed to areas on the screen. "And here is the head and the brain. See the blood flow?"

Alaria laughed. "If you say that's what it is." She reached out and pointed to an area on the screen. "What's that?"

"Your bladder." Marci giggled. "These are hard to read for the average person." She made several clicks on the machine and studied the numbers. "It looks like you're exactly on track for a January thirty-first due date. You're measuring precisely eleven weeks and three days, which is fantastic." She held the cursor on the computer over a flickering light on the screen. "This is the heartbeat. Would you like to hear?"

Alaria looked at Braxton before nodding. "If you don't mind."

Marci laughed again. "You're the mommy, silly. Of course I don't mind."

She flipped a button and a swooshing sound filled the room. She adjusted the wand and the noise changed to a rapid heartbeat. Alaria closed her eyes and let it wash over her, the fast beating of her child's heart. Tears prickled her eyelids, and she tightened her grip on Braxton's hand. She was so preoccupied by the sound of the beating that she almost didn't hear Marci speak.

"Everything looks perfect. I'll print you some pictures, update your file, and let the doctor know. He'll check in for a second, but you're doing just great. You'll need to be seen again in a few weeks. Congratulations." She turned off the machine and the beating immediately ceased. "You can get cleaned up and dressed."

Alaria didn't open her eyes until the other woman was gone and when she did, she and Braxton were alone in the bright room, left staring at the dark screen of the ultrasound machine.

"What are you doing?" Gage stood at the bottom of the stairs, glaring up at Alaria as she hefted a large duffel bag and slung the strap over her shoulder. "You shouldn't be carrying that."

Alaria dropped the bag and put her hands on her hips. "I'm pregnant, not an invalid." She returned Gage's glare. "I'm still going to have to fight and run and train and do everything we've been doing."

"That doesn't mean you should do things when you don't have to." He climbed the stairs and took the bag. "Enjoy the break. You have an excuse to be lazy and get us men-folk to do your bidding."

Alaria snorted and tugged the bag out of his hands. "I don't need you men-folk to do my bidding." She loped down the stairs. "Brax! You ready?"

Braxton leaned back on his stool in the kitchen. "I've been ready for an hour." He drained his cup of coffee and sat it down. "The car is loaded out front, and the plane is fueled up and on the runway." He stood and stretched, his black t-shirt riding up to expose a sliver of tanned skin and a skinny trail of blond hair.

Alaria ignored the pool of desire at the sight of his skin and swallowed. "You should have said something, and I would've been quicker."

Braxton shrugged and slid past her in the hallway, bending to take her bag and moving toward the door in one smooth motion. "No biggie." He held the door for her and slung the duffel into the trunk.

"We're ready now, aren't we?"

Alaria looked over her shoulder to where Gage leaned against the door frame. He touched two fingers to his forehead in a half-salute and walked back inside, his voice carrying over his shoulder.

"Be careful."

Alaria nodded and turned back to Braxton. "Yeah, we're ready." She slid into the front seat and closed the door.

Braxton dropped into the driver's seat and turned the key in the ignition. He maneuvered the car out onto the main road and turned toward the small, private airport. They rode in silence, both preoccupied with their own thoughts.

When Braxton turned into the airport and parked the car, they both exited the vehicle quickly and headed for the plane. Braxton loaded their bags into the cargo container, and they both climbed the steps into the cabin. The captain had already done the safety check, and in ten minutes, the plane was rolling down the runway.

Braxton leaned back in his seat and cast a look around the plane. "Gage doesn't do anything halfway, does he?" He chuckled. "The jet sinks so he has a bigger one built."

Alaria looked at the plush leather couches, the thick carpet and the sleek granite counters. In one corner was a fully stocked bar. Against one wall was a huge television and stereo system. To the rear was a huge bedroom and bathroom, and toward the front was a spacious office, a second bathroom and a smaller bedroom. It was the exact same layout as the previous plane but a third larger.

"He gets extreme joy out of being rich." She chuckled and pulled her feet up onto the couch. "How long is the flight to Colombia?"

"It'll take us two days of travel. It's eight hours to New York, where we'll refuel. Then I need to make a stop in Philly. It'll take a couple hours, then we'll be on our way. There will be one more stop in Mexico to fuel again, and then we'll be in the air until Bogota."

Alaria tucked a long strand of her hair behind her ear and stared at Braxton, her eyes narrowed and her gaze unwavering. "How long are we planning to stay down there with Dooley?"

Braxton picked up the remote control and flipped through channels idly. "I figured we'd give ourselves a day to rest from the trip before starting it over again, and then we'd be on our way. It'll be Thursday when we get there, so I'll be happy if we leave Sunday to head back, get back to Scotland Tuesday." He settled on a movie. "Is that okay with you?"

She nodded. "I don't care how long it takes. I don't think we have a deadline on this task like we did on the last." She rolled her shoulders. "I can tell you from personal experience that this task is going to involve a lot of pain."

His gaze darkened as he remembered Alaria's screams as her back was carved open. "That is going to haunt me for a good long while, I think." He patted the couch cushion next to him. "It was all I could do not to stop Damon from hurting you."

Alaria slid down the couch and curled up against Braxton's side, resting her head on his shoulder. "I could tell." She sighed deeply. "Why are we going to Philadelphia?"

He exhaled slowly and ran his hand over her hair. "I need to have a talk with Griffin."

The last time Braxton had visited Griffin's grave, it had been cold and snowy. This time, the heat was oppressive and sweat beaded on his forehead as he walked through the rows of headstones to the place where Griffin lay.

He stooped and laid the bouquet of flowers he carried on the grass near the headstone and took a step back. Fifty feet behind him, Alaria waited patiently. He looked at her briefly before turning to the chunk of stone, feeling only slightly silly about what he was going to do.

"I don't know if you can hear me or not, but there's something that I need to do here. Some things I need to say to you." He paused, sighed, and laid his hand on the stone. "I wish you were here to look at me and talk to me. Well, part of me does. The other part is glad that I get to spill my guts to an inanimate object. Regardless, I'm here to talk, and I'm going to choose to believe you're going to listen."

Braxton took a deep breath and closed his eyes. When he opened them, he was in the white room Gabriel kept. There was a white chair, couch, and glass coffee table with a pitcher of iced tea and two glasses sitting on it. A cheerful fire crackled in the fireplace in one corner. Standing near the hearth, her blonde hair falling over her shoulders and dressed in a white suit was Griffin.

Braxton shook his head to clear it, and when she was still there, he sighed. "I didn't expect you to come when called."

Griffin smiled. "I told you Gabriel had made arrangements for me to be around when he thought I was needed. Obviously, he thinks you need me. How long has it been since we were in the garden together?"

"A week."

She looked surprised. "That's not long at all." She reached out and took his hands, drawing him down onto the couch and sitting next to him. "What's going on, Brax?"

"I went to visit your grave." He closed his eyes for a moment and looked pained. "I went to let you go."

Griffin blinked rapidly. She was silent for fifteen seconds, and when she spoke, her voice was soft and sad. "I think I expected that to gut me." She squeezed his hand. "Every time we talk, it becomes clearer that I'm different. That didn't hurt my feelings. I didn't feel anything." She studied him carefully. "What made you realize you need to let me go?"

Braxton took another deep breath. "I think this is a cruel trick by Gabriel. It would have been so much easier to say this to a rock." He stood and paced the room. "I'm tired of being sad. I'm sick of spending my life missing you. I want to wake up in the morning and not feel guilty that you're dead. I want to lay down to go to sleep and not feel guilty that I'm alive." He plowed his hands through his hair. "I want to have a life. I've been plodding along like I'm already dead. Not making plans, not moving on, all because I've convinced myself I'm as good as dead, or should be, and it's only a matter of time before I join you. The problem is that I don't want to. I want to start living again, Griffin."

Griffin's brows drew together. "Then live. It's not like you need my permission." She chuckled. "I'm dead, Brax. I can't be mad at you."

"No, but I've been mad at both of us. I'm mad at you for being dead and at myself for having survived."

She sobered. "I hate that I've affected you this way. If I could, I'd go back and change it. I'd have stopped myself from ever starting this."

"I don't want to change it. I don't regret being with you. I regret everything else. I regret the Choosing and not just running off and enjoying the few months you may have had. I regret you dying, I regret not being able to change it, and I regret that I wasn't able to be there with you when you died. I think that's the biggest problem I've been having." He rubbed his hands over his face. "I didn't get to tell you goodbye."

Griffin stood and crossed the room to stand in front of him. She reached out and laid her hands on his face, forcing him to look at her.

"I want you to listen to me, and I want this to be the last time I have to say it. You are what got me through the last year of my life. I was going to die no matter what either of us did. You made me strong enough to do what I had to, and I'm glad you did. I'm happy, Braxton. I like Heaven. I don't want to come back to Earth. I don't want to be alive again. You haven't died. You have a chance to make a life for yourself and to die an old man. That is what I want for you. I want you to be happy." She kissed him gently, her taste familiar and comforting. "I'm letting you go. You can tell me goodbye now. Do whatever you need to do to let me go, and do it now."

Braxton leaned his forehead against hers. "I think the thing that's been the worst for me is Alaria. I want to wish she was still a Devil and you'd been able to ask for your own life. I want to want her dead, but I don't." He closed his eyes. "I don't have the same feelings for her as I did for you, but I do have feelings."

Griffin huffed. "Braxton, you've known her for two years. You knew me for nine months. Of course the feelings are different. We were all chemistry and circumstances. Anything with her is going to be different because you've had two years of getting to know one another."

"This isn't something new. It started a year ago."

"So?" When he looked at her blankly, she laughed. "It's like you're hoping I'll be mad about it." She kissed him again. "I want you happy. If she makes you happy, I want you to leave here and go get her and never let her go." She stepped back. "Alaria told me once that it seems like you have to know exactly why every little thing happens and why you feel every little thing you feel. I'm telling you the why isn't important. It doesn't matter if it's because you went through something horrific together, it doesn't matter if it's only because I'm not there, and it doesn't matter why else. All that matters is what you feel, and what she feels." She squeezed his hands. "Go away, Brax. Tell me goodbye, and forget about me."

Braxton smiled. "I'll never forget about you, Griffin. I couldn't even if I wanted to." He stared at her intently. "I hope you really are as happy as you're telling me you are. I want you to be."

"I want you to be happy, too. You deserve to be. Just because I'm dead doesn't mean you have to act like you are. Go and live, Brax. I won't be mad. Hell, I won't even know, but even if I did know, the thought of you moving on makes me happy. I want you to leave here and move on with Alaria, or someone else, but move on. Let me go."

"I'm going to. It's what I came here to do." He stepped back and studied her face. "I'll never forget you, but I'm going to live without you." He sighed. "I thought this would be harder."

"Which means you should have done it a long time ago." She smiled gently. "Goodbye, Braxton."

Braxton returned the smile. "Goodbye, Griffin."

The sunlight was blinding when Braxton returned to the cemetery. He blinked rapidly to adjust to the brightness and turned around, finding Alaria standing fifty feet behind him, in the exact same position she'd been in. When he turned to look at her, she lifted her eyebrows.

"Did you do what you needed to do or do you need to stand there for a while longer?"

Braxton shoved his hands in his pockets and trekked back to Alaria. "I'm ready."

"What was the point of this trip?" She turned toward the car they had rented at the airport and began walking toward it. "I know it had to be something other than for you to stand there and stare at her grave for half an hour."

"I wanted to tell her goodbye." He opened the door to the car and sat down, waiting until Alaria did the same before he continued. "You told me to work quicker on getting my shit together. This is what that looks like." He started the car. "I came here to get my shit together."

Alaria nodded slightly. "And did you?"

"I don't think I'd have ever been able to do it on my own. I have too much guilt and too many emotions, but it seems Gabriel isn't as icy as he'd like me to believe because he's now brought Griffin from Heaven twice to talk to me. Talking to her and seeing her happy and still at least somewhat alive, well, that's helped a lot with the getting together of the shit."

Alaria stared at the side of his face. "What do we do now?"

Braxton grinned and reached out to squeeze her hand. "Well, right this minute, we have three hours before we take off for Mexico. We could go get something to eat before heading back to the airport." He looked at his watch. "It's Happy Hour."

Alaria giggled. "I can't drink." She patted his knee. "Food sounds good."

He turned out onto the main road and merged into traffic. "The question then becomes—is this just dinner, or is it a date?"

Alaria took several deep breaths in an attempt to calm the nerves that rose up within her. She wiped her palms on her jeans and swallowed. "I've never been on a date."

Braxton slid a glance her way and smiled, the expression only slightly rakish. "Then I think it's high time you found out what it's like. Date?"

Biting the proverbial bullet, she nodded. "Date."

Alaria had never seen Braxton be charming. She'd seen him wallow in guilt. She'd seen him fight violently. She'd even seen him caught up in a moment of passion, but she'd never seen the man be charming.

Despite everything going on—talks with dead people, hunting for Devils, and the trip to South America—he seemed relaxed at dinner. He had taken her to a quiet restaurant with dark wood and big steaks and slid into the same side of the booth after she got in so smoothly she didn't notice his presence until she turned to take the menu from the waitress.

Conversation at dinner flowed easily. They talked about simple things, both making an effort not to mention Devils or anything going on in the world. They ate in companionable silence, comfortable with one another. When it was time to leave for the airport, Braxton held her arm to help her out of the booth and easily tucked it into the crook of his elbow as they walked to the car.

The plane was lit up on the runway, the door open and the steps already pulled down. They climbed them slowly, and Alaria stopped at the top, rubbing her hands on her jeans. Braxton had one hand on either handrail, and he slowly backed her into a corner at the top of the steps.

"This feels weird." Alaria crossed her arms. "I'm not sure what I'm supposed to do."

Braxton chuckled. "It's good to be out of your comfort zone every once in a while."

"Everything about this whole thing is out of my comfort zone. If this were inside my comfort zone, there would be no conversations or dates, and we'd be naked and sweaty. I've never done this before, and I'm not sure how to act or what to expect. I swear I feel like some sort of teenager."

"Alaria, I don't want you to act any way other than how you normally act. We've known each other too long and been through too much shit to pretend to be anyone other than who we are." He reached out and pushed a lock of her hair behind her ear. "Now, if you don't mind, could you be quiet for a minute so I can end this date correctly?"

Alaria laughed softly. "What's your definition of ending it correctly?"

He hummed deep in his throat and curved one hand around the back of her neck, pulling her forward to align her body with his, molding her curves to him. She was tall, even in tennis shoes, and the top of her head came nearly to his nose.

"The only way to end a good first date is with a kiss goodnight." Braxton laid his hands on her hips. "It's all about building anticipation for the next time, so it's all you can think about for at least an hour afterward. It should be hot but not too passionate because the goal isn't sex." He leaned forward and ran his mouth along her jawline. "The goal is to see if there are sparks." He nipped her jaw sharply and pressed his lips to her ear, his voice a whisper. "I know we've done this part before, but this is the first time we're both making a conscious decision to do it. No one's crying, no one's drunk, and unless Gabriel is waiting for us inside, which would not, for the record, surprise me, there's no one here other than you and me."

Alaria's eyes drifted nearly closed. She gripped Braxton's shoulders to balance herself and sucked in a deep breath. His lips teased the sensitive skin under her ear, and a maelstrom of emotion whipped up inside her. Desire and need mingled with nervousness and a touch of fear, leaving her trembling and weak in the knees.

"I want you to be ready for this." Braxton's breath was warm on her skin. "I'm going to kiss you, and it's going to be a good kiss. It's going to be one of those kisses that changes everything. It's going to be hot and deep, and it's going to make you feel things. Are you ready?"

Alaria had never had the experience of being unable to speak. But in that moment, with Braxton pressing against her, his arms hard and un-yielding on either side, his breath caressing her skin and his scent filling her head, she couldn't come up with a single word. She inhaled a deep breath—leather, pine and spice—and nodded.

That was all the answer he needed. He took her mouth confidently, pressing her back against the railing and wrapping his arms around her, crushing her to him. His tongue swept into her mouth, brushing against hers and flooding her with his taste. Her hands clenched his arms desperately, and her knees went weak, making her sag against him.

Braxton took his time with the kiss. He explored her mouth leisurely, using his lips and tongue to learn every crevice. He relished her taste—chocolate and sin—and groaned deeply, running his hands over her body and sliding them around her to rest on the perfectly firm curve of her ass.

Alaria couldn't think, and she couldn't breathe. She was at Braxton's mercy. She returned the kiss eagerly, pressing herself against him fever-ishly and digging her nails into his arms to hold herself upright. When he pulled back and set her away from him, it took her several seconds to clear her vision and catch her breath enough to release his arms.

She looked up at him, her fingers pressed to her swollen, bruised lips, and let out a deep breath. When she spoke, her voice was raspy. "If you were really dropping me off at home after a date, this would be the point where I invited you in."

Braxton laughed warmly and pressed a kiss to her forehead. "You never have sex on a first date if you intend for there to be a second." He waved her into the plane and followed her inside. "I think we can both agree there should be a second."

The captain spoke over the intercom. "We've been cleared for flight, folks. Please have a seat and strap in for takeoff."

Alaria was distracted enough by the announcement that she turned around to look at the cockpit and forgot all about Braxton's statement. "Since when do we have to strap in for takeoff?"

"New pilot. The last one needed to sleep, and I didn't think we want-ed to be grounded that long." He dropped into a chair and clipped the seatbelt into place. "I think we might have time to see a little of Bogota before we fly back. Not a full day, but at least a few hours. We could see some of the sights, maybe eat some local food and then see what stuff might be going on."

Alaria sat down slowly and pulled the strap across her lap, snapping it into the metal receptacle. "Somehow I assumed we would sort of be like you and Griffin or the others. They didn't go on dates. Gage and Aradia went from avoiding to banging in one day. Greer and Damon maybe had a little more get-to-know-you time, but it was still very fast."

Braxton crossed one leg over the other and looked at her steadily. "We're different people, and I know how I want this to go. If you have a problem with it, then we can talk about it, but I don't want to base how we do things on how the others have, or how I did things with someone else in the past. I want to figure out what feels right for us, and given how far we've come and how hard we've fought both to get here and keep from getting here, I think we should at least try to take advantage of the opportunities we have to date." He shrugged and looked sheepish. "God knows this might be the only chance and we'll just feel it out after we get back, but I'd like the chance to take you out if you'll let me."

Alaria nodded hesitantly. "I don't know how to date."

"I'll teach you." He grinned and reached out to lay his hand lightly on her knee. "This isn't going to be easy. There's a lot we're going to have to get through."

She laughed nervously. "Like the fact that I'm knocked up with a Nephil?"

Braxton chuckled. "There is that." He sobered. "In all seriousness, putting all the personal stuff aside and talking just about the baby, I want you to know that no matter what happens between us, I will do whatever it is you want me to do with that child. Not because it's a Nephil, and not because God says it has to exist, but because it's your child and even without the romantic shit, you and I are friends and I care for you."

Alaria leaned back and laughed. "Does that include changing diapers and mushy green beans?"

His gaze serious, Braxton nodded. "If that's what you want, I'm there." He squeezed her knee and leaned back. "I'm already going to be raising Finley once we're through this. I have no clue how to do that, but I'll damn well do my best."

"I promised Sam that I'd help you, and I will." Alaria nodded once, definitively. "I don't relish the thought of being called 'Mommy.'"

"I can't imagine you being called that, and I can't imagine myself raising a child, but here we are. We don't have to make big, sweeping decisions tonight, or even in the next six months. All you need to know is if you ask me to be there, I'll be there. Labor, two a.m. feedings, or nothing at all. Whatever role you want me in."

She stood as the plane leveled out and bent over to kiss him once, hard and short. "We both know how this is going to go, Brax. You've come to the conclusion the same as I have. We're stuck together for better or worse, and we're going to be raising children together." She paused at the door to the bedroom. "I told you once that you're a good man, and I meant it. But being willing to raise two kids who aren't yours just because it's the right thing to do is so far above and beyond that I don't even know words for it." She leaned against the doorframe and cocked one eyebrow at him. "If you decide you want to break the first date rule, I'll leave the door unlocked, and I'll be sleeping naked."

Braxton groaned as she shut the door and let his head fall back so he could stare at the ceiling. His pants were uncomfortably tight, and he shifted restlessly. "That woman will be the death of me yet."

Turning off the lights, he moved through the cabin of the jet toward the other bedroom, crossing through the small office and into the room. Stripping his pants off, he unzipped his bag, withdrew a small bottle of lube and dropped onto the bed.

Alaria waited for nearly an hour, hoping Braxton would change his mind. She laid in the dark, the covers pulled up to her chest and her hands folded on her stomach. There was a small sliver of light coming under the door, and she heard him moving around in the main cabin. When she heard him entering the other bedroom, she sighed. The sliver of light disappeared, and she groaned in frustration.

Damn that man.

Her whole body was strung tight with desire. It had been months since she'd had sex, and the pregnancy hormones were making her want it more than she had previously. She squirmed on the sheets and tried to get comfortable despite the want.

Making a low noise of frustration deep in her throat, she rolled to the edge of the bed and leaned over, unzipping the small side pocket of her duffel bag and stuffing her hand inside. She found the slim wand inside and pulled it out. The vibrator was about four inches long and made out of discreet white plastic.

Sighing in contentment, Alaria slipped her hands beneath the blanket and shifted so that her knees fell apart. She placed her right hand at the juncture of her thighs, forming a V shape with her fingers to part the lips to the entrance of her body, her desire making her wet and hot. She twisted the dial on the end of the vibrator with her left hand, and ran the device over her entrance, rubbing it against her clit and rolling it back and forth to get the most sensation.

Pleasure speared through her, and she whimpered softly. It wasn't going to take much. She lifted her right hand and skimmed it over the skin of her abdomen and up to the mounds of her breasts. She rubbed her fingertips on the tightly beaded point of her nipple and pinched it lightly between two fingers, grunting at the bolt of sensation that resulted from the contact.

She rubbed the vibrator against her clit harder, slipping it down and slightly inside her body, using the bent end to caress the entrance to her body while maintaining the contact with her clit. She rolled her nipple between her fingers, tugging and squeezing gently, the touch increasing her race to climax.

Alaria felt her orgasm building and panted softly, desperate for it. She pressed the vibrator into her body harder, rubbing it up and down vigorously. She licked her fingers and used the moisture to create more friction on her nipple, holding her breath and straining for the climax that was just out of reach. She lifted her hips slightly, slid the vibrator farther inside herself and scraped her fingernails over her nipple lightly.

Her orgasm rolled through her, hot and slow. She sucked in a breath and collapsed against the mattress. Her chest was covered in a sheen of sweat and her internal muscles undulated in response to the climax. She sighed deeply, and rolled to fish in the bag for a disposable wet wipe, cleaning the vibrator before putting it back in the bag.

She settled into the pillows and gave herself a few moments to catch her breath. She closed her eyes and smiled softly, feeling much more relaxed and much looser than she'd been ten minutes before.

As her heart rate slowed and her breathing returned to normal, Alaria felt sleep closing in on her. She let her eyes drift shut and sank into the cool oblivion of sleep.

Alaria woke with a jerk when the door to the bedroom flew open and light streamed in. She squinted and blinked rapidly, lifting her hand to shield her eyes. Braxton stood in the doorway, wearing a black t-shirt and jeans, with his hair still damp from a shower, and stubble darkening his jaw.

He raked his eyes over her, taking in her mussed hair, and her tanned skin, bare where it was exposed by the rumpled covers. The blankets had slipped down to her waist, giving him a clear view of her breasts. He tore his eyes away from the dusky globes and forced himself to look at her eyes.

"We'll be landing in about an hour." Braxton coughed and rubbed one hand over his jaw. "I thought you might want to get a shower."

Alaria nodded and propped herself up on her elbows, giving him an even better view of her chest. "You thought right. Did I miss the stop in Mexico?"

"I did, too. The captain tells me it went without a hitch. We both slept the better part of ten hours."

She gaped at her watch. "I haven't slept that long in as long as I can remember." She lifted one eyebrow and smiled wickedly. "Enjoying the view, Braxton?"

He returned the grin. "If I'd known you were serious about sleeping naked, I'd have had a much harder time going to bed in the other room."

"I never joke about being naked." She sat up and threw back the blankets, rising unabashedly and bending to get clothes from her duffel. She brushed by Braxton's arm and looked over her shoulder, grinning at the look on his face. "Maybe next time you won't go to bed in the other room and we can have fun together instead of me having fun with my vibrator."

Braxton's jaw fell open. "You didn't."

Alaria laughed and rose onto her tiptoes to brush a light kiss across his mouth before whispering, "Just because you've taken a vow of celibacy or some other stupid notion doesn't mean I have. I like sex. I love orgasms, and if you won't give me one, there's no reason I can't do the job all by my lonesome."

Braxton stared after Alaria for several moments. Shaking his head, he went to the small kitchen and put on a pot of coffee to percolate. He took two cups out of the cabinet and tapped his foot impatiently while waiting for the brew to be ready. After four minutes, the light turned from red to green. Distracted by self-generated images of Alaria in the throes of orgasm and what she might look like writhing on the bed, he reached for the pot without looking and swore when he grabbed the carafe instead of the handle, burning his hand and splashing coffee on the counter.

Alaria was fast in the shower. By the time Braxton had managed to clean up the mess, place the coffee cups on the table and toast four pieces of bread for their breakfast, he heard the water shut off. Five minutes later, dressed in jeans and an olive green camp shirt, with her hair hanging in damp curls down her back, she emerged from the bathroom and walked toward him.

At that moment, with bare feet and no makeup, with droplets of water still visible on her skin, Braxton was struck by how young she looked. Alaria was always gorgeous and ageless, but he'd never before noticed that when she was relaxed and comfortable, her face could be soft and pretty instead of the intense, hard look she normally had.

"What're you staring at?"

Alaria's voice startled Braxton from his reverie, and he shook his head. "Nothing." He gestured to the table. "I made some toast. I thought with the nausea you could probably keep it down."

She smiled and dropped into one of the chairs, picking up a piece and biting into it. As she chewed, she studied Braxton from beneath her lashes. "Did you ever want kids?" When he looked at her in shock, she waved her hand. "Meaning, when you and Griffin were together, did you ever daydream about what might have been? Talk about how many kids you'd have had? Anything like that? Or, hell, been even a little excited when your college girlfriend's period didn't arrive on time?"

Braxton chuckled and finished his own toast. "Griffin and I talked about it, though I think that was way more for her than it was for me. If things had been different, and she had survived, I imagine we'd have had children, though I don't know if it's because I wanted them or because she did and I wanted to make her happy. As far as before, I was never really with anyone long enough to feel anything other than sheer terror if the words 'I'm late' were ever mentioned." He nodded pointedly to her stomach. "Did you ever want to be a mother?"

"Yes." She chuckled when he looked surprised. "Didn't think the bitchy Devil woman would want to have kids?"

Braxton struggled to find the right answer. Finally, he sighed. "You don't seem like the maternal type. I'd heard you mention it a time or two when you talked about being made human, but, to be honest, I always thought it was talk."

Alaria swallowed a gulp of coffee. "Don't get me wrong. I never wanted to be a mom this way. What Gabe did to me isn't right, and I don't think I can ever forgive him for it, but I did want children at some point. I had no idea if I could have them, or if I'd be a good mother, or if my babies would even be human, but I felt a tug to try anyway."

He reached out and covered one of her hands with his. "I think you'll do a fine job." He tugged on her hand until she stood, and he directed her into his lap, releasing her hand and burying both of his in her hair. "What's between us isn't just sex, and as much as I want to bury myself in you over and over until neither of us can walk, I'm not going to. That doesn't mean I don't want you because I do." He brought her face down so he could nibble at her lips gently. "I want to taste and touch every fucking inch of you and then fuck you until you're a puddle of post-orgasmic bliss." He pulled back farther and stared into her eyes. "But I never want you to ask the same questions of me you did of Gabe. I never want you to doubt where we stand, and I never want you to question whether or not I'm invested or whether I would fight for what's between us. You need to know those answers, and be sure of them, before we take this any further."

Alaria let his words wash over her, soothing and soft. She shifted to straddle his lap instead of perching on it, and pressed her body against his tightly, wrapping her arms around him and nestling her head in his neck. She felt his heart beating against hers, and closed her eyes, enjoying the feel of him pressed against her.

"I think part of me does know that." Her voice was a whisper next to his ear. "You make me feel safe, Braxton, and I never knew I didn't already feel that way. I told Gabe once that he and I weren't some epic love story. We weren't Romeo and Juliet or any of the other thousands of couples destined to be together, whether in life or in death. I don't think you and I are that epic love story, either. You make me feel safe and comfortable, and we *can* be together long term. We make sense, and we fit well." She sat up to stare into his eyes. "I'm not in love with you. I wish I was, but I'm not. Maybe someday, but today, I can say for sure I love you because you're a phenomenal friend and because of all of the things you do and who you are, but I don't feel the same way that I did for Gabe. With him, it was hot and all-consuming, and with you, it's warm and comfortable."

Braxton chuckled and wrapped his arms around her, pulling her toward him to capture her mouth in a kiss. "I'm not in love with you either." He tucked her hair behind her ears. "I want you. I like you. I will be here for you for as long as you'll have me, in whatever way you want me, but I don't feel the same for you as I did about Griffin. I don't think we're supposed to. It's different because we're different people. We make sense, Alaria, and in this world, living the lives we do, that's the most I think either of us could ask for."

They stayed like that for several minutes before Alaria climbed out of Braxton's lap and held out a hand. He cocked an eyebrow and took it, allowing her to pull him to her feet. When she immediately pressed herself against him and ran her hands up his chest to loop casually around his neck, he looked down at her curiously.

"What are you doing?"

She fisted her hands in his shirt and backed up until he was sandwiched between her and the wall. She yanked him forward, pressing her body against his. "Just because you won't have sex with me doesn't mean we can't fool around." She wiggled her eyebrows. "Don't human teenagers derive pleasure from groping and rubbing?"

Braxton laughed. "Yeah, but for us adult men, it really only breeds tight pants and discomfort."

"Well then, maybe that'll get you where I want faster."

Alaria clamped her mouth on Braxton's in a searing kiss. Her tongue swept into his mouth, rubbing against his, and she nipped at his mouth with her teeth. Her hands, small and graceful, grasped the hem of his t-shirt, and she wrenched it over his head.

Nearly growling, she splayed her hands on his chest and scraped her nails over his skin, enjoying the varying textures of the dusting of coarse hair, the smooth skin, and the flat discs that were his nipples. She pressed the heels of her hands into his shoulders and used his leverage to hike herself up, wrapping her legs around his hips.

Braxton turned so he was the one pressing her into the wall with his thighs, holding her up. His hands gripped her hips tightly, and he ravaged her mouth with his own. She groaned deep in her throat and dug her fingers into the tightly corded muscles of his back.

Alaria tore her mouth free and stared at him, her chest heaving as she struggled to catch her breath. Slowly and deliberately, she unbuttoned her shirt, each button that slipped from its loop exposing another inch of creamy skin.

Her breasts were encased in black lace. The bra was cut low enough that Braxton could see the dusky points of her nipples peeking out above the fabric. The clasp was in front, and Alaria met Braxton's gaze and held it as she ran her own hands over her chest, kneading the globes of flesh and tugging the lace down enough to bare the tightly beaded tips.

Braxton expelled a raspy groan and shifted slightly, trying to ease the pinch of his jeans biting into his swollen erection. "You're not making this easy on me, woman."

Alaria laughed and slipped one hand between their bodies to rub against him. "I can make you feel better." She leaned forward and bit his ear sharply. "Touch me, Brax."

His hands covered her breasts, and he worked the clasp to free them, casting the scrap of fabric aside and reveling in the feel of her flesh filling his hands. He rubbed his thumbs over her nipples and dipped his head to suck one into his mouth, swirling his tongue around the point.

Alaria unwrapped her legs from around him and slipped her hands down his body to the button on his jeans. She slipped it from its hole with a slight pop and lowered the zipper slowly, sliding her hands inside his boxers and wrapping her fingers around his long, hard penis.

They both jumped when she encompassed him with her hands, and Alaria hummed in satisfaction as she ran her fingers over his length. She shoved his pants and underwear down his legs and encircled him with one fist, running it up and down the smooth skin. Braxton groaned softly and leaned his head against the wall over her shoulder, his eyes heavy lidded and nearly closed.

Alaria leaned forward and ran her tongue around the sensitive shell of his ear. "By the time I am done with you, you are going to be begging me to let you fuck me."

Braxton curled one hand around the back of her neck and brought her mouth to his in a deep, searching kiss. When he pulled away, he spoke, his voice husky and rough. "I don't doubt that, but I can make you just as desperate."

She grinned. "Good. Let's see how much fun we can have without dick in pussy."

The raunchy words made his cock jump, and they both groaned when she ran her thumb over the tip, massaging the soft flesh. Alaria dropped to her knees and leaned forward, taking him deep into her mouth.

Braxton's knees went weak as she surrounded him with wet heat. She sucked strongly, swirling her tongue around him and moving her head back and forth, driving him in and out of her mouth.

Once he was slick and wet with saliva, she wrapped one fist around the base of his penis and concentrated her licking and sucking to the head while pumping her fist up and down, tight and fast.

She tasted salt as a bead of liquid appeared, and she sucked harder. Braxton's hips jumped, and he fisted his hands in her hair, his eyes closed tightly. She felt his whole body tense, and she knew that it wouldn't be long until his orgasm tore its way through him.

Alaria lifted her head and looked up at him, a seductive smile on her lips. She slowly licked him from base to tip, her fist pumping up and down. The veins that ran up the appendage stood out from his tanned skin, and the head of his penis grew dark red as blood rushed to it. Alaria hummed softly and swiftly lowered her head, taking him all in and sucking deeply.

Braxton felt release start deep in his belly, and he closed his eyes in anticipation of the rapture. Before it hit, though, the plane lurched, and they were both tossed to the side. Alaria hit the ground, her face smashing into the carpet, and Braxton hopped awkwardly from foot to foot, trying to avoid stepping on her while also trying to keep his balance. Within seconds, the captain's voice filled the cabin.

"Sorry, folks. We're starting our descent, and it looks like we're coming down on a bit of weather. I'd suggest strapping in for the rest of the trip. We'll be on the ground in about fifteen minutes."

Alaria rolled to her back and stared up at the ceiling, rubbing her jaw gingerly. A bruise was already forming where she'd struck it, and she moved her mouth to make sure nothing was broken. Braxton appeared in her line of sight, his hand extended and his pants pulled up. She grudgingly took the proffered hand and allowed him to heave her to her feet. They stared at one another for a long moment, neither sure what the appropriate response was. Finally, Alaria giggled.

"I'd say it'd be a story to tell our grandkids, but I really don't think you'd like me telling them about that time I failed at giving you a blow-job."

Braxton chuckled and dropped onto the couch. "I can honestly say, Alaria, that turbulence is a fantastic erection killer." He grinned when she buttoned up her shirt and sat next to him. "Though until the turbulence, it was fantastic."

Alaria settled against his side and smiled. "I'm glad you enjoyed. What time is it on the ground?"

"About one in the morning, I think. They're several hours behind us, and it's just seven in Scotland. We'll land shortly, and then it'll take an hour or two at the airport to unload everything. We'll get into a jeep, and our guide will take us out to the monastery. From what I know, it's about a hundred and fifty miles outside of Bogota, so it'll be a five-hour drive to get there. Once we're there, I'll meet with the Warriors and check in on some things. We'll meet with Dooley tonight and tomorrow, take Saturday to rest, and then head back Sunday morning."

"Has Gage texted with any news on the Devils?"

Braxton nodded. "He's found Beelzebub and Lilith, and he has a line on Abaddon and Abalam. Azazel is the only one who's evading him right now, and he's hoping to have him pinned down before we get back. Greer and Damon are developing infiltration plans to get to them." He absently toyed with her hair. "Greer wants to go after Lilith, then the twins, and then Azazel, if we've found him by then."

Alaria sighed deeply. "Azazel will be anywhere there are lots of willing men and women. He likes sex and doesn't care who it's with. I wouldn't be surprised to find him at Miami Beach or in some brothel somewhere. It would amuse him that people would pay to fuck him. He's been chained up a long, long time."

The Captain's voice filled the cabin again. "Again, sorry about the bumpy ride, but we're coming in on the runway now. The local time is one-seventeen a.m., the temperature is eighty-two degrees with ninety-one percent humidity. Welcome to Colombia."

Chapter Eight

Michael looked around the thatched hut and groaned. Only Lilith had ever summoned him there. When a flash of light filled the room, he turned, expecting to see the blonde Devil. Instead, he faced Gabriel.

"Brother, I apologize for calling you on such short notice, and to this place, but I needed to assure myself we would have complete privacy." Gabriel snapped his fingers, and two chairs appeared in the middle of the room. "Please, sit and let us talk."

Suspicious, Michael arranged himself in one of the chairs and crossed his legs. "Why have you brought me here? We always speak in the garden, or in your room, but never here. I didn't know you were even aware of its existence."

"I wasn't until recently." Gabriel smiled. "Don't worry, Michael, Father does not know about it. However, it is a move being made by Him I wish to discuss with you."

"I haven't been made aware of any change in strategy."

Gabriel sighed. "The time you brought me to the garden to tell me Alaria had been chosen as the vessel for a Nephil, I was angry at you. Now that I find myself in a situation similar to the one you were in, I feel guilty for having felt that way. I know how hard it must have been."

Worried, Michael leaned forward. "What is going on? What's happened?"

"Much as I impregnated Alaria in order to ensure the survival of humanity, Hell has made a move to extinguish it. It has become clear this battle may be fought beyond the six who have been chosen. We must take steps to make sure there are safeguards in place to deal with the moves the others are making."

Michael sighed deeply. "What have they done?"

"The male Devils were enchanted by Garrick before he died to allow them to father children. They've all been having intercourse with multiple women—as many as they can—in order to create Cambion who will continue their cause should they be defeated."

"There have been Cambion before, Gabriel. They rarely survive birth, the same as Nephilim."

"It's different this time. Devils haven't been the father before, only demons. They're creating an army, Michael. I've been made aware of several thousand pregnancies via the four Devils, and several warlocks are experimenting on pregnant humans. They're feeding them Devil blood in order to allow the demons to father Cambion that will survive. Add to that the thousands of demons still trapped on Earth, along with the wolves and vampires, and we're dealing with an army which has the potential to be nearly a million strong. It will continue to grow as they make more."

Michael rose to pace, panic rising up within him. "What has God ordained be done?"

"We don't have the Angels to fend off an insurgency of such magnitude. He fears there will be another siege against Heaven. He has ordained the Angels must take steps to ensure there will be a large number of Nephilim to fight against the Cambion and demons. He's withdrawing all Angels to Heaven to guard the gates." Gabriel turned to make sure he and Michael were looking in each other's eyes. "He's ordered us to abandon Earth. Angels are now only allowed to go to Earth to create Nephilim with human women. They are to be impregnated as quickly as possible. Even the female Angels have been given the ability to carry children. We are going to have a war, Michael, whether the six succeed at this task or not."

Michael held up a hand. "I need a moment, Gabriel." He crossed the room to a cabinet and withdrew a bottle of scotch. Foregoing the glass, he tipped up the bottle and drained it with three gulps. Cursing his inability to be truly drunk, he leaned his head against the wall. "The fifty-year time limit?"

"Has been lifted. God is going to give them the war they want."

Michael's wings shuddered, and he expanded and contracted them anxiously. "We can't let this happen. There has to be a way to stop it. We've spent millions of years protecting these creatures. We can't allow them to just be exterminated."

Gabriel sighed. "I'm sorry, brother. We're under orders to return to Heaven. We have little choice in the matter. You'll still be allowed to advise the six in their task, but after the task is complete, you will not be allowed back on Earth."

Michael gripped the mantle on the fireplace so tightly the wood cracked and splintered beneath his hands. "You intend to go to Heaven and stay there?"

Gabriel looked guilty. "I've spoken with Father. I'll be allowed to keep an eye on the child Alaria carries. Beyond that, yes, I intend to stay in Heaven with the rest of the Host."

"I won't. I swore to guide and protect them, and Heaven help me, I'm not going to abandon them in their hour of need. Without us, they will all die."

"For generations, humans have left God's grace. Humans wove the spell to undo the Choosing. They follow Lucifer in droves. God grows weary of it. With this army of Cambion, they will siege against Heaven. Every sword is needed to protect our home." Gabriel laid a hand on his brother's shoulder. "Come home with me, brother."

"You would watch your child die?"

"My child will be spared. I've spoken to Him of it." Gabriel returned to his chair. "Greer and Aradia have been chosen to host Nephilim as well. God feels that their abilities would allow the children to be nearly as powerful as the child Alaria carries."

Michael closed his eyes and shook his head. "Which is it, brother? Has He given up on them, or is He still trying to save them?"

Gabriel sighed. "I know it seems as if He is sending mixed messages. When the Choosing failed, God was heartbroken. He had devised a way to eradicate Lucifer's influence from Earth in a way it hadn't been since the Garden. Humans found a way to negate that and let demons back onto Earth. Humans continue to be involved in serving Lucifer as hosts for the demons and now as willing, even eager hosts to the Cambion children. These women aren't being forced, Michael. They're volunteers. Our Father sees Earth as a lost cause and Heaven as our only chance. The Nephilim are a way to both give Earth a chance if the humans want it and help protect Heaven when we need it." He looked at Michael sadly. "It is not our job to understand, brother, only to serve."

"I cannot serve a master who will subjugate the free will of the very creatures He created and purports to love. When it was one woman, for a very particular purpose, with His hand upon it, I could swallow my objections and allow it to happen. I will not stand by and allow the women who have given up everything short of their very lives to serve Him to be robbed of their choice. I can't abide it, Gabriel. I can't abide any of this."

"You're the Angel of War. You should be relishing the chance to watch a war the likes of which has never been seen."

"I would enjoy it were I leading our Host into battle alongside them. Regardless of how we feel about the human race as a whole, the specific humans we guide are very special and undeserving of being abandoned. I enjoy fighting wars, Gabriel, not watching them from Zion."

"I do not agree with everything being done, but we were made to serve, and serve we must. If you do not do as has been decreed, you may be punished."

"This would not be the first time I have risked the wrath of Daddy dearest, and I doubt it will be the last." Michael stalked to the door. "I won't stand for it. I haven't spent the last years fighting alongside these creatures who risk their lives daily to please Him, only to watch the one they seek to please turn His back. I won't allow those women to be impregnated against their will. You do what you have to in order to clear your conscience, and I will do what I have to do to clear mine."

Gabriel followed Michael with concern in his eyes. "Brother, if you defy him, I can't promise you'll be safe."

Michael whirled around "Would you come after me, Gabriel? Drag me back to Heaven kicking and screaming? Would you lead a squad to find me and capture me?"

Gabriel shook his head. "No, I would not, but I cannot assure you others might not feel differently." He sighed deeply. "Is this it, then? The point where you part with Heaven?"

Michael shrugged carelessly. "If He is so willing to throw away what we've protected for millions of years, then I will be parting ways with Him, yes. As insignificant as I think humans are, I can't stand by and idly do nothing while the people I've learned to respect fight and die in a war they cannot win."

"You know as well as I do it is a war that can never be won. All we can do is strive to keep the balance, and we have been outmaneuvered. If we continue as we are, we will all die a slow, painful death. I have secured a better future for my child. I won't apologize for that, Michael."

"Do what you feel you need to. You'll receive no judgment from me. As long as there is even a glimmer of hope, they will keep fighting, and I will fight alongside them." Michael opened the door. "This is where we part ways, brother. I regret this is how it ends."

"What will you do?" Gabriel crossed his arms and regarded his brother coldly, resigned to their disagreement.

Michael glanced over his shoulder. "I'm going to give Aradia and Greer a chance to make their own decision before someone can take it away from them." He glared at Gabriel, his eyes hot with anger. "I won't stand by and allow the Host to brutalize and rape the women of Earth."

Gabriel reached out and grasped his brother's arm. "I don't want you to believe that this is as it was with Alaria. What I had to do with her was different than how it can be for the human women selected."

Michael shrugged off Gabriel's grasp. "What are you talking about?"

"The very nature of human conception requires sexual intercourse. A sperm must meet an egg and be fertilized into a zygote which grows into a fetus and is eventually born."

"I don't need a biology lesson, Gabriel. I know how sex works. Get to the point."

"The point is that we are not Devils, and God is not Lucifer, regardless of your desire to see him in that light. I created my child with Alaria through sex, but there is a way to create Nephilim without intercourse."

"How?"

"God has given us the ability to touch a human woman with the intention to transfer Angelic essence. It will remain inside her until the next time she has sexual intercourse with a human man. At that time, she will become pregnant, and the child resulting will be Nephil. The nature of reproduction requires there to be intercourse in order to create life, but your assumption that the Heavenly host will be forcibly raping women is incorrect."

Michael glared. "Forcible or not, you are still stripping them of their choice. What of the female Angels?"

Gabriel waved his hand dismissively. "If they desire to carry a child, which I doubt any will, they will have to find a man to have sex with. I don't know the vernacular for a singular sexual encounter, but I know humans have them quite frequently." He examined his lapel for any imperfections. "Michael, this is war. We need an army to combat the Cambion. Greer and Aradia are very strong and talented. While an Angel would not harm them in order to plant within them a Nephil, do you really think one of the Devils, or a demon would hesitate?"

Michael tipped his head back and stared up at the sky, thinking things through for several moments before speaking. "This is it for me, brother. I will not abide by this decision. If He ever decides to fight, I will lead His army against the Cambion in a war so bloody it will be remembered for all the days of this Earth, but I will not cower behind the gates with the rest. I am the Angel of War, so it is to war I will go."

Gabriel nodded curtly. "These women are receiving a gift. They are being chosen by God for an incredible purpose. They will carry Nephilim, brother. When presented with the option, do you not think they will agree to it?"

Rubbing his hands over his face, Michael sighed deeply. "I fought with myself over the decision regarding Alaria. I was told that it would be one time, and that the child could kill Lucifer. Actually kill him. You and Alaria already had a sexual relationship. My—reservations—could be overlooked in that situation." He paused to think about what he wanted to say for a long moment before continuing. "I don't doubt that the majority of the human women you approach will consider this a great honor. I also do not doubt that they will not be given the whole story. They will likely not be told that raising a Nephil may cost them their lives, that they will send their children off to war, or that God is abandoning them. And what if they say no? Will they be given this gift anyway? Even if they don't want it? Would the Angels impart upon them their essence regardless of the desires of the humans who must carry, birth, and raise the Nephilim? It would be as much a rape as if they tossed them down and forcibly penetrated them."

"The women won't know, Gabriel. Those chosen for this will not know anything. They will continue with their normal lives. Any who are already pregnant will be touched with Angelic essence and the child will become a Nephil. Those trying to conceive will have the miracle they have been begging God for. Couples around the world will celebrate the conception of children."

"And what of those trying to prevent pregnancy? What of those who do not wish to be mothers?"

Frustrated, Gabriel paced. "What would you have me do? Go to each of them and ask their permission to place a soldier in their womb?"

"Yes!" His anger bubbling over, Michael's voice rose to a yell. "The Warriors wouldn't refuse! They would consider it their duty and be among the only ones capable of protecting the children God has ordered be made. There are witches like Aradia, Healers like Greer, Hunters like Damon who would all think the same. The special people that God would choose for this would likely be the ones the most willing to do it!"

"What if they say no? Are you going to be the one to tell Him?"

Michael laughed bitterly. "It wouldn't be the first time I've pissed him off and I highly doubt it would be the last." He stared at his brother. "Consider your decision carefully. This is where I break with Heaven. What you do next determines whether this is where I also break with you."

Michael appeared in Gage's kitchen with a flash of light. The four people at the table looked up in surprise. Gage held up his mug of blood in a mock salute.

"At least you popped in at dinner instead of the middle of the night." Gage gestured to an empty chair. "Have a seat. Might as well be comfortable while you tell us the inevitable bad news you have."

Michael smirked and dropped into the chair to which Gage motioned. "I wish I had good news. I don't like coming to you only to make your lives more difficult than they already are, but unfortunately, I am again in the position to do just that."

Greer set down her wine glass and folded her hands under her chin. "What's going on?"

Michael smiled sadly. "I don't know all the details, and when I say that, do not think I mean I won't tell you, because if I knew, I would disclose it. Truly, I have little knowledge of what is going on. Gabriel hailed me to him today to speak to me of orders coming down from God."

Damon sighed. "It's never a good thing when God issues orders. What does He want this time?"

Michael raked his hands through his hair. "He has issued an edict requiring all Angels to retreat behind the pearly gates and abandon Earth. From what I have been told, Beelzebub, Azazel, Abaddon, and Abalam have been impregnating all the women who will lie with them. By doing this in conjunction with a spell cast upon them by Garrick, they are producing thousands of Cambion. In addition, they are feeding women pregnant by demons their blood in order to allow the offspring to survive past birth. They are siring an army."

Gage whistled softly. "That's certainly some bad news. Why has God issued the retreat order?"

"Because He believes there are enough humans involved with our adversaries that they have taken an affirmative step toward Hell. He believes that by abandoning them and leaving humans to their own devices, He is allowing them an opportunity to have the fate they desire. However, to allay the evil on Earth, he has authorized—demanded—the Angels begin impregnating human women at the same rate as the Devils are. He is requiring an army be raised to allow humanity a second chance."

Aradia sucked in a breath. "I thought God had only allowed that to happen once because of what Alaria was in the past. To allow the violation of so many women is obscene."

Michael nodded. "I agree with you. I stand apart from Heaven in this decision. However, there is nothing I can do to keep it from happening. I do not know for sure, but given the manner in which this was explained to me, I believe the women to be impregnated are being chosen because they have some talents or abilities that, when combined with the power of the Angels, will create very talented and powerful Nephilim. Greer, both you and Aradia have been chosen to carry Nephilim."

There was an eruption of anger as all four humans began talking at once. Greer rose to her feet, her eyes flashing with anger, and she slapped her hands against the table. "If a fucking Angel comes after me, I'll chop his dick off and shove it down his throat."

Aradia nodded in concurrence. "I'll turn them into a statue if I have to."

Michael held up his hand to get their attention. "I knew what the reaction would be when I came here. I know what you're going to say, Gage." He cast a dark look at the vampire, who had also stood, his jaw set out of fury. "And you're right. You can put up Angel wards. That'll help. Yes, Aradia, you could maybe kill some Angels if you want to.

The problem is there are very powerful Angels out there, some more powerful than either Gabriel or I. We tend to be the ones who interact with humans the most, but that doesn't mean we're the best, or worst, there are. There are Angels who could turn me into a pile of ashes. They could walk right through those wards and never feel a thing. The Angel of Death is one of them." He sighed deeply. "The problem is not the Angels. They are not going to rape you. Angels do not do such a thing. There is a way by which we can create Nephilim without penetrating a woman. However, it has been pointed out to me that while the Angels do possess this restraint, those serving Lucifer do not, and your talents have likely not escaped their notice. They could be coming for you as well, and likely are."

Gage sat back down, though his expression was still angry. "Then what to you propose we do? You wouldn't have told us if there wasn't some way for us to stop it."

Michael nodded. "You're right. There is only one way I know of to completely stop them, at least for now. I cannot promise you they will not come after you again later, but it will buy us some time."

Damon waved his hand. "Let's hear it then."

"You would need to already be pregnant."

Gage laughed bitterly. "I'm a fucking vampire, Michael. Even if I wanted to, I couldn't sire a child. You know that."

Michael smiled grimly. "I also know what I am capable of, and sterility and death are within my realm of powers, at least temporarily. I won't do anything without your permission, but what I would ask from you is for you to allow me to bless you both. It would provide a small amount of Angel essence, but enough to make the child a Nephil." He tapped his fingers on the table. "You may say no, and I will not force you. I will do everything in my power to protect you from the fate God has ordained, but I cannot guarantee we will be successful, and I don't know how much time you have to decide. What I do know is that we are in a time of war, God fears a siege upon Heaven, and He is casting aside many of the rules under which we have operated for millions of years in order to be able to have the best chance possible of winning that war. The two of you are very powerful, and I do not believe He will ever leave you alone until you birth a Nephilim." He looked concerned. "Even if He would, there is the problem of Lucifer as well."

Greer was the first one to speak. "How much Angel essence are we talking? I mean, I'm not saying yes to this, but I want to know how much of this potential kid would be mine and Damon's and how much would be yours." She laughed nervously. "Don't get me wrong, I like you just fine, but I don't want to have to share custody with you or have a kid with your eyes and nose. It would be too much for me."

Michael smiled reassuringly. "Don't concern yourselves with that. I am not suggesting I become some sort of third parent. In order to give Angels a way to sire children without requiring intercourse, we have been given the ability to transmit our essence with a touch if we want to. The material I would provide has nothing to do with appearance or personality. It would allow them to have Nephilim abilities. I have no desire to father Nephilim and even less to take away the joy of parenthood from someone who would enjoy it. It would be enough that the children would be Nephilim despite having been born of two human—at least for the most part—parents."

Gage cleared his throat. "And what about vampire DNA? What would that do to a baby?" He raked his hands through his hair. "I'm not crazy about fathering a child I would have to watch grow old and die, but I think I'm even less crazy about the idea of having a fleet of Devils coming after Aradia and Greer with the intent to forcibly impregnate them." He cursed softly. "You fucking Angels are great about giving us choices that aren't really choices."

Michael looked pained. "I hope you believe me when I tell you I do not agree with what is being done. I am not returning to Heaven with the rest, and I will fight alongside all of you for as long as is necessary. It seems that I, not unlike Alaria, found my breaking point with Heaven. I cannot stand aside and let this be done, and I won't take part in it. Because of that, I must actively oppose it."

Aradia reached out and covered Michael's hand with hers. "I know it must be hard for you, and I'm sorry for it. I wish there was something I could do."

"It's hard only in the sense that I am disappointed in my brethren and in my Father." Michael sighed deeply. "There's nothing any of us can do to change the present. Gabriel has elected to join the Host behind the gates. He will remain there other than brief trips to check on his child."

Gage snorted. "He's always been a pansy." He looked at Aradia. "What are you thinking?"

Aradia smiled sadly. "That I hope now, more than ever, we find a way to earn your humanity so you don't have to watch our child die." She patted Michael's hand gently and continued to speak to Gage. "I don't believe we have a choice in this matter. It seems as if God is prepared to take free will from us in order to raise this army to confront the Cambion." She lifted one shoulder in a delicate shrug. "I suppose the end is worth the means if the war is won by the Nephilim, though I loathe the thought of birthing a child I know I will send off to war."

Greer sighed. "As much as I want to say no, and as much as a part of me wants to have a shot fighting off anything that would want to come after me, I know we have more important things to worry about at the moment." She looked at Damon. "We wanted kids someday anyway."

Damon laughed wryly. "This isn't exactly how I thought we'd plan our family, babe." He leaned back in his chair and looked at Michael. "If you were Gabriel, I'd accuse you of being a liar. I never know what to think of him, and I always get the feeling he's only in it as far as it's good for him. You, I trust. So you tell me this—if we say no, are we going to be targets? Are they in real danger of being attacked?"

Michael's gaze was steady and steely. "Yes, to both of those questions. I think God knows I would not sit idly by and allow this to happen, and that is why He has not allowed me an audience with Him lately, so I cannot give you precise answers from the lips of God. What I can give you is my knowledge and experience with Him and with the rest of the Host. The one thing God will not allow is another siege on Heaven. With the Devils raising an army of Cambion, that is the only purpose. They are violent and powerful, and they are born with a burning desire to kill. There are not enough Angels to stand against such an army, and the Nephilim are a counterweight to Cambion in every way. Raising His own army is the only way to achieve two important goals. First, it ensures there will be a readymade army to stand against the siege. Second, since they are half-human, it allows humanity a way to earn their way back into His grace through fighting for Him during the coming war. The tasks you have are now secondary to God. He already sees this as a lost cause."

Gage cursed again. "This is why I hate God. He makes the edicts and decrees that affect our lives, and He stays up there in His castle and never cares what His decisions are going to do to the rest of us. I get that He's disappointed over the Choosing. We all were. We all fought hard to make that happen. Hell, most of us nearly died and a shit ton of people did die. Then, Lucifer plays dirty and we're back here. God pits six people against Hell itself, and just as we're about to beat those fuckers, Lucifer makes another move, and instead of giving us more people or more ammo or more anything, God in all His infinite wisdom decides it's *our* fault this happened, and He cuts us off at the knees. I get that He's unhappy. We're fucking unhappy, too! But that does not give Him the right to take away every weapon we have just because He's got His feelings hurt over a few assholes picking the wrong side! He is no better than Lucifer. What happened to being a loving and merciful God?" Gage slammed his hands onto the table and stared at Michael, becoming aware that he had stood at some point during the diatribe.

Michael chuckled. "Well, you're still alive after having said all of that, so I don't think He's as bad as you seem to think He is. He's also a jealous and vengeful God, who has destroyed this Earth once already. You're only surprised because you weren't alive while the Bible was being written."

Aradia rubbed the back of Gage's neck softly as she looked at Damon and Greer before answering for them all. "We'll do it. Whether God's given up on us or not, we still have a chance to win this, and we don't need to be distracted. We were already racing against Alaria's pregnancy, so this won't change anything for us." She smiled softly. "It won't affect our abilities to do our mission. We're going to prove God wrong. We can do this. We *will* do this."

Michael nodded and reached out, pressing his fingers against each of their foreheads. "It is done. The next time you lie together, you will conceive a child." He began to fade, then reappeared, standing awkwardly and staring at Gage. "I know I came with bad news, but I fear I am no longer welcome in Heaven..."

Gage chuckled. "I've got plenty of rooms. Pick one."

Chapter Nine
July 31, 2031 - Colombia

Alaria lowered her sunglasses to shield her eyes from the harsh Colombian sun. Her hair was plaited into a braid hanging down her back, and she was already regretting her choice of jeans instead of shorts. Braxton hopped out of the Jeep on the other side, his boots sending up puffs of dust from the dirt driveway. Together, they looked at the monastery.

It was flush against a rock cliff, with the Rio Negro less than a hundred yards from the front gates. They were deep within the jungle and very close to the eastern border with Venezuela. Vines covered the cast iron gates and climbed the stone walls, covering most of the windows and doors. Armed sentries patrolled the gate, and people were stationed on the roof at every corner.

Alaria put her hands on her hips and studied the building. "Will we be safe here?"

Braxton nodded. "For a day or two, we will. We're only sixty miles from the nearest village, but it's small and mostly made up of farmers, fishermen and a few shopkeepers. There aren't any big cities between here and Bogota, so the odds of anyone being able to find us out here are slim. This place has been a Warrior stronghold and training ground for nearly a hundred years. It's never been breached."

"It'll have to do, I suppose." She looked at her watch. "It's already eleven. We'd better get inside, get settled and let Dooley get his stuff gathered up while you talk to the leaders." She plucked at the already damp fabric of her shirt. "I'm going to change into something more revealing."

Braxton chuckled and slid his arms around her waist and into the back pockets of her jeans. "You're about to walk into a commune of Warriors and Hunters who are overwhelmingly male. Don't wear anything too revealing or you might have to kick some ass."

Alaria rose onto her tiptoes and brushed a kiss over his mouth. "I can kick plenty of ass."

"Brax! Alaria!" Father Brad Dooley rushed from the monastery, wearing jeans, sandals and a ball cap in addition to the white collar and flowing black shirt of the priesthood. He drew to a stop when he saw the way they sprang guiltily apart. "It's not as if I've never seen a kiss before." He smiled widely. "Just because I'm celibate doesn't mean you have to be." He leveled a glare at Braxton. "I'd like to think Griffin would approve. I know she wanted nothing more than to see you happy, and I know she considered you a friend toward the end, Alaria. You've come a long way from the first time she asked me about you." He swiftly embraced them both. "Come in. I know it's been a long trip."

Braxton picked up his duffel and slung it over his shoulder. "I'll need to meet with Calder and Lex for a while to go over how things are holding and work on a plan for keeping this place safe moving forward. I'm a bit out of touch with the Warrior network, but from what I understand, things are getting pretty dicey out there and there are more and more people who need a safe house between missions." He looked to Alaria. "I think some of the guys are a little uneasy with you being here, so as much as I hate it, I'm going to have to meet with them on my own and catch up with you later."

Alaria shrugged, though it was obvious it stung that the Warriors didn't want her there. "If they don't trust me, they don't trust me, and we don't need to give them a reason not to trust you, either." She picked up her own bag. "I'll get settled, have some lunch, take a bath and see you later tonight. Is it okay to look around, or do I need to stay in my room and not be seen?" She sighed when Father Dooley shifted from foot to foot and looked guilty. "That answers that. Will you at least show me to my cell?"

Braxton sighed. "Alaria—"

She held up a hand. "You can't help how they feel, and there's nothing I can do to change their minds. One would think risking your life every day for nearly two years would be enough to put a couple checks in the 'trust' column, but they don't know me, and the odds are I've killed someone they knew. I get it."

Father Dooley smiled. "I'll take you up to your room and stay with you for the afternoon. We won't get into anything substantive without Brax, but I hate the thought of you staying by yourself because these guys can't see past who you used to be." He patted her arm. "It'll be fine. Promise."

Braxton looked at the computer screen in front of him and the map spread out on the table. The two Warriors in charge of the Colombian base stood on either side of him, their faces matching expressions of grimness.

"This is worse than I thought it was going to be."

Calder Leftwich laughed. "Dude, you've been living in a mansion in Scotland for the last bit. You haven't been in the trenches lately." He held up his hands when Braxton glared at him. "Don't get me wrong, I think what you're doing is more important than what we're doing, because if you win, this all stops. All we're doing is trying to plug the holes while you work. Unfortunately, they're getting more numerous and harder to plug. We're training new guys as quickly as we can, and they're dying faster than we can train them. It isn't going to be long before this spills into the real world. We're monitoring the news stations and the internet and we're trying to scrub anything damning, but at this point, I'm beginning to think it might be better to let some stuff get out so the humans have a chance to be prepared."

Alexia Renaud crossed her arms and stared at them both. "What we need is for those fucking Angels to get off their asses and start working with us instead of sitting on the sidelines with a goddamned bucket of popcorn."

Braxton frowned. "It's about to get worse. Gage, one of my group, called me after we landed and told me the order has gone out— the Angels are to pull back to Heaven. Apparently our not-so-friendly Devils are impregnating every woman they can stuff their dicks in, and the only reason Angels are allowed out of Heaven from here on out is to do their version of the same." He took a deep breath. "At least the Angels give the women a choice. And there's no sex involved, so really it's not at all the same thing, is it?"

Calder looked at him in disgust and shook his head. "They're still no better than the ones we're fighting. If the Angels would come down here and fight, there would be no need for Nephilim at all." He sighed and turned back to the screens. "We knew from when your soldiers came back from the future that eventually we'd be left alone. I guess I was hoping we'd change that, or even delay it, but it looks like we haven't managed to do much."

Braxton nodded. "We knew it could happen." He picked up a computer printout and studied it. "How are you holding up here?"

Alexia sighed. "Good so far. We've had a few demons get close, but our sentries have killed them all before they've gotten in. There has been a lot of activity picking up around here, and the local tribes are getting antsy, to say the least. We're really just using this as a base now because of how often our guys are getting killed and sending newbies out as soon as we get them trained up. I don't think it'll be long before we end up on their radar, but it hasn't happened yet."

Calder brought up another map on the computer screen. "I know you've been out of touch, so I'll catch you up. There used to be sixty Vatican sponsored Warrior bases and another hundred informal ones. All fifteen in the States are still standing. We're still good. A few others haven't been breached yet, but Europe is struggling. Twelve of the bases have been completely wiped out, and eighteen sanctuaries have gone up in flames—some literally." He leaned back in his chair and ran his hands through his hair. "Africa is gone, dude. We're the last one in South American, and both Canadian bases are gone. There are a lot of Warriors breaking with the Vatican and going out on their own. A few have gone to ground and are hiding their families away. The general consensus is this could be the End of Days. The signs are lining up, and it's getting very bad very fast."

Braxton rubbed the bridge of his nose and closed his eyes for a moment. "Thoughts?"

Alexia pulled her hair into a ponytail before stuffing her hands into her pockets. "We've been talking about abandoning the bases. Stick with the informal network so we can still keep in touch with each other and there isn't the big target of these places. We could mobilize some of the Warriors who train our new guys and set up temporary places. I think we have to accept the fact that the more mobile we are, the better off we'll be."

Braxton nodded slowly as he processed the notion. "I'm not sure how I feel about that. Have we been getting any direction from the Vatican?"

Calder shook his head. "None. I think half of them have their heads buried in the sand in denial this is happening, and the other half are too busy trying to make their own preparations, or they're out trying to stem the flow of occurrences the best they can." He looked out the window and stared off for several moments. "There's no right answer. We have to do something or they'll come and kill us all. Then again, if we leave, we leave the indigenous people here completely defenseless, and we would be giving up the way of life that has sustained us since the Dark Ages. If this mumbo jumbo about quasi-rapist Angels is true, then we're also giving up an opportunity to be there to train these poor bastards when they hit puberty and realize they aren't human but Ne-philim."

Alexia snorted. "We've always known we were the redheaded step-child of the Vatican, but when they're faced with either denying they know about us or having to admit they've hidden this shit from the general populace for centuries, we all know they'll let us die out before they admit we belong to them." She cocked her hip to the side and stared at Braxton. "Where's the she-Devil you brought with you? I thought you'd want to keep an eye on her."

Braxton ignored the flash of anger that rose in him at Alexia's words and forced himself to remain calm. "She's in her room hanging out with Brad Dooley. For the record, she's not a threat. She's as human as I am, and she's putting her ass on the line trying to save this world the same way we are."

Calder studied Braxton carefully, sensing there was something more going on. He shook his head at Alexia. "If Winslow says we can trust her, we trust her. I can't make the troops like her, but as far as I am con-cerned, if you vouch for her, we're good." He idly flipped through the maps on the table. "Dooley has refused to tell us what he's looking for and will only say it's something you need. Do you want to fill in some of the holes there?"

Braxton chuckled. "I don't know what he's got since we have a policy of not disclosing important shit on the phone. What he's looking for is another door to Hell. From the way he talked, I would be willing to bet he's found it. We need to know where it is so we can keep the Devils from opening it. From what we've heard, it's the only door through which they can resurrect Lucifer."

Calder whistled. "You really think they can do that?"

Braxton nodded. "I think they'll give it everything they've got if they find it."

Alexia's brows drew together. "Then why don't we try to destroy every trace of evidence it exists? If no one knows where it is, then they can't find it and we can't lead them to it."

"Because I need to access it. One of the parts of these fucking tasks has to do with the damn door. Lucifer is damn near breaking out on his own, and this may be our only way to ensure he stays down there forever. He's so powerful that even if he's the only one out, he can create new demons from here on Earth. We'd never be free of them." Allowing several moments for that to sink in, Braxton sat silently while Lex and Calder exchanged a long look, then glanced down at his watch. "There're still a couple of hours before dinner. Why don't you guys show me around the grounds and let me take a look at what you've got going on here? We'll talk again this evening and see if we can't come up with a solution for the bases. I don't want to make a unilateral decision, but in the same breath, I know if someone doesn't tell some of the others what to do, they'll treat it as a suggestion and not an order."

Calder stood and stretched. "I think a break sounds like a great idea." He picked up a pair of sunglasses and perched them on his face. "You get to make the call because you're the Warrior who confers with Angels. If it comes from you, they'll listen."

Father Dooley looked out the window and down at the glimmering blue water of the pool. "We get crocodiles in there occasionally. Just baby ones, mostly, though the morning after I got here I went down for a morning swim and just jumped in without looking. Damned ten footer almost ate my ass for breakfast."

Alaria smirked as she unzipped her duffel to rifle for cooler clothing. "Haven't you ever heard the phrase 'look before you leap'?"

Dooley chuckled. "That has never been truer than when there's a hungry croc chasing you." He turned and perched on the window sill, his gaze sympathetic. "Not everyone can forgive and forget like a priest, Alaria. The Warriors live in a very unique world."

"I'm not mad at them." She laid a pair of shorts and a tank top on the bed. "I understand why they think what they do. It's nothing I haven't thought about myself a hundred million times since I was made human." She looked sad for a moment. "God left me with the guilt of everything I did when He made me human. If I think about it too much, it consumes me, so I can only imagine I did something to some of them they should hate me for."

"That doesn't mean you're the same person you were back then." He looked back to the pool. "I think a swim sounds like heaven. Do you want to go?"

Alaria looked into her bag and toyed with the lone bathing suit she'd brought. "Well, I figured a bathing suit would be necessary in the jungle, but that was because I was anticipating outdoor, communal showers, not swimming pools." She shrugged and sighed. "Why not? Watching them drain and refill it after I've sullied it with my Devil germs will be amusing."

She changed into her bathing suit and covered up with a large towel she found in the bathroom. Dooley had stopped by his room and changed into swimming trunks covered in blue and pink hibiscus flowers and a baggy black t-shirt. Together, they wound their way through the cavernous monastery and exited the building into the courtyard containing the pool.

There were several Warriors lying on chairs around the water, and four men who looked as if they were still teenagers were throwing a Frisbee amongst themselves. When they saw Alaria, all but one woman immediately left. Dooley saw a flash of something equal measures of hurt and anger flash across Alaria's face before she dropped her towel on the cement and slipped off her sandals.

Alaria looked down at herself and smiled. Pregnancy had its benefits, and the early curves were one of them. Her breasts had already grown half a cup size and her hips flared out slightly more than they had. Her stomach was still flat, though instead of belying the muscles from her hours and hours of training, she was softer and curvier.

Dooley rolled his eyes and did a cannonball into the pool. Alaria jumped and squealed when the cool water splashed her. She scraped wet hair off her face before glaring at him. The priest shrugged and held out his hand to her.

"You're getting wet anyway. Come on in."

Alaria stooped and slid into the pool, sucking in a breath as the water enveloped her. She kicked off the wall and glided from one end to the other, enjoying the feeling of weightlessness. Dooley found a beach ball floating on one end and grabbed it. When Alaria stood and turned to face him, he batted it to her.

"First one to score ten points buys coffee?"

Alaria grinned and twirled the ball. "You have no idea what you've just gotten yourself into."

Braxton walked between Calder and Alexia, taking in the pairs of Warriors sparring under the close watch of several more experienced ones. The leaders called out instructions and critiques, and the younger ones quickly readjusted.

"They look good." Braxton drew to a stop and nodded. "There's a lot of new blood lately."

Calder crossed his arms. "Unfortunately, there are a lot of people finding out our world exists because their families are getting murdered. We keep a close eye on all the news outlets, and we manage to get to most of them before they do anything stupid. Occasionally we miss and they get themselves killed, but we've got a pretty good success rate with it."

Braxton lifted his eyebrows. "The Vatican wouldn't be happy to know we're actively seeking people out."

Alexia snorted. "They abandoned us long ago. Their edict is to keep the existence of these creatures as quiet as possible. What better way to do that than to bring the people finding out into the fold, teach them how not to get killed, and impart on them what they need to know to not only protect themselves but other people? Even if they learn for a few weeks and go home, the odds are they'll be able to stay alive."

"How many become fully trained Warriors?"

Calder shrugged. "Around a third, I think. Most don't have what it takes to be a Warrior, so we send them home better trained. Others want nothing to do with our mission, and we respect that as well. Some, though, are angry or vengeful, and they're the ones easiest to train and use." He reached out to touch the arm of a man stomping by them. "This is Dominic. He got here about six months ago. He's leaving on his first official assignment next week."

Dominic scowled. "The sooner the better if you ask me." He glared at them. "I can't believe you let him bring a fucking Devil in here, Calder.

We'll all be dead by the time they leave if you don't get rid of her. Heart-beat or not, she's still a Devil, and she'll betray us all."

Braxton lifted his eyebrows. When he spoke, his voice was calm and steely. "You're new, so I'm going to choose to believe you don't know any better. The next time you insult Alaria in my presence, I will rip your fucking tongue out of your head, boy. She traded immortality for a chance to help save all our asses and may very well die while she's doing it."

Dominic drew his shoulders back and puffed up. "Once a Devil, always a Devil. Just because she fucks a Warrior doesn't make her one of us."

Calder had time to utter one sentence before Braxton reacted. "Dom, you have no idea what you've just done."

Braxton struck out and punched the younger boy in the nose. The sound of crunching cartilage echoed through the yard and blood spurted from both nostrils. Dominic dropped his shoulder and charged Braxton, tackling him to the ground. Braxton flipped him to his back in one motion and smashed his head against the ground.

Dominic brought his knee up into Braxton's groin, and the older man's grip loosened slightly as his breath expelled from both lungs and he groaned in pain. Dominic got in two punches, one to his jaw and one to his ribs before Braxton's vision cleared and he punched both fists into Dominic's face.

Alexia took a step back to avoid getting rolled into the fight and looked at Calder. "How long do we let them go?"

Calder pulled off his sunglasses. "I was hoping one would knock the other out right quick so I wouldn't have to get in it." He sighed deeply and handed her his glasses. "Hold these. I don't want them broken." He gave the two men on the ground one glare before pushing his sleeves up and wading in to the fray.

Alaria heaved herself out of the pool and wrapped her towel around her body, sliding her feet into her flip flops. She heard a shout followed by the sound of fighting and lifted her eyebrows. Dooley, still floating around the pool, seemed oblivious to the sound. She debated going to investigate then looked back toward the doors leading inside.

She listened hard to the fight, and when she heard Braxton's voice, she struck off toward it. Rounding the corner of the building into the main training area, she saw Braxton rolling around on the ground with a younger man, both trying to pummel the other, and a large man trying to pull them apart while a pretty blonde stood back and shook her head at the whole situation.

Alaria stopped when she was next to the blonde. "What happened?"

"Dominic is a moron and is getting his ass beat." The woman held out a hand. "Alexia Renaud. You must be Alaria."

Alaria nodded and shook her hand. "I am." She cocked an eyebrow. "Can the other one handle those two?"

"That's Calder Leftwich. He can handle them. He's the one who runs this place." Alexia sighed lustfully. "What is it about hot men pounding on each other that makes me want to get naked?"

Alaria chuckled. "They are nice to look at." She put one hand on her hip and tried to look stern as Calder yanked Braxton to his feet. "Though he'll be regretting this tomorrow. That eye's going to swell up nice and big." She smiled at Alexia. "I'd better drag him off to lick his wounds. It was nice meeting someone who will actually talk to me."

Alexia laid a hand on Alaria's arm. "You're not what I thought you would be. Let me know if you need anything while you're here."

Alaria nodded and crossed to Braxton. She slid under one of his arms and wrapped one of hers around his waist, tugging firmly in the direction of the monastery. "Let's get you cleaned up and changed."

Braxton glared at Dominic before addressing Calder. "I expect you to deal with that."

Calder chuckled and heaved Dominic to his feet. "I think you dealt with it, dude, but I'll reinforce the lesson once he's fully conscious again."

Alaria dragged Braxton through the doors and pulled him toward the stairs. "What the hell was that about?"

Braxton rubbed his jaw. "He needed brought down a peg or two. Idiot came up to me spoiling for a fight and trying to push all my buttons." He looked at his bloodied knuckles in satisfaction. "I don't think he'll be doing it again."

Alaria led him up the stairs and down the hall toward her room. "Are you hurt?"

He shook his head. "Nah, just a little bruised. He got a couple good hits in, but nothing's broken."

"Was it because of me?"

Braxton ran his hand over her hair and bent to nuzzle her. "Don't worry about it, Alaria. I took care of it."

Hurt and anger flooded her eyes, and she stepped back. "You can't beat the hell out of everyone who says something mean about me." She opened the door to her room and led him inside, pushing him down onto the bed while she went to the bathroom for a washcloth.

Braxton grinned rakishly. "Sure I can. I'm bigger and stronger than most people, and I like kicking ass."

Alaria smiled as she pressed the wet cloth to the cut on his eyebrow and he hissed. "Well, if you keep picking fights, you're going to have to kiss mine. I think it's stupid to take shit so seriously."

Braxton reached around her and laid his hand lightly on her butt. "I'll kiss yours anytime you want me to."

She snorted. "What happened to this plan of celibacy you have?"

"Hey, you're the one who decided we could fool around without breaking the rules." He tugged her towel away to ogle her in her red bikini. "I happen to think you had a great idea." He ran his hands over her thighs. "Saturday is all ours. We'll work with Dooley tomorrow and go over his stuff, do our thing Saturday, and head home first thing on Sunday. By then, hopefully Gage will have a better idea of what's going on with the Devils and where they all are, so we can get on with this task and get it done."

Alaria studied his head. "The bleeding's stopped. From what I understand, our rooms share the bathroom, so I suggest you go get some clean clothes and take a shower to wash the blood off." She swatted at his hands when he tried to pull her down into his lap. "I'm not fooling around with you while you're bloody and dirty. Go."

She waited until he had retreated into the bathroom and shut the door before she changed out of her suit and into shorts and a tank top. She'd only been in Colombia for eight hours and there had already been a fight because people hated her. It was going to be a long weekend.

CHAPTER TEN

AUGUST 1, 2031 - COLOMBIA

FATHER DOOLEY laid out the papers he'd written notes on and looked between Braxton and Alaria with an expression of nervousness and excitement. He muttered to himself quietly as he organized, and after several minutes, he stepped back.

"It was written in Atlantean, which is a language we don't exactly have a translator website for. I was able to find a couple things in the archives that gave me a few words, and from there I was able to put a few things together. I was lucky enough Michael sent one of the lesser Angels down here with some Greek to Atlantean translations, and I was able to figure it out after that. Once I had it into Greek, I could bring it to English. I have to tell you, I was shocked not to find Aramaic since that's what people spoke in Biblical times, but I've certainly seen stranger."

Braxton smiled in amusement. "What did you find, Brad?"

"The third gate was in Atlantis. Graciela built her portal on top of it and used its power to amplify her own in order to escape before the city sank. When it sank, it had to be relocated. Because God didn't want any of the Angels to know where it was—apparently He is still afraid that some of them are going to betray him to Lucifer, even after all these years—so He used humans to relocate it. Specifically, He used priests in Greece." Dooley shook his head and grinned at them in amazement. "I never knew the Gods and Goddesses were really Angels and demons until I started looking into this, but it makes sense."

Alaria rolled her eyes. "I could have told you that. They made up stupid names and held court. Some liked Rome, some liked Greece, a few lived in Atlantis, still others in Sumer. They had tons of fun back then. God wasn't too happy when he found out some of the lesser Angels were playing at beings Gods and Goddesses, and thus Mount Olympus came to a bloody end."

Dooley gaped at her. "One of these days, when all this is over, I'm going to tie you to a chair for a month and make you tell me everything you know." He shook his head and looked back at the papers. "Anyway, back to the point of the whole matter. They moved it to the one place God protected above any other because it is the one place He needed to keep standing."

Braxton swore and stood. "Mother fucker. It's under the Choosing Place, isn't it?"

Dooley deflated. "You had to take my thunder, didn't you? All this research and you figure it out before I can tell you. That's no fair, Braxton." He sighed deeply. "From what I can tell, it's under the chapel, and there's a pretty damn good chance it's directly underneath where Griffin sacrificed herself. There's an energy emanating from it that would have drawn her to it."

Alaria chuckled. "A Hell Gate under a church floor. That is not what I expected to hear."

Dooley nodded. "It wasn't what I expected to uncover either, but if you think about it, there's really no better hiding spot. God knew the only time there would be Devils in there was during the Choosing, and there was so much magic and energy going on there that it would be almost impossible for them to tell what it was. Once the Choosing was over, they had no use for the place and no reason to go back. It's pretty perfect."

Braxton leaned back in his chair and nodded. "You're right. It is a good hiding spot." He ran his hands through his hair. "Makes things a little easier for us. We'll be able to do all the rituals right there in the chapel. The only trick will be keeping the Devils we capture from getting loose and warning the others about where we're at. If they catch on to us, we're screwed."

Alaria rubbed her temples in a futile attempt to fend off a headache. "The problem we're going to run into is that not all Devils can be contained in traps. Azazel, Beelzebub, and Lilith can all get out of them.

Abalam and Abaddon will get stuck in them, but the other three can walk right through, which is not good for us. We have to find a different way to trap them."

Braxton swore under his breath. "I didn't even think about that." He looked at Alaria. "Do you know how to keep them in? Or have any ideas?"

She shook her head. "I never looked into it, and because I'm now human, I really can't. Aradia can strengthen the protections, and Michael gave us the info about using blood to paint everything, so maybe that'll be enough to keep them in, but I can't tell you for sure. With Hell closed off, we can't send them back without going to the backdoor in New Zealand and opening it, and then we run the risk of them giving information to Lucifer about how far we've gotten on the task. At least if they're out, they aren't communicating with him. The downside, of course, is keeping them contained for any appreciable amount of time is going to be extremely difficult—if not impossible."

Braxton rose to pace the room, his expression belying his tension. "Do you have any ideas, Dooley?"

Dooley shook his head. "I'm not out there fighting. I didn't know they couldn't get past Devil's traps until thirty seconds ago. I'd suggest combining the blood idea with the liquid silver to see if they amplify one another, and perhaps integrating some Wiccan symbols. Aradia could likely help you. She'd know which ones are the most powerful when put together. Otherwise, I'm kind of at a loss what you could do." He shrugged. "If I think of anything, I'll let you know, but can we get back to what I found?"

Braxton stopped pacing. "There's more?"

Dooley grinned and punched his fist into the air. "Ha! You don't know everything before I tell you. Yes, there's more. In addition to finding the location of what I've termed the Lucifer Gate, I've also discovered you're going to need more than the wings of the Devils to put him back once you've called him forth." He leaned forward and bounced in his chair, excited about what he'd discovered. "See, when you open up the door and pull him out, you're breaking all his chains. This means you have to have something powerful to put him back in. You are going to have to recreate the chains and rechain him to Hell in order for this to work."

Alaria's breath whistled between her teeth as she exhaled. She leaned forward and braced her elbows on her knees. "This just keeps getting better and better. I suppose you found out how we're supposed to do it?"

Dooley handed her a paper. "There's a spell which is simple enough. I'd let Aradia do the casting, though, since she's the one with the most power over that sort of thing. It's what you need to do the spell that's interesting. You need Lucifer's blood, Michael's blood, and Griffin's blood—which you can get from the knife if I'm translating things correctly—and it has to be mixed in the vessel in which Christ's blood was caught."

Braxton laughed. "The Holy Grail? The fucking Holy Grail? So you're telling me we have to capture the five nastiest creatures on the planet, carve their wings off, and keep them secured while we do all the others. Then we have to summon Lucifer from Hell to take his wings and then take his blood, and now we have to find the goddamned motherfucking Holy Grail?" He made a frustrated noise in his throat and glared at the priest. "Do I look like Monty Python or Indiana Jones to you?"

Alaria cleared her throat. "Brax, darling, getting the stupid bowl is the easiest part of the whole thing." She lifted one shoulder in a careless shrug. "Michael can fetch it from Heaven." When both men gaped at her, she held out her hands. "Don't look at me like that. I didn't know we'd need it. It held the blood of Jesus in it. It's too powerful to leave on Earth, so the Angels took it up to Heaven, and it's been there ever since." She gestured to the papers. "What I want to know is how this Atlantean knew what was going to happen all these years ago but the rest of us are just now finding out about it."

Dooley smiled. "I can answer that one." He rubbed his hands together. "Goodness, I like having the answers much more than looking for them." He shuffled several pieces of paper. "This particular prophet had visions—pretty good ones from what I can tell—and he writes of having foreseen these events and being given information from God on what to do. Given how accurate his accounts are, I'd be willing to bet the farm he's right about what you need to do."

Alaria stared at him blankly. "You don't own a farm."

The priest laughed. "It's a saying. It means I'd bet everything I have he's right about it." He looked through the papers. "I think that's all I have about stuff. I found your gate, and I figured out how to put him back and keep him there."

Braxton nodded. "I assume you also found out how to open the Lucifer Gate?"

Dooley nodded. "I forgot about that. Yes, it's in here, too." He organized the pages again and handed them to Braxton. "It's easy enough. Only Michael can open it. His blood is the key to it. He'll know how to do it." He sighed and sat back down. "All of my notes are there. If you have questions, well, I'm not going anywhere anytime soon. I'm public enemy numero uno for escaping them, and I have no desire to find out what they do to people who piss them off."

"Calder and Lex will take good care of you for as long as they can. If it gets so bad we have to shut this place down, then the odds are good you aren't even blipping on their radar and we're all dead, so yeah, staying here is a good idea." Braxton cast a slow glance around the room. "I wish I could make it so you can go home, Brad. I know you have to miss it."

Dooley shook his head. "Here is nice enough. I teach the kids some exorcisms and give them weapons they can't ever drop in battle. This is me doing my part to make sure the world doesn't end." He stretched and put his feet on the desk. "Besides, they have amazing coffee, and the weather is always warm. There are worse places I could be."

Alaria tossed in her bed, unable to sleep. Moonlight poured in through her window, spilling across the floor and onto her bed. Sighing, she threw back the covers and crossed the room to look out the panes of glass.

The water from the pool glowed from the cold white light, and fireflies twinkled outside the window. She smiled at the pretty bugs and looked over her shoulder toward the room where Braxton was sleeping. A glance at the clock told her no one else would be awake at such an hour, and she headed to the bathroom to change into her bathing suit.

Three minutes later, dressed in sandals, a long t-shirt and holding two towels, she opened the door to Braxton's room and slipped inside, going to the edge of the bed quietly. He stirred as the light from the bathroom hit his face and opened his eyes, yawning sleepily.

"Hey. Everything okay?"

Alaria nodded. "Everything's fine. Get up. I want you to come somewhere with me." She bent and rifled through his bag, tossing him his swim trunks. "Put those on. We're going swimming."

Braxton looked at the clock. "It's three in the morning."

"Exactly. We have a couple hours before anyone will be up, and then we'll start our day together on the right foot." She shifted her weight from foot to foot and smiled at him sheepishly. "I'm trying to give you what you want with the dating. This is me being spontaneous and fun, so take it or leave it."

He laughed and tugged her down for a slow kiss before hopping out of bed and walking to the bathroom to change. "Oh, I'll definitely take it."

Alaria waited while Braxton exchanged boxers for trunks and handed him a towel before grabbing his hand and dragging him down the hall, down the steps, and out the door. She carefully closed the door so as to make sure the creaky, ancient wood didn't wake anyone else up and bit her tongue to muffle a squeal when Braxton grabbed her around the waist and carried her toward the pool.

"Hold on. Don't throw me in." She squirmed in his arms. "Dooley told me there are crocodiles in the pool every once in a while, and the last thing I want is to be crocodile bait."

Braxton set her down carefully and peered into the water. "There's nothing in there." He looked around the yard. "I don't see any large, toothy reptiles coming our way, do you?"

Alaria shook her head. "I didn't get the feeling it happens very often, but if you see one, we run."

He lifted one eyebrow. "What? Big, tough Devil woman can't take on a reptile with a brain the size of a walnut?"

She snorted. "And that could be fifteen feet long and weigh three tons? No thank you. Crocodile Dundee I am not." She dropped to sit on the edge of the pool and slipped her feet into the water. Leaning back on her elbows, she peered up at Braxton. "It's nice and warm."

Braxton stepped to the side and dove in, his body slicing through the water. He swam nearly the entire length of the pool before surfacing and paddling back to where Alaria sat. He used one hand to brush his hair back from his face and grinned up at her.

"I don't think I've really let loose and had some fun in over two years. At least not until the past couple days." He ran his hands over her smooth calves. "Thanks for playing along, Alaria. I know this isn't how you would have chosen to handle things, and it means a lot that you're going along with it."

Alaria lifted one shoulder and blushed. "It seems my way is much more Devil than human, so I'm content to let you set the pace. I can be patient as long as I know I will eventually get what I want."

He chuckled, the sound warm and rich. "I can promise you will. Now get in here."

Without warning, Braxton grabbed her by the thighs and yanked her into the water, completely dunking her before hauling her against him and lifting her up until they were eye to eye. Alaria swiped both hands over her face, wiping droplets of water from her skin and tucking her hair behind her ears. She lifted her legs and wrapped them around him loosely. Slowly, she leaned back until she was lying flat with her arms spread out and her hair flowing behind her in the water. Braxton kept one hand on her lower back to balance her and let the other drift up and down one of her thighs, enjoying the feel of her skin in his hand.

She stared up at the sky, enjoying the view of the inky blackness dotted with stars. Chill bumps rose on her skin from the cool breeze on her nearly bare body, and she shivered slightly. The water surrounded her and she relaxed into it, feeling weightless and free. She lifted one hand from the pool and laid it on her stomach, her mind turning to the life growing inside her.

"We have to win, Brax. I don't want my child born into a world not worth living in." She righted herself and studied him seriously. "I know it exists to kill Lucifer, and it's a failsafe, but if we win and rechain him to Hell, there's no reason our children ever have to fight. By the time they're grown, we can kill all the Cambion. I want to make a world where Finley and this baby never have to wonder if they'll be killed in their sleep."

Braxton sighed deeply and pulled her close. "I have a feeling they're going to have to fight anyway. There is always going to be evil out there, and there will always be a need for people who can fight it. We'll teach them everything we know, pray they're stronger than we are and worry every second they're out of our sight." He nuzzled her neck with his nose. "I want the same world you do, and I believe we'll make this one better and our children will make it better still, but I don't know if it'll ever be a fight that can be completely won." He ran one hand over her hair and let the other rub the skin at the small of her back. "We're supposed to be relaxing and having some fun, not standing here talking about heavy shit."

Alaria smiled and leaned her head against his. "I know. I'm sorry. I came and got you thinking this would be fun and flirty, and here I am getting all serious on you." She shook her head and looped her arms around his neck. "I'm done with it for the next thirty hours, I promise."

Braxton pressed a kiss to her forehead. "It'll all be okay. No matter what happens, we'll get through it." He ran his hands down her sides. "Now, what kind of red-blooded man would I be if I didn't take the opportunity to at least cop one feel of you in that bikini?"

She chuckled and reached between their bodies, cupping him in one of her hands. She stroked the ridge of his penis gently, making a soft noise of satisfaction when he hardened and lengthened to fill her palm. "Looks like I'm copping one first." She used both hands to stroke him through his shorts, rubbing gently until he was fully erect and rock hard. She leaned forward and scraped her teeth over his earlobe.

Braxton groaned and leaned against the side of the pool, his eyes half-closed and bolts of pleasure rocketing through his body as she massaged his dick. "I didn't think we came out here to do this." He looked around nervously. "Not that it doesn't feel amazing, but I don't exactly want to get caught with my pants down by another one of the Warriors."

Alaria laughed and trailed kisses over his neck. "That's the thing about starting something with a Devil, Brax. I have a lot fewer inhibitions than most human women."

Proving her point, she slipped both hands inside the swim trunks and wrapped her hands around his cock. The cool water offered an amazing contrast against the heat of her skin and Braxton's hips jumped as she stroked him. She rubbed the tip of him with one hand and pumped the other fist up and down slowly. Wickedly, she leaned in and pressed her mouth to his ear, her tongue lapping at the lobe and caressing the shell before she whispered to him.

"I'm going to make you come." She caught his ear in her teeth and nipped sharply. "There are a lot of things we can do without fucking. I'm going to get you off and then we're going to go inside and you're going to return the favor." She nearly purred when his penis twitched in her hand. "I love the feel of you, Brax. Hot and hard and thick. I can't wait to wrap my legs around you and let you pound into me until we're both spent and then pin you down and ride you senseless."

Braxton closed his eyes completely and let her raunchy words wash over him. Her hands worked their magic on him, and he felt himself getting closer and closer to orgasm with each stroke of her fingers. He reached out and slipped his fingers inside the cup of her bathing suit top, rolling her nipple between his fingers and tugging it gently.

Alaria pressed their bodies together, rubbing herself against him and speeding up the movements of her hands. She sucked and nipped at his neck and throat while rubbing one thumb around the head of his cock. His head fell back and his whole body tensed in anticipation of release. She chuckled softly and tightened her grip slightly.

"Don't fight it. Come for me." Her lips were hot against his ear. "I love how your cock feels in my hands. I loved the taste of you and the feel of you in my mouth. I want you to take me hard and fast." She smiled in satisfaction when he groaned loudly. "Come, baby. Do it for me."

His orgasm rolled through him like a tidal wave. His cock jerked and twitched, and he emptied himself into the pool. He groaned raggedly as he climaxed and relaxed as the tension in his muscles ebbed and flowed out of him.

Taking ten seconds to breathe, Braxton swiftly switched their positions and pinned Alaria to the side of the pool, tucking himself back inside his trunks before claiming her mouth in a searing kiss. He tore his mouth away and quickly tugged her bikini top aside, baring her breasts.

"I don't need to take you inside to return the favor." He grinned. "Hold on tight, baby, 'cause this is going to be a hell of a ride."

He cupped her breasts in his hands, rubbing the soft globes of flesh. He thumbed both her nipples before blowing on them, his cool breath raising bumps on her skin. Slowly, his gaze never leaving hers, he stooped and sucked one nipple into his mouth, rubbing his tongue against the tightly beaded tip.

He gently slid her bottoms down her thighs until he could get one hand between her legs. He nudged her thighs apart and separated her folds, finding her clit with his thumb. Finding her hot and wet, he rubbed the exposed bud, sending shockwaves of need through her. He sucked on her nipple while he rubbed her and hummed when she tangled her hands in his hair and tugged sharply, holding her to him.

Braxton eased one finger inside her, her body wet and slick. He positioned his hand so the heel of it rubbed her clit while he stroked into her with his middle finger. Alaria groaned deeply and moved her hips in time with his thrusts.

He released her nipple with a slight pop and used his free hand to grip the back of her head, bringing her forward until he could kiss her, letting his tongue brush against hers, tasting her. Her legs spread father as he offered her pleasure, and she whimpered softly.

"You think you're the only one who can talk dirty?" He shifted his head to the side so his lips touched her ear, and his breath blew across it as he spoke. "I am going to bury myself in you, Alaria, and fuck you until neither of us can walk. I'm going to make you scream my name, and I am going to lick every inch of your body."

He thrust into her harder with his finger, smiling in satisfaction when she cried out from pleasure and tipped her head back, her eyes closing. Her hips moved with his thrusts, encouraging him.

"When we go to bed, it's not going to be quick. By the time I slide into you, you'll be weak-kneed and begging me to take you." Braxton scraped his teeth over her earlobe. "Jesus Christ, I can't wait to have your thighs wrapped around my head and my face buried in your pussy." He pulled back to meet her gaze, his hot with passion. "I am going to eat you alive."

Alaria exploded around him, her orgasm hitting her unexpectedly and wrenching a surprised yell from her. He continued to thrust into her, wringing every bit of pleasure from her he could until she collapsed boneless and sated into his arms. Gently, he pulled her bikini bottoms back up and tucked her breasts back into the cups of the top. He stroked his hands over her back, holding her as the tremors from her release worked their way through her. The water around them was warm and lapped gently against their skin, helping hold them up.

"Braxton."

There was something off about her voice. Instead of being relaxed and dreamy, it was tense, with a note of fear. He pressed a kiss to her neck. "What is it?"

"Don't panic."

"Dammit. I knew someone would see us out here." He sighed and turned around.

On the cement across the pool stood a crocodile. Its gaze was focused on them, and it moved slowly to the edge, heading directly to the water. Braxton measured it with his eyes and swore under his breath. If he was right, and he was, it was at least twelve feet long.

Alaria's nails dug into his arm. "What do we do?"

Braxton pulled her hands off him. "We get out of this pool and run for the door. They can't move fast on land for very long, but if it gets in this water, we're fucked." He took two steps backward and felt the edge of the pool against his back. "On three." He took a deep breath and waited until Alaria was right next to him. "One. Two." They both braced their hands on the concrete. "Three!"

The crocodile slid heavily into the pool as Braxton and Alaria heaved themselves out. They were merely inches from the edge when the reptile surfaced, teeth flashing as it tried to capture one of them. They scrambled to their feet and dashed across the lawn. Braxton wrenched open the door and ushered her in ahead of him. They skidded to a stop in the entry.

Father Dooley stood at the bottom of the stairs, talking to Calder. Both men looked at them curiously. Calder cleared his throat.

"Do I even want to know?"

Alaria giggled. "There's a crocodile in the pool."

Calder swore hotly. "Motherfucker. Not again!"

Alaria was standing in her bathroom in her underwear and a bra when someone knocked on her door. Sighing, she wrapped a towel around her body and crossed the room to open the heavy wooden door. Alexia stood on the other side. Alaria lifted one eyebrow and leaned against the frame.

"Something I can help you with, Lex?"

Lex shook her head. "Not a thing. I heard Brax telling Calder the two of you were going into the village today, and I thought maybe I'd keep you company while you get ready." She looked a little sheepish. "There aren't many women here—just me and two others, and they're a couple—so it makes it impossible for me to get any time with someone not in possession of a penis."

Alaria held the door open. "Come on in." She closed it behind Lex and returned to the bathroom. "Take a seat if you want. I was just putting on makeup and braiding my hair."

Lex perched on the edge of the bed. "How long have you and Braxton been dating?"

"About five minutes." Alaria chuckled and rubbed foundation into her skin. "This will technically be the second date. Is that a problem?"

"Honestly? Yeah, it's going to be a problem for him. Not with me, or with Calder, but with people like Dominic—the dude Braxton pounded on—it'll cost him legitimacy. They won't want to follow someone who is tangled up with a Devil, even if the distinction is former." She sighed and tapped her fingers on the mattress. "I'm not sure how much damage it will do, but I know it won't be good."

Alaria felt a pang of guilt, knowing what Lex said was true. "I told him it was stupid to date. I told him we should just sleep together and get it over with and see what happens, but no, the silly man wants to go to dinner and fool around."

Lex crossed one leg over the other and bit her lip to keep from grinning. "He must really like you." She lifted her eyebrows out of curiosity. "How do you feel about him?"

Alaria looked over her shoulder. "I'm not sure you and I have known each other long enough to have girl talk. No offense, but I barely do that with Aradia and Greer."

"None taken. But if I were you, I'd be jumping from the rooftops if a guy like Brax wanted to take me out. I've been banging Calder for three years, and we're still sneaking around behind the guys' backs. He thinks admitting we're together will make the other Warriors, especially those that are still training, think less of him. I obviously disagree, but I'd rather have the man than the public acknowledgment, and for whatever reason, I can't have both."

Alaria smiled softly and turned around so she was fully facing Lex. "I was with someone before Braxton. Someone I loved and who I had pined for much longer than you've been alive. He refused to choose me over his other obligations. I thought I could deal with it, but eventually it got to be too much, and I had to let go."

Lex met Alaria's gaze steadily. "Is that the father of your baby?"

Without thinking, Alaria laid her hand on her stomach protectively. "How did you know? I'm not showing yet."

Lex smiled. "I had two kids. A boy and a girl. They were two and five when demons broke into our house and killed my husband and my babies. They'd have killed me, too, except I was running late coming home from work and got to the house while the demons were there. I was trying to fight them off when Calder and Braxton found us. They saved my life, brought me here, and showed me how to defend myself. I never wanted to leave. I swore I'd never stop until I killed the demons who took my family. That was eight years ago." She crossed her arms and stared at Alaria steadily. "The point, before I got distracted by my own sordid past, is that a mother sees the signs of pregnancy way before anyone else will. How far along are you?"

Alaria shifted uncomfortably, unsure talking to Lex was a good idea. "Twelve weeks and a couple of days."

Lex smiled softly. "Second trimester is right around the corner. All the nausea stops and instead of being tired, it seems like you have more energy than you know what to do with." She sobered. "You're very brave to carry a baby during this. I don't know if I'd have made the same decision, even with having had children before. Not because I wouldn't want another one, but because I don't know if I could bring a child into a world that might not exist to see them grow up."

Alaria rubbed her hand over her stomach. "I guess I just have faith we're going to succeed at what we're doing. If we fail, the odds are good I won't be alive to raise it, and I can't accept that." She dropped the towel and pulled up a pair of jeans. "Lex, one thing we've always said, and I'm learning is true, is that we can't stop living just because we're involved in this. We're still human, and we still need things. Nothing will ever change that, no matter how bad things get. Living doesn't make us weak. It shows the bad guys we're strong enough not to let them take our lives away." She yanked a tank top over her head and then hopped on one foot, then the other, pulling on a pair of cowboy boots.

Lex stared at Alaria for a long moment. "I didn't want to like you. I wanted to hate you like the rest of them, but then we met yesterday when Brax and Dom were pounding on each other, and I didn't hate you. I should have stayed away today because, dammit, now I genuinely like you." She stood and smiled brightly. "Don't let the others get to you. Braxton deserves to be happy more than just about anyone I've ever known. Dealing with what happened in Romania, then Griffin, then losing his sister and parents, well, he's had a rough go of it." She reached for the door. "Have fun tonight, and don't worry about making noise. These walls are thick."

Alaria chuckled and followed Lex down the stairs to where Braxton was talking to Calder and Dooley at the bottom. He looked up when he heard them descending and smiled. Alaria stood next to him and laid her hand on his arm. He reached up to pat her hand and nodded to Calder.

"We'll be back in a few hours, and then we'll be leaving tomorrow morning to head back. It's a long trip back to Scotland, and we need to get things going so we can finish this up."

Calder nodded. "No problem. We're here holding down the fort." He smiled brightly. "Just no more middle-of-the-night swims. That's when the crocs are the most active." He shook his head and laughed. "There are several Jeeps in the garage, and the keys are in the cabinet on the wall. Take whichever one you want and just follow the road heading south. After about twenty miles, it'll fork. Take the left branch, and about forty miles up it, you'll come to a decent-sized village. There're a few restaurants, a nice market, a small hospital, couple bars, that sort of thing. It has enough to occupy yourselves for three or four hours."

Braxton tucked Alaria under his arm and touched his fingers to his temple in a mock salute. "Don't wait up."

"This is surreal." Alaria looked around the market, her eyes alight with curiosity. All around her people mingled and bartered over the various goods set out for purchase. "I don't remember the last time I did any shopping." She fingered a rack of brightly colored peasant skirts. "Before, I just conjured whatever I wanted, and now Gage takes care of all that. He's got good taste, thank God."

Braxton laughed and reached for a wide brim straw hat, a pair of over-sized sunglasses and a silk scarf. He looped the scarf around her neck, tying it loosely, and then set the hat on her head and slipped the glasses on her face. Alaria bent her knees slightly to look at herself in the small mirror set up and laughed.

"I look like a really crappy private detective."

Braxton kissed her nose. "You look like a really cute private detective." He pulled out his cell phone and took a picture of her in the items before she pulled them off and laid them back down.

The market in the village was much larger than either of them had originally thought. They walked from table to table, picking up trinkets for the four back in Scotland and making fun of one another while posing with outrageous clothing and jewelry. Alaria insisted on buying Braxton a brightly patterned Hawaiian shirt, and he repaid the favor with a neon pink straw cowboy hat.

Laughing and more relaxed than either had been in months, they scarfed down plates of red rice, chicken and vegetables and washed the food down with margaritas. Then, slightly tipsy, Braxton dragged her into the center of the village where a local band played guitars and several couples danced.

He swung Alaria around the dance floor, spinning her in a circle before pulling her close and sliding his arms around her to hold her. Braxton was struck with a memory of doing nearly the same with Griffin several weeks before her death when they'd been in Peru and he'd managed to talk her in to venturing out of their hotel room.

Instead of feeling guilt about being there with another woman, or the gut wrenching grief he'd been plagued with since Griffin had died, he felt only a warm fondness for the memory. Smiling, he buried his face in Alaria's hair and inhaled her scent before spinning her out from him and twirling her around. Laughing, she wrapped her arms around his neck and rose onto her tiptoes to press her lips to his ear.

"Take me back to the monastery, Braxton, and then take me to bed." She brushed her lips over his cheek. "We've both waited long enough."

The drive back was long and tense. Braxton maneuvered through narrow streets and then over a bumpy dirt road, covering the hour trip back. The sun had set while they'd been eating dinner, and the route was much slower in the dark. The headlights from the Jeep were narrow beams that barely cut through the dense jungle, and it slowed them to just a little over half the speed they'd had on the trip in.

Finally, after nearly two hours, they pulled through the gates at the monastery and Braxton jerked the vehicle to a stop in the garage. Alaria cast him a seductive look with her gaze hot and inviting as she climbed out. Entering the main building, Alaria reached out and seized his hand, pulling him up the stairs and walking quickly down the hallway. She pushed open the door to her room and slammed it shut behind them, shoving Braxton against it and feverishly pressing her own body against the hard planes of his.

She attacked his mouth with hers, sweeping her tongue inside and nipping at his lips with her teeth. Her fingers worked the buttons on his shirt free and she shoved the garment off his shoulders, down his arms, and pulled it off, dropping it to the floor where it was forgotten. Relishing the feel of smooth skin dusted with coarse blond hair under her hands, she ran her nails over his chest and scratched them over his small nipples. Braxton's hands slid down her sides and over the curve of her bottom, gripping firmly and holding her tightly against him, his eyes closed and head tipped back as he enjoyed her assault.

Alaria nimbly unbuckled his belt and yanked it from the loops before popping the button loose and sliding the zipper down. He kicked off his boots and stepped on his socks to pull them off one at a time while she gripped his pants in both hands and grinned up at him while beginning to lower the garment. The fabric caught at his hips, and she tugged at it in frustration, stooping to lower his jeans down his legs before tugging them off his feet and casting them away to join his shirt.

Braxton's boxers received the same treatment his pants had. Alaria ran her hands up his legs, enjoying the feel of rough hair on her soft palms. She skated her fingers over his hips and brushed them through the dark blond hair that covered his groin. Her fingers danced over his protruding erection, teasing him as she gently touched him with only her fingertips. Braxton leaned heavily against the wall and pushed his hips forward slightly, enjoying her ministrations.

Alaria leaned forward and pressed her mouth to the tip of him in a whisper-soft kiss before dropping to her knees in front of him. His dick jumped at her touch, and she chuckled softly before leaning forward and engulfing him in her mouth. She swirled her tongue around his engorged head and wrapped one hand around his base, using the other to cup his balls.

She bobbed her head up and down, sucking strongly each time her mouth wrapped around the tip. His cock reddened as blood flowed into it, and she hummed deep in her throat from satisfaction as she ran her tongue down his entire length. She turned her head to the side to suck and nip at the skin near the base of him and licked him slowly when he groaned loudly.

Braxton tangled his hands in her hair, running the silky strands through his fingers and holding it tightly as she sucked on him. His eyes closed and pleasure swarmed him, clouding his mind and making it hard to do anything other than feel.

He tugged sharply on her hair to get her attention. "You need to stop, or I'm gonna lose it."

Alaria looked up at him, her lips swollen from the blowjob she'd been giving him. "That's the point of blowing you, last time I checked." She pumped her hand up and down, using the saliva left from her mouth to lubricate him. "Do you not want to?"

Braxton groaned and struggled to think despite what she was doing to his penis. "I want to be in you, Alaria, not jizzing on the carpet like some fifteen-year-old." He tugged her to her feet and began efficiently undressing her. "Besides, you might be able to have multiple orgasms, but I am not that young anymore. The body wears out way faster than the mind wants to."

Alaria shrugged. "Your loss." She tugged her shirt over her head and stepped out of the jeans he lowered down her legs.

She'd put on black lace. A skimpy thong showed off the delectable curve of her ass, and the bra dipped down low enough to show him the top of her areolas. The rest of her breasts were covered in lace so thin he could easily see the dusky points of her nipples jutting out. Her black hair flowed over her shoulders, and she lifted one eyebrow at him before cocking one hip and placing her hand on it.

"See something you like?"

Braxton smiled slowly and laughed huskily. "I know you think you can handle me, but you'd better get yourself ready, lady. This is about to be a night you'll never forget."

Alaria grinned. "Bring it on, baby. I'm not some wilting flower. I can take whatever you want to dish out." She reached out and took his hands in hers, placing them on her breasts. "I want this. I want you, and I want it tonight. I'm tired of waiting. We've waited long enough."

He massaged the mounds of flesh in his hands gently, enjoying their weight and the way they filled his palms. Her breasts were large and curvy, sitting high on her chest and topped with pink nipples. He ran his thumbs over both tips through the lace and smiled when she moaned softly. He leaned forward to press his mouth against her ear, his cock steely hard against her thighs.

"As much as I'd love the BJ, I don't want to waste an orgasm when I could be inside you. I'm going to fuck you, Alaria. I'll have you so many ways and so many times neither of us will be able to walk by the end of it." He gently pinched her nipples, chuckling when her hips jumped as bolts of pleasure darted through her. "First, though, I'm going to tongue-fuck you until you come so hard you go limp."

Braxton reached down and gripped her hips, lifting her in his arms to carry her across the room to the bed. He laid her on the mattress, arranging her so her feet were still on the bed. He stretched out next to her, flicking one finger over her right nipple before dipping his head and sucking it into his mouth.

The sensation of him sucking her nipple through the lace created delicious friction that made Alaria gasp and groan. He cupped her other breast in his hand and slipped his fingers inside the bra, rolling the hardened tip between his fingers while he flicked his tongue over the other.

He sucked deeply, using both teeth and tongue to wring every bit of pleasure from her that he could. Her fingers tangled in his hair, holding him to her chest, and her hips arched toward him. Chuckling, Braxton eased his free hand inside her panties and palmed her, rubbing her clit gently and sliding one finger inside her.

He stroked into her slowly, using his hand to apply pressure to her clit then removing it before she came, withholding orgasm while he sucked her nipple. After several minutes, knowing he couldn't keep her from climaxing much longer, he released her nipple and stilled his finger inside her, still rubbing her clit gently for several seconds before withdrawing his hand completely.

Braxton took her mouth in a heated, gentle kiss. He stroked one hand down her cheek and along the side of her body, giving her time to settle down. When her breathing slowed and she stilled, he stood and drew her underwear down her legs, tossing them aside and running his hands up her calves, over her knees and up her thighs.

Alaria's eyes drifted shut, and she gave herself over to Braxton. His touch was confident and strong, and he didn't hesitate to touch her or need to ask how to bring her pleasure. He knelt between her legs, placing her feet on the floor so he could look at her. He drew one finger down the cleft of her body before leaning forward and pressing a hot, open-mouthed kiss to the inside of her thigh.

He inhaled deeply, taking in the musky, feminine scent of her. He nuzzled her thighs with his nose before sticking out his tongue and giving her a long, leisurely lick. Alaria's whole body jerked on the bed, and he laughed softly. He held her hips in his hand and dragged her toward him, spearing her with his tongue and tasting her fully.

She groaned and lifted her thighs, tightening them around his head. Braxton licked and sucked at her, driving his tongue inside and rubbing slowly. She thrashed on the bed as he caressed her. He massaged her legs with his hands while he flicked his tongue over her clit. Slowly, he released one of her legs to use his finger inside her while continuing to stimulate her with his tongue. Alaria gasped and moaned from the new sensation, and she clenched around him, on the verge of orgasm.

He licked her again, slow and soft, then jabbed his tongue against the small bundle of nerves. She exploded around him, her back arching and lifting her body off the bed. Her hands fisted in the sheet, and her eyes rolled back in her head as white-hot pleasure speared through her.

Braxton continued to thrust his finger into her while she came, not letting her rest before he sent her over-sensitized body back up the crest. When she stopped trembling and began groaning again, he withdrew from her, surreptitiously wiping his mouth and finger on the sheet before standing and looking down at her. Alaria took several deep breaths before rolling to her knees. She twisted her arms behind her back to unfasten her bra, tossing it to the floor.

Braxton reached out and trailed one finger across her shoulder and down her chest to stroke across one of her hardened nipples. He slid onto the bed, pulling her into his arms and kissing her deeply. His hands slid down to grip her ass, and he held her against his body tightly. Slowly, he broke the kiss.

"I'm having a bit of an issue."

Alaria's gaze went to his crotch and his very hard penis. She grinned and shook her head. "Everything looks like it's working to me." She looped her arms around his neck and met his gaze. "What's wrong? Are you having second thoughts about doing this?"

Braxton shook his head. "Not at all. More that I'm not sure which way I want to fuck you first." He looked at her heatedly. "I want to take you doggie-style, I want you to ride me—hell—even fucking you against the wall is a thought that makes my head spin."

Alaria smiled slowly and reached between their bodies to cup his cock in her hand, running her hand up and down slowly. She pumped him several times before releasing him and turning around. Slowly, she bent over until she was on her hands and knees. She spread her knees wider and lowered herself to her elbows, opening herself to him. She looked over her shoulder at him and cocked one eyebrow.

"Let's try it hard and fast this first time to burn off some of the horniness. Then, when we aren't both so primed we're ready to explode, we'll try it sweet and slow. Right now, I want you in me, and I want it rough."

Braxton grabbed her hips and yanked her back, impaling her on his penis in one hard stroke. She yelped from the unexpected and sudden invasion, then groaned and rolled her hips, nearly purring from the feel of him inside her. She panted softly and jerked her hips twice, trying to create the friction she needed.

Braxton spread his hands on her ass, squeezing gently and stroking the silky skin. He ran his hands up her back and around to cup her breasts, rubbing both nipples with his fingers as he rocked his hips slowly, doing nothing more than driving her crazy.

Slowly, he withdrew until he was completely out of her. He wrapped one hand around his cock and rubbed it against her. Alaria groaned and arched backward, trying to envelop him in her heat. He sank into her an inch, then rocked back and forth, barely stroking in and out. When she was incoherently begging him for more, only then did he spear into her and drive deep.

Braxton leaned forward and gripped the headboard as he thrust into her. He drove hard, seating himself completely inside her with each pump of his hips. Alaria groaned and panted as he fucked her, striving for her own orgasm. He quickly learned her body, discovering which movements made her clench around him from pleasure.

His own orgasm approaching, he drove himself into her faster and harder. Her body was wet and hot, and each stroke was a smooth, silky descent that made his eyes cross. She gripped him tightly and urged him on with whispered pleas for more. The bed moved back and forth as he thrust, and their sweaty bodies made a slight slapping noise as they collided over and over.

Desperate to bring her release before he took his own, Braxton let go of the headboard with one hand and pressed the pad of his thumb against her clit, rubbing firmly. She cried out and came apart, flying into orgasm. He stroked into her several more times, relishing the feel of both her muscle contractions and the moisture created by her body as she came before giving into his own climax and emptying himself into her.

He collapsed to the side, falling to the bed and heaving her against him, wrapping both arms around her and holding her tightly. Alaria snuggled into his arms, her breathing heavy and shallow. She rolled far enough to wrap her arms around him, cradling him against her chest, and relaxed into his arms.

"That was amazing."

Braxton smiled as Alaria's words washed over him. He kissed her softly and rubbed her back. He grinned wickedly. "You ain't seen nothin' yet."

Chapter Twelve

Alaria was sleeping in Braxton's arms when the first explosion threw them both from the bed. They awoke in a panic, fumbling for each other and their clothes as their sleepy brains tried to make sense of what was going on. She clenched her fist and conjured her war apparel of leather pants, stiletto boots, a red and black leather bustier and whip.

"What the fuck is going on?" Braxton hopped on one foot to drag on his pants.

Alaria went to the window and pushed back the curtains. "Mother fucking son of a bitching bastard." She looked over her shoulder. "It's Beelzebub."

"Beelzebub is out there?"

She shook her head. "No, but I recognize his demons."

Braxton looked up from buttoning his shirt. "Why are they here? I can't imagine Beelzebub coming after a Warrior base in South America. That seems way below him."

Alaria pushed off the windowsill and turned to face Braxton. "I don't know. What's here that they could want?" She snapped her fingers as realization dawned. "Son of a bitch. They're after Dooley and the papers to find out where the Lucifer gate is."

Braxton tied his boots and went to his room for weapons. He returned with a short sword, a pistol and four spare clips. "You get the papers, I'll go for Dooley, and we'll meet out front to help with the demons."

Alaria nodded and opened the door leading into the hallway. Already, bodies littered the floor and the sound of battle was unmistakable. She glanced over her shoulder. "Don't die."

Braxton smiled. "Don't you die, either."

Alaria took off running, heading for the small library on the top floor where Dooley had kept his papers. She passed several Warriors running down to the front of the monastery to battle off the demons. She beheaded three demons as she strode down the hallway to the library doors and burst into the room.

She conjured a small knapsack and shoved the scrolls and documents Dooley had been using into it. She took the time to light a fire in the hearth and throw everything else she could into the flames, hoping to destroy anything she didn't know about that the demons could possibly use. She strapped the bag to her body with leather cording and raced back down the stairs toward the exits.

One look told her Beelzebub had sent everything he had. She spotted Dmitri, Beelzebub's second in command, and a demon several thousand years old, standing just outside the gates of the monastery, commanding what looked to be at least three hundred demons, half that of vampires and fifty Hellhounds.

Alaria used her whip to beat back the demons swarming her as she came through the door. She exchanged the whip for a sword and hacked her way through the throng. Before she'd made it even a quarter of the way across the yard, a second explosion rocked the whole building. Alaria was thrown off her feet and landed hard on her shoulder, hissing as she heard the bone snap.

Cursing, she rolled to her back and thrust the sword up, running a demon through with it and buying herself enough time to climb to her feet. Her left arm hung uselessly at her side, and she gripped the sword in her right hand, gritting her teeth against the pain and turning in a slow circle to assess the situation.

Lex came at her from the left, a wicked looking buck knife in one hand and a .44 magnum in the other. She turned to press her back against Alaria's. "Looks like we could both use someone to watch our backs." Lex set her mouth in a firm line. "Do you have any idea what's going on?"

Alaria nodded. "As far as I can tell this is Beelzebub's crew. I recognize the head honcho on the other side of the fence. Nasty little bugger. Long story short, we think they know we have the information about where the third gate to Hell is and they want to get it back before we figure it out. That's the only thing that makes sense. I can't believe it's coincidence that they show up here when Braxton and I are here and you're the ones hiding Dooley. Nothing else makes sense. If they manage to get the information and stop us, we'll be dead in the water on trying to cast out the demons on Earth. If we win, there will be no more demons. If they win, Lucifer will walk free."

Lex swore under her breath. "They're here for the priest, then. Have to be, cause he's the only one who can tell them what they need to know." She leveled her gun and fired three shots, killing two demons. "We have to get to him and then up to the library."

"Brax went to get Dooley, and I've already been to the library. All we can do now is beat them back." She gritted her teeth. "Fuck us both. Here come the dogs." Alaria clenched her hand and used her waning powers to conjure a second sword, which she handed to Lex. "My left shoulder is broken. I'm no good on that side, so watch it if you can. Bullets annoy these fuckers unless you get them in the head. Sword works best. Whatever you do, don't let them get their teeth in you."

Lex lifted the sword. "I've fought dogs before. I've got this."

Together, the two women braced themselves for the six hounds barreling toward them. Alaria leaped a split second before the first one would have been on top of her, slashing her sword along its back and slicing it open, revealing the spine, which gleamed white and pristine against red, mangled meat. She landed on her feet and twirled, blade flashing, and drove her weapon into the hound's head, extinguishing its life in a heartbeat and wrenching her sword back out of it to face the next.

Lex took one down quickly, thrusting her dagger through its eye as it leaped at her. She squealed when the propulsion of the four-hundred-pound-animal ripped her knife from her hand. Adjusting, she whirled to the side and gripped her sword tightly, holding it in front of her body. The third hound charged her, teeth dripping saliva and eyes gleaming in the moonlight. She let it get close enough she could smell the putrid stench of its breath before lifting her blade at the last second and slicing forward, separating its head from the rest of it.

"Nice job." Alaria grunted when the fourth hound slammed into her and hacked wildly, trying to avoid its powerful jaws as she struggled. She managed to slice off a paw, which landed with a hard plop, and split open the dog's soft underbelly, spilling its intestines on the ground in a greasy, bloody pile.

Steam rose off of the pile of guts and both women were assaulted with the scent of rotting eggs. Alaria gagged and swung her sword, ending the squealing, writhing animal in one stroke. She turned to face the final two with Lex but slipped in the intestines and fell hard, landing on her already broken shoulder. She cried out from the jarring pain, and Lex turned to look at her. The other woman extended a hand to help Alaria up, not paying attention to the hound leaping at her.

Alaria screamed a warning and yanked hard on Lex's arm, jerking her down into the entrails and keeping her out of reach of the snapping jaws. Alaria struggled to her feet and stood between the last two hounds and Lex, who was trying to get up.

"Thanks for the save." Lex picked up her sword and pressed her back against Alaria's. "Let's end this."

Alaria planted her feet and twirled her sword, waiting for the inevitable assault. She saw Calder out of the corner of her eye and sighed in relief. Having a third person would make it easier for them all. She slashed at the last two hounds, blood slickening her grip on the weapon. Lex took out the fifth hound by driving her sword deep into the chest cavity and jerking upward, nearly ripping the beast in half.

Alaria rushed forward and charged at the final dog, who ran straight at her. An instant before they would hit one another, she dropped to the ground, plunging up with her sword as she slid in the bloody intestines on the ground, breaking through its ribcage and exiting through its mouth.

Satisfied they'd killed the hounds, Alaria yanked her sword loose and turned to grin at Lex. Before she could utter even a word of warning, a seventh hound raced toward them out of the woods and leaped onto Lex, knocking her to the ground and clamping its jaws around her.

"No!"

Alaria wasn't sure if the yell belonged to her, or to Calder, who was approaching from the direction of the building, but they both raced forward, trying to reach Lex before the hound killed her. They were both too late.

The dog crunched through her ribs, ripping shards of bone and strings of flesh. Blood sprayed out onto the ground and into its fur, and Lex's eyes went flat and dark in the span of a heartbeat. The hound swallowed a mouthful of bones and organs and lowered its head to rip into Lex's softer belly.

Calder reached it a half second before Alaria did, throwing himself on top of the animal, hacking with a dagger and desperate to kill it without stopping to consider what he was doing. Alaria grabbed Calder to yank him away, but he clung to the hound. She pulled hard, using her bad arm to slash at it with her sword to keep it from killing them both.

Calder bucked Alaria off and continued his assault. The dog rolled, striking up with its claws and ripping Calder's off the skin and cartilage from his face in one swipe. Alaria closed her eyes in one moment of profound grief before she lifted her sword and charged it, driving the blade through its skull and into its brain.

She dropped to her knees next to Calder, her fingers pressing against his jugular to check for a pulse she knew wasn't there. His eyes stared up at her, blank and dead, and she gagged at the sight of his mangled skull. Two feet to her left, laid a mound of skin and cartilage she thought was his face.

Alaria slowly climbed to her feet and surveyed the yard. All around, bodies lay on the grass. Smoke from the two bombs and uncountable gunshots hung thick in the air, and the grass was slick with blood. Several Warriors stood around, and the sound of moaning permeated the air. She saw Dmitri shaking his head in the woods before disappearing, undoubtedly on his way back to tell Beelzebub they had failed.

Alaria looked around, searching for Braxton and Dooley. Her shoulder throbbed, and she noticed for the first time that she was bleeding from a deep cut on her thigh. Sneering at the jagged flesh, she limped toward the monastery to find the two men.

She saw Braxton coming out the front door. His hair was stained red with blood, and he was limping. His shirt was soaked and his pants splattered with fluid. He met her eyes and shook his head.

"No." Alaria's denial was fast and adamant. "No, he's not dead."

Braxton's voice was heavy with tears. "They got to him before I did. Fuckers didn't want to take him, they were here to assassinate him. I don't know why. He could've told them what they wanted. If they'd been trying to get the information from him, I'd have been there in time."

Alaria choked back tears. "What happened? Where is he?"

"He's in his room. You don't want to go up there. The hounds ripped him to pieces." Braxton ran his hands over his face. "I think I killed fifty fucking vampires." He looked around. "How is it out here?"

"No better than in there. Calder and Lex are both dead. Lex went down to a hound and then Calder went ape-shit crazy trying to hack it to death with a four inch pig-sticker." She sniffled. "I tried to drag him off, but it swiped him across the face and ripped half his throat out. He was dead before he hit the ground."

Braxton looked around the yard where the two dozen Warriors left standing were beginning to look their way. He saw Dominic yelling and gesturing wildly toward Alaria. Though they were too far away to hear what was being said, Braxton had no doubt it would lead to violence. He grabbed Alaria's hand and dragged her inside and up the stairs, heading toward their rooms.

"What are you doing?" Alaria trailed behind him, confusion in her gaze.

"The shithead who made me knock him out is down there getting everyone riled up thinking this is your fault. I have some sway over them but not enough given how many bodies there are laying on the ground. We need to leave now, or we'll be the next ones they try to kill."

Alaria gaped at him. "They're Warriors, Braxton. They won't kill us."

"If they think you're responsible for the deaths of all these people, they won't hesitate. They wouldn't come after me, but I'd never let them do anything to you without going through me first, so that leaves both of us dead." He locked the door and slid the dresser over to block it. "Gather what you need and see if you can get Michael down here to give us a lift out of here. If not, we've got a hell of a long hike in some very dangerous jungle."

Alaria threw the few things she'd unpacked back into her bag and dumped the bloody, barely legible papers she'd gotten from the library on top before zipping it up and glancing up at the ceiling.

"Michael, get your ass down here now! I need you!"

There was a shimmer and Gabriel appeared. "Michael is preoccupied at the moment. What assistance is it you need?"

Alaria glared. "We need to be zapped out of here. There's an angry mob of Warriors who think I'm responsible for a lot of bloodshed."

"Are you?"

"Even if I was, you would have no right to judge me for it." She glanced into the other room. "No, I didn't do it. Beelzebub sent a death squad in, and they did their fucking jobs very well. But I'm the former Devil, and as such, it must be my fault. If we don't get out of here soon, it's going to get very messy very fast."

"Who is we?"

Braxton came into the room with his duffel in one hand. He shook his head and sighed when he saw Gabriel. "I told her to call for Michael."

Gabriel looked at Braxton darkly. "I'm the only one available. If you'd prefer not to ask me for help, I can certainly leave you to the angry mob after your blood." He smiled saccharinely. "Your choice, of course."

Alaria grabbed her bag and strode to the middle of the room. "Enough with the testosterone poisoning. We need a ride out of here, and you're the one who showed up." She reached out and wrapped her hand around Braxton's wrist. "You'll take the ride because I need to get back to Greer before I fucking bleed to death."

Gabriel blanched. "Why didn't you tell me you were injured?"

Alaria waved him off. "Because it's none of your business. I stopped being your business when you tricked me into fucking you for the sole purpose of knocking me up with a child I never wanted to have and impressing upon me a fate I never would have accepted. Now are you going to take us back to Scotland or not?"

Gabriel nodded tersely. "As you wish." He reached out and touched each of their foreheads. With a flash of light, they were standing in the middle of the yard outside of Gage's estate.

Braxton hefted both bags in one hand and wrapped his other arm around Alaria, supporting part of her weight against his side to help her limp toward the house.

Within twenty seconds, the door flew open and Aradia ran out. She dashed across the yard barefoot, her red hair flying behind her and a look of concern marring her face. She went to Alaria's other side and wrapped her arms around the woman, taking over the brunt of her weight from Braxton.

"I felt the flash when Gabriel dropped you off. What happened?"

Braxton slowly let go of Alaria and switched one of the bags to his free hand. "We ran into some troubles in Colombia and had to get out in a hurry." He looked down at Aradia. "You got her?"

Aradia glared up at him. "I've got her." She started toward the house. "Greer was in the shower when I felt you drop in, so she'll be able to fix you right up. The boys went to town to stock up on groceries and some magic stuff I need. We've been working on ways to trap the Devils at the Choosing Place."

Alaria grimaced as she limped. "Any luck with that?"

Aradia nodded. "I think so. The problem is that we have no way of knowing without testing it out, and the only Devils capable of breaking regular traps aren't exactly going to volunteer to let me experiment on them."

Alaria gritted her teeth and hissed as they climbed the stairs up to the front door. Aradia half-dragged her to the living room and deposited her on the couch. Alaria sank into the cushions gratefully.

Aradia raced to the stairs and yelled up to Greer. "Greer! We need you! Alaria's hurt!"

Greer, her hair wet and wearing a bathrobe, ran down the stairs and over to Alaria. She looked at the injuries carefully before speaking. "I need you to take your pants off. The shoulder I can do through your clothes, but the last thing you want is for me to seal leather inside your thigh."

Alaria looked sheepish. "I don't think I can manage to get them off on my own. I've only got one good hand right now."

Braxton stepped forward. "I've got it."

He knelt in front of her and untied the laces on the front of her leather pants. He pulled off her boots and laid them aside then gently peeled the fabric off, taking care not to jostle the deep gash on her thigh more than necessary. Greer and Aradia exchanged a look over their heads, but neither had the nerve to say anything in front of Braxton.

Greer cleared her throat and reached out, laying her hand on Alaria's leg. Alaria felt a burst of heat followed by an intense burning sensation as the muscle reformed itself. She grabbed Braxton's arm and struggled not to cry out. When Greer healed Alaria's arm and the bone snapped back into place, she yelped and buried her face into Braxton's shoulder, biting down on him to allay some of the pain.

Greer sat back and rubbed Alaria's shoulder gently. "All done. I know you're supposed to be pretty much indestructible with the Gabe spawn in there and all, but I'd still recommend resting for the rest of the day." She looked to Braxton. "What happened?"

Braxton sighed deeply and moved to perch on the coffee table. "Beelzebub sent a fleet of monsters to get back the information Dooley had that we stole from them a few months ago in Florida. I knew they'd be looking for it, but I didn't think they'd ever find it down there. After the attack was over, most of the Warriors who survived were the ones who thought trusting Alaria was going to get us all killed."

Greer nodded. "They were going to blame her so you made a quick retreat. Makes sense." She stood and ran one hand through her wet hair. "Well, if I might make a suggestion, Brax, there is plenty of new info on the Devils and where they are in Gage's office. You also might think about calling and having his jet sent home. Aradia and I can help Alaria up to her room and get her settled in bed for some rest, and the boys should be home in a few hours. I know once they are, we need to discuss our first move." She looked at Aradia nervously. "There's a lot you two don't know, a lot you two know that we don't, and I'm sure none of us want to go through it more than once, so I imagine that we're going to have a lot to talk about once they get home."

Braxton looked over at Alaria. "Is that okay with you?"

Alaria nodded and chuckled softly. "It's fine. I could use a shower—so could you, by the way—and they're both dying to ask me questions about you and why we're so touchy feely that they don't want to ask in front of you."

Braxton nodded and bent to kiss her gently. "I'll be in Gage's office if you need me."

Aradia waited to speak until Braxton was out of sight. She leaned forward excitedly. "Forget the shower. When did that happen?"

Greer snorted and helped Alaria stand. "More importantly—how is he in bed?"

Alaria laughed and headed for the stairs. She grinned wickedly and lowered her voice so that Braxton couldn't hear. "I think all I need to say is he made me scream like a porn star, ladies."

Greer pointed to an area on the map projected onto the wall in Gage's library. "Lilith is living in a mansion outside of Rio de Janeiro. She's up on a hill, and the back of the house is on a cliff overlooking a lake. It's well guarded and has some super heavy-duty security systems." She moved the laser pointer to another spot. "Here is the main gate. There's a hand print and retinal scanner here and armed guards in the shack there. We believe them to be demons but don't know for sure.

"Gage has done some infrared scans of the area, so we know there's a tunnel system underneath the place leading down to a boat dock. I think that's the way we're going to be able to get to her. It's not patrolled, and it seems like the easiest way in. I think we're going to have to split up to neutralize the guards. We should probably use tranqs on them since we don't know if they're human. Once we have her, we zip back to the Vatican and take care of the wings. Aradia has been working on all that stuff."

Aradia nodded. "I've been working with Michael to make the traps strong enough to hold her. We've been using blessed blood I'm boiling with salt and herbs, and then we're lining all the traps in liquid silver. I've also figured out that while she can walk through the traps, she is not completely impervious to them. I believe if we tattoo a trap on her lips, it will keep her from shedding her human form. I'm using the theory on the shackles I've made. I forged them out of steel lined with salt, then I cooled them in Holy Water and etched the traps into the metal. I think they'll hold her."

Braxton crossed one leg over the other. "What about the rest of the Devils?"

"The only other two who can get out are Azazel and Beelzebub. We don't need the special precautions for Abaddon and Abalam. With Lucifer, I'm working on a combination of a Devil and Angel trap. It's a lot of work since I'm making it from scratch, but I think I'll have it ready in a few days. However, I've been doing some research, and I think we need to avoid Samhain. It's the point when the veil between Earth and Hell is the thinnest, and Lucifer would have more power to draw on. If we shoot for the Autumn solstice, which is September twenty-first, I should be able to tap into the natural power of the seasonal change, and it'll help super charge me."

Alaria chuckled wryly. "Then we definitely want to do it then. That gives us seven weeks to get all of this done, which is a tall order. We're going to have to move quickly on them and we won't have much time to rest or recharge between." She looked between the other two women with a droll expression. "I know neither of you have been through it, but the first few weeks of pregnancy make you nauseous, tired, and generally miserable. With three pregnant ladies, it's going to put more of the burden on the guys, so it's going to be tougher on all of us."

Braxton sighed deeply and ran his hands through his hair. "It's like God gets a kick out of this. He sits in His palace watching us try to maneuver through the last thing getting pitched at us, and just as soon as the end is in sight and we start feeling like we might actually survive this shitstorm, He tosses something new at us."

Michael shifted forward in his seat uncomfortable. "You have no idea how greatly it pains me not to be able to disagree with you, Braxton. However, at this moment in time, I fear I'm in complete agreement." He looked at the map. "I wish I could accompany you on your missions, but if I get too close, Lilith—or one of the others—will sense I'm there. What I can do is take you in close enough it would only take you a couple of human hours to reach the house. Once Lilith has been captured, I could also transport you all, including her, to the Choosing Place." He looked around the room. "If I might offer a suggestion—when you go to this place, you should send two to the tunnels, two to the front gate and two to the roof. That way the ones above and beneath can paint traps in an effort to keep Lilith in. I know it's a hassle with the hoops through which you must jump to make sure they work on her, but it is a worthwhile endeavor in my opinion."

Gage chuckled and sipped a glass of whiskey. "Good idea." He stood and walked to the window, looking out at the sprawling lawn. "There's a lot we have to do in a short period of time." He looked back at Michael. "Is it still safe for you to be storing the wing roots? I know you can't go up to Heaven."

"I took precautions before I came to see you with the news of what God is doing. The roots have been removed from Heaven and are being stored somewhere very safe. I will protect them all, have no doubt of that."

Aradia stretched her arms over her head. "I think Alaria and I need to be the ones painting the symbols. We know the most about them, and frankly, we're the best at them. Greer obviously needs to be somewhere with a sniper rifle, and we likely need one of the guys to go in after Lilith. Gage is the strongest, so I think he and Alaria should come up from the tunnels. I'll go to the roof with Greer so she can snipe people while I paint, and Damon and Braxton can charge the front gates to get in that way. I can easily transport myself, Greer, or both of us inside if Alaria and Gage get into trouble and need help."

When no one objected, Gage nodded decisively. "Okay, then. We'll finish the painting at the monastery tonight, get some sleep and leave tomorrow as soon as it gets dark. I'll keep an eye on the infrared scans to make sure Lilith doesn't leave, but she's typically banging some random man most nights, so we shouldn't have to worry."

Alaria laughed. "That bitch has quite a sex drive."

Before he could stop the words, Braxton spoke. "You have no idea. She damn near wore my dick off."

When everyone in the room turned to look at him with identical expressions of shock, save for Alaria, who, smirked and shook her head in amusement, Braxton looked sheepish. He shrugged his shoulder petulantly.

"What? Like none of you have ever had a stupid one night stand?"

Damon chuckled and stood. "Bro, we've all done it, but you might be the only one who ever fucked someone whose pussy came complete with a set of fangs."

Alaria leaned back against the bathtub and pressed her hands to her stomach. Nausea rolled through her, twisting her guts until she squeezed her eyes closed and prayed to God to let her die in peace.

"That particular prayer is going to fall on deaf ears, Alaria, and you know it."

Alaria groaned and turned her head to the side. "What are you doing here?"

Gabriel straightened the cuffs to his shirt and smoothed his hands down the sleeves of his coat. "I have come to offer you a reprieve from this task. I've been cleared by Father to release you from your duty to the others and take you somewhere safe where I can care for you while you gestate."

Alaria closed her eyes. "Go away, Gabe."

"I wish you would be reasonable. This is a lost cause. You will fail this task. God has already declared the mission futile. He is raising an army to fight the Cambion. This will be decided by the child you carry, not by you. There is no need to continue to struggle and risk your life."

"Stop pretending you care about me." Alaria climbed to her feet and filled a glass with water to rinse out her mouth. "You only care about the baby. I'm just a vessel to carry it."

"Like it or not, we are going to be parents, and my top priority is caring for my child. I'm not going to disappear quietly into the night and pretend this isn't happening. If I wanted to, God would let me take the child when it is born and raise it in Heaven where it would be safe. You'd do well to remember that and watch your tongue when you talk to me." Gabriel watched with cold anger as she stalked into the bedroom and yanked clothes from the dresser, pulling them on over her naked form.

Alaria whirled to face him, her eyes flashing with fury. "If you try to take my child, so help me God, I will storm the gates of Heaven myself and rip you limb from limb." She jabbed him in the chest with one finger. "You're lucky I believe you care for this baby, or I'd put you on your ass right now."

Gabriel closed his eyes with a pained expression on his face. "I cared for you, too."

"Past tense." She crossed her arms over her chest and glared at him. "We knew it would end like this. You knew what would happen when you made the choice to impregnate me without my knowledge or consent. You had no doubt what you did would rip us apart, and you did it anyway. I know you think you had no choice, but that still didn't give you the right to take mine away, too." She glared at him. "Maybe it's better this way. Instead of wondering how we could have fixed things, I hate you."

Gabriel winced and closed his eyes for a brief moment, the pain caused by her proclamation clearly evident on his face. "I would like to repair the damage done to our relationship. I know things are rather contentious right now, but I don't think they have to be that way. If you could find it within yourself to forgive me, we could move on and at least raise the child together." He stared at her intently. "We don't know what she will be like. I'm immortal. It's possible the child will be as well. Do you really want to leave it alone with no one once you die?"

Alaria laughed bitterly and placed her hands on her hips as she thought about how to respond. "Even if that happened, it would be several decades old and not a child." She shook her head. "You can't come in here asking me to abandon the people I have learned to care about because it would be better for me, and you can't threaten to kidnap my baby and then expect me to forgive you and move on. Forgiveness would require you actually be sorry for what you've done, and I don't believe for a second you're sorry about this. I think you're sorry I'm this mad, and I think you're sorry I'm not willing to fuck you anymore, but not for a second do I believe you're sorry you did this to me."

Gabriel lifted his shoulder in a shrug and smoothed his face into a calm façade. "I'm not sorry about the child. It was necessary, and one day you will see that."

Alaria scoffed. "What I see is a God so desperate to preserve this Earth that He is stooping to the level of Lucifer. They're different, but I'm beginning to think one is no better than the other."

"It is necessary. The Cambion would be strong enough to siege against Heaven, and without the addition of Nephilim, there are not enough Angels to hold them off if the demons and Devils join with them." Gabriel sat down on the end of the bed. "I know you don't agree with it, and I know you probably don't even really understand it, but this is a war. Lucifer is rising up against Heaven once again, and this time, without Heaven doing something drastic, he will win. There is no choice but to do what we are. We need more troops."

Alaria leaned against the dresser and crossed her arms over her chest.

"We might still succeed. If we accomplish this task, then there's no reason for this to happen. Even if there is an army of Cambion, the Host could handle it with all the demons sent back to Hell. If you were to convince Him to help us win this task, nothing that is happening would be necessary."

"I wish we had that option, but God fears Lucifer has grown too strong. He has decreed this task a failure."

"He hasn't given us a chance to try. We have all the information we need now, and we're moving on Lilith tonight. We might still win."

Gabriel looked pained as he answered, knowing Alaria would be angered. "Even if you were to capture all five of the Devils, you still have to win against Lucifer, and God says he has grown too strong for you to contain, even with Aradia. We made the mistake of not having a backup plan the last time. Heaven trusted Lucifer would abide by the rules and the Choosing would be the final say in the matter. He will not be caught in that position again. If you do succeed, and the Nephilim are not necessary, He will destroy them as they are born as He has always done. If you do not succeed, it will ensure our victory against the siege when it occurs."

Alaria's eyes flashed with anger. "I thought you were different. I trusted you. I loved you. I had hoped that over these millions of years God had changed, but He hasn't. He's going to allow the Angels to cause human women to be impregnated because the Nephilim *might* be needed at some point, and if we win and they aren't, he's going to kill them. I don't fucking know which way is worse."

Gabriel sighed deeply. "Could you at least try to understand? If you fail at this task, the child you carry could *kill* Lucifer. Not just chain him up but *kill* him. Isn't all of this worth the chance? Humans have been moving toward Hell for centuries. Most of the women carrying the Nephilim think it is an honor for them to be chosen to do this. Angels are not brutalizing women as you seem to think they are. Most of the Angels are causing it to be done the way in which Michael did to Greer and Aradia and for the others, their partners have been more than willing. Eager, even."

Alaria snorted. "And do the ones so eager to drop their panties for an Angel know the result of the one night stand is going to be a Nephilim?" She nodded when Gabriel looked guilty. "I didn't think so. At least the ones doing it like Michael are fully disclosing what the baby is going to be. The ones having sex, that's just plain dirty."

"They do not need to know. If they were aware, they might do things differently. This way, the children will be relatively well-hidden until they reach maturity and can be taken to train. I wish you would just try to see it from our perspective. We played by the rules on the Choosing, and this is what we got: an Earth full of demons, Griffin dead for no reason at all, and Lucifer on the verge of breaking out because of how many humans have been trying to free him. Garrick and his fleet of witches came within a hairsbreadth of breaking the chains. You have nearly died trying to stop this, and now that we're on the verge of winning again, Hell makes another move that would not only negate what we've done, but put us in a worse position than we've ever been in before."

Alaria stared down at the floor for a long moment, then looked up at him with eyes shining with tears. "Hell is always going to make a move. They will always have something up their sleeves. If we kill Lucifer, Beelzebub will take over, and he'll have more moves. There is no winning this war now. All we can do is keep fighting and keep trying to make Earth better than it was the day before. Angels need to work with the humans, not leave them to die. What you're doing is giving them a death sentence. What happens if, once the Cambion are defeated, they come up with something else to spring on us?"

"Then we would find a counter to it and continue to fight."

"The only way to win is to get the prize on your side. Heaven and Hell are fighting over Earth, so you need to work with the humans and make them see what's going on. If they help, you could turn the tide. Continuing to keep them in the dark and use them as pawns is going to ensure this continues happening. The only way to stop it is to work with the humans."

Gabriel sneered. "God doesn't need help from a mere human, and neither do the Angels. We have made the decision, and that is the end of it. If you and the others insist on continuing this useless mission, that is your choice, but I won't stand by and watch it. If you ever change your mind and want to come to Heaven where I can keep you safe, call for me. Otherwise, be careful, Alaria. If I ever feel as if you're endangering my child, I will come and take it, and you'll never see it again."

GREER STRAPPED a black utility belt around her waist and slid a buck knife into the sheath on her thigh. She fastened six clips of ammunition to the belt and shouldered her rifle before stooping to holster a pistol to one ankle. Checking the scope on her weapon, she deftly tested the slide and barrel, making sure of the action before slinging the strap over her head to hold it close against her body.

"Okay, everyone has the gear, and I've showed you all how to use it." Greer looked around the hotel room at the other five people. "Gage and Alaria, the two of you have hollow point rounds. They make a hole coming out three times the size of one going in, so don't shoot at anything you don't want to kill. I've put half a dozen cans of spray blood in your bags to draw the symbols, and one of liquid silver to line them. There's also a couple boxes of salt and a half dozen bottles of Holy Water in there. In the front pocket is a map of both the tunnels and the house. I've marked on there the rooms where Lilith is the most likely to be.

"Brax and Damon, I've given you both tranquilizer guns to try and keep from killing the guards, at least until we know whether or not they're demons. There are shotguns and rifles there, and I've color coded the boxes of ammo just in case. Red is for salt-crusted, blue is for silver, and green is for wood, just in case some other monsters show up. Once you're through the gate, sweep the yard, clear it, and then head in the front and back doors and secure them behind you. Alaria and I should be in the house by then, and from there it's hopefully only a matter of time before we find Lilith."

Alaria cleared her throat. "Try to use silencers as much as you can. I don't know how likely it is Lilith will be able to bust through these traps since we've never tried them before, but we'd might as well up our odds in every way we can, and that means being quiet and getting in before she knows we're there." She tossed a walkie-talkie to Braxton and one to Greer. "We'll keep in touch via these. I know Greer and Damon can do the psychic thing, but for those of us without someone in our heads, the radio will let us keep on the same page. Whatever any of you do, do not expose yourselves until the traps are in place. If we get found out before they're set, Lilith will flash out, and we might never find her again."

Greer snapped a clip into her weapon and reached for the door leading out into the parking lot. "Let's get this show on the road."

Alaria had nearly made it to the door when Braxton reached out and snagged her hand. He held her back until the other four had gone ahead and closed the door.

"I won't keep you but a second, but I wanted to make sure to tell you to be careful." He looked meaningfully down at her stomach. "I know you aren't a hundred percent, and I don't want anything to happen to you."

Alaria smiled. "We'll all be fine. It's six of us against one of her. She doesn't stand a chance." She squeezed his hand. "Let's go before they think we're in here having a quickie or something."

Braxton grinned. "That wouldn't be so bad." He leaned down and brushed his mouth across hers. "Do you want to have a quickie?"

She chuckled and pushed him back. "I'll tell you what, if we all get home in one piece, tomorrow night I'll ride you until you're unconscious. Sound like a plan?"

He swatted her ass and reached around her to pull open the door. "Works for me." He pulled it closed behind him and strode across the parking lot to the others. "Let's get this show on the road."

Aradia shook the can of blood and depressed the sprayer, drawing Devil's traps on the roof of Lilith's house. Her back ached from being bent over so long, and her hair was already coming loose from its braid. Sweat ran down her back and into the waistband of her jeans as the oppressive heat bore down on her.

"This is ridiculous. It's one in the morning, and it's still ninety degrees."

Greer giggled softly and looked over her shoulder at Aradia. "Welcome to South America, honey. It's hot all the time down here." She pressed her eye back to the lens of her sniper rifle. "I see Damon and Braxton in position. So far, it looks like there are four guard posts with four guards in each making a total of sixteen. The boys are splitting up to try and tranq them, and I'll pick off the rest from up here if I need to."

Aradia shook the can and stepped to the left to start a new trap. "I'm almost done here. Has anyone checked with Gage or Alaria to find out how it's going down there in the tunnels?"

Greer reached out with her mind toward her husband. *"Hey babe, you there?"*

"Everything okay?"

"Fine. Have you heard from Gage or Alaria on whether or not they're done with the traps? Aradia says we're almost good up here, and we need to get this thing started. The longer we wait, the bigger the chance we get caught."

"Nothing's come through on the radio, and last I knew, Alaria and Brax don't have the psychic stuff going on yet, so I'm gonna guess no one's heard from them. I'll have Braxton radio down and see what's going on. Make sure your radio is on, but keep it turned down low."

Greer rolled her eyes at the sarcasm. *"Got it."*

Damon turned to Braxton and gestured toward the radio. "The girls are almost done with the traps. Why don't you check with Gage and Alaria and make sure they're good so that we can get this going?"

Braxton picked up the radio and pressed the button, his voice a slight whisper. "Gage, Alaria, either of you there?"

Alaria's voice crackled through. "We're here. We're painting the symbols on the ceiling of the tunnels now. We'd better hope Lilith is standing still or asleep because if she isn't, she's going to know sooner rather than later that we're here."

Braxton looked down at the computer set up on the ground and studied the infrared image. "I'm picking her up on the third story and there's no movement, so I'm going to assume she's asleep. There are three heat signatures in there, but none are moving."

"She's probably having a fucking threesome." Alaria chuckled. "Is that all you needed?"

"Aradia and Greer are nearly done with their symbols. We're waiting for you guys to get through the tunnels and up to the entrance into the basement before we move. Just keep us updated on progress."

"Will do. Talk to you soon."

Alaria tucked the radio back into her pocket and picked up her backpack, slinging it over one shoulder. Gage put the cap back on a can of blood and zipped up his own bag, standing.

"You ready to do this?"

She nodded. "As ready as I'll ever be. Did you hear what Brax said?"

"I heard." He turned off the flashlight and led her farther into the tunnels.

Quietly, they crept up the damp stairs, their backs pressed against the wall and each clutching a gun. There was a small sliver of light creeping underneath the door at the top of the steps. Gage held up his hand to stop Alaria and pressed his ear to the door. He listened intently for ten seconds before gripping the doorknob and turning it slowly.

They entered the basement and shut the door softly behind them. Alaria went to the left, sweeping the basement quickly and meeting back with Gage near the stairs that would lead them up into the main house.

"Ready?" Gage paused on the third step and looked down at her.

"Let's get this done."

They ascended quickly, and Gage opened the door. Together, they emerged into the dark kitchen. Gage listened for several moments, straining to hear any indication that anyone was in the house. Hearing nothing, he nodded to Alaria.

"Third floor, right?"

Alaria nodded and fished the radio out of her pocket. "Brax, we're in the house and ready to go get her. Check with Aradia and make sure they're ready up top."

There was static for fifteen seconds before Braxton's voice came over the radio. "You're all clear to proceed to the third floor. Damon and I are neutralizing the guards. We'll come in through the back door and be three minutes behind you in case you need help with Lilith. Be careful and let us know if you get her in the shackles. Aradia will come in to do the tattoo."

Alaria smiled tensely. "Will do. See you soon." She turned to Gage.

"Do you want to do a full sweep or go straight to the third floor?"

"I don't sense anyone else in the house besides the three up there. There are only two heartbeats, so the other ones are human, which means we'll have to try not to kill them unless we have to."

"I know, Gage. I'm not a Devil anymore. I don't just kill people for the hell of it." She pursed her lips. "Let's just get this done. The longer we have to stay here, the greater the risk we run of getting caught."

The third floor of the mansion had a long hallway with several doors on either side. Gage stood in front of each, listening for movement. At the third door on the right hand side, he held up a hand and gestured for Alaria.

"In here."

Alaria picked up the radio. "We've located Lilith and are moving in."

She reached out and turned the knob, pushing the door open and standing back. On the bed were two naked people. The blankets were in a tangle on the floor and there was an array of brightly colored sex toys laying on every available surface. Alaria lifted one eyebrow in amusement and scanned the room for Lilith.

"Did you really think I wouldn't hear you coming?"

Alaria froze and turned, finding Lilith standing behind them. The blonde Devil wore a tight leather catsuit that zipped up the front. Her breasts threatened to spill out the top of the leather, and she tapped one finger against her chest.

"Long time, no see, Alaria. How's humanity taste?" Lilith stuck her index finger into her mouth and curled her tongue around it seductively. She cocked her head to the side. "Well, my goodness. One vampire, one Devil, a witch, three humans, and four heartbeats. Either Gage has figured out a way to be mortal or you're carrying a child?" She giggled. "Alaria's pregnant. Well, that's an interesting development. Who's the father?" Her eyes lit up with glee. "Could it be Gabriel?"

Alaria yawned and snapped her fingers, changing her clothing from army fatigues and boots to the red leather corset and black leather pants. She cracked her whip loudly and studied Lilith with mild interest.

"I have wanted to kick your ass for millions of years. So when I tell you that you can either come the easy way or the hard way, know I really, *really*, want you to pick the hard way."

Lilith grinned. "Ooh, goody. A fight. It's been far too long since I got to strangle a whore bitch." She held up her hands and watched in delight as her nails lengthened and sharpened into points.

Gage lifted his eyebrows. "That's a new one."

Lilith turned her head to look at him. "Sorry, sweetheart, but this is between us girls. No boys allowed." She tossed out her hand and a ring of flames sprung up around Gage, trapping him, unable to get out unless he wanted to die. She turned her attention back to Alaria. "You don't have your powers anymore. You know I'll kill you."

Alaria conjured a ball of fire in her hand and lobbed it at the Devil, striking her in the stomach and throwing her back several feet. "Just because I'm not an evil bitch doesn't mean I can't still wipe the floor with you. I have enough tricks left to take you out."

Lilith looked down at herself and swore at the melted leather and burned flesh on her abdomen. "You whore! This is a ten-thousand dollar garment!"

Alaria had to choke back a laugh as Lilith charged and tackled her. She hit the floor hard and grunted when Lilith used her claws to slice deep furrows in one of Alaria's thighs. She kicked out, striking the Devil in the pelvis, and scrambled to her feet, only to screech in frustration when Lilith threw herself onto Alaria's back.

"Seriously, Lilith?" Alaria bit back a scream as her hair was yanked savagely. She felt several clumps of it come loose from her scalp and swore. "Fucking hell, you fight like a girl!"

Alaria slammed Lilith against the wall several times, trying to shake off the Devil. Lilith clawed at her head and neck, too furious to do anything else. Even in her enraged state, Lilith was much stronger than Alaria, and Alaria was unable to get her off.

The sound of doors slamming trickled up from downstairs, and Alaria knew Braxton and Damon were on their way up. Gage was watching the fight with a steely hatred in his eyes, fury bubbling up at being contained. Alaria gritted her teeth and reached behind her, grabbing Lilith by two handfuls of blonde curls and wrenching her off her back. She slammed Lilith into the floor and twisted her arms behind her back savagely, placing one knee on the back of her neck.

"Hold still, you fucking cunt!"

"Is name calling really necessary?" Aradia lifted her eyebrows as she regarded the situation in front of her.

Alaria looked up and grinned when she saw Aradia and Greer appear in the middle of the room. "You have no idea."

Aradia looked over at Gage and waved her hand, extinguishing the flames. She glanced over to Lilith and sighed. Her eyes turned white as she let her power rise up within her, and Lilith's hands snapped together, the shackles flying out of the bag and fastening themselves on her hands and feet. Aradia shook her head when Lilith tried to shed her human form.

"Oh, I don't think so. See, I painted my traps large enough that you wouldn't know you were stuck unless you tried to leave the room, which is why you've been able to fight Alaria, but I think you'll find you're stuck, Lilith."

Lilith glared at Aradia. "How? I'm immune to traps."

"Not to my traps, you aren't." Aradia clutched a chunk of citrine in one hand and a slim metal pen in the other. She grabbed Lilith by the chin and held her still as she carved a small Devil's trap into the inside of Lilith's bottom lip. "Now you can't leave unless I let you, and I'm not going to let you."

Fear rising in her eyes for the first time, Lilith snarled. "What the hell do you want with me, anyway? You have to know that doing something to me is just going to get the others after you."

Alaria chuckled. "They aren't coming to save you. No one is. They're running scared, just like you were. We're here for your wings, and you know it. And once we're done with you, we're going after the rest. We're sealing Hell shut and casting you all out, Lilith, and you're going to help us do it."

Lilith giggled. "Even if you get my wings out, there's no way you'll find all the rest before Lucifer sheds his chains. He's getting out, and when he does, you're the first one he's coming for."

Michael appeared in the room with a slight rustling sound and appraised the situation quickly. "Hello, Lilith. I see you got into a bit more than you can handle tonight, hmm?"

Lilith sneered at the Angel. "Don't even start with me, you self-righteous asshole. You're going to let them carve me to pieces, so don't bore either of us with the pleasantries."

Michael pushed up the sleeves on his button down and smiled at her. "That's where you're wrong. I fully intend to carve out your roots myself."

Lilith paled. "You wouldn't dare."

He grabbed the shackles and yanked her toward the door, breaking the Devil's traps with one flick of his hand. "Oh, I would."

Braxton stepped beneath the hot spray of water and stuck his face in it, bracing one hand against the wall and letting the water sluice over his body. He closed his eyes and relaxed for a moment. It had been a long couple of days.

Capturing Lilith had been easier than expected. Alaria had been the only one hurt, and Greer had healed the claw marks with little fuss. Michael had transported everyone to the Choosing Place, where they had chained Lilith to the spot where Griffin had died, and Michael had proceeded to carve out the roots of her wings.

It had been bloody and horrible, just like they had all known it would be. The Devil had screamed and begged as the roots were ripped from her back. After they had been removed and placed safely inside the box where Michael was keeping them all, Greer had laid her hands on Lilith's back, intending to heal her.

It hadn't taken them long to realize Greer's abilities didn't work on Devils, which had left them with Lilith flayed open and her spine on display through what was left of the muscles on her back. Taking sympathy, Michael had used his powers to close the wounds, but the healing had left him drained and tired.

Lilith, difficult as always, had taken to shrieking at the top of her lungs incessantly. Michael had volunteered to stay with her at the Choosing Place to make sure she didn't escape, which allowed everyone else to travel back to Gage's estate for some well-deserved sleep and a thirty-six hour reprieve before they went after Abalam and Abaddon.

Braxton sighed again and straightened, reaching for the bar of soap. His whole body was tense, and he knew it would be a miracle if he slept, despite how tired he was. Absentmindedly, he rubbed the bar between his hands and then skimmed his hands over his body, spreading the suds around.

He gritted his teeth when he washed his penis, glaring at the organ when it hardened and jumped from even that platonic touch. One bout of sex in twenty months was not enough. He wondered briefly if it was too late to sneak down the hall and into Alaria's room, but he knew it was. He and Gage had stayed up until two a.m. going over strategy, and he was almost entirely sure Alaria had been asleep for hours.

Resigning himself, Braxton reached out and turned the water from hot to cold, hoping it would kill the erection so he could go to sleep. He fleetingly considered masturbating but decided against it. He was as tired of his own hand as he was of being horny. No, the only one that would take the edge off was asleep down the hall.

He turned the water off five minutes later when it became apparent he was just going to have to live with the discomfort. Grabbing a towel, he dried himself quickly and walked into the bedroom, coming to an abrupt halt, his mouth dropping open in shock.

Candles covered the dresser and the two nightstands—the only light in the room. The curtains were drawn shut, and the blankets had been removed from the bed, leaving it covered with only a sheet.

Sitting on the edge of the bed was Alaria. Her hair was curled and flowing over her shoulders. She wore a black lace negligee that left nothing to the imagination. It hugged her body, molding to her curves and displaying peeks of her skin. It cupped her breasts, caressing her smooth skin and hard nipples and clearly showing her areolas through the lace. It skimmed over her slightly rounded stomach and stopped high on her thighs, leaving her long legs bare.

Her toenails were painted blood red. For some reason, that more than anything sent Braxton's blood pressure climbing. He took in every inch of her several times, his mouth practically watering as he tried to decide what to do with her first and in what position he wanted to do it.

Alaria stood and pointed to the bed. "I call the shots tonight. I guarantee you'll like everything I do, but I'm in charge."

Braxton grinned. "I have absolutely zero problem with the suggestion."

"Lay down."

He crossed the room hurriedly and laid down on the bed. Alaria went to one side and used silk straps he hadn't before noticed to tie his hands loosely to the headboard and his feet to the footboard. Standing back, she raked her eyes over him, taking in the muscles, the scars, and his very erect penis.

"This is going to be fun for both of us." She crawled onto the bed next to him. "First, I'm going make you pant. If I measured right, you should have enough slack on those ties to sit up."

Obligingly, Braxton slid up the mattress until he was sitting up. "You measured right."

Alaria grinned wickedly and ran her hands over his dick. "If I wasn't going to make you feel so good when I'm done with you, I'd feel bad for what I'm about to do." She stood and walked to his dresser, where he noticed for the first time that she had laid a small bottle of lubricating gel and a slim vibrator.

She pulled the chair from his desk to the middle of the room and perched on the edge of it, the bottle and wand on the floor by her feet. Meeting his gaze and holding it, she slowly ran her hands up her own body, cupping and lifting her breasts, rolling her own nipples between her fingers. Braxton groaned, and his cock jumped at seeing her touch herself.

"This is cruel, Alaria."

Alaria giggled. "I told you there's nothing off limits with me. I like pushing the boundaries and trying new things. You don't seem shy, so I figured you might enjoy playing."

Braxton groaned when she pinched her nipples and spread her legs to give him a view of her. "Oh, I plan to enjoy." He felt desire knotting deep down in his gut. "Touch yourself for me."

She lifted an eyebrow. "I told you I call the shots tonight. I'll touch myself when I'm good and ready to."

"Do it." His voice was low and raspy. "First, I want you to tug your nightie down so I can see your nipples."

Alaria smiled at the bolt of want spearing through her. She reached up and slipped the straps of the negligee down, pulling it down just far enough to expose her breasts. Rubbing her fingers over her nipples, she looked back up to Braxton.

"Well then, since someone is feeling bossy, you can just talk me through this. What do you want me to do now?"

"Pick up the vibrator and the lube. Slick it up and turn it on."

Doing as he said, Alaria twisted the knob at the top of the white wand and turned it on. "What now?"

His eyes hungry, Braxton devoured the sight of her bare breasts. "Lift your skirt up a couple inches and spread your legs. I want to see you." He waited until she slid forward to the edge of the chair and lifted the skirt to expose herself to him. "Now I want you to open yourself up and put the vibrator on your pussy."

Alaria groaned slightly and did as he told her. She had always enjoyed being in control of sexual encounters. Never before had she realized how hot it was to have someone else calling the shots. She pressed the vibrator to her center and gasped as the vibrations made her jump.

"I want you to slide it in and out slowly. While you do that, use your other hand to rub your nipple. I want you to come, Alaria. Hard and as fast as you can. Come hard so you're good and wet when I get in you." He watched her chest flush with color and her eyes close as she concentrated on finding her release. "Fuck yourself for me. Imagine it's my cock sliding in and out of you. You're hot and wet and so goddamned beautiful. I want to get my tongue on you again and taste you."

Alaria let his words wash over her. She rubbed the vibrator against her clit, desperate to find her orgasm. What had started out as a plan to tease Braxton had quickly turned into something else. Even tied to the bed, he was calling the shots, and instead of being annoying, it was sexy as hell.

She opened her eyes as her orgasm swept through her, her hips lifting and a groan escaping her. She sagged in the chair, panting, and quickly twisted the vibrator to turn it off. Braxton smiled hungrily and pulled at the scarves.

"Come untie me. I want to touch you."

Alaria shook her head as her vision cleared. She stood and pulled the straps back up on the lingerie, concealing her breasts once again. "No." She crossed the room and slipped onto the bed with him. "That was fucking sexy as hell, but it doesn't change my plan for the night. I'm going to ride you like a pony, and you're going to lie there and let me do it."

Braxton moaned deep in his throat. "I want to touch you."

Alaria grinned wickedly. "You can touch me the next time. This time, hands off. No touching allowed. I'm going to use your cock like I just did the vibrator. I'm going to fuck you. Hard and fast and so good your head will spin."

She climbed on top of him and impaled herself on him before Braxton could think of a retort. He filled her, stretching her body and spearing up into her. They both groaned when she was fully seated on him, and Braxton rocked his hips, using what little range of motion he had to bring them both pleasure. She slid herself back and forth in his lap, wet and easy. He glided in and out of her body, hard and thick and hot.

Alaria rode him slowly, driving them both up the crest of release. She leaned forward, gripping the headboard in her hands and rocking her body against his. Braxton groaned and murmured to her, tugging his hands against the straps, half-heartedly trying to get loose so he could put his hands on her. Both knew he could break them if he wanted to.

She climaxed first, the delicious heat sweeping through her and carrying her away on a wave of sensation. Every nerve ending fired, her body spasmed around him, and she threw her head back on a groan, jerking her hips as she came.

With a raw groan, Braxton let her orgasm trigger his own, spilling himself inside of her and arching his hips to bury himself in her fully.

Smiling and sated, Alaria took the time to free his hands before sinking to the bed next to him and settling into his arms. Braxton drew her close, pulling her up for a kiss and wrapping both arms tightly around her body.

"You should do this every day of the week and twice on Sundays."

Alaria giggled. "Surely we can find other things to do occasionally."

Braxton closed his eyes. "I might not survive them."

"Then I know I'm doing my job right." She leaned up and nipped his chin with her teeth. "I'm not boring."

"I wouldn't care if you wanted missionary every single time." He ran his hand over her arm. "I want you because of you, not because you're a sex goddess."

Alaria lifted her eyebrows. "Sex goddess, huh? I could get used to that." She slid one arm across his chest and laid her head on his shoulder. "For the record, I'd still want you if you were boring and vanilla, too. It wouldn't be as much fun, but I'd still want you."

Braxton laughed. "I'm glad to know it's not my sexual prowess that keeps you coming back."

"Oh, it helps." She giggled. "It also doesn't hurt that you're easy to look at and fun to talk to."

Braxton had opened his mouth to answer when a light filled the room and Gabriel appeared. Alaria scrambled for the blanket folded on the floor, trying to cover them up before he could see what had happened, but she knew as she did it that it wouldn't be quick enough. The Angel took in the situation and charged across the room.

"You bastard!"

"Gabe, no!"

Alaria's cry fell on deaf ears. Gabriel grabbed Braxton and lifted him off the bed, throwing him across the room. He crashed into the dresser and hit the floor, his nose bleeding. Alaria rushed forward, grabbing Gabriel's arm. Lost in his rage, he swept his arm to the side, sending Alaria flying into the window. The glass shattered, and she nearly went out it.

Braxton stood and reached for his pants, yanking them on with one hand before facing the Angel. "You need to calm the fuck down, Gabriel."

Gabriel snarled. "You had to have her, didn't you? Taking my place by her side wasn't enough for you. You had to take my place in her bed!" He swung at Braxton and landed a punch on the Warrior's jaw.

Alaria used her powers to conjure herself clothes and again went toward Gabriel. He held out his hand and blasted her back with a bolt of energy that tossed her to the bed.

"I'm going to kill him, and you will not interfere. I've put up with the embraces, I've put up with the feelings, and I've put up with the grief I feel at losing you, but I will not put up with another man defiling you!"

Braxton dodged a punch, still not wanting to fight Gabriel. "Calm down."

"I'll calm down when you're a pile of dust." He glared at Alaria. "He's the reason you won't come to Heaven with me, isn't he?" Gabriel sneered. "Or has he always been the one you wanted? First you steal Griffin's life, then you steal her husband and have the family with him that she should have had. Tell me, Braxton, do you picture Griffin's face when you bury yourself in her?"

Braxton clenched his jaw shut. "You need to stop talking now."

"Finally, something we agree on."

The two men clashed violently. Gabriel conjured his sword and swung it at Braxton, intending to kill the other man. Terrified, Alaria raced for the door and threw it open.

"Aradia! Help!"

She ran back inside, where Braxton was using the chair to fend off Gabriel. Doors slammed from upstairs and down the hall, but Alaria feared the others would be too late. She watched in horror as Gabriel slashed the chair in half. Braxton dodged one slash of the sword and went for the gun he kept near the bed. Alaria saw the glint of light off the blade and screamed, throwing herself between Gabriel and Braxton.

Gabriel thrust the sword out, intending to run Braxton through with it, his vision red with fury. The blade met flesh, and he roared triumphantly.

Alaria stumbled back one step, her eyes wide and mouth open. Her hands went to her chest, where the blade from the sword had entered her ribcage and protruded out between her shoulder blades.

"No! No!" Gabriel shrieked, grabbing her as her knees buckled.

"Greer! Get your fucking ass in here NOW!" Braxton's voice was loud and panicked. He hit his knees in front of Alaria, placing his hands on her face. "It's okay. You're okay. Greer can fix it. Hang on, baby, don't you dare die on me!"

"Move!" Greer shoved Braxton out of the way. She gripped the sword in both hands and wrenched it out of Alaria. She tore at the pieces of fabric to get a clear shot at the wound.

Aradia raced into the room and threw out one hand, tying Gabriel hand and foot and slamming him against the wall. Without pausing, she pressed her hands to Greer's back, lending the Healer her strength.

Alaria tried to speak, but nothing came out other than a stream of blood. She looked around the room, scared. Greer had her eyes closed and the skin on Alaria's chest was slowly pulling closed. Aradia was muttering under her breath, her eyes pitch black and power rolling off her in waves.

As soon as the healing gave her the ability to, Alaria screamed, her ribs knitting themselves back together. She tried to breathe and found she couldn't suck in a full gasp. It felt as if she was being stabbed by a thousand daggers, and she screamed until her throat bled.

Eventually, the pain faded and a warmth filled her. Alaria wobbled, unable to balance herself when Greer let go of her. She fell forward and would have hit the ground had Braxton not been there to catch her, gathering her in his arms and crushing her to him.

Gage turned to Gabriel, his eyes flashing heat and anger. "Alaria, how do I kill an Angel?"

Alaria was sobbing in Braxton's arms. She looked up toward the ceiling, tears streaming down her face. "Michael."

Whether Michael was paying close attention or if there was enough desperation in her plea that it carried to him, the Angel appeared in the room with them. He looked at the bloody sword, which he recognized as Gabriel's, at Alaria's half-naked body and the still angry-looking pink scar on her chest, and at Gabriel, tied with witch-rope in the corner. Disbelief in his eyes, he shook his head.

"Brother, what have you done?"

Gage answered. "What he did is run Alaria through with a sword and nearly kill her. If Greer hadn't gotten here exactly when she did, Alaria *would* be dead."

Horrified, Michael crouched in front of Gabriel. "Why? Why would you do such a thing? She is the mother of your child."

Braxton cleared his throat from the corner. "He was trying to kill me, Michael. He walked in on us in bed together. Alaria was trying to help me, and Gabriel stabbed her by mistake."

Gage's voice was a growl. "Get him out of my house, Michael, and do not ever let him come back. If he ever steps foot in this house again, I will not stop until he is dead. NO ONE comes into THIS house and hurts one of MINE!"

Michael rose and laid his hand on Gage's shoulder. "I won't let him disrespect your home. I'll take him back to Heaven." He looked at Aradia. "Could you drop the witch-rope?"

Aradia hesitated. "What will you do with him?"

"I'll take him back to Heaven. He'll be punished for hurting a human outside of the sanctions of God."

Gabriel was sobbing on the floor. "I'm sorry, Alaria. I'm so sorry."

Michael reached down as Aradia let the ropes drop and gripped Gabriel by the shoulder. With a sad look around the room, Michael disappeared, taking Gabriel with him.

Alaria took a trembling breath. "The baby. Greer, the baby."

Greer smiled reassuringly. "Is fine. I'm sure Gage can hear the heartbeat, and it felt good and strong to me."

Gage nodded. "The heartbeat is strong, sweetheart. Don't worry about it." He stooped and combed her hair back from her face. "I won't let Gabe in here again. Aradia will start putting up wards immediately."

"If you do that, Michael won't be able to get in."

Alaria coughed weakly. "Michael won't let him come back. He can handle Gabe." She looked around. "I'm tired."

Gage stood. "Braxton, take her into her room to rest. I'll get the room cleaned up." He sighed and looked at Greer. "How long will it take her to be back up to full strength?"

"A few days, maybe a week."

"Get her settled into bed and come downstairs. We need to reevaluate our plan to go after Tweedle Dee and Tweedle Dum."

Braxton stood, Alaria lying in his arms. She weakly looped one arm around his shoulders and laid her head on his shoulder. Her eyes were barely open, and her skin was pale and clammy. Each breath hurt as she sucked in and expelled air. He carried her from the room and into the bathroom.

Gage rubbed his eyes and looked at Greer. "How close was she to dying?"

Greer's expression was grim. "Without Aradia lending me some of her power, I don't know if I could have brought her back. Her heart was nearly cut in two. The only thing on our side is it takes a few seconds for the message to get to the brain, and she still had some synapses firing. If I'd been five seconds later, it would have been too late."

Aradia cleared her throat. "What do we do about Gabriel?"

Damon lifted his lip in a sneer. "I think I'm with Gage on this one. We should've killed him. I know he and Alaria have a complicated relationship and they had an even more complicated breakup, but there is no excuse out there good enough to make me think he should be forgiven for trying to kill Brax."

Greer sighed. "We're also a bit prejudiced because Alaria and Brax are ours. We don't know what Gabe might have been feeling or why he was even here to begin with. Do we know if he knew they were together?"

Gage shook his head. "It doesn't matter. Damon is right. There's no excuse. Gabe's a big boy. He should be able to handle himself, and he should know better than to do what he just did." He headed toward the door. "If any of the rest of you want to figure out how the fuck to make this delay fit in with our plan, be in my office in an hour."

Alaria placed her feet on the floor and took a deep breath. Her chest still burned with the remnants of the trauma from being stabbed in the chest. For the most part, she was back to normal, but there was still some pain when she tried to breathe too deeply. Greer thought it was because her body was preoccupied with a pregnancy and had been unable to heal as well as she normally would have.

Alaria didn't care why she still hurt, she just wanted it to stop. They had already pushed off going after Abalam and Abaddon because of what had happened, and she didn't want them to continue to be delayed because of her.

A knocking filled the room, and she looked around in confusion. She heaved herself to her feet and went to the door, opening it. Finding no one in the hall, she cast her eyes toward the ceiling and wrinkled her brows.

"Who is it?"

"It's Gabriel. May I come in?"

Unable to stop the smile at his disembodied voice, Alaria crossed her arms over her chest. "Gage will behead you if he finds you here, but yeah, it's your funeral. You can come in if you promise to leave the sword in Heaven."

Gabriel appeared in the room, looking disheveled for the first time Alaria could remember. His hair was greasy and messy, his suit rumpled, and lines creased his face. He stood awkwardly, hands shoved in his pockets and his shoulders hunched over.

"Are you well?"

"Greer managed to fix most of the damage. I'm still sore, but I'll be fine."

Gabriel raked his hands through his hair. "I've come to apologize to you."

She quirked an eyebrow. "You were trying to murder Braxton. I hardly think I'm the one you should be apologizing to."

"I'm not interested in speaking with the human." He sat on the bed. "Will you sit with me?"

Alaria perched next to him, picking up a pillow and placing it in her lap before leaning back against the headboard. "I don't think we can come back from this."

Gabriel hung his head, his eyes sad. "I know." He looked at her with tear-filled eyes. "I want to explain to you why I did what I did. Not that there is an excuse, but to try and make you understand."

Alaria hesitantly reached out and laid her hand over his. "You were jealous. We've been fighting over the baby and our relationship, and then you were faced with the naked evidence of me and another man. I understand why that hurt you. I didn't mean to."

"You didn't hurt me. I did. It's taken me these last few days of forced retrospection to realize nothing that has happened has been due to anyone other than me." He stared down at the floor. "I never really believed you when you told me we wouldn't end up together. I kept telling myself you would get tired of being human and ask me to help you regain your wings. I imagined I would go to God and take up your cause, and He would grant the request."

Alaria's voice was a whisper. "I don't want to be an Angel."

"I know that now." He ran his hands over his thighs nervously. "I realized it when you asked me to choose you. I felt like I was losing you. I had built it up to be this sure thing, and there you were, crying and begging me to stay with you—to choose you over God—and everything came crashing down on me. I behaved reprehensibly toward you, and I'm sorry. Then, when Michael came to me and told me about the edict requiring the child, a part of me truly believed it would be the thing that could bring us back together."

"Gabe..."

"I know." Gabriel tipped his head back and looked up at the ceiling. "I know now it was a stupid thought. My emotions confused me. All of the things we did together…they made me feel guilty and wonderful all at once. I loved you and hated you for doing that to me, but I wanted to keep you. I thought the baby would bring us back together, and when it had the opposite effect, I didn't know how to handle it. I've been working on dealing with that, and I actually came here to discuss the situation with Braxton. I needed to assure myself that if I wasn't going to be involved with the child, he would take care of you both the way you deserve to be taken care of."

Alaria's heart constricted. She tucked her hair behind her ears and sighed deeply. "I hate this. I hate that we're sitting here like this, and I hate like hell that it's ending like this. It shouldn't have."

Gabriel smiled slightly. "I think it had to. If it hadn't ended in flames, I don't know if you ever would have been able to let go. I don't want for you to be human, but I do want you to be happy, and for some reason outside my comprehension, those two things seem to go hand in hand."

"You don't want me unless I want to be an Angel, and I needed you to pick me over Heaven." She ran her hands over her hair, tugging sharply on the ends before turning her head to face him. "Braxton is a good man."

"I know he is." Gabriel laughed bitterly. "He's going to be raising my child. I'll never get to hear her refer to me as 'Daddy.' It'll always be in reference to Braxton."

Alaria's brows drew together. "We are not nearly to that point. I'm not trying to replace you, but I don't know if I can forgive you for what you've done. You impregnated me without my knowledge or permission and then you stabbed me with a fucking sword."

"I'll pay for what I did to you for the rest of my life, however long that ends up being." He reached out and laid his hand on hers. "I just want you to know I did love you as best I could. It wasn't nearly what you deserved, but it was all I had."

"I know." Her voice was soft.

"Will you let me watch over the child? As an uncle, or family friend, but something. I need to be able to make sure it's okay. I know you don't believe me, but I love the baby, and I would lay my life down protecting it. Can you do that for me? If you have to leave, or be gone, will you let me be the one to watch over it?"

Alaria's heart twisted painfully in her chest. She nodded through her tears. "I can do that." She didn't object when Gabriel pulled her into a hug. She wrapped her arms around him and breathed in the familiar scent. A small part of her wished they could have made things work, and she felt one tug of longing to go back to how it had once been. She rubbed his back gently and sat back. "You should go before Gage or Braxton find you here. They aren't so happy with you right now."

Gabriel nodded. "I'm not too happy with me, either." He stood. "Before I go, you need to know nothing has changed with the tasks. God still views this as a waste of time. If ever you want to be taken to Heaven to remain safe, all you have to do is call for me, and I will come get you no matter where you are."

"I won't."

"I know, but I had to offer." He smiled sadly. "Goodbye, Alaria."

Alaria didn't answer until he had disappeared from the room. "Bye, Gabe."

"Hold on." Damon leaned forward and glared at Gage. "Three days ago, Abaddon and Abalam were in some hotel in Las Vegas, and now you're telling me they're in Purgatory?"

Greer crossed her legs. "Forget how they got there. How do *we* get there and how to we get them back out?"

Alaria sighed. "Purgatory is an interesting place. It's kind of like a holding tank. It doesn't surprise me that they went there since it's as close to Hell as they can get right now. Do we know where the other ones are?"

Gage nodded. "We know Azazel is in a brothel in Amsterdam. Alaria, you were spot on with thinking he would want to be where there's a lot of sex. He's apparently been one of the most popular male prostitutes in the city for a few months now. Beelzebub is slick as spit and still evading us. Every time I tug a line, he's gone before I've pinned him down."

Alaria smirked. "He's sneaky. He'll be the hardest one to catch, and he's the most dangerous because he's the smartest." She tugged on her hair in frustration. "I really wanted to go after the Wonder Twins next. Abalam is a vicious motherfucker, but he and Abaddon make one another weaker. Azazel is tough."

Greer's eyes lit up. "Unless we take a different approach. The important thing is we get to him, not how. What if we were able to go in and get him without a fight?"

Gage folded his arms across his chest. "What are you thinking?"

"I'm thinking that sex is Azazel's weakness. He was deprived of it for so long he's desperate for as much as he can get, and the side effect is he's spawning a whole fleet of Cambion while he's being rented out by the hour. We need to take advantage of that." Greer grinned brightly. "Azazel has met Braxton and Gage, he saw me in Hell, and he knows Alaria. He doesn't know Aradia." She turned to Aradia, her eyebrows lifted and her gaze hopeful. "Has he ever seen you?"

Aradia shook her head, a sinking feeling in her stomach. "No, he's never laid eyes on me. None of them have. Garrick and Javal did, but they're both dead, and Lilith, but she's locked up."

"I didn't think so. What I'm thinking is Alaria and I slut you up and send you in to the brothel. You flash a lot of money, pretend to be some Greek heiress or something and ask to see the beef. Then you pick Azazel, go back to his room and use some of your witchy-wiles to knock him on his ass, and use your witch-rope to capture him." Greer snapped her fingers. "He's never seen Damon, either, so maybe we send Damon in as your husband who likes to watch. That way there's someone else there in case you get into too much trouble to handle."

Alaria pursed her lips. "I don't think he'd see it coming. For one, he's too cocky to think he could ever get trapped by such a simple plan. Two, he's going to be expecting us all to come, guns blazing, and try to take him out by force, which is why he thinks he's safe at work. There are too many people there, and he knows we wouldn't want to risk the potential casualties." She nodded decisively. "I like it."

Gage looked at Aradia. "What do you think? You would be the one in danger, so you're the one who has to say yes."

Aradia was pale, but her eyes were determined. "I think if we have a chance to get even one of these Devils without risking our lives or risking the lives of innocent humans, then that's what we have to do."

Damon huffed a deep breath and rubbed his hands on his thighs, turning to grin at Aradia. "Well, fuck. It looks like we're a married couple now."

Gage guffawed and rolled his eyes. "We are not swinging, Mackenzie, so keep your paws to yourself." He stood. "I'll work on getting some IDs for the two of you. The place where he's at is very high-end, and you'll need to provide some information." He looked to Alaria. "Do you feel strong enough for us to leave Tuesday?"

"That gives me two more days to get better. I think that'll be fine." Alaria folded her hands over her stomach before shifting to address Aradia. "You're going to need to look sexy. Heels, short skirt, low-cut top, and a push-up bra. Damon, you're not a pretty boy, so you aren't really Azazel's type, but we can address some of those issues. Go get a manicure to get rid of some of those callouses, get a haircut and learn how to slick it back from your face. We'll get you a slick suit, skinny tie and a snug shirt. He'll like the physique." She arched her eyebrows. "You'll have to act like a couple. You want to attract Azazel. Gage can correct me if I'm wrong, but I imagine the workers can turn down a client."

Gage nodded. "Azazel seems to be the most popular attraction, but there's a huge waitlist and only a small percentage of clients see him. I hacked into their books to look at his schedule."

Alaria chuckled. "I know his type, for both men and women, so I'll fix both of you up, but you're going to have to put on a good show. Slap her ass, make out at the bar, giggle like newlyweds. Anything you can think of to make yourselves look like two people who want to get fucked. I would suggest, Damon, you be the one to make eye contact with Azazel. Study him, then you're going to nudge Aradia toward him. From there, she needs to act coy and cute. Flirt with him. Tell him you're on vacation and your husband gets off on watching you with another man. Ask if he works there. He'll like that you don't assume. Then, you want to let him lead. Trust me, he will."

Aradia was taking in everything being said, her face drawn and pale. "I think I might be sick."

Gage reached out and held her hand. "You don't have to do this. We can find another way. If you don't feel like you can, or like you would be in too much danger, you don't have to. No one would be mad at you."

"I can do it. I have to." Aradia rubbed her hands over her face. "I'll be fine. I don't know how well I can act like I'm into Damon, but I'll do my best."

Damon chortled. "No offense, Red, but I'm much more into sassy blondes." He winked at Greer, who smacked his arm. "Seriously, it'll be fine. It's playing a part. I'm not going to think you're in toit, Gage and Greer will just choose not to watch, and they're not going to be mad at us for it. This is a job. I can promise you it won't affect any of the relationships around here."

Aradia took a shaky breath. "I trust you all with my life. I know I'm a bit different in that I had never had any relationships of the romantic sort before Gage. I don't want to have any other than him. The thought of letting anyone, even if it's Damon or Braxton, whom I love and trust, touch me in anything other than a platonic manner, makes me feel odd." She smiled at Damon. "Please don't take offense. I'll do what is necessary, but I just feel as if I need some reassurances these things won't be held against me later on."

Gage reached out and covered Aradia's hand with his own. "Aradia, my love, you are agreeing to do something very brave and strong. I'm proud of you for being strong enough to go after Azazel like this. I swear to you nothing will change between us. I know it's hard for you—harder on you than it would be for any of the rest of us—but I never want you to think this would come between us. It won't."

Aradia squeezed his fingers and smiled. "Okay." She shifted her eyes to Damon. "Have I offended you?"

Damon laughed and shook his head. "It would take a lot more to offend me." He rose. "I don't know about anyone else, but it's getting late, and I'm hungry. I think there's a pack of beef in the fridge, and I intend to grill it."

Braxton shook his head emphatically. "Fuck that. The last time you grilled it was cooked to death." He shot to his feet. "You can stand back and watch the master. God knows you have a lot to learn."

Greer giggled as the two men left the room. She leaned back on the couch and slung her arm around Aradia's shoulders. "We're a family. Dysfunctional as hell with a shit-ton of issues, but we're a family. We take care of each other. There isn't going to be some cat fight between us after it's done. Besides, Damon has a magnificent ass, and it's a crying shame no one else gets to experience the glory that is grabbing it."

Aradia choked on a gulp of water, and Alaria laughed, holding her chest to combat the pain at the movement. She reached out and patted Aradia's knee gently. "It's fine. With any luck it'll be a little kissing, a little groping and we'll be done. No big deal, I promise."

Aradia rolled her eyes. "I think I'm going to need a glass of wine before dinner, with dinner and after dinner."

Gage laughed and stood. "That can be arranged."

A SLEEK, black limo pulled up to the curb. The lights from the sign on the top of the building glowed blue and yellow in the dark, spelling out two words: Clover House. Aradia studied those words as she waited for the driver to come around and let her out of the limo. Damon sat next to her, his hair slicked back from his face and dressed in a navy blue pin-striped silk suit and a lavender button-down shirt with a blue and purple striped tie. His shoes were black with a pointy toe, and Aradia was having a hard time not giggling at him.

Damon reached over and laid a hand on Aradia's knee. "Are you ready?"

Aradia sighed deeply. "As I'll ever be. The hardest part is going to be not laughing at you."

He scowled. "If you look up the word 'metrosexual' in the dictionary, there would be a picture of me dressed like this next to it."

The driver opened the door and held out a hand for Aradia, who took it, allowing him to help her out of the car. She squinted against the bright lights coming from the brothel and offered a nervous smile as Damon tucked her hand into the crook of his arm. She took a deep breath and closed her eyes for a moment, gathering her strength and dampening her power so Azazel wouldn't sense she was a witch.

"Let's get this done."

Damon led her to the door, casting a furtive glance from side to side before pulling it open and slipping three folded bills to the doorman. Within moments, a scantily clad woman with long blonde hair, large breasts and dangerously high heels approached them.

"Welcome to Clover House. My name is Dixie. If you'll follow me to the desk, we'll take care of scanning your IDs and getting a tab opened. Are we operating on a budget this evening?"

Damon shook his head and guided Aradia in the direction the woman led them. "No budget." He slipped a black credit card from his wallet and handed it to Dixie, along with the two fake IDs Gage had had made for them. She took them swiftly, scanning them into her computer and swiping the credit card. She smiled up at him.

"Again, welcome to Clover House, Mr. and Mrs. Trent. Straight through the main doors you'll find our complimentary bar. There are beer, wine, cocktails, and liquor available there gratis for our guests. The ladies and gentlemen in our employ are all wearing a red bracelet to help you identify them. Each has their own rate, and each their own preference. Is there something in particular I can help you find tonight?"

Aradia giggled, and Damon smiled at her indulgently before speaking. "We're interested in whatever strikes my wife's fancy. I think for now we'd prefer to mingle and meet some of the staff."

Dixie nodded and pushed a button to open the door into the main part of the building. "Enjoy your stay at Clover House. Don't forget to close your tab on your way out."

Damon dipped his head to whisper to Aradia as they went through the doors. "You're going to have to sex it up, babe. You're the one who's going to get his attention, not me."

Aradia gritted her teeth and reached down to tug up the hem of her skirt a couple of inches, exposing her thighs. She unbuttoned two more buttons on her shirt, allowing the red silk and black lace of the corset she wore underneath to spill out, displaying her breasts for all to see. She fluffed her hair, arranging it around her shoulders and cocked one eyebrow at Damon.

"Better?"

"Take the shirt off." He reached out and finished unbuttoning it, tugging it from her shoulders and off her arms. He handed it to a passing waitress, who smiled and tucked it over her arm. "That's better. Alaria and Greer did a good job with the lingerie." He narrowed his eyes. "Do

I recognize that corset?"

Aradia flushed red. "It's not like *I* have any of this stuff." She ran her hand down his arm. "Let's get this over with."

Damon wrapped his arm around her waist, slipping his hand down to cup her ass. He led her to the bar, swiftly ordering a glass of champagne and a scotch. Once the drinks were in their hands, he turned to survey the men and women in the room with casual disregard.

"He's the one in the armchair by the fire place. With the long hair and arms as big as my thighs."

Aradia nodded. "I see him. Should I go over to him?"

"No. Let him notice us first. Don't hit me."

Aradia wrinkled her brows at that but didn't have a chance to respond before Damon jerked her into his arms and kissed her deeply, cupping one of her breasts in his hand and placing the other on the small of her back. She tried to relax into him, but the entire experience felt unnatural. After several moments, he released her mouth, leaning forward to press his mouth to the skin under her ear.

"It's as weird for me as it is for you, but we have to get his attention. You need to grope me."

Hesitant and near tears, Aradia reached between them and let her fingers graze over his crotch. The lack of anything protruding was a relief to her, and she giggled despite herself, then reached around and cupped his ass in one hand, squeezing gently. Damon murmured softly to her.

"He's looking. Turn around and look around the room. Drag your finger between your boobs and get him to notice you. Make eye contact if you can."

"Alaria said for you to."

Damon chuckled, his breath warm against her ear. "I already am."

Aradia turned to look over her shoulder, trying to be as seductive as possible. She scanned the crowd, stopping to look at several of the people before allowing her eyes to settle on Azazel. Her eyes skated up his body, taking him in, and sought out, found, and held his gaze. When he lifted his drink and nodded in her direction, she felt a greasy knot of worry form in her stomach.

"You're going to have to go over there."

"I know." She lifted one shoulder and shivered when Damon ran his hand up her arm. "When?"

"We're discussing it. You need to look a little excited and a little nervous. See, I'm looking patient and excited at the same time. You're telling me you like him."

"Am I?"

Damon laughed again. "That's what he thinks. Now I'm telling you I like him too and you should go talk to him. You're telling me you don't want to go alone—you think I should go with you."

Aradia glared at him. "That's pretty damn accurate." She squealed when he swatted her butt and nudged her away from him.

"Go get him, Aradia. I'll watch from here."

Aradia stumbled one step before getting her balance. She cast one look at Damon, who made a shooing motion with his hands. She sucked in a breath, held it, and forced herself to saunter across the room, swinging her hips and trying to look as seductive and sexy as possible. The way Azazel was watching her made her sick to her stomach.

He smiled as she approached and gestured to the seat across from him. Without a word, she dropped into it.

"I'm Ally." The lie tasted bitter in her throat.

"Azazel." He reached out to shake her hand. "Pleased to make your acquaintance."

Aradia smiled shyly and lowered her eyes slightly, looking up at him through her lashes. "Do you work here?"

Azazel laughed and held up his wrist, showing her the red band. "I certainly do." He leaned forward and stroked his fingers over her knee. "You don't look like the type who normally comes in here."

"What type normally comes in here?"

"Well, not Greeks for one. That's a very pretty accent you have, Ally. What part of Greece do you hail from?"

Aradia laid her hand on top of his. "I was born in Athens and grew up outside the city. I've been in the States for a few years, though. My husband is a New Yorker."

Azazel looked over at Damon, who was watching them with a heated look on his face. "Your husband is very attractive."

"I certainly think so. Tell me, why do you do this? Someone as handsome as you, surely you don't have a problem sexually."

He laughed. "I don't. In fact, my wait list is several months long. I work here because I enjoy sex, and I want to have it with as many people as I can. It amuses me that people pay me to enjoy myself."

Aradia shifted nervously. "Well, if you're that booked up..."

Azazel grabbed her hand as she started to rise. "Tonight is technically my night off. I hang around here while I'm off to see if anyone interesting comes in, though I don't schedule appointments. Sit for a few minutes."

Her heart pounding in her chest, she dropped into the chair again. "We're heading back to New York tomorrow. We thought a place like this might be fun."

He lifted his eyebrows. "Looking to experience a cock other than your husband's?"

Aradia flushed bright red. "Something like that."

Azazel folded his hands beneath his chin and studied her. "It doesn't bother you he's going to fuck a whore?"

Seeing the challenge in his eyes, Aradia jutted her chin up and met his eyes. "Actually, he's going to jack off while I fuck the whore."

The Devil laughed and stood, holding out his hand to her. "I like you, Ally. Get your husband and come upstairs with me. He can watch me make you scream."

Knowing she had to finish what she had started, Aradia reached out and boldly cupped his penis in her hand, her tongue darting out to wet her lips. "I think I'll be the one making you scream."

Azazel grinned and bent, capturing her mouth in a heated kiss. Aradia forced herself to kiss him back and press her body against his. When he pulled back, his eyes were clouded with lust, and his erection was pressing into her belly.

"What's his name?"

"Brandon."

Azazel turned and met Damon's eyes through the crowd and jerked his head toward the stairs, keeping hold of Aradia's hand and pulling her along behind him. Damon pushed off the bar and followed them. Aradia knew he was keeping Greer updated on everything through their link, and she swallowed her nerves as she trailed up the stairs behind Azazel.

Azazel led them into a large bedroom. The wood floors were dark and shiny, and there was a huge custom-sized bed in the middle of the room. A cabinet was against one wall with an array of sex toys Aradia imagined would make even Alaria blush. There were heavy straps tied to the headboard and the footboard, and there was one nightstand covered in different boxes of condoms and bottles of lube.

Damon closed the door and crossed the room, standing near the only chair. Azazel smiled at him hotly and took Aradia's hands, pulling her body close to his and dipping his head to taste her skin.

In an instant, the locks on the door turned, and Aradia's eyes went from green to black. She chanted under her breath and long strands of rope appeared, rising up from the floor and wrapping themselves around Azazel's body, curling around him until he was tied securely.

Azazel roared as he was caught and hurled himself at Aradia. He knocked her over and landed on top of her, managing to sink his teeth into her shoulder before Damon grabbed him and wrenched him off. Azazel opened his mouth and tried to expel his essence. Aradia shook her head.

"I don't think so." She began whispering in Latin, chanting an exorcism backward. Each time she repeated it, her voice rose in volume. The black and red fog hung in the air for a long moment before retreating back inside of Azazel.

Aradia quickly used her metal rod to tattoo the Devil's trap on the inside of his lip before taking a step back and looking at Damon, a jubilant smile on her face.

"That was the most disgusting thing I have ever done."

Azazel glared at them. "You cunt. I am going to rip you in half when I get out of these ropes. A fucking witch! You think you can really trap me?"

Aradia sneered at him. "I killed Garrick. I think I can handle one lowly Devil. I'm not susceptible to your mind control, and you're trapped with that tattoo. I've neutered you, Azazel."

"You're one of them." Azazel laughed. "Fucking bitch, you're one of the six trying to keep Lucifer from rising!"

"Looks like you're finally getting caught up." Damon looked at the ropes suspiciously. "Are you sure those will hold him?"

Aradia nodded. "I'm sure. They won't last long, but we've got enough time to get him to the others and put the shackles on. Witch-rope isn't supposed to be a permanent solution, but I have enough power that I can contain him for a few minutes. If he'd known who we are beforehand, I'd have never been able to because he could deflect the magic." She tugged her skirt down to cover her thighs. "Let's get him out of here before someone comes in. I really don't want to have to explain this to someone else."

Damon grabbed Azazel by the ropes and shoved him. "Let's go."

Azazel snorted. "Do you intend to just parade me out like a prize through the front door? I think someone will notice, don't you?"

Aradia smiled. "I'm not taking you out through the front door." She tipped her head back. "Michael! We're ready!"

Azazel swore. "Son of a fucking bitch."

Michael laughed as he appeared. "Your penis got the best of you after all." He crossed his arms. "I always knew your love of sex would be your downfall."

"Your cock has gotten you in trouble before, too, Brother." Azazel grinned. "Tell me, do they know it was you who told Lilith that Braxton's family had been taken into protection? Would they trust you so greatly if they knew you were the one responsible for those deaths?" He grinned when Damon and Aradia turned to look at Michael, surprise flitting across their faces. Aradia lifted one hand to press her fingers to her throat. Azazel laughed. "That's right, big protector Angel-boy here was so busy fucking Lilith that he let her find out where his sister and parents were."

Michael efficiently snapped the shackles on Azazel's hands and feet. "Do us both a favor and shut up." He disappeared with Azazel in a flash.

Damon looked at Aradia. "Do you think that's true?"

Aradia rubbed her throat with her fingers while she though through the situation. "I don't think for a second that Michael betrayed any of us. Not for a single moment. Whether Azazel is lying or there is more to the story, I don't know, but I do know he would never betray one of us."

"I'm thinking the same thing." He tucked her arm in his. "Let's get out of here. The limo should be waiting outside, and it'll take us back to the jet. Greer says to tell you that you did a nice job."

Aradia blushed. "Is Gage angry at me?"

Damon glared at her. "Greer says to stop being stupid, and I agree with the sentiment. You did an amazing job. You had him wrapped around your little finger. Without you, there's no telling how bloody this could have gotten." He led her down the stairs. "You'll feel better once you can change into your own clothes." He smiled as the hostess handed him back his credit cards as they passed.

"Thank you for coming to Clover House. I'm sorry you didn't find anyone to your liking."

Damon nodded at her. "Have a nice night."

Aradia didn't speak again until they were in the limo. Once in there, Damon helped her out of the corset and thigh-high boots so she could change into her normal clothes. Giggling, she yanked her leg from the leather and fell back against the seat.

"How is it I'm perfectly comfortable with you seeing me like this, but one kiss had me on pencils and knives?"

Damon laughed. "I think you means pins and needles, babe." He handed her the blouse she'd brought from her own closet to change into. "And it's because there's nothing sexual about this. Greer is right. We've become a family over the last year, and you know I would never do anything to disrespect you or Greer and Gage." He yanked on the other boot and pulled it off her leg. "So, tell me...I'm a better kisser than Gage, right?" He wiggled his eyebrows at her and sent her into gales of laughter.

Once Aradia had caught her breath, she leaned over and hugged Damon tightly, planting a smacking kiss on his cheek. "I love you, Damon. I really, truly do, but kissing you is how I imagine it would be to kiss a brother."

Damon tucked her under his arm and relaxed against the seat. "Greer says to tell you she just laid one on Gage, and it's no contest. I'm the better kisser."

Aradia giggled again and settled her head on his shoulder. "Then it's a good thing she's the one who has to kiss you."

They rode in companionable silence back to the airport. By the time the car pulled out onto the runway, Damon had removed his tie and jacket and unbuttoned the top two buttons on his shirt. Aradia had pulled her hair back into a messy bun and replaced the boots with sandals. The other four had been waiting in their own car in the alley behind the brothel but had left as soon as Michael had taken Azazel, having them arrive several minutes before Damon and Aradia did.

Gage went straight to Aradia, enveloping her in his arms and holding her tightly. He placed one hand at the back of her head, pressing her face into his shoulder. "You did amazingly well, darling. I am so proud of you." He kissed her forehead gently. "You and Damon both did a phenomenal job."

Aradia clung to him, breathing in his scent and closing her eyes to calm herself down. "I'm just glad it went like we planned." She pulled back and looked at Greer. "I know you've already told me to stop being silly, but I can't help it. Stuff like this may be just a job for the rest of you, but for me, it's frightening and out of my comfort zone."

Greer reached out and hugged Aradia. "It would be boring if we were all the same. You have your beliefs, and we all respect them. We're just grateful you were able to work through the anxiety to do this. Without you, we'd all be hurting right now."

Aradia returned the hug tightly. "Thank you. That means a lot to me." She looked up at the plane. "Should we head for home? We have a Beelzebub to find."

Alaria wrung her hands nervously as she watched the time on the stove-top clock. She shook her head in disgust at herself and tapped her fingers on her coffee cup. There were twenty minutes until she had to leave.

Braxton stumbled into the kitchen, his eyes sleepy and jaw covered in scruff. He snatched a mug from the cabinet and poured it full of coffee. Dumping sugar into the cup, he pressed a kiss to Alaria's hair before sliding onto the stool next to her.

"You're up early."

"I have an OBGYN appointment this morning."

Braxton took a deep drink of coffee. "Did I know that?"

"No. I've been debating on whether or not I want to go to it. I have to leave in about twenty minutes if I'm going."

"Why wouldn't you?"

Alaria looked over at him, her nervousness evident on her face. "Because we've done a lot of stuff in the last four weeks, and even though I know this baby is supposed to be pretty indestructible, I'm scared to death that something's wrong with it. I mean, what if that fucking sword cut it in half?"

Braxton bit his cheek to keep from laughing. "Do you want me to go with you?"

"I don't want you to feel like you have to go."

"I don't feel like I have to." He ran his knuckles down her cheek. "If we're going to be together, I'm going to be involved in the baby's life. There's no way around that. It doesn't make me uncomfortable to go to the appointments with you if it doesn't make you uncomfortable."

Alaria laid her head in her hands. "I know that. I want you to be involved, but I also know it's a selfish want. I need for you to know I can do this on my own. I don't want you thinking we're going down this road because I feel like I need a father for the baby. That's not it at all."

He did laugh then, warmly and richly before kissing her gently. "We started down this road long before Gabe knocked you up, sweetheart. We don't have to figure out all the specifics today or even in the next few months. I will take whatever role you're comfortable with. For better or for worse, it looks like we're going to be raising kids together with Finley and now this baby. I'm okay with that. It doesn't freak me out to go with you to appointments or to be there in the delivery room, but if it does you, that's no big deal, either."

Alaria leaned her head against his shoulder. "I just feel like this could be too much too fast if we aren't careful. I don't want to end up fucking everything up because I'm in a tough position."

Braxton squeezed her knee and climbed to his feet. "I'll go grab a quick shower and get dressed so we can go." He brushed a gentle kiss over her hair. "We live in a world where we could both die tomorrow. I feel okay about things. If you don't, then tell me, but if you're just worried about me, please don't be. I'd be making the same offer to you if we were still just friends."

Alaria nodded slowly. "Okay. We need to be walking out the door in fifteen minutes to get to Glasgow by ten."

It took Braxton twenty minutes to get ready, but his driving on the trip in made up for the five minutes. At ten o'clock on the dot, Alaria was signing her name on the sign-in sheet and handing over the credit card Gage had given her to pay for the appointment. Several minutes after, she was ushered back into an examination room, Braxton's hand clutched tightly in hers, to have her blood pressure and temperature checked.

The nurse, whose name tag read Tami, quickly handed her a sheet. "Just take off your pants and underwear and drape this over your legs. The ultrasound technician will be in shortly, and then the doctor is going to do a physical exam just to get a pap smear on file since we don't have a record of you having had one. How far are you?"

"Fifteen weeks today."

"Okay, well it might be possible to tell you the sex of the baby. Do you want to know?"

Alaria's eyes widened in surprise. "I hadn't really thought about it. How sure can you be on a blurry little machine?"

Tami giggled. "More accurate than you'd think. If the tech isn't sure, she'll tell you, but we're right about ninety-seven percent of the time as long as you're over fourteen weeks along."

"Sure. Let's find out." She shrugged. "Why not?"

Tami gestured to a button. "Just push this when you're ready and the tech will be in."

Alaria efficiently stripped out of her boots, jeans, and panties. She slid up onto the examination table and draped the sheet over her legs. "Push the button for me, would ya?"

Braxton depressed the yellow button with one finger and lifted his eyebrows at her. "Nervous?"

"A little. Between these appointments, honestly, I can almost forget I'm pregnant. I'm not throwing up the past few days, and I feel pretty good, so it's easy not to think about it, but here, it's all I can think about. I don't know when to start buying stuff, or when to let Gage start buying stuff, or even what I need to get." She sighed deeply. "I don't know how much longer I can let Gage take care of me."

Braxton snorted. "You're not. We're saving the world. It's not like we can hold down a day job in the middle of all this, and if we fail, there won't be any place for us to work at. Besides, Gage isn't the only one who has money. I inherited all of Finn's money when Sam died, since I'm the one taking care of Finley. Would it make you feel better if I started paying for it?"

She wrinkled her nose. "No. Not one little bit."

"I didn't think so. Don't worry about it. Gage has more money than God. He owns six casinos, last I knew he has thirty-seven restaurants, a dozen hotels, and four resorts. Which will do no one any good if society falls apart the way it might if we lose."

"I don't know. Greer and Damon said they still got paper money as pay from their duties as soldiers. I think it's hard to know what it'll end up being."

There was a knock on the door, and a slender man dressed in teal scrubs and black tennis shoes entered the room. His hair was pulled into a ponytail, and he held a clipboard in his hands. "Good morning, Ms. Windsor. I'm Thad, and I'm going to be doing your ultrasound this morning. I see Tami was in to see you. Do you have any questions before we get started?"

Alaria shook her head. "I don't think so."

"Good! Okay, I need you to lie back, and I'm going to pull the sheet down enough to get to your lower abdomen. Can you tuck your shirt into the band of your bra for me?" He smiled brightly when she did as instructed. "Fantastic. Okay, there's some warm goop here to make it easier to see inside, and Dad, you can stand here by Mom's head so you can see, too. Now, I'm going to take a lot of measurements to make sure everything is okay, then I'll show you some parts of your baby, and then you can hear the heartbeat, and we'll see if we can tell if you need pink or blue. Sound like a plan?"

"Sure." She glanced up when Braxton laid his hand on her shoulder and smiled.

The grainy picture on the screen cleared, and Alaria was captivated by the squirming baby on the screen. Even her novice eyes easily found the head and arms as they waved wildly. Thad dragged a line across the screen on several places, taking measurements of different areas of the fetus. After several moments, he turned a dial and a whooshing sound filled the room.

"The heartbeat is one hundred and fifty-six beats per minute, which is perfect. The size of the baby is exactly on track for fifteen weeks. Looks like the baby weighs about fifteen ounces right now, which is good for this stage in development. Estimated due date is January thirty-first. This stuff can and does change during gestation, but right now it looks like baby will end up being right at seven pounds and about twenty inches long. Now, Tami said you do want to know boy or girl, right?"

Alaria nodded. "If you're sure. I don't want you to guess at it, but if you're positive you're right then go ahead and tell me."

Thad moved the wand around her stomach, rolling the picture on the screen to several different angles. "Well, Mama, break out the pink. It looks like you're having a little girl."

Braxton's hand tightened on hers and he grinned despite himself. "A girl."

Thad returned the smile. "Daddy's little girl, I think." He pushed a button and printed off a string of pictures. "Here are the photos from today. Dr. Levitt will come in to do a physical really quickly, and I'll have Tami set you up for next month. We like to see patients every four to six weeks through the first two trimesters and then every two weeks during the third. Unless there's a problem, we'll do another ultrasound at twenty weeks for the anatomy scan and one at thirty-six weeks to gauge the size of baby before she comes."

Alaria nodded slowly. "Okay." She looked up at Braxton. "It's a girl."

He chuckled softly. "So it is."

Braxton blinked, and when he opened his eyes he was standing in a white room. Gabriel already sat in one of the chairs, and there were two glasses of iced tea sitting on the coffee table. Gabriel gestured for him to sit.

"Don't worry. I don't have my sword with me, and I've calmed down since I saw you last."

Braxton dropped onto the couch. "What do you want?"

"I want to talk to you about my daughter." Gabriel looked pained and sad. "Your daughter."

"I'm not looking to replace you. I won't tell Alaria whether or not to let you in her life. It's her call."

"She's made it." Gabriel reached out and took a drink of his tea. "I can't blame her for it. I understand why she's made it, and I will abide by it. I provided the genetic material for the child, but I will not be raising her. You will."

Uncomfortable, Braxton shifted in his seat. "I'm not sure we should be having this conversation."

"I know the future. Some things are not set, like the outcome of the tasks you are doing, but other things are, and your relationship with Alaria is one of them. I cannot see whether or not you stay together, or what form your relationship takes, but one thing I can see is that you will raise this child. Are you ready to be a father?"

"I'll do whatever Alaria needs me to do."

"In the glimmers I've seen, you are raising my child. I want you to know I know, and that I have come around to accept it as what will happen. I made my decisions, and for better or for worse, this is the result of those decisions. I am not going to be a father. I am a sperm donor. As much as that grieves me, there is nothing to be done about it. I will honor Alaria's wishes, and unless she asks me for more involvement, I will limit my role to Guardian Angel."

Braxton leaned forward and braced his elbows on his thighs. "I'm not interested in this being a constant pissing contest between us. Alaria and I were not involved while she was involved with you. We didn't sleep together until well after the two of you had split up."

"I know. I am sorry for what I did. I was angry, and Alaria tells me I was jealous. It is an emotion I had not before felt. I do not like it, and I can assure you it will not happen again. I never wanted to hurt her, but it seems the longer I am around her, the more I hurt her, and I want to stop it. The only way I know how is to fade into the background and let the two of you be together. She's right. I took her choice about the child away. I imposed my will and the will of God upon her without her permission or knowledge. It was unforgiveable. After everything else, I then ran her through with my sword because I was blinded by rage at seeing her with you. It is not a healthy relationship for either of us, let alone a child. Besides, I don't feel emotions the same as you humans do. Frankly, the strength of what I felt scares me, and I have no desire to feel such a thing again."

"I never tried to replace you, and I never would if you and Alaria decided differently. If she wants me to, I will be involved in the baby's life, and I will take on whatever role I need. I don't want you to stab someone if you hear her call me 'Daddy.'"

Gabriel smiled sadly. "You will be. You and Alaria have chosen each other. I know Griffin was forced upon you, and you bore that weight with dignity. I don't like you, but I do respect you, and I know you to be a good man. If you weren't, I'd have killed you to keep you away from my child. I loved Alaria in the best way I could, and in the end, that is not enough for either of us. I hate that it isn't, but there's nothing to be done about it. She is human, and I am not. It was doomed before it began, and we were both aware of the risk. I don't like the turn of events, but neither does it make me sad. I will have no issues moving on from this, and in many senses of the word, it brings me great relief to return wholeheartedly to the service of my Father. I struggled with being away from Him, and it is a weight off me to be back in His Grace. I have no desire to ever leave it again."

Braxton leaned back in the chair and stared at the Angel. "You might be the strangest being I have ever met." He shook his head and frowned.

"I'll take care of them, but not because you asked me to. Because Alaria is my friend, she's a good person, and I care for her deeply. I'd help her if the baby were the result of a one night stand with a bartender. It has nothing to do with the parentage. We're going to help each other."

Gabriel smiled sadly. "I want her to be happy. Please, make her happy, Braxton. Give her what I could not. Give her your heart. She deserves it."

Braxton stared at him intently. "I'll give her whatever she needs."

In the span of a heartbeat, Braxton was again standing in the room at the doctor's office, holding Alaria's hand. She looked up at him, an odd look on her face. He shook his head to clear it and squeezed her fingers gently.

"Did you say something?"

Alaria narrowed her eyes. "Where did you go?"

He smiled and helped her sit up as the tech left the room. "Gabriel."

"Oh God. What did he want?"

"Nothing bad, don't worry. He just wanted to talk. I imagine it's along the lines of the same conversation he had with you. Didn't you think you oughta tell me he popped in after the whole stabbing thing?"

Alaria blushed and looked down. "I didn't want to cause more problems, and he just came to apologize, so I didn't see the big deal about it. He was pretty torn up about everything."

"Well, as much as an Angel can be torn up, I suppose." Braxton dropped into the chair. "He told me he's backing off and he'll respect what we decide to do."

"He told me the same thing. I think he got scared when he did what he did with the sword."

Braxton reached out and touched her hand. "We'll just play it by ear and see how it goes. We'll be fine, one way or the other."

Alaria smiled as the doctor entered the room and pulled her hand from his. "We always are."

"A GIRL!" Greer wrapped Alaria in a hug and squeezed her tightly. "I can't believe it's a girl! Congratulations!"

Aradia hugged Alaria as soon as Greer let her go. "Yes, congratulations. I'm happy for you!"

Alaria laughed and pulled free. "Well, it was either going to be a girl or a boy, so I'm not sure why this is such a big deal."

Greer scoffed. "Girls are fun. You can dress her up and do her hair and not have to worry about all the gross things that come along with being a boy."

Braxton chuckled as he moved through the room on his way to Gage's study. "As long as she looks like her mama, I'll be happy."

Greer watched until the door was shut. "How is that going to work? What does Gabriel think? Is he going to be okay with you and Braxton after everything? What do you want Braxton to do? Is he going to help raise the baby?"

"Whoa, way too many questions." Alaria dropped onto the couch. "We've talked about it some. Gabriel isn't going to be involved. He and I discussed that when he came to apologize, and I guess he took Braxton to the white room and talked to him about the same thing today. He's going to watch over the baby, but he will not be involved in any of the day-to-day. I don't want him to be after everything that's happened, and I'd like to give the baby as much of a normal childhood as I can. To me, that means having a dad who's there all the time."

Aradia sat next to Alaria. "So Braxton is going to help with the baby, then?"

"He says he will, and he also claims he would be making the same offer if we weren't sleeping together. Knowing him like I do, I believe him. I think he would. There's also the issue of his niece, who he will get back once this is all over. I don't think either of us are equipped to raise kids on our own, so it makes sense for us to do it together as much as we can."

Greer stared at her drolly. "Well, the two of you are nothing if not practical." She rolled her eyes. "When will you admit that you two are in love with each other? We've watched you try and figure this out for over a year now. I know you don't think you are, but you and Braxton are going to be together."

Alaria sighed. "I don't think I get a happily ever after. I've done too much for God to let me be happy. I care for him, I want him, and I will likely spend the rest of my life with him, but not because we're crazy in love with each other. We'll do it because it makes sense, it will keep everyone safer, and we get along."

Aradia lifted her eyebrows. "You didn't see him when we thought you were going to die. That was the face of a man who was terrified he was going to lose you." She reached out and rubbed Alaria's shoulder. "I know you're scared, and I know you don't want to get hurt again, but for what it's worth, I think you and Brax are great together. I know you loved Gabriel, and part of you probably still does, but I think you seem much happier now than you were before."

Alaria scowled. "I don't want to talk about it anymore. I killed almost an entire day having some kid look inside my uterus when what we need to be doing is finding out where Beelzebub is. Without knowing where he is, we can't go after the Wonder Twins. With them being in Purgatory, we have to go after the puppet-master first."

Greer drew her knees up into her chest. "Gage is working on it, but Beelzebub is tricky and hard to handle. The other thing we need to deal with is Gage. We still don't know if he's going to be cast out with the rest of the demons."

Aradia paled. "I can't believe Michael would allow that to happen. Gage has given up so much for this."

"Is there a way to put his soul back into his body?" Alaria reached out and snagged a bag of chips from the coffee table. "If we give him a soul, then there's no problem."

"There's also the prophecy that he could be made human. A love like no other vampire has experienced and being cleansed by fire. I wish we knew what that means."

Alaria chewed thoughtfully. "Well, if I had to guess, I'd say the love like no other part of it is probably where the baby comes in. I don't think a vampire has ever fathered a child before." She reached back into the bag for more chips. "Don't worry about it too much. I agree with you, Aradia—Michael won't let Gage go anywhere."

She stood and stretched, reaching toward the ceiling with both hands. Casting a glance at both the other women before looking longingly toward the kitchen, she sighed deeply.

"I'm going to go start dinner. I'm hungry." She rolled her eyes. "We wouldn't have been gone half as long had Braxton not decided I needed to go buy something for the baby before we came back."

Greer squealed. "What did you buy?"

"Some clothes, diapers, and blankets mostly." She moved into the kitchen and washed her hands in the sink. "Apparently, I'm supposed to get excited and buy a lot of stuff for a baby. Though why something that starts off so small needs so much stuff is beyond me."

Braxton wanted a cigarette. He patted his pockets from habit, scowling when he realized he didn't have any. Gage quirked an eyebrow and smiled at him knowingly. Damon nodded sympathetically and scowled before speaking.

"Believe me, when he told me where Beelzebub is, I did the same damn thing."

Gage leaned back in his computer chair. "We knew Beelzebub was smart. He makes the others look like slavering idiots, but this is beyond what even I thought he would do."

"Have you told Aradia and Greer?"

"Not yet. I know Greer will likely have a plan to deal with it because she's great at stuff like this. I just told Damon because he was in here when I found it, and then you came in asking." Gage chuckled and leaned back toward the desk. "Greer and Alaria have accused us more than once of keeping them out of the decisions. I know this is going to end up causing more 'penis club' comments, but really it's just they like to hang out when we have down time, and I have work I need to keep up on." He reached behind him and picked up a folder, handing it to Braxton. "Speaking of work, I got those stocks of Finn's reinvested. I think you'll be pleased with the outcome."

Braxton rolled his eyes. "Thanks, but that's so not important right now. We need to figure out how in the hell we're going to get to Beelzebub and if we go for him first or if we go for Abaddon and Abalam first."

Damon ran his hand through his hair. "That's where I think it gets complicated. If Beelzebub is keeping an eye on them, which I think he probably is, then he'll know if we go for them. It wouldn't surprise me if he's put them in Purgatory as a safety measure. He's keeping them safe to keep himself safe. Lilith and Azazel wouldn't have listened to him—Azazel because he'd have thought Beelzebub would be trying to save his own ass and Lilith because she doesn't listen to anyone."

Gage tipped his head back and stared up at the ceiling. "I don't know if going after them both is a good idea. That's three Devils at the same time, which very well could be stretching us too thin." He tapped his fingers on the desk. "Why don't you bring in the girls? We probably shouldn't try to figure it out without them or they'll get mad."

Damon rose and left the room, returning seconds later with the three women. They all chose chairs and looked at Gage curiously. Alaria was the one to break the silence.

"Well, what did you find out?"

"I found Beelzebub."

Greer grinned. "Fantastic. Where is he? Do you have schematics? I'd like to take a look at them before we go to see the best way to get in. We'll need to get some infrared scans for me to get a count of how many things are in there with him."

Gage cleared his throat. "It isn't going to be that simple."

Alaria sobered. "Where is he?"

"He's in Hades."

Greer snorted. "Isn't that just another name for Hell?"

Alaria shook her head. "No. Fuck, I should have thought about that. Back in the ancient Greek and Roman eras, all those gods and goddesses? Yeah, they were Angels and Devils. They figured out really early on if they were exposed to humans, the humans would think they were gods. A lot of them really liked the idea of being worshipped, if only to see why God liked it so much.

"They had temples built and created a mountain where they all got together and had parties and talked. There were some who did it in Rome, some in Greece, others in Atlantis, still others in Egypt and Sumer. Everywhere you hear of gods and goddesses, rest assured they were Angels and Devils. Mostly lesser Angels and Devils, the ones you never hear of and who are just members of the Host or run-of-the-mill Devils. Nothing special. Except for Beelzebub and Lilith. Lilith loved being worshipped. She became Venus, the Roman goddess of love, and enjoyed having a line of potential lovers going out the door of her temple. Beelzebub wanted more than idle worship. He wanted to be feared, and he was comfortable in Hell, so he became Hades, the god of the underworld. People back then had no understanding of Heaven and Hell, but they were eager to develop an idea of where you went when you died."

Aradia sighed deeply. "I knew the gods and goddesses were Angels and Devils, but it never occurred to me it might have been the Devils we seek."

Greer shifted in her seat. "What does it mean, though? What does Beelzebub being all worship-y thousands of years ago have to do with anything?"

Alaria bounced her knees nervously. "When Mount Olympus fell during the rise of Christianity, it wasn't because the gods killed each other. It was because God struck them down. He had allowed the dalliance for a while, thinking it was harmless enough, and well, it was before Jesus, so people were still going to Paradise and being offered a choice of Heaven and Hell. Once humanity proceeded toward Lucifer enough that God wanted to wipe the Earth out, He sent Jesus. At the time, He decided there was no use for gods and goddesses, and He destroyed most of them. Some slunk back to Heaven to spend the next part of eternity begging for forgiveness, and some of the Devils were cast back to Hell. Beelzebub was smart enough to know what was going to happen, so he closed off Hades right before God went on His rampage and was able to escape punishment. If Gage is right, he's opened it back up and is using it to hide."

Greer ran her hands through her hair and stretched. "What does that mean?"

"It means he's had time to plan how to keep us out. He's had time to put up protections and to arrange for lots of things to make it harder for us to reach him." Alaria gnashed her teeth. "The first of which will be fucking Charon and the river Styx. If you get in it, you die. Incinerated. Charon will only give you a ride across if you have gold, which I'm sure Beelzebub has now figured out a way to make sure he won't let anyone across. So we're going to have to make a goddamned fucking boat to get in there, too. Then there's the three layers. There's the Elysian fields, which is pretty and a lot like Paradise was." She paused. "Just to be clear, people didn't actually go there when they died. Beelzebub would put people in a coma and take their consciousness down there until they died. It gave him something to play with. He may be slick, but he is a sadistic bastard. He would play at being judge, jury, and executioner. He had the Fields, where he would let people go to play and romp. Then there was the plain old Underworld, which is where he stayed. It was dark and damp and dreary, but nothing spectacularly horrible went on there. He kept his slaves there. Then there was Tartarus. That is where the fun stuff happened. He had cells set up for torturing people, he had rape racks, pits of hot oil, guillotines—basically anything nasty you can think of."

Aradia shivered. "I grew up in ancient Greece. Tartarus is a place we were told horror stories about as children."

Alaria nodded. "He took enough people down there and let them return that they were able to convince everyone the Underworld is where you went after death. The more people who believed it, the more power Beelzebub held over them. I think it's pretty likely it was Beelzebub playing around so much that got God's attention in the first place, and then he abandoned it fast enough to avoid being punished for it."

Gage cleared his throat. "Is there a way for us to get down there?"

"You can't." Alaria spoke directly to Gage as she rubbed her hands on her thighs. "The River was created so Beelzebub is the only thing without a soul allowed across. If another soulless being tries to cross without being with him, the River will rise up and destroy it. You wouldn't make it in the front door."

Braxton swore. "Well, fuck. He's smarter than we gave him credit for. He's gone to the one place we can't all go."

Alaria chewed on her lip thoughtfully. "Beelzebub's powers are magnified down there. It's his baby. He controls every aspect of it. Absolutely every single aspect. It's going to be hard. Likely the hardest thing we'll have to do aside from chaining Lucifer. We can get in, but we won't be able to get out from the inside, so Aradia is going to have to stay here, too. She has to be able to drag us back out when we're done. It won't be easy."

Gage rose to get a bottle of scotch and three glasses. "You three can't drink, but I think we boys could use a little something." He poured the scotch and passed them out. "So the four of you will go down. Aradia will control the door, and I'll sit twiddling my thumbs while waiting to see if you live or die?"

Alaria shook her head. "No. If I'm right, and I'm pretty sure I am, Abaddon and Abalam will be notified if we go after Beelzebub. I think you need to get Michael and go after those two while we go after Beelzebub. Damon can go with you, and Michael, and Braxton and Greer will come with me. Vampire blood has some healing properties, and Michael can help with it, so we definitely need the Healer going to Hades."

Gage drained his drink. "I don't like the idea of splitting up."

"Which is exactly why they're making us do it. There are six of us, and six against one or two is good odds for us. Two against two is not good odds, though Michael will be able to even those a bit. Damon and Greer can keep in contact via the mental link they've got, and we're basically just going to have to go balls to the walls on this one. There isn't any other choice."

Greer rocked back and forth, thinking. "Can we take weapons into Hades?"

"Your guess is as good as mine." Alaria shrugged. "I would suggest trying, of course, but there's no guarantee. It's been a long time since I was down there. I went a couple times when he first made it to see what the fuss was about, so I know the basic layout, but other than that, we're just gonna have to play it by ear."

Damon put his snifter down with a clack. "Where is Hades? I mean, we all kinda get Heaven and Hell. They exist, but they're not on Earth. Where is Hades? Detroit?"

Alaria laughed. "Close, but no. Archangels, and therefore a few Devils, have the ability to make places. They exist around Earth. It's kinda like another dimension, if you want to think about it that way. Michael has a garden, Gabriel has his white room, Lilith kept a castle, and Beelzebub has Hades. His is by far the most in depth, but it exists around us. Aradia will have to use magic to find it and pry the doors open to let us in and then again to let us back out."

"Any idea how I'm supposed to do that?" Aradia delicately sipped a cup of tea. "I've never done anything like this before. Don't get me wrong, I'm game to try—I just don't want to mess it up."

Alaria shook her head. "I wish I could tell you for sure. Generally, you have to have an invitation from the person who made the area. They're our private spots, but I imagine if you can find Beelzebub, then you can just whip up enough power to blast a hole through the door." She turned to Gage. "How did you figure this out, anyway?"

Gage lifted his feet to place them on the desk and leaned back in the chair. "I have my own set of contacts. Believe it or not, there are some demons left out who don't like Beelzebub too much. I just tugged on some strings until I found one willing to talk. Apparently he needed some help opening it back up and used a coven of witches from Germany. He killed them all when it was done, but not before one of them had told her lover, my demon, what she was doing. He's pissed his piece of ass got killed and was happy to spill the story for some financial incentive and a guarantee we aren't coming after him."

Braxton let out a low whistle. "Well fuck. This just got really complicated. When do we leave?"

Gage sat up. "In a few days. I need some time to do some research into the things we need to take with us. I don't know how effective guns will be, so there's going to be an emphasis on knives and such. Greer, how do you do with a bow and arrow?"

Greer shrugged. "I haven't used one in years, but I do fine with one. I don't know how many arrows I could possibly take down there, though."

Gage laughed. "Well, you'd need to try not to lose them all, but we could send quite a few. We'll need to send food and water in case it takes a while to get through whatever nasty surprises Beelzebub has in store for you down there, and we need to make sure you three have the firepower to be all right."

Aradia smiled gently. "You're forgetting me. If I can reach them, I can send them things. My abilities have only gotten stronger. There's very little I can't do now, which is why they have made it so I can't go on either trip. No offense to the rest of you, but I'm the strongest of us all, and they know it."

"It doesn't hurt that Beelzebub has been dying to get his claws into me." Alaria stood and stretched before looking at Gage. "The solstice is approaching. We have a little less than a month to be ready for Lucifer.

We can't waste too much time doing this. I say we need to be moving on this within a week. It might take us a few days in each place. Aradia, do you feel comfortable holding down the fort that long? You'll be guarding Lilith and Azazel and making sure we all have what we need while we're gone."

Aradia shrugged. "I can do it. The traps are holding so far, and Michael hasn't reported any weakening. If anything, I can always hail Gabriel to help if need be. I'll be fine."

Alaria laughed as she exited the room and headed back toward the kitchen. "Famous last words."

Chapter Twenty
August 27, 2031 - Scotland

"Brax?"

"Hmm?"

"Are you happy?"

Braxton rolled onto his back to look over at Alaria, his eyes heavy from sleep and his body radiating heat from being wrapped in the blanket. "What's wrong?"

Alaria lifted one shoulder in a shrug. "Nothing really. I just wondered if you're happy."

"Aren't you?"

She stared at him for a long moment before answering. "I think so. I don't know if I've ever experienced it before." She laid her hands on her stomach. "My pants don't fit now, and that irritates me a bit, but I feel...content here, I think. I don't want to leave. I have an urge to make sure you're happy, and I smile when I wake up in the morning and see you. Is that what happy feels like?"

Braxton reached out and covered both of her hands with one of his. "It sounds like it." He rubbed his thumb over the back of her left hand. "I'm happy we figured things out. I'm glad you're here with me and that I was able to work out my shit enough to get us to this point. I don't regret doing what we've done. I don't know if *I'm* happy, but that's nothing to do with you and everything to do with what we're trying to accomplish." He laughed softly. "I don't think we're happy people."

"Greer thinks I'm in love with you."

A tidal wave of emotions rose up within Braxton at her words, filling him with a mixture of confusion, hope, and grief. He continued to rub her thumb and concentrated on making sure his voice was calm when he answered. "What do you think?"

"I think I like you, and I respect you, and I want to go to sleep next to you at night. If I'm selfish and just think about what's good for me and not you, I want you with me for this baby. I can do it alone, but I want to do it with you. I don't have the same feelings for you I did for Gabe. That was a hurricane. I couldn't stop it. With you, I don't want to stop it. I don't think I'm in love with you, but I know I want to be with you. You and I can have a future, whatever it might be, together. We can help each other and protect each other, and we can be happy together."

"I don't think everyone needs all-encompassing love. For some people, companionship is enough. I think we're like that. Neither of us needs the heat and the insane emotions. We both had it, and it didn't work for either of us." He tugged her until she was laying in his arms. "I could be content like this forever. I enjoy just being together and not having the super intense emotions get in the way. I think we both need this."

Alaria shifted up and pressed her mouth to his in a kiss. "I'm a bit nervous about tomorrow. There's a lot that can go wrong."

"We'll be fine." He ran his hand over her hip and rubbed the hem of her t-shirt between his fingers. "Don't worry about it tonight. We've done all we can, and all that's left is to try and get some sleep." He slipped his hands beneath her shirt and brushed the curve of her breast. "Or do other fun things."

Alaria moaned softly when his fingers slid over her nipples and rubbed them gently. "You understand I'm going to be huge and hideous soon, right?"

Braxton nibbled at her throat. "You aren't going to be huge and hideous. I think you'll be gorgeous." He slowly lifted her to straddle his hips. "Besides, it'll just give me a preview for how you'll look when I'm the one doing the knocking up."

Alaria's gut tightened. "You would want that?"

"You always talk about how you wanted to be human so you can find someone and have babies with them. I knew what you wanted before I got into this. So, yeah, if you want it, I'll give it all to you." He ran his hands over the slight curve of her stomach and the barely discernable protrusion where her child grew. "Besides, if I'm going to raise a couple kids, I might as well get to make at least one of them." He stroked his hands over her ribcage and up to cup her breasts. "I'll never treat her differently. I know we'll tell her eventually who her father is, but I want you to know I'll love her the same way I do Finley and the same way I would any child we have. We may be cobbling together a family in a very nontraditional way, but we'll still be a family."

Alaria bent to kiss him gently. "Why don't we do some practicing for when you're doing the knocking up?" She ran her hands over his chest. "This is new for me. Even when we've been together, it's always been so much about the sex, but tonight, it's because I want to be with you. I want you to take me slow and gentle and make me fly."

Braxton laughed against her mouth. "Ask and ye shall receive, babe."

He rolled her until they were lying side by side. He slipped her t-shirt over her head and tugged off her shorts. Running his hand over her stomach, he smiled against her mouth as he traced the ridge of her protrusion. Alaria reached up to press one hand to his face, caressing his skin gently with her fingers.

He pulled her against his body, kneading her back muscles in his hands and slipping them down to caress the curve of her ass. Her breasts were pressed against the wall of his chest, and her legs wound in between his.

Braxton pulled back slowly, pressing short kisses to her nose and eyelids. He ran one hand down her neck and over her collarbone before cupping her breast and lifting it slightly, stroking her dusky skin gently.

"I love the way your skin tastes." He bent his head to her breast, sucking her nipple into his mouth and winding his tongue around it, brushing the sensitive nub with the slightly rougher texture of his tongue.

His free hand came up to cover her other breast, and he tugged on her nipple gently, rolling it between his fingers and gently scraping his fingernail over it. Alaria moaned softly and twined her fingers through his hair, tugging sharply and holding his head to her. She slid her legs up his and wrapped them around his waist, bringing their hips together.

"I want you."

Braxton laughed and sucked harder before releasing her long enough to drag his tongue over the other nipple. "What happened to soft and slow?"

"It can be soft and slow once you're in me. Right now I'm hot and horny, and I want you naked."

She used her legs to flip him beneath her and yanked off his boxers, baring his body to both her gaze and her hands. Groaning softly, she cupped his swollen penis in her hands and stroked her fingers over him, tracing the veins and enjoying the heaviness. She dipped her head and took the tip into her mouth, rubbing her tongue over the sensitive skin and tasting the salty tang of the clear liquid forming there.

Braxton relaxed into the pillows and closed his eyes. "Feel free to keep going, but if getting me inside you is the most important goal, I'm going to need to use that."

Alaria lifted her head, her eyes heavy-lidded with passion. She skimmed her fingers up and down, teasing him. "I like doing this for you. It's fun for me to see the reactions I can get. It turns me on that I turn you on."

She slowly ran her tongue from base to tip, swirling it around the top and sucking gently. She wrapped her lips around his cock and sucked strongly. Braxton's hips jumped, and she hummed in the back of her throat as she slid her mouth up and down on him.

She massaged his thighs with her hands, and her breasts brushed against the hair on his legs as she moved slightly while sucking him. His skin was smooth and silky as she laved attention on his penis, and Braxton's groans grew louder the longer she used her mouth on him.

He flipped her to her back in one smooth motion. Using one hand to part her thighs, Braxton slid heavily into her, thrusting slowly and rocking his hips against hers gently. Pleasure rose up in them both, and he stilled within her, enjoying the feel of her body wrapped around him.

Alaria wrapped her legs around his waist, cradling his hips between her thighs and running her hands over his back, stroking the smooth skin gently. He pressed his face against her neck and began to move.

Slowly, he rocked his hips against hers, barely moving as he stimulated her body with his own. He used his knees to support himself and gripped her thighs with his hands, pulling her harder against his body and driving farther into her..

Alaria reached up and palmed her own breasts, running her fingers over her nipples to increase her stimulation. She met his eyes with hers, brown to blue, and lifted her fingers to lick them, applying the dampened digits to her nipples to aid in her pleasure.

Braxton grinned down at her and slipped his fingers between their bodies to flick them against her clit. She groaned and jerked her hips against his, her head thrashing on the pillow as her orgasm built.

"Harder." Her voice was a desperate whisper.

Braxton chuckled and continued his slow, torturous pace. "No. You asked for slow and soft, and that's what you'll get."

He looked down and watched himself slide in and out of her, his dick slick and wet from her body. His own climax threatened, and he moved his fingers faster against her clit to help her find hers before he was swept away. Alaria dropped off the cliff of release with a ragged cry and a spastic tightening of her body, and pleasure speared through her and radiated through every inch of her.

He buried himself in her completely, relishing the silky slide into heat as he came, his body tightening and a raw grunt tearing its way from his chest. Alaria's legs fell to the sides as Braxton collapsed to the bed next to her, rolling to drag her close as he hit the mattress.

Emotional and sated from their lovemaking, Alaria cuddled close to him, pillowing her head on his chest and slipping one arm around his waist. She leaned up and brushed her lips over his jaw. His eyes were already heavy with sleep. She settled into his arms and let herself relax into him.

"I don't know how this is supposed to work, but I'll love you the best I can and I'll do my best to make you happy."

Braxton smiled and hugged her snugly. "I know, baby. Me, too. Go to sleep."

Breakfast the next morning was subdued. Aradia was tired from five days of near constant preparations for prying the doors to both Purgatory and Hades open. There were black smudges beneath her eyes, and her skin was paler than normal. Greer, however, seemed the opposite. She was energized, going through their packs with a clipboard and a checklist while absently munching on toast and bacon between making checks on the paper.

"Gage, how many bags of blood do you need?"

Gage looked up. "Blood won't keep long unless we can find a way to keep it cold. There's a small cooler in there I put dry ice in, and that'll help, but it only fits about a half dozen bags. I can go a couple days without and it won't be a problem."

Damon lifted his shoulders in a careless shrug. "Push comes to shove, you can just feed off me if you need to. I make more."

"I don't want to do that. I don't make a habit of feeding off real, live people. It makes the bagged stuff taste worse than normal." Gage shuddered and forced himself to swallow the rest of his blood. "What we can take with us will last me seventy-two hours. I can go without for another forty-eight to seventy-two. If we're there more than six days, we're likely going to have bigger problems than my being hungry."

Braxton bit off a chunk of sausage and glanced to Greer. "Don't forget the prenatal vitamins. The three of you all need to take care of the smallest members of the family."

Greer checked her clipboard. "Already got it. Gage, did you call ahead to make sure the Choosing Place is stocked for Aradia? I'm not making her a pack, but I can if I need to."

"It's fully stocked. The kitchen works, the pantry is full, and I had the Priest's office turned into a witch room where there's anything in the world she could need for any spells. There's also a complete weapons array just in case."

Aradia wrinkled her nose. "I don't need guns. You know that. If I can't fight it off with my magic, then the odds are good it'll kill me. Nothing to be done about that, unfortunately."

Greer tapped her pen against the clipboard. "I think we're all set. I've got weapons lined up on the couch for us all. Everyone is getting a utility belt with a machete, dagger, three stakes and an aerosol of Holy Water. It'll make more efficient use of what you can take in. There's also a rosary in each bag so you can bless water if you run out of what you have. There's a thigh holster with a pistol, a hip holster with two guns, and a shoulder holster I've modified to hold a sawed-off and a short sword. Because I believe in multi-tasking, all the weapons for the semis are solid silver forged in Holy Water and crusted with salt. They're good for anything other than vamps, and the bullets for the pistols are wooden, so that covers that. Questions?"

Braxton drained his cup of coffee. "How many rations do we have?"

Greer looked concerned for a moment. "There's eight MREs each and two gallons of water. The problem is the weight of water, so I'm including some nutrition powder to mix in. It helps with hydration and calories. You guys can carry a bit more, but Alaria and I have about an eighty to ninety pound limit, and that's pushing it. That's over half our body weight. I've put Gage at one-thirty in his pack and you and Damon at one-ten, Brax. If you're not out in three days, water will be a concern more than food. Food should last you four days, five if you stretch it. Gage got some freeze-dried stuff I'm supplementing it with. It's lightweight and doesn't take up much room, so there're a few of those that'll buy you another day or two. Just try not to let it take you very long. That's the only advice I can give."

Alaria tied her hair back into a ponytail. "I can carry as much as Gage. I still have some Devil strength, and we might as well not waste it. That'll get my crew a few more gallons of water, at least."

Gage nodded. "I can do better than one-thirty. I'm a vampire, not a human. I can't get out of breath." He chuckled wryly. "The fact is we don't know how long we're going to be gone. I think there may be food and water to be had in Purgatory, but I have no idea about Hades. Alaria?"

Alaria shrugged. "Maybe. Maybe not. There used to be in the Elysian Fields, but Beelzebub can control everything in there. He doesn't have unlimited amounts of strength, and it took him centuries to make Hades, but it could have changed a lot since I was down there the last time. Or, it could be exactly the same. The only way to know is to go down there and find out for ourselves. If it is like it used to be, we'll be on our own for the first part, then there'll be berries, fruit, water, lots of stuff in the fields, and then once we get to Tartarus, there's nothing but misery. The worst thing is we're not going to be able to tell where we're going to land. Beelzebub organized it so the three chambers wrap around the core, which is where he would be. I have no idea which is on the outside, which is in the middle, and which is the innermost layer."

Braxton whistled softly. "So how are we supposed to get from one of these layers to another?"

Alaria shook her head. "We'll have to figure it out when we get there. I don't know." She looked over at Gage and Damon. "You two will be fine. Purgatory still has creatures in it, at least a few. Long story short, before there was Hell, when people died, they went to Paradise. Demons and Devils who died were sent to Purgatory. Over time, Lucifer has occasionally brought things out and back in to Hell, but until the meeting to arrange the Choosing, there was no way for dead supernatural creatures to go to Hell, so God created Purgatory as a jail, basically. Anyway, it'll be nasty, but there will be corporeal demons and Devils there and maybe a few other vampires you can feed on if you absolutely need to."

Gage grimaced. "Yuck." He sighed deeply, expelling the unneeded air from her lungs with a whoosh. "I wish there was a way you could be both places. You know way more about this than any of the rest of us."

Alaria stood and stretched. "If you get into a bind, just tell Aradia, and she can relay the message to me." She looked at Aradia. "I'm assuming, of course, that you'll be able to keep an eye on us while we're in?"

Aradia nodded slowly. "To an extent. I'm going to give each of you a citrine and a spell. The citrine will magnify the little bits of magic you have. It'll allow you both to talk to me. There's also a slim chance Damon and Greer will be able to talk to one another, and I'm assuming Michael will be able to get in touch with me if you need something. Again, we won't know until we get there."

Damon slapped his hands against his knees and stood. "Then let's get going. We can talk this to death, but we're just going to keep coming back around to the same place, which is that we need to get down there to find out what we're going to have to do."

Chapter Twenty-One
The Choosing Place

Aradia stood in the center of the blood-stained floor, her citrine pendant clutched in her hand. "This spot has a lot of power. It's not just the Hell Gate beneath—it's Griffin's blood here. It's pure and full of power."

Michael smiled softly from where he sat in the front pew, waiting for Aradia to open the door to Purgatory. "That's why the rituals with the Devils must be done with the knife she used. I'm hoping the power will bolster yours enough to allow you access to Hades. It's not Purgatory I'm concerned about. Getting there, while not simple, is not much of a challenge for a witch with the power you possess. Hades will be the issue."

Aradia rolled her shoulders. "I'm going to open up Purgatory first." She glanced at Damon, Gage, and Michael. "You guys ready?"

Gage nodded. "Let's get this done."

Aradia tipped her head back and closed her eyes. She let her magic rise up within her and whip around the room. When she opened her eyes, they had gone completely white. The citrine in her hand glowed until it was painful to look at. Her voice low and rich, she began to speak.

"Gates of Heaven, Gates of Hell. Angels on high and Devils that fell. Hear my demand, obey my cry. Turn the lock, open the door. Grant me access to that which exists no more. Purgatory deep, Purgatory black.

Open your gates, ascend through the black. Hear my cry, answer my plea. Swing open the gates, and open to me!"

A loud crack filled the room, and Aradia stumbled back two steps, the magic falling around her like a curtain. A stone door appeared in the middle of the room with a wrought iron handle and elaborate carvings. Michael smiled grimly.

"This is our exit." He waited until Gage and Damon had shouldered their packs and weapons before turning and speaking to Aradia. "I'll reach out if we need you. Gabriel has been notified to be on standby should something happen here. If he does not answer, you should call for the Angel of Death. He is the most powerful of all Angels and will answer if you call out for him."

Aradia nodded. "Thank you. Please, all of you, be careful. I'll do what I can, but I don't know how much power I will have to assist once I reach through the door. Come back to us safe."

Damon reached out and tugged Greer close for a hug, laying one hand on her stomach. "You take care of both of you." He kissed her forehead. "That's my whole life going to Hades, and I'd rather die than see anything happen to you. We'll try to keep in contact with each other."

Greer brushed her hand over his cheek. "We'll be fine. Come home to me, Damon."

"I will."

Aradia smiled at the exchange before looking at Gage. Neither of them spoke, the gaze between them conveying what words could not. After a long moment, Gage nodded and stepped to the door, reaching for it and pulling it open.

"Ready or not, here we come."

Within seconds, the three men had disappeared and the gate slammed shut, disappearing into the floor as quickly as it had risen up. Aradia sighed as the portal closed and squeezed her eyes shut for a second.

"It is so hard to watch all of you charge out into battle and know I must stay here. I so wish I was going with you."

Greer wrapped her arms around the other woman. "I know. It's the hardest to be the one getting left, but we couldn't do this without you." She rubbed Aradia's arms briskly. "Do you need a little time to recharge before you pry open Hades? Or can you do it now?"

Aradia squared her shoulders and strode back to the center of the room. "I can do it now. I want all of you to stand back just a little bit. I'm not going to be able to do this without accessing black magic, and I don't know what form this door is going to appear as, so it's safer if you give me a little space."

She planted her feet and pulled a slim dagger from her waistband. Aradia rolled her eyes back into her head, and when she looked forward again, they had gone black. She concentrated on channeling the black magic through the prism of her citrine until it was cleansed into power she could bend and use. The sky outside rumbled in response to the sheer amount of power she was harnessing to work the spell.

She dug the tip of the dagger into her palm and sliced downward, opening up a large cut. Blood welled and spilled out onto the floor, hot and thick. It boiled and bubbled where it struck the concrete. When Aradia spoke, her voice was filled with power and rose to echo throughout the room.

"Hades black, Hades deep. Secrets held, still to keep. Gates of iron, gates of stone. Peel apart, bring us home. Wind rise, water flow. Take them now, down below. Heavenly mission and Godly quest. Allow them access, take no rest. Feel my power, taste my wrath. Blow out windows, open gate. Beelzebub blind and filled with hate. Obey my will, hear my plea. Power of God, magic of Earth, spill forth and pull the gate to Hades from the Earth! I beseech thee! Blind Beelzebub to the sieging force. I command it! With my power, through my plea, as I command it, so shall it be!"

The monastery groaned and trembled on its foundation. Lightning cracked through the sky and thunder rumbled menacingly. Rain pelted the windows. The lights flickered, and every candle in the sanctuary lit, flame flaring and sparking though no one touched them. Aradia threw her head back and her arms out, letting power pour from her. It streamed outward, burrowing into the ground and visibly wrenching a swirling black and purple portal to the surface. Aradia groaned and used her magic to support the portal.

"I don't know how long I can hold it. Go now before I lose control of the magic!"

Alaria shouldered her pack and strode through the portal without a backward glance. Close behind her, Braxton did the same. Greer grabbed her bag and rushed after them, disappearing into the purple and black.

They emerged onto a strip of rocky beach. The sand was gray, and the ground was littered with chunks of rock and broken branches. Fog covered the river, thick and white, and they could barely discern dead trees jutting out of the water. When Greer took a step toward the shore, Alaria's arm shot out and knocked her back.

"Don't touch the water. If you get even a drop on you, it will steal your soul, and you'll end up in there forever. Charon comes once an hour to check for new souls. All we can do right now is wait until he shows up with the boat."

Braxton let out a low whistle. "This place is something else. It's like a scene from a nightmare."

Alaria laughed. "This is just the foyer. Just wait until you see the basement." She shifted the load on her back. "This is not going to be easy, nor is it going to be fun. If Aradia's spell worked, Beelzebub might not be able to see us clearly, but there's no way to know that yet. Maybe no way to know that at all."

Greer shifted from foot to foot. "I hope the others are okay."

Braxton laid his hand on the back of Greer's neck and rubbed it soothingly. "They will be. Can you hear Damon?"

She shook her head. "No. The link went black. I think we're either too far apart or there's too much interference to get through. I can tell he's there, and he's alive, but that's it."

"It's better than nothing." Alaria looked out over the river. "Here he comes. Get ready."

Braxton's hand went to his gun. "Is this guy a threat?"

"It's an illusion, programmed by Beelzebub. His only job is to collect the toll and take people across. We're all human and we all have souls, so we should be safe." Alaria took a step forward as the boat came ashore. She handed a gold coin to both Braxton and Greer. "For the toll."

Greer shuddered as she saw the captain. Charon was a tall, skinny figure, emaciated as if it hadn't eaten in weeks. Its cheeks were hollow, and bones protruded through the paper-thin skin. Chunks of skin and flesh hung off him, the sores left behind filled with pus oozing out of them. Alaria lifted one eyebrow and put her hand on her hip.

"Long time no see, Charon. We're here to take the boat across."

Charon's lips peeled back to reveal yellow, jagged teeth. "We've been expecting you."

Alaria gestured to the other two. "Make sure not to get in the water as you board the boat. Give him the gold coin before you step on and sit down quickly."

Charon held up one hand. "Place your toll in my hand and board the ship."

Braxton handed over his coin and stepped up, sitting near the back. Alaria slapped her coin into Charon's hand and stepped up. Before she boarded, Charon shook his head.

"This is not sufficient coin for the passage. You have three coins amongst you and five souls. Two souls must stay behind."

Alaria paled. "The baby. I didn't even fucking think the embryos had souls already."

Greer nodded and handed Alaria her coin. "Take mine. I'll have Aradia send me two more and come across on the next ferry."

Charon cleared his throat. "We are leaving in one minute, whether I have one passenger or three. Make your decision."

Braxton looked pained. "You can't come back through this on your own. It'll be at least an hour before you could come across and there's no telling what's waiting on the other side. If we land in Tartarus, it could be bad. Give us your pack, keep your weapons, and just have Aradia yank you out. We're going to have to do it just Alaria and I."

Greer grimaced and glanced back toward the boat. "I don't want to leave you guys alone. What if you get hurt?"

Alaria leaned over the edge and hugged Greer. "We'll have to not get hurt. I'll heal quickly if I do. It's the joys of having some Devil left in me. Go back and help Aradia any way you can. We'll be fine."

"Are you sure?"

Alaria nodded. "I'm sure. Get out of here and stay safe. We'll be back as soon as we can."

Greer reluctantly handed over the coin and her bag to Alaria, who took it and sat down. Charon pushed off the bank with a long pole, and the boat slid into the water and away from the shore. She watched until the boat had receded then looked up.

"Aradia? Now would be a fantastic time to yank me out of here."

It took five minutes, but Aradia's voice broke through the haze. "What's going on? You've only been down there two hours."

"Two hours? It's been half an hour. Time must move differently. Can you pull me out? We didn't bring coins to cover the babies, so one of us had to stay behind."

Aradia sounded annoyed. "Why didn't you just ask for more fare?"

"Because Charon wouldn't wait that long. It was a split second decision. Now can you yank me out or not? It's fucking weird standing here talking to the sky."

Alaria sank down into the bench and stared out over the deep black water. "Charon, where is Beelzebub?"

"Master has disallowed me to talk to you about such matters."

"What can you tell me?"

"Master has requested I make it known to you that he is looking forward to your confrontation. He has imagined this day for many months and has masturbated many times to the fantasy of ripping your head from your shoulders."

Alaria grimaced. "That's gross."

"I am merely the messenger."

Braxton cleared his throat. "Can you tell us where you're dropping us off?"

"The first layer of Hades is where most of the souls go. It is barren, but there is nothing there to hurt you. Followed by that are the Elysian fields, and finally, you shall enter Tartarus. Should you succeed in traversing all three of those areas, you will cross into the Core of Hades, where Master keeps his castle. I think you will find it rivals the onyx castle kept by Lucifer in its greatness."

"What exactly is in Tartarus?"

"First, you will need to fend off the crows. They have no food other than the souls that cross through Tartarus, and if they capture you, they will eat your eyes and organs for the rest of time. Then, you will face the Sea of Souls. It is the remnants of all of the souls Master has brought here to feast upon. They will grab at you and attempt to enter your bodies in order to ride you out. After that is Cerberus—the three-headed dog worse than any Hell Hound you have ever met. It is ten feet tall with razor sharp teeth and saliva that will burn your skin and eat through your muscle if it gets on you. Should you pass through all three of these, you would then face the castle gates. I don't believe I need to tell you what is inside those, do I?"

Alaria shook her head. "I think we can take it from there, thanks." She stood as the shores came into view. "What happens if we win?"

Charon cocked his head to the side. "If you are to capture Master, then you would be able to bring him back to the shores here and return to the other side. Your witch will only be able to reach you from those shores. Should you lose, you will be sentenced to eternity in Tartarus and my Master will have forever to play with you both." He tipped his hat as the boat hit the shore. "Have a nice day."

Braxton leaped out first, taking Greer's pack and placing it on the rocky ground before returning to help Alaria climb out. They stood and watched as Charon pushed the boat away and disappeared into the mist. Alaria sighed deeply.

"Honestly, it's not as bad as I thought it was going to be."

Braxton lifted his eyebrows. "Not as bad? Killer birds, disembodied souls, and a three-headed, giant Hell Hound? What part of that isn't bad?"

"I didn't say it isn't bad. I said it isn't *as* bad. The only things we need to watch out for here are some stray demons that might be wandering around. Beelzebub kept a lot here to act as guards, and to let them play with the souls. Anyway, when he had to close up shop and flee, he didn't give any of the demons warning, so they've been down here for a couple thousand years with nothing to do and no one to play with. That'll make them dangerous and hungry."

"Those are not words I like hearing in the same sentence as demons." He stooped to transfer boxes of ammo and rations from Greer's pack to each of theirs. "We need to find out if guns work down here. If they don't, we can lose about seventy pounds of weight by dumping them."

Alaria reached down and drew the .45 on her hip. She slid back the slide and fired a shot into the ground, the bullet burrowing into the sand and smoke rising from the barrel. "They work. If they work in Hell, they should work here." She bent to dig through the packs as well. "We can leave Greer's sleep sack here. We won't need it. Leave the guns themselves. We have the same caliber, so we don't need more guns, just the ammunition. You can leave her sword. We each have one. Same with the machete. Other than that, I think we should keep everything."

Braxton continued to dig through the bag, dispensing the weight evenly between his pack and Alaria's. Once that was done, he shouldered his and turned in a circle. "Any fucking idea which way we go?"

Alaria laughed. "Yes, actually. Don't you humans take Greek or Roman mythology anymore?" She shook her head. "The river Styx wraps around Hades. It runs the perimeter. The river Acheron, which is the river of pain, runs straight through. If we find it, we can follow it directly to the Elysian Fields. There, we would need to follow the Lethe straight through the Fields past the Isle of the Blessed to where it connects with the river Phlegethon—the river of fire—which goes straight into Tartarus."

"That all sounds great, but first, can we drink from any of those? Second, how do we find the Acheron? And lastly, when you say river of fire, you're just meaning its name, right? It's not actually made out of fire."

"We follow the Styx until it intersects with the Acheron. The Acheron flows out of it and into Hades, so we need to follow the beach for now. We could hypothetically drink from the Lethe, but it's the river of oblivion. We'd forget who we are and why we're here and would spend forever there, so I don't recommend it. However, unlike the other two, it won't kill you if you fall in. Just don't swallow the water. The Phlegethon is made out of lava, not fire, so I guess technically it just means the name."

"How the fuck are we supposed to go down a river of lava?"

Alaria scowled. "Not a fucking clue. We'll figure it out when we get there." She lifted her shoulders in a shrug. "Once we get into Tartarus, that Sea of Souls Charon told us about is actually the Cocytus, which is the river of wailing. It was named that because of the sound of the screams of the souls lost in it. We literally have to swim across it. It won't kill us, either, but the souls will try to drag us under and drown us." She strapped her pack across her chest. "The Fields of Asphodel are where we are now. Let's get into the Elysian Fields and get this underway. With any luck, Rhadamanthus still rules there. He might give us a hand."

"Who the hell is Rhadamanthus?"

"He's a Devil who was in charge of the Elysian Fields. He supposedly got trapped here with everyone else. He was just a minor Angel and has very few powers as a Devil, but he liked to be down here, and he liked the Elysian Fields. Most people said it was because it reminded him of Heaven. If he did get trapped down here for a couple millennia, he's likely going to be pretty pissed at Beelzebub, and we might be able to use that to our advantage."

Braxton sighed as they started walking along the shore of the Styx. "How do you know so much about this stuff? It's like you're my seventh grade Latin teacher reincarnated."

Alaria looked at him darkly. "You seem to forget I was around for it. It's not hard to know a lot when you saw it happen."

He huffed another breath. "Only me, getting involved with a chick who was already alive when Adam and Eve were born." He turned his head and stared at her drolly. "Please tell me you weren't alive when Earth was created."

Alaria laughed. "I could, but it would be a lie."

"WHAT DO you mean you're in the monastery with Aradia? Why aren't you in Hades?"

Greer sighed inside Damon's head. *"We didn't take the babies into consideration. Apparently they already have souls, and Charon could sense them. He wouldn't wait, and Alaria didn't know where the boat would drop them off, so I gave them my pack and Aradia pulled me back out. I'm here with her. I've been trying to reach you since I got out."*

"How long have you been out?"

"Three days."

Damon's voice was filled with surprise. *"It's only been about eighteen hours down here."*

"It seems like time moves about four times slower down there than it does up here. That means that tops you guys have about five days down there your time before we're pressing up against the Solstice. We need those three sets of wings before we can hail Lucifer, and Aradia will have the most power over him on the Solstice."

"We haven't found them yet. Gage has been trying to scent them, but so far no luck. We just hunkered down to get a few hours' sleep, but knowing what I know now, I'll wake them after just a couple instead of a few. Six hours' sleep down here is a day up there, and we can't waste that much time."

"Have you run into any nasties?"

"It's been quiet so far. Nothing to report. How's it going for Alaria and

Braxton?"

"As far as we can tell, they're fine for now. They're in the first layer, heading up river toward the second. It'll be when they get to the third layer that the fun starts. Get some sleep, babe, and be careful. Now that I've found the link, I'll keep in close contact with you on stuff."

"Okay. Love you."

"You, too."

Damon cut off the link to Greer and looked around the clearing where Gage slept and Michael sat staring into the embers of the fire they had built. He shifted closer to the Angel so as not to disturb Gage.

"Greer says time moves differently down here. It seems like it's going a quarter the speed down here as up there. That means we only have five days to get this done before we're out of time."

Michael sighed deeply. "Come first light, I will fly out and scan for the Devils. Once I've found their hiding spot, I can return for the two of you and take you in. Purgatory is huge, and I cannot fly for an unlimited time, but doing it that way will save time. I had hoped they would have a trail easy to pick up on, but I was incorrect on the assumption."

"I don't know if it's a good idea or not. Logically, it works, but if something were to happen, you're the only one with an ability to do any sort of healing if we get hurt."

"I can be reached via mental link as easily as you reach out to Greer. If you need me, I will hear you, and my powers of teleportation do still work down here. Finding them is the problem. I cannot sense their location, though I can sense their presence." Michael shifted slightly. "I suggest you get some sleep. I'll only allow you four more hours in this time before we must be awake again. Do you wish for help going to sleep?"

Damon blinked rapidly. "What do you have in mind?"

Michael reached out and touched Damon's forehead, smiling as the man slumped to the forest floor. "Sleep well."

The Archangel kept watch over Damon and Gage until the sky began lightening. There was no sun in Purgatory and no moon, so the nights were pitch black and the days were little more than dreary gray. The water was thick and oily black, and the trees produced blood instead of sap. The air—thick and oppressive—bore down on them incessantly.

Michael was grateful he had no need for oxygen as he rose to put out the fire and wake the two men. Gage awoke instantly, rolling to his feet and looking around to make sure there was no threat. Michael chuckled and patted the vampire on the back.

"I'm not going to let you get attacked in your sleep, boy. Have a little more faith in me."

Gage laughed and reached down to help Damon to his feet. "It's not you I don't trust, it's everything else in this place." He bent and pulled a packet of blood from his bag. "Let's eat on the road, shall we?"

Damon gulped half a bottle of water and bit into a protein bar. "Michael is taking off to try and find Tweedle Dee and Tweedle Dum. I got in touch with Greer last night, and they told me time is moving a lot slower down here than up there. We've been here almost four days already."

Gage swore under his breath. "Of course we have. Why in the world would they make anything fucking easy?" He paused. "Wait, how does she know time moves differently? Has she talked to Aradia? Is she okay?"

"Greer didn't say anything, so I assume so. I'll talk to her again in a bit." Damon rubbed his hands over his face. "Here's the thing: we didn't consider the babies when we sent them into Purgatory. There was only enough passage for Brax and one of the girls, so Alaria went with him since she knows her way around and Greer had Aradia pull her back out, so Greer is at the Choosing Place with her."

Gage blinked rapidly. "Well hell."

Before the vampire could say anything else, Michael stretched out his wings and spoke. "I am going to leave you now and try to locate the two Devils. If you need me, call for me and I will come back. Once I have found them, I will return for you."

Gage scowled. "What do you want us to do? Wait here?"

Michael looked incensed. "Certainly not. It is not safe for you to remain in one place for any amount of time. We have been in this place as long as we may remain up to this point. You must continue to move forward. In order to maximize the amount of time we have left, I will transport myself to the far end of Purgatory and work my way back to you. You continue on the path we charted. Call for me if you need help."

Michael was gone in a flash, and Damon sighed as he shouldered his pack. "It's boring down here, dude. We've seen half a dozen demons and that's it. They ran when they saw us."

Gage chuckled and started walking. "The only problem is if they ran straight to Abalam and Abaddon to tell them we're on our way to get them. If they did, then this gets harder, and we're going to be pressed for time." He shook his head in disgust. "I can't believe time works differently." He ran his hands over his face. "And how did we not think about the babies being souls?"

Damon clapped Gage on the shoulder. "Lesson learned. None of us thought about it at all. Alaria and Braxton can handle it. They have to. Beelzebub is the baddest ass of them, but Alaria has his number. She's known him for millions of years."

"I hope so, but he has all of his powers, and she has a shadow of hers. He was stronger than her when they were both Devils, let alone now that he's been ruling Hell for the last several million years."

"Braxton is with her. He's good. He can help her." Damon sighed deeply. "Would you stop worrying, please? We've got a job to do, and we need our energy on this one, not on Alaria and Braxton. They can handle it."

Gage held up his hand and dragged Damon behind a tree. He pressed a finger to his lips as he peeked out from behind the tree. Ducking back, he reached to the holster on his hips and withdrew a wicked buck knife.

"Half a dozen demons. They've got Hell Hounds with them. They're different than the others we've seen."

Damon drew his pistol and checked to make sure it was loaded. "How so?"

"They're looking for something."

"Probably us." Damon stuck his head out and looked at the group coming down the path. "Plan?"

"Kill all but one. Keep the one and make it take us to Abalam and Abaddon."

"Those two cannot possibly think six demons and four Hounds could take us down."

Gage looked at Damon with a dangerous glint in his eyes. "If I had to bet, they've been watching and waiting until Michael left us. There will probably be more waiting in the wings." He sniffed deeply. "I smell vampires. About ten, heading this way from the south. We need to get these guys taken care of before they get here." He looked around quickly. "Get up in that tree and take out those dogs. I'll go for the demons."

Damon loaded the rifle quickly and swung up into the low branches of the nearest tree. Gage wrapped his fingers around the handle of his dagger and strode out into the clearing, putting himself directly in the line of sight of the demons and hounds. One of the demons held up a hand to stop the rest and took several steps forward before addressing Gage.

"It's pretty stupid of you to come down here."

Gage smiled. "I think it's pretty stupid of you to come here looking for me. Or have you been down here so long you don't know who I am?"

The demon sneered. "You know as well as we do that we've been here since before the first vampire walked the earth. They're such a new, interesting invention. Almost as strong as a demon, but not quite, and not like a human at all. It is odd."

Gage smiled. "Being odd doesn't change the fact that I am going to kill you all."

"Where's your companion? We were told there were two of you once the Angel flew off." He shook his head. "I still can't believe Michael was desperate enough to come down here. Things must be really bad up top for them to let that happen."

Gage cocked his head and, ignoring what had just been said by the demon, continued musing out loud. "What do you get out of this, anyway? If I kill you down here, your soul doesn't go anywhere. You don't go back to Hell, you certainly don't go to Heaven, and you aren't reformed in Purgatory. You will completely cease to exist. What appeal does that hold?"

For a moment, there was a flash of fear in one of the demons' eyes, and Gage knew he'd found the one he would let live. The demon in the front of the group lifted his shoulders in a careless shrug and sighed deeply.

"There is one of you, or two, when we find the Hunter and drag him out from whatever hidey-hole you've put him in, and ten of us, with more on the way. Do you really think you're a match for us?"

Gage grinned viciously. "Let's find out, shall we?"

Damon's shots rang out through the clearing with a loud crack. Four shots, one on top of the other, proving he was as good a shot as Greer, and two of the Hounds dropped, two holes in each head. Before anyone could react, two more shots rang out and the other two dropped.

Gage charged into the demons, slashing the leader's throat with his knife as he did. He ripped into a second using nothing but his teeth, sinking his fangs into the soft flesh of its throat and ripping, the acidic putrid blood of the demon running down his throat.

His face covered in blood, Gage elbowed a third demon in the face as it charged him. Damon fired twice more, and a demon fell to the ground, a perfect round hole in his forehead. Gage spun the creature around and slammed its face into a tree until it slumped, unconscious. Casting it aside, he turned to the final demon, the hairs on the back of his neck standing up as he heard the vampires approaching.

Damon dropped from the tree lithely, a stake in one hand and a sword in the other. Gage locked eyes with the demon and held up his hands to show he wasn't going to attack.

"I could have killed you, but I didn't. I won't if you'll show me where the two Devils who sent you are."

The demon shook his head rapidly. "I can't. They'll kill me if they find out."

"I'll kill you if you won't. At least this way you have a shot. If we win, we'll take the two of them out of here, and you'll never have to worry about them again."

"I want out of here. I've been stuck here for thousands of years."

Damon looked over his shoulder. "No offense, but I could use a hand with these vamps. Either tie him up and bring him with us, or we need to move on. There's no time to negotiate." He glanced at the demon. "Dude, there's no way for us to let you out. The best you can hope for is to survive, and that's even pressing your luck. If you run back to Abalam and Abaddon with your tail tucked between your legs, they'll kill you. If we lost and they find out you helped us, they'll kill you. If you won't help us, we'll kill you. You can't go all foggy and jump ship down here, so you can't run. The only way you survive is to help us win. So what's it going to be? Dead for sure or maybe get to live?"

The demon looked pained. "It doesn't sound like I have a choice, now does it?" He sighed deeply and nodded to Gage. "Okay. I'm in."

"Good choice." Gage withdrew a length of rope from his bag and used it to bind the demon.

Damon was locked in battle with three vampires by the time Gage got the demon secured. He beheaded one with a smooth slash of his sword and jammed the wooden stake into a second's chest before it could reach him.

His mouth set into a grim line, Gage waded into the battle. He ripped the head off one vampire, letting it drop to the ground with a wet plop before it burst into ash. The next one managed to land a punch to the side of his face before Gage plunged his hand into its chest and ripped the heart out, casting it aside carelessly as he turned to face the one behind him.

Damon hacked through two vampires with his sword, his brow creased. "Gage, man, these are like fucking newborns. They're so crazed it's like whacking them as soon as they rise."

"No blood down here. Once the blood lust sets in, it's hard for them to escape it. They can drink demon blood if they can find them, but in case you haven't noticed, Purgatory isn't exactly heavily populated anymore." He stabbed the final vampire with his stake. "Our two favorite Devils likely gave them enough blood to wake them up—vampires go catatonic if they go too long without blood and will eventually wither away into ash, but that takes hundreds of years—but not enough to make them function fully."

Damon looked down at the coating of dust on his boots. "It's almost enough to make you feel sorry for them." He sighed deeply. "What now?"

Gage smiled. "Now he takes us to Abalam and Abaddon." He jerked the tied up demon to his feet and cut the rope around his ankles. "Do you have a name or shall we call you 'it'?"

"When I was human, I was named Ronald. No one has called me anything in a long time, though."

"Well, Ronald, we need to hurry up and get to the place where the two idiots who sent you are." Damon prodded the demon in the back. "Lead the way."

Gage picked up his pack and strapped it across his chest. "Do you think we should call for Michael?"

"Let's wait until we have something to tell him. How far is their base from here?"

Ronald began walking. "It's about a day and a half hike from here. Years ago some of us tried to put together a colony. We built some houses, trying to establish something, but it didn't work out. The vampires attacked every chance they got, and demons started feeding on each other. This *is* Hell for us. There's no way out, and there's no relief. There's no food, very little water, and it just hurts all the time." He shook his head morosely. "Some of the buildings were left standing. Abalam and Abaddon are there with some of the demons left. I rather think they're enjoying it. They brought some people and food, which we hadn't seen in decades. It's been a very quiet group for the last few days. Because of what they brought, most of the things here swore allegiance to them immediately."

Gage whistled. "I don't know if we should wait that amount of time. That's nearly a week up top, and time is short as it is."

Michael appeared in a flash of light, his wings folded close to his body. "I have found them."

Ronald blanched. "I was going to lead you to them! I swear it!"

Gage looked at the Angel. "Is it about a day and a half hike from here?"

Michael looked perplexed. "How did you know that?" He shook his head. "It's of no importance. I discovered, rather unfortunately, that my powers of teleportation are severely limited here. I'm afraid we will have to walk. I can transport myself, but I fear I do not have the energy to transport the two of you as well."

Damon laughed and spoke to Gage. "That answers your question." He looked at Ronald. "If I let you go, you're going to run as fast as you can in the other direction, do you understand?"

Ronald nodded. "I won't say a word, I swear."

Gage slashed the ropes. "If we catch you trying to sneak back and warn them, you'll be dead."

The three men watched as the demon raced the opposite way down the path. Michael sheathed his sword and looked around the carnage. "Didn't I tell you to call for me if you got into trouble?"

Damon chuckled. "If we'd been in trouble, we would have."

Chapter Twenty-Three
September 1, 2031 - Hades

Alaria wrapped the thin solar blanket around her shoulders more tightly and shivered in the cold. Braxton sat behind her, his arms wrapped around her and his own blanket tight around him.

"This cold is ungodly." She blew air into her hands. "We should get to the Elysian Fields about an hour after dawn. Once we're there, it'll be much more pleasant."

Braxton chuckled. "It doesn't get much more unpleasant than this. Who would have predicted literal snow in Hades?"

"Beelzebub." Alaria's voice was dry and humorless. "He liked the phrase 'when it snows in Hell,' so he made it snow here." She shook her head and chuckled wryly. "I'd forgotten how annoying that bastard could be."

A warm light filled the cave, and Aradia appeared. She was transparent but fully visible. "Oh good. It worked this time. I've been trying to reach you for hours. There's something you need to know."

Braxton sighed deeply. "Why do I have a feeling you do not come bearing good news?"

Alaria laughed. "There is no such thing as good news for us. What's going on?"

Aradia looked solemn. "It is September first."

Alaria blanched. "That's impossible. We've only been down here a day and a half."

"Time moves differently for you in Hades and for the others in Purgatory. Greer was able to ascertain that through her mental link to Damon. I knew it was imperative to tell you once we found out."

Braxton rapped his head against the wall of the cave. "Why can nothing ever go right?" He sighed. "Okay. How is it going for the others?"

Aradia smiled grimly. "They have discovered where Abalam and Abaddon are hiding and are on their way there. However, it will take a day and half down there to reach the place, which is nearly a week up here. That was yesterday, so we have at least five days to wait before we'll know whether or not they've been able to get them." She looked around. "Where are you?"

Alaria rubbed her hands over her thighs to warm them. "The Fields of Asphodel. We're following the Acheron straight through until it leads us into the Elysian Fields. We've got about four hours until sunrise and another hour past that before we'll get there. It's too fucking cold to sleep, so we'll be heading out as soon as it's light enough to see. No moon down here."

Aradia put her hands on her hips. "I don't want to panic you, but I do want to impress upon you that I must call Lucifer forth during the Solstice. That means you have twenty days up here to accomplish your goal, which is five days down there. I know it's a tall task, but there's no other choice."

Alaria slapped her hand against her thigh in frustration. "Well, fuck. It's been a long, long time since I've been here. Once we get over into the Elysian Fields, our only chance at meeting the deadline is if Rhadamanthus is still there. If he is, we might be able to talk him in to zipping us through to the Phlegethon so we can get into Tartarus and get this show on the road. Once we're there, we've got to get through all of Beelzebub's ridiculous tasks. If Rhadamanthus isn't there to bring us through or if we can't convince him, it could take a day or two to follow the Lethe through the Fields and to the junction with the Phlegethon. At that point, we still have to figure out how to get through a river made entirely out of lava, which is going to be fun—note the sarcasm—in and of itself."

Braxton reached over and clamped a hand over Alaria's mouth. "Enough rambling. Aradia, do you have any idea how we can get through a river made of lava?"

Aradia pursed her lips. "I have never been faced with that issue before. I'll have to give it some thought. Give me a few hours."

Braxton chuckled. "Your hours or ours?"

"Likely yours. I'll try to have something for you by the time you reach the Elysian Fields." Aradia cocked her head. "How do you intend to cross the barrier between the Asphodel and the Elysian?"

Alaria reached up and pried Braxton's hand from her mouth. "We don't have to. Remember, this place isn't really the after-life. It's Beelzebub's mirage. The barriers are all for show. There are big scary gates that are tall and intimidating, but they don't have any real power over us. The Acheron will intersect with the Lethe at the gates. We'll dive into the Lethe and swim under the gates. That river won't hurt you if you get wet."

Aradia nodded. "As long as you have a plan." She looked between them. "Be careful. I'll be back as soon as I have something to tell you about the lava problem." She sighed. "If I was down there, I would just cast a protection spell, but my magic won't fully translate to where you are."

Alaria smiled. "We'll manage. Don't worry about us."

"I'll be back. Stay safe." Aradia looked at the floor of the cave and held out a hand, her eyes going black. There was a flash, and a crackling fire burned in the spot where she had stood.

Braxton grinned. "I knew that witch was good for something!"

Alaria moved closer to the fire and held her hands out. "We should try to log a couple hours' sleep once we thaw out." She groaned at the stiffness in her fingers. "I guess we now know what it feels like with no sun and no moon to regulate things. It's fucking cold down here."

Braxton dug through his bag for two bottles of water and an MRE. "Want to eat while we have heat?"

Alaria scowled at the brown plastic. "I never thought I'd see the day one of those would look good."

Braxton ripped into the package. "Baby, that day is here."

The black iron gates separating the dull gray of the Asphodel Fields from the lush green of the Elysian Fields rose up out of the rocky earth and pierced the sky. Spirals of metal intertwined with one another, forming a complex design. Through one section of it flowed a slim river, barely fifteen feet across and eight feet deep. Its water was a rich teal, and it jutted off the Acheron and bisected the Elysian Fields.

Alaria went to the bank and looked down in it. "This one won't hurt you if you get in it. It's just made of water. No nasty surprises here. You have to be careful to get in on the side of the blue. If you touch the black water, your soul stays here and that's no good for anyone. The current will move pretty fast, and it's not going to be a bad ride once we're in. Whatever you do, do *not* drink any of the water. Don't even let it get in your mouth. If you do, you'll forget everything about yourself from who you are to why we're here. Again, no good for anyone."

Braxton looked at her in amusement. "You explained this to me once before. I've got it."

"It bears repeating. We can't be too careful." She sat on the side of the water and slowly slipped into it. "Follow me. We'll ride the current a ways to shorten the trip."

"What about this Rhadamanthus?"

"Oh, he'll know when we cross into his domain. If he's here and he wants to see us, he'll pop up. Have no doubt about that."

Braxton slipped into the water and marveled briefly at the temperature and consistency. The water was warm and pleasant, but it had the viscosity of half-set Jell-o. As he approached the gates, he ducked under the water—his mouth firmly closed—to keep from beheading himself on the spears jutting down into the river from the gate. The current was brisk and swept him under the gate and into the bright greenery of the Elysian Fields.

"Are you sure we can just trust this Devil is going to show up? He *is* one of the bad guys."

Alaria grinned at him over her shoulder. "I used to be the bad guy, too. Jesslyn was technically one of the bad guys. Just because we ended up on the wrong side of this doesn't mean we're all like the idiots. Rhadamanthus fought with the rest of us, and he was wholeheartedly on Lucifer's side, but after the Fall, he got his jollies down here playing at being a god. He's relatively harmless."

Braxton opened his mouth to speak and found himself standing on the grass, completely dry. Alaria was beside him, also dry, and in front of them was a tall, gangly man. He was nearly seven feet tall, with shoulder-length red hair and a thin build.

"I don't know if I would describe myself as being harmless, Alaria, my love, but I do appreciate being remembered."

Alaria smiled. "Rhadamanthus."

Rhadamanthus embraced her tightly, kissing each cheek. "Darling, call me Rhad. Times have changed since I was last up top, and I do believe being 'rad' is now something desirable." He extended a hand to Braxton. "Who are you?"

Alaria interjected. "He's a Warrior. We need your help."

Rhad lifted his eyebrows. "My help? What possible help could I have to give? In case you've forgotten, I got stuck down here when Big Brother Bub shut it down. I've been here alone with a few dozen wandering souls trying to waste several hundred years. There isn't much I can do."

"Beelzebub is back in his castle. He's here hiding from me."

"Why is he hiding from you? No offense, but Bub is—or was—stronger than you. What's happened?"

Alaria sighed. "Briefly? I changed teams. The Choosing happened."

Rhad paled. "So there are no demons on Earth?" He reached out and touched her throat, feeling the pulse. "You got what you wanted. You're human. Oh, sister. How do you think you're going to defeat Beelzebub human?"

"I got to keep some of the abilities. Long story short, Lucifer found a way around and cracked open the main gates. I've been working with Gabriel and Michael to plug it up. The last thing we need to do is reinforce Lucifer's chains. Doing so will cast out the demons left on Earth and make sure Lucifer can't get out."

Rhad raked his hands through his hair. "Damn, girl. A man gets trapped in Hades for a few centuries, and the whole fucking world changes." He paced back and forth. "I don't know what to do here, Alaria. I'm not even sure what you want."

"All I need from you is to transport us to the Phlegethon. Once we're there, you can pretend you never saw us."

"Just how do you intend to get through a river made of lava? As a Devil it would have been a piece of cake, but it'll boil your flesh from your bones now that you're human, love

"You oughta figure it out fast." Rhad turned to Braxton. "You don't say much, do you?"

Braxton shook his head in amazement. "I'm just taking it all in. Honestly, I'm wondering why you haven't tried to kill us yet. You're a Devil, aren't you?"

Rhad waved his hands dismissively. "Oh, boo. I was a very minor Angel with some very simple powers. I came down here because it was fun and because I generally like to make people happy. Unlike most of the others, I never much cared for pain, and I knew what would happen if we lost. Let's just leave it at...I was better at seeing the big picture. I'd like to get out of here, of course, but I've no interest in either wings or humanity. In fact, given that it's been far too long since I've been out of this place, I'll make you a deal."

Alaria frowned. "No contracts."

"Of course not, darling. I think I can trust you to be good to your word."

Braxton crossed his arms. "Let's hear it, then."

"I'll go with you, help you get across the Phlegethon, and even help you subdue Big Brother Bub. What do you want with him, by the way?"

Braxton sighed. "The only way to cast out the demons is to have the wing roots from the original fallen Archangels for a spell. We have to get Beelzebub's."

"Just the two of you and a witch?"

Alaria smiled. "No. There are six of us. The others are after Abaddon and Abalam. They're hiding in Purgatory."

Rhad shuddered. "Horrific place, that. Now, back to my offer. I'll help you with your suicide mission, and providing we don't all die horrible deaths, you get your witch to spring me from this place, too." He held up three fingers to his temple. "Scouts' honor that I won't cause destruction and mayhem—much, anyway."

Braxton's brow creased. "How do you know what a scout is?"

"I can watch Earth. Want to see?" He nearly skipped to a pool that had formed alongside the Lethe. "This is my scrying pool." He waved his hand over it and a picture of a bustling city appeared. "Tokyo." He waved again. "There's New York. I keep up on current events."

Alaria looked at Braxton. "What do you think?"

Braxton shook his head. "Oh, no. You don't get to put this on me. You know him—kinda. I don't like to trust Devils, but the first time I tried it worked out pretty well. Your call, babe."

Rhad perched on a boulder. "I'm not after betraying you, love. I've never been one for the backstabbing. I've been down here a long, long time, and Bub didn't even stop by to let me know he was back. You're the first real people I've seen in thousands of years. The only thing that keeps me sane is that scrying pool right there. I want to be a part of the world. I don't care if I ever see Hell again. I fought the first time, and I've paid for it ever since. I'm not going to make the same mistake twice."

Alaria rubbed her hands over her face. "Beelzebub has set up some traps for us before we can get to him. We have to get past the crows, Cerberus, and the Sea of Souls."

Rhad shrugged. "Those aren't specifically for you. Those are just a part of Tartarus. If I had to wager a guess, I'd say it took a lot of his power to open this back up. He might be drained, or he might be putting his energy into keeping the castle itself safe. Either way, some Devil powers might come in handy. What powers do you have left?"

"Some strength, my ability to conjure weapons, and a bit of teleportation. I can still get onto the dreamplane, too. I didn't lose anything completely other than making deals and controlling people. Everything is just a bit weaker." Alaria tossed Braxton a bottle of water. "We're on a tight timeline, to be honest with you. I don't know if you've figured it out, but time down here and out there moves differently."

Rhan nodded somberly. "Yeah, it's four hours up there for one down here. It sucks, but it's what we have to deal with. What's the timeline you're dealing with?"

"We need the power of the Solstice for our witch to pull Lucifer out to do what we need. I think it's September second up there, so we've got nineteen days their time. That gives us almost four days down here."

Rhad laughed. "Darling, we can do what we need to do in two." He started walking. "My powers are muted this close to the Fields of Asphodel, so we'll hoof it an hour or two into the Elysians before I can port us out. This is a big area, and I'm not a super strong Devil on a good day, so we'll have to stop for a moment on the Isle of the Blessed for me to rest, and then we'll continue on to the edge. We won't cross over until I'm at full strength."

Alaria laughed. "I haven't told you'd we'd help you yet."

Rhad looked over his shoulder. "Oh, boo. You would have already headed out instead of wasting precious time here chatting with me if you weren't going to at least try. I know it's not a sure bet. Your witch might not have the power, Bub might have done something to keep me here, hell, I might have been down here so long that it kills me to leave. I don't care. I'm sick of being here alone with the only thing keeping me sane a picture in a puddle. I'm ready to break out."

Braxton shook his head and chuckled softly. "One of these days the world is going to make sense again."

Rhad chortled. "Don't bet on it. From my not insignificant knowledge of the world, it's going to make less and less sense." He looked at Alaria. "So Lucifer is trying to break out?"

"He's almost out. There have been a few thing loosening his chains. We have to use him to get the demons and Devils cast back to Hell, and then we have to rechain him. If we can do that, then things will settle down."

Braxton cleared his throat. "Why aren't you jumping for joy at the prospect of Lucifer getting out?"

Rhad drew to a stop. "Are you kidding? For the same reason none of the Angels want God to walk the Earth. It's no good for anyone. That much power? No, thank you, sir. I want Lucifer to stay right where he is, especially if I'm getting out. Think about it this way. With him down there, we get some autonomy to choose our existence. We can do basically whatever we want. Pretend to be human, be a mobster, anything. If he's out, we'll have to do what he says. If we don't, we'll likely die. I don't want to fall in line, and I don't want to stop existing. Besides, a lot of us *like* Earth. Not many want to see it destroyed and a good portion genuinely want to stay there. If Lucifer gets out, we don't get to play anymore. I don't want that."

Braxton frowned. "I don't think that's a very popular opinion among your species."

Rhad laughed. "That's because the majority of my kind are so short-sighted they can't see anything other than whatever it is that gives them instant gratification. What do you think Lucifer will do once there are no more humans to play with? I'll tell you what. He'll move on to us, and that is something I most decidedly want to avoid."

Alaria stopped to pull out a bottle of water. "I told you we wanted to find him."

Braxton smiled grimly. "You were right."

Rhad chortled and slapped Braxton on the back. "They always are, my boy. They always are. Congratulations, by the way!"

"On what?"

"The baby, of course! Once I started paying attention, the third heartbeat was super obvious. What will you name her?"

Alaria cocked her head to the side. "How do you know it's a girl?"

"I can tell. Any of us could if they tried." Rhad shook his head in amusement. "Have the two of you talked about names?"

Alaria sighed. "No. We've had a few things on our plates without worrying about that, too." She took another gulp of water and raked her hair back into a tight ponytail. "I'd forgotten how hot it got in the Elysian Fields."

"It's better than the cold in the Asphodel."

They walked in silence for the better part of two hours. Rhad led them through a heavily wooded area, across a field filled with flowers, and over three bridges. Finally, he drew to a stop and reached out to grab both of their arms.

"Here we go. Hold on to your hats, folks."

ABALAM GROANED loudly. His hands tangled in the hair of the two women on their knees in front of him as they simultaneously licked his cock. He thrust his hips slightly, smiling when the women giggled and playfully fought over which one got to suck on him.

He slid onto the pallet serving as a bed and lay flat. Crooking one finger at the women, he grabbed the blonde by the hips and guided her down onto the ridge of his penis, sliding inside and moaning from pleasure at the feel of her body surrounding him. The brunette leaned down and kissed him slowly, letting her tongue play in his mouth and gently scratching her nails down his chest.

"Straddle my face. I'm going to tongue-fuck you while she rides my dick."

The woman moved to obey, and the two seductively stroked each other's breasts. The blonde bounced enthusiastically on him, bringing orgasm closer and closer as she moved. Just as he was about to come, the door opened and Abaddon came in. Not stopping, the woman continued rocking, making eye contact with Abbadon as she rode Abalam.

Abalam gripped the hips of the woman on his face, pulling her tighter in and stroking his tongue in and out of her. He rolled his eyes sideways to see Abaddon and met his companion's eyes, holding the gaze as he came, surging up into the woman he penetrated and stabbing his tongue against the clit of the other, sending her into the spasms of orgasm before roughly shoving her aside and knocking the other woman away, not knowing, or caring, whether or not she had experienced an orgasm.

"I told you that you would get your turn with them! Leave us! I wish to fuck them at least one more time so I can experience both pussies before you take over."

"I apologize for the interruption, but our enemies are approaching." Abaddon gathered clothes for the other Devil and handed them over. "It would appear we're going to have to fight."

Abalam pulled on his clothes and looked between the two women. "Get dressed and make yourself ready to do battle." He stooped to tie his shoes. "Are all six coming?"

"No, only three. The vampire, the Hunter, and Michael."

"Michael? What the fuck is he doing down here?" Abalam strode through the house to look outside. "I don't see them."

"The sentries spotted them about a half a mile out coming this way. We should leave now while we have a chance to do so. They'll be here within minutes."

Abalam growled. "We'd have to fucking run like humans down here. Our powers are muted. If I'd known that we'd be no stronger than demons down here, I'd never have agreed to come down."

"They will be weaker too, then."

"We don't know that for sure. We can assume, but if we're wrong, we're screwed." Abalam scrunched up his face. "Why in the world would there only be three of them?" He smiled. "Unless they were stupid enough to split up and go after Beelzebub at the same time. That would explain the split, and the witch would have to be on Earth to hold the doors open. Can we get in contact with Earth?"

Abaddon nodded. "Yes, why?"

"Go get word to them that the witch is alone. If they find her quickly and kill her, then even if they get our wings, they'll be as stuck down here as we are."

"I'll do my best. Who do you want me to tell?"

Abalam considered that carefully. "I think it might be time to utilize one of our agents left in Heaven. Call for Bartholomew. He's been sitting in Heaven waiting to do something for millennia. It's time we gave him his chance."

Abaddon smiled widely. "I'll complete the spell to hail him immediately."

When he had left, Abalam looked around the yard. Within seconds, the demons left in the compound poured out. There weren't many of them. He'd sent half of his troops to kill the attackers before they got to the buildings. The fact that Damon, Gage, and Michael were still alive was all he needed to know about the state of his demons and Hounds.

"I know you're coming! This is your one chance to turn around and leave before we kill you!"

Michael's voice came back, penetrating the forest. "If you could kill us, you wouldn't be warning us. Make this easy on yourselves and come out. If you cooperate and let us have the roots, we'll leave you alive."

Abalam snorted. "You can't kill us anyway. Hell is closed, in case you haven't noticed."

Michael emerged from the trees, his wings spread behind him and his hand on his sword. "Don't you know? If you die down here, you cease to exist. No Hell, no Heaven, no reforming."

Fear flickered in Abalam's eyes for an instant before it smoothed into nonchalance. "You're bluffing."

Michael lifted one eyebrow. "Am I? Are you sure? Or are you just hoping I'm bluffing?" He scanned the crowd of ten demons. "Is this all the backup you have? Son, I could defeat you all on my own." He drew his sword and twirled it absently. "Where's Abaddon?"

"Oh, he's around. Where are your two friends?"

Gage and Damon came out of the woods. Damon held a rifle close to his chest, while Gage clutched nothing but a buck knife. Michael smiled wickedly.

"They're here. Do this the easy way. Save us all the hassle of fighting and just let us have the roots."

"I'm no more going to give you those things than you're about to willingly let me cut your wings off. Keeping those where they are on my back is the only way Lucifer's plan stays alive." He looked over his shoulder as Abaddon fell into line with him. "Why can't you just leave us alone and let us do this? You stupid fucking Angels and your damned human helpers have to interfere in everything we do."

Michael bristled. "Because you were never meant to exist! If the plan my Father had designed had taken shape in the way it was intended, Devils would never have existed! We will always try to stop you because you should not be!"

Abalam grinned. "How could you say such a thing about your own son?"

Michael's brows drew together. "Are you ill?"

Abalam's eyes lit up with joy. "Lilith never told you, did she?

Gage cleared his throat. "He's just trying to rile you, Michael. Don't listen to anything he says."

Michael held up a hand. "You have thirty seconds to speak your mind before I run you through with my sword."

"We all knew you were fucking her. Every last one of us knew about it. I'm sure by now you know about the Cambion, so you know we found a way to make ourselves fertile. It worked on the female Devils, too. When God found out about it, He immediately made the Angels fertile even though you didn't find out about it for a while after. You knocked her up. She delivered a son a few months ago."

"Liar!" Michael teleported himself across the clearing and seized Abalam by the throat. He lifted the Devil off the ground and laid his hand flat on Abalam's head, using his powers to reach into the Devil and access his memories.

He didn't notice Gage and Damon rush into battle. He didn't notice the blood and mayhem around him as his companions hacked their way through the demons. All he could see were the images flowing out of Abalam.

Lilith in a panic. Lilith with a bulging stomach. Lilith screaming as she labored and the look of adoration on her face when she reached down and pulled her child from her body. The tuft of white-blond hair and bright blue eyes so much like his own.

Roaring with fury and grief, Michael ripped the knife Griffin had used from his waistband and threw Abalam to the ground, pinning the Devil with his knees and stabbing him, shredding through skin and muscle. He wrenched fibers of muscle apart and tore out the silver rods where his wings had once anchored.

"NO!"

Abaddon threw himself on Michael, hacking at the Angel with a dagger. Still blinded by fury, Michael stabbed Abaddon in the throat with the knife. Blood gurgled up and spilled onto the ground in a red river, splashing in the dirt.

Gage's voice managed to penetrate the rage slowly. "Get his roots before he dies! If he dies, he disappears! Get them!"

Michael efficiently made slices in Abaddon's back and ripped out the roots. Before he had even climbed to his feet, Abaddon disappeared, leaving nothing other than a bloody puddle on the ground. Abalam curled into a ball and sobbed piteously.

Damon put his hands on his hips. "Why the hell did we come down here if you were just going to do that on your own without even needing our help?"

Gage laid a hand on Damon's arm. "Not now, son." He went to Michael and gripped the Angel by the shoulders. "You couldn't do anything about it when you didn't know. Now that you know, you can do something. We'll find him, and we'll get him for you." He looked over his shoulder, speaking to Damon "Don't let Abalam run off. We need him for more information."

Michael covered his face with his hands. "I have a son! I've let that Devil bitch birth my child. What do I do?"

Gage crouched when Michael slumped to the ground. "You find him, and you raise him. When was the last time you were with Lilith?"

"Before the funeral for Braxton's family."

"Then the child is no more than three months old. That's an infant. This baby isn't going to know who its mother is or what she is. He'll have you, and that will be enough."

Michael looked sad. His eyes filled with tears, and his brow was wrinkled. "I'm immortal. What good can I be to a child?"

"Perhaps the baby is, too. He's born of two immortal parents." Gage stood. "You can be a father. We'll help you with whatever you need."

Michael climbed to his feet and stalked toward Abalam, who was still writhing in pain on the ground. He stood over him and glared down at the Devil. "All I need to know is where my child is."

Abalam gasped for breath. "Lilith hired a fucking nanny. She didn't actually want to raise the whelp, she just wanted to keep it to use against you later."

"What is the caretaker's name?"

"If I tell you, will you let me go?"

Michael nodded. "I don't have time to waste torturing it out of you. Tell me the name and we will both walk away to fight again another day. But heed this. If you lie to me, I will make it my only mission in life to find you and slice you to ribbons. What Alaria did to you will be nothing compared to the pain you will experience at my hand."

Abalam rolled onto his back. "Monica Peters. She's an American. Lives in California."

Michael looked at Damon. "Get Greer through your link and have Aradia open the gate. We have both sets of roots, and I have something very important I need to take care of."

Greer rifled in the fridge absently, trying to find something to eat that didn't require cooking. She jumped when she felt a familiar tugging on the mental link she shared with Damon and smiled.

"Hey there, stranger. How's it going?"

"We got the wing roots. We need Aradia to let us out. Abaddon is dead. Michael has a son. Apparently he knocked Lilith up."

Greer choked on an olive and coughed, hacking until the offending vegetable dislodged itself from her throat. *"I didn't see that one coming. Lilith hasn't breathed a word. Where is it? Is it alive? Is it human?"*

"It's alive, but I don't know if it's human. Can you just get Aradia to open up the portal before Michael has a heart attack?"

"Can Angels have heart attacks?"

"I suppose it's just as likely as them having children with Devils, but I don't want to find out for sure. Go ask her."

"Okay, okay. Hold your horses. I'll be right back."

Greer climbed the steps to the room where Aradia worked and entered it softly. The redheaded witch was perched in her chair, studying a spell book. She looked up when Greer entered the room and smiled.

"Come sit and join me."

"Damon just got me on the link. They have the wing roots, and they need the portal opened back up."

Aradia smiled. "Oh, thank goodness. Now we just need for Braxton and Alaria to get Beelzebub and bring him through. I checked with her two hours ago, and their companion was very nearly to full strength. They've been resting on the Isle of the Blessed until that happens. They'll likely move within eight hours their time." She picked up her citrine. "Let's go down to the chapel to do this."

There was a rustling and a white light filled the room. An Angel appeared, dressed all in white, with white hair and white wings. He nodded to each of the women in turn.

"My name is Bartholomew, and I am an Angel of the Lord."

Greer lifted her eyebrow. "I gathered the Angel part. What do you want?"

Bartholomew sighed. "It has come to my attention that you have been left unprotected. I am here to offer my services as a guard for you while you wait for the others to complete their tasks."

Greer looked at Aradia nervously. "I thought Heaven was on lockdown. We were told to call for Gabriel if we needed anything, which we don't. Everything is fine."

Bartholomew smiled coldly. "Gabriel sent me. I am an Angel. Surely you can trust me."

Aradia brushed past the Angel and headed for the stairs. "You can leave. Michael will be returning shortly. I'm going to open the gate to Purgatory to allow them to come out as we speak."

"Michael is a traitor. He abandoned Heaven in its hour of need and has left the Host to dally on Earth. You'll have to excuse me if I don't particularly care what Michael is doing." He reached out and grabbed Aradia's arm. "You're going to stay here with me."

Aradia's eyes flashed red. "It didn't take you long to drop the good Angel act. Gabriel would never send someone we don't know without at least warning one of us first. Why are you really here?"

Bartholomew laughed. "You're smarter than I gave you credit for. I'm here to kill you. If I kill you, Michael and those roots are trapped in Purgatory forever."

Aradia drew up her power and blasted out a wave, sending Bartholomew crashing into the chair she had been sitting in. She smiled saccharinely. "No one told you how powerful I am, did they? You're a minor Angel. They've sent you here on a suicide mission."

Bartholomew sent out a lightning bolt, which Aradia deflected with a careless swipe of her hand. It broke one of the windows with a loud crash before hurting outside and striking a tree with a ground-shaking bang, splitting it in half. She threw out both arms and sent magic ricocheting through the room, picking him up and rapping his skull against the stone wall.

Greer ran for the desk and snatched up a knife, opening a cut on her hand quickly and allowing the blood to drip out onto the wood. "We can't kill him. Only a Devil can rip out their Grace. We're going to have to settle for sending him somewhere else!"

Aradia smiled darkly. "I can still try to kill him. Where's your Grace, Bartholomew?"

"Fuck you, you witch whore." Bartholomew flung out bolts with both hands, haphazardly striking them on anything he could.

Greer drew a symbol in the blood and wrapped her hands around Aradia's citrine, ducking her head and whispering under her breath. She slammed her hand down into the symbol and looked at her palm, the intricate drawing emblazoned in her skin. Aradia whipped a bolt around and threw it back at Bartholomew, and Greer charged him, planting the hand with the symbol firmly in his chest and muttering an exorcism under her breath. There was a loud crack, and Bartholomew disappeared.

Aradia was rushing down the steps before the air cleared. "We have to get the portal open. He must be one of the spies for Lucifer that is in Heaven. He'll be back with more quickly. That spell only sends him somewhere else. It doesn't stop him from coming back, and if we can't kill him, we need someone who can."

Greer swore under her breath. "No one ever taught us how to fight off fucking Angels."

"I don't think we can. From what I know, the only things that can kill an Angel are another Angel or a Devil. I don't think a human can do it, which is what makes this guy so dangerous. Put up some Angel wards while I do this. I can yank Michael through them."

Aradia went to the front of the sanctuary and stood on the blood-stain left from the Choosing. She closed her eyes and tipped her head back, opening them to stare up at the ceiling and knowing they had turned from their normal blue to white. She began chanting, her voice deep and low.

"Gates of Heaven, Gates of Hell. Angels on high and Devils that fell. Hear my demand, obey my cry. Turn the lock, open the door. Grant me access to that which exists no more. Purgatory deep, Purgatory black. Open your gates, ascend through the black. Hear my cry answer my plea. Swing open the gates and open to me!"

The wrought iron doors appeared, and Aradia ran forward, yanking it open. Michael immediately shoved his way through it, followed closely by Damon and Gage, who held the slim silver roots in one hand. Michael looked around the room appraisingly.

"Why are you warding against Angels? Do you no longer wish for me to help you?"

Greer shook her head. "An Angel named Bartholomew is a traitor.

He's spying on you. Someone sent him to kill us. He's not a very good actor."

"Bartholomew? He's among the lowest ranking of the Angels." Michael closed his eyes and moved his head from side to side in a sad shake. "I would have never guessed." He looked around. "Gage, the child?"

Gage smiled softly. "Will be waiting for you or on its way before you get back. You have my word."

Michael nodded curtly. "I'll return shortly. It would appear as if I have an Angel to murder."

Rhad stood and stretched. "Okay, I'm recharged. Let's get this show on the road."

Alaria slowly climbed to her feet. "Well, it's about time." She picked up her pack and strapped it across her chest. "Not that I'm complaining—much—since we'd have no way across the Phlegethon without you, but we're down to less than three days down here to get through this."

Rhad sighed. "Darling, I doubt we'll be here a day. Once we get to Tartarus, we have no choice but to keep moving. If we stop, we die. Beelzebub will sit up and take notice once we've crossed the Phlegethon. I don't think he has enough energy to throw more at us than is already there, but I've been wrong before. Opening this place back up had to take massive amounts of power, and if he's the only one who did it, then he's going to be zapped for a long time. I'd bet weeks."

Braxton unzipped his pack. "We need to lighten the load before we go in. Ditch anything we can—the blankets, all the food except a couple power boosts. The lighter we are, the faster we move." He began setting things aside. "We need to lighten up on ammo, too, but we'll do that after Cerberus."

Alaria laughed. "We might not have any ammo left after Cerberus." She helped him unload the packs and zip them back up. "Okay, Rhad, let's get this over with."

Rhad reached out to grab them both. "Rules, kids. Once we land, you fight. Those crows are going to be on top of us before you know what's going on. Whatever you do, don't get separated and don't stop moving. I'll lay down some fire cover to buy us some time, but the only way to get through is to take out what we can while we move. If we stop, we die." He snapped his fingers and a rope curled around all three of them, linking them together. "We're about to get swarmed. Weapons ready?"

Braxton loaded the shotgun, and Alaria checked the clip in her pistol. Braxton nodded. "I think we're ready."

Rhad laughed ruefully. "Boy, you're not the slightest bit ready, but we'll see what we can do anyway."

The Devil teleported them over the Phlegethon, the heat from the lava reaching up to scald them as they passed through it. They landed on dry, cracked earth. Braxton had time for one look around before the crows swarmed.

There were hundreds of them. They descended upon the three in a flood. The sky turned black, and they were overwhelmed with the sound of wings flapping. Beaks pecked at them, razor sharp and fast. Braxton looked from side to side, and the only thing he saw was feathers.

He fired the shotgun rapidly, taking care not to shoot Alaria or Rhad. Each blast created a small hole in the flock of birds, and he was able to drag the other two forward several inches before more birds swooped in to fill it.

Alaria fired thirteen times in rapid succession, and eleven birds fell to the ground. She scrambled to snap in another clip, unable to do so without first using her knife to stab at the birds as they encroached on her. When one brushed against her face, she realized they had feathers as sharp as their beaks. Blood bloomed on her cheek from where they had touched her, and she brushed it away in annoyance.

Fire erupted from Rhad's hands and multitudes of birds fell to the ground, scorched and smoking. The smell of burning flesh and feathers filled the air, and Alaria nearly gagged from the stench as it flooded her nose.

Braxton shouldered the shotgun once it was out of ammo and yanked his pistol from its holster on his hips. He grabbed three birds that managed to sink their claws into his shoulders and broke their necks, casting the bodies aside before firing.

As they moved through the cloud of crows, it slowly began to thin.

Braxton pushed forward, drawing his machete and carving a path through. Alaria's pistol hit the dirt, and she resorted to tearing at the birds with her bare hands. Bloody cuts and punctures riddled both of her arms, and there were several rips in her clothes.

"How much farther?" Alaria's voice was nearly panicked as she ripped two birds from her face and stomped them to death beneath her boots.

Rhad sent out another stream of fire, sending dozens more spiraling to the ground in heaps. "We've barely started, love. Braxton, my boy, you're the head of this line and I strongly suggest you move faster! If you want me to have any power left for Cerberus, we need to be going a lot quicker than we are."

Braxton's voice was tense and harsh. "If I could see where I'm fucking going, I would." He swung his machete haphazardly, slicing one crow in half. "So this is where Hitchcock got the idea, huh?"

Rhad made a strangled noise as one bird drove its beak into his crotch. "I have not one fucking clue what you're talking about. Either move or cut yourself loose so we can!"

Braxton charged forward ten feet, crunching birds under his boots and stabbing blindly into the cloud of black. Fire blasted from Rhad as he tried to clear the way using his powers. They stumbled through, hacking and fighting until finally, the air cleared, and they were free of the birds. He sliced through the rope, falling to his knees and rolling to his back.

Behind them, thousands of crows sat in a group, waiting for them to come back and completely oblivious of the hundreds of dead birds interspersed with the live ones. Alaria collapsed next to him, covered in bloody peck marks and scratches.

Rhad was the only one relatively unharmed, though his face was pale and drawn and his knees wobbled as he dropped onto the hard, cracked ground. Placing both hands on his waistband, he pulled the fabric out and peered down at his penis, verifying the bird hadn't done any permanent damage. Satisfied, he laid his hands over his face for a long moment before speaking.

"I didn't mean to yell at you, love, but it was getting hard for me to maintain my fire power to deal with those damn things."

Braxton shook his head. "Don't worry about it." He took several deep, gulping breaths. "How long can we lie here?"

Rhad looked around. "We're on the edge. The crows can't get us, but we're not quite in Cerberus' territory. It's a thin line between the areas in Tartarus that allowed for Beelzebub to bring people to watch the torture without actually being subjected to it. If we stay here, we'll be okay for a couple hours. I'll need at least a three hour nap to recharge after that." He looked sheepish. "I know you want to get going, and so do I, but I'm no good if I have nothing of my powers left to give you and if we charge on without giving me a chance to shore myself up, that's precisely what will happen."

Alaria waved her hand dismissively. "No complaints here. Brax and I could occupy half that time cleaning up the puncture wounds. Take your nap. We'll be ready when you are."

Rhad rolled over and was asleep within ten seconds. Braxton shook his head in amazement. "How does he do that?"

"It's how he recharges. He was a relatively minor Angel and a pretty minor Devil. He has some tricks that come in handy, like the talent with fire that you saw, but overall, he's weak. Over the years, he's trained himself to fall asleep almost instantly when he needs it. It's efficient."

"It's weird." Braxton dragged his pack to himself and opened it up, pulling out the first aid kit. "How badly are you hurt?"

She surveyed her arms and legs. "Mostly little nicks. They'll heal within a few hours." She glanced at him. "You look a little worse for wear."

He sighed deeply. "Nothing life threatening, but it's enough to be annoying. I would kill for a bottle of scotch and a couple Vicodin right now."

Alaria laughed. "We're not getting drunk or high." She ripped into a plastic packet. "I can do two aspirin, but that's the extent of the med kit."

Braxton took the aspirin and swallowed them. "It's better than nothing." He unscrewed the cap on a bottle of water and wiped blood from her face and arms. "There are a lot of pecks, but I don't think any of them are deep."

She grabbed the rag and did the same to his face. "You're the same way. I'll be fine in a couple hours. I think we should use the alcohol wipes to clean yours out so you don't get infected."

He shrugged. "Do what you want. We've got three hours before he's ready to go, so we've got time to waste. Is there going to be a break like this on the other side of Cerberus?"

"I'm not counting on it. The Sea of Souls is on the other side, and it's too wide for him to transport us across. We have to swim, and that's going to be dangerous. If I remember correctly, and it's been so long I may not, I think there's a skinny strip of in-between like this, but it's prone to flooding."

Braxton shook his head. "How does it flood? It's not like it rains down here or anything."

"The riverhas a current and it's so wide and so long it can get waves, which sometimes cover the neutral zone." Alaria dabbed at the punctures on Braxton's face with an alcohol pad. "We'll get through this."

"I know we will." He reached out and brushed his knuckles down her cheek. "Just a few more days and this will all be over for good. We'll get to concentrate on having real lives instead of saving everyone else's."

Alaria laughed and turned her face into his hand slightly. "I don't know what I'm even going to do after this. I don't exactly have any marketable skills." She looked at him pointedly. "What do you intend to do when there are no more demons to hunt?"

"We'll figure out something." Braxton winced when she cleaned a particularly deep wound. "Maybe we can be mercenaries or something. We have marketable skills, they just aren't legal skills." He chuckled. "Or maybe I'll put on a suit and run Finn's companies. Corporate shark tank and all that."

"I don't see you in a suit. If we don't get this done soon, there won't be society left. The United States and Europe are still okay, but we know from when we were in Colombia that it's getting harder and harder to keep this stuff under wraps. It won't be too long before it gets really bad, especially if we don't succeed at keeping Lucifer in Hell."

"Don't borrow trouble. We'll get through this fine, and then we'll figure out what we're going to do. Hell, we might be so busy raising babies that neither of us wants to do anything else for a while. We have time, and we have the means. We can figure it out together." He looked over at Rhad. "Can we trust him out in the world?"

Alaria nodded. "He's not a bad guy, and he's been trapped in here so long most people would be insane. I don't think he's really a danger to anyone, and he knows the score. He knows that if we win, he goes back to Hell. Fuck, if we win, Gage goes back to Hell, too."

"I'm still not convinced Michael doesn't put a stop to that." Braxton twisted to look over his shoulder. "How far into that is Cerberus?"

The air around them shimmered, and Aradia appeared. She smiled brightly before she saw the still oozing wounds covering both Braxton and Alaria. The smile faded into an expression of worry.

"What happened? Are you okay?"

Alaria nodded. "We're fine. We got past the crows. What's up?"

Aradia clasped and unclasped her hands. "There have been a couple new developments. First, it seems as if the Devils are getting desperate. They brought down one of the Angels spying on Heaven to try and kill Greer and I. We were able to hold him off long enough until Michael came out of Purgatory. They got the wing roots from both Abalam and Abaddon."

Braxton grinned. "That's great! We still have to get past Cerberus and the Sea of Souls before we can get to Beelzebub, and we don't have the knife, obviously, so we're probably going to have to drag him out with us."

"I'm working on sending the knife. You should have it in a few minutes. I'm going to practice with a couple little things first before I send the dagger. There has been another development."

Alaria's eyebrows drew together. "What's wrong?"

"Abalam informed Michael that Lilith has birthed a son. About three months ago, apparently. Gage has located the child and is sending for it."

"Who knocked her up?" Braxton looked disgusted. "There's one Cambion we can kill before it's old enough to kill us."

Alaria shook her head slowly. "No." She looked at Aradia. "It was Michael, wasn't it? Michael has a son."

Aradia nodded sadly. "It would seem as if he does. He is going to be raising the child here on Earth, at least until we can ascertain whether or not the child is immortal or human. No one knows what it's going to be since typically neither Angels nor Devils can reproduce. He's not really welcome in Heaven right now, anyway. Regardless, we're dealing with it. Do you have a timeline in mind for when you'll need me to open up the door and let you out?"

Alaria sighed deeply and wrapped her arms around her knees. "Rhad needs a couple hours to recharge before we fight Cerberus. We're stronger with him than without him, so I think the time is a small price to pay for the increased chance of survival. Once we go into Cerberus, we have to keep moving, but we've got what's likely going to be a four or five hour swim ahead of us and then we have to go after Beelzebub. I'm hopeful we'll be done within twelve hours down here, so that's two days up there."

"Okay. I'm going to try to get rest between now and then. It's draining just to come down here like this, and I know I'm going to need a lot more firepower heading into these last few days." She looked around. "Is there anything you need before I go?"

Braxton laughed. "If you have some magic trick for getting past a giant three-headed dog then that would be great, but other than that, I think we're okay for now."

Aradia looked thoughtful. "I don't know if my magic would translate down here even if I could figure something out. It's the same problem I ran into with the river of lava. However, there are stories from my time about Cerberus. One man was rumored to have defeated him by lulling him to sleep with a flute, and another drugged him with poisoned food. Now, unless Beelzebub has several three-headed dogs named Cerberus, I doubt that either of those rumors are true. Hercules captured him, too, but that version was much smaller than the one you're going after." She shrugged helplessly. "I would suggest cutting off its heads. Three people, three heads."

Alaria made a small noise in her throat as she considered that. "If it can't concentrate on all three of us at once, that might not be a bad idea. It's worth a try, anyway." She laughed. "Believe me when I tell you Hercules was just a man, and no one ever sang this beast a lullaby or fed it poisoned honeycakes."

Aradia grinned. "So you're familiar with the myths, then?" She looked around. "I need to go. My energy is waning from being down here so long. I'll check in with you in a few hours to see where you are. I don't know if I can hear you if you call for me, but it can't hurt to try if you need something. I'll work on getting the knife down to you as fast as I can."

Braxton ran his hands through his hair as Aradia disappeared. "I wish she could help us more. I know she's doing everything she can, but it just seems like the world's most powerful witch oughta be able to do more than just pop in to check."

Alaria laughed. "You have to remember she's not really here. She can't be down here and open up the door to let us out. If she came down here, she probably could help us do all of these things, but then we'd be stuck down here. Once you're down here, unless Beelzebub opens the door, you're not getting back out." She glanced around. "How much longer until we can wake sleeping beauty?"

Braxton looked down at his watch. "Two and a half hours. Why don't you lie down and try to take a nap, too?"

She glared at him. "We slept last night. I don't need sleep every three hours. I'm fine."

He held up his hands in mock surrender. "Fine, fine. Far be it for me to try and be helpful."

Alaria sighed and stretched. "I think we should ditch the guns. Cerberus isn't going to be something we can take down with a rifle, and we can't use them in the Sea of Souls because nothing there is corporeal. Once we get to Beelzebub, the odds of guns working after being submerged in the Cocytus for hours is slim to none, and the weight will make it easier for them to drag us down."

Braxton nodded. "Let's wait until we're past Cerberus to do it, though. I'm willing to try shooting the damn thing before we go hand to hand combat on it." He began unpacking their bags. "I'm going to make sure everything is completely loaded and clean. That'll kill a couple hours until we have to head out."

ALARIA JUMPED to the side and rolled to the ground, hitting her shoulder on the red clay and bounding back to her feet before the spiked tail of Cerberus could take her out. She leaped over the back swing of the tail and drove down with her sword, anchoring the swinging appendage to the dirt and buying Rhad and Braxton a precious few seconds to go after one of the three heads.

She clenched her hand and conjured another sword, using her petty amounts of magic to light the blade on fire. Twirling it and striding forward in her spiked heels, she reached deep within herself and formed what she could of her waning Devil's powers into a fireball. She held it in her palm, nurturing and fostering it as it grew larger and larger. She knew she would have only one shot with the fireball, and she had to make it count.

Braxton battled two paws, whacking at them with the edge of his sword and making pitifully little progress. Rhad sent out wave after wave of fire, trying to drive back the two heads coming after him simultaneously. He brandished a sword in one hand and a writhing white ball of flame in the other, using them in alternating fashion to fight Cerberus.

Alaria slashed with her sword, trying to get the beast's' attention more than she was trying to do any damage. They had learned within seconds that its skin was as hard as stone and their blades did little more than scratch. She hissed with pain when one of the spikes from the tail caught her in the leg, cutting deep into the muscle on her calf. Limping, she dodged two feet and managed to get between the dog's legs, looking up at its chest.

Braxton saw what she was doing and dashed across the front of the animal, yelling and swinging his sword, trying to get its attention. He nearly tripped over his shotgun, which had been discarded ten seconds into the battle when he'd realized bullets bounced.

"What the hell are you trying to do?" Braxton grunted when one of Cerberus' heads sent him flying ten feet. He hit the ground with a bone-shattering thwack and blinked rapidly to fight off the black spots swarmed in front of him.

Alaria moved with the dog, keeping herself underneath it and waiting for the right time. "I have a plan! Rhad, get back! I'm going to blow it up!"

Rhad looked up from where he was scorching the fur off one of the three faces. "How in Lucifer's name do you intend to do that?"

She held up the still growing fireball she held in one hand. "I'm going to turn it into a furnace, but get back! This is going to be messy!"

Rhad leaped over the tail as the animal pivoted and shrugged. "What do you need us to do?"

"Keep it busy!" Alaria hefted the burning sword and ran to keep up with the wildly swinging beast. "Keeping it still would be good, too." She gritted her teeth. "This had better work. If it doesn't, I'm going to end up blowing us up, too."

Rhad grunted as he hit the ground. "Make it fast, Alaria!" He rolled from side to side, trying to avoid the massive jaws as Cerberus tried to bite him. Braxton leaped to his feet and raced to help, using his sword to bat at the beast.

Alaria said a quick prayer she was right about how to kill it and drove the flaming blade up into the softer underbelly. Blood—black and thick as tar—oozed out and covered her arm. She squeezed her eyes shut and thrust her arm up, implanting the ball of fire as deep into the abdominal cavity as she could. Holding her breath, she sprinted away, stopping to help Braxton drag Rhad behind a boulder. She ducked down, her eyes closed and her concentration fully on making the inferno into a bomb.

She felt it building, felt it growing and spinning, gaining momentum as it burned. Cerberus stopped moving, a confused look on each of its three heads. It made a strangled noise and took two steps backward, yelping and whimpering. Alaria forced every bit of Devil magic she had into the fireball and erupted it.

They watched in awe as the fire engulfed the dog. Rhad held out his hands and sent a stream of fire at the beast, keeping the flames from going out. The stench of burning flesh filled the air and Alaria gagged, bending over to retch from the assault on her nostrils. The stream Rhad sent rose up to encompass the entire animal, melding with the heat from Alaria's fireball and increasing the intensity. When the fireball exploded, the earth shook from the force of the blast. Bits of bone and blood rained down on them, showering all three with the remnants of Cerberus.

Covered in guts and dirt, Braxton swiped at his forehead. "Well, a swim will feel nice after that." He unzipped his bag and pulled out a cloth to wipe his face. "Everyone okay?"

Alaria nodded. "I'm fine. Rhad?"

Rhad was wiping bone fragments from his shirt. "I don't think I've ever been this dirty. If you were inquiring as to whether or not I'm injured, then no, I'm fine. Sore, of course, but that's to be expected." He grinned. "And is nothing that won't be cured by a long, leisurely swim." He looked down at the two backpacks. "I think you should lighten your loads. Keep some water for once we reach shore, and the knives, certainly, but I don't believe guns are going to be your friend in this."

Braxton dumped out all of the MREs and protein bars and all but two bottles of water. He set aside all of the ammo, both his pistols, the shotgun, and the rifle. He looked over at Alaria, who had done the same.

"I think we can probably use only one pack. Mine's almost empty."

She nodded. "Yeah, mine too. I think we need to find a way to keep the salt, though." She pulled out a dagger triumphantly. "Aradia did it. This is the knife Griffin used, so we'll be able to take care of Beelzebub down here, which will make things easier."

Braxton combined the contents of the two bags and shouldered the half-full one. He looked between Alaria and Rhad. "Where to now?"

Rhad led them past the bloody field where Cerberus had been to another small strip of red dirt. "This is the safe zone. About fifteen feet on the other side is the Sea of Souls. It drops off a couple hundred feet as soon as you're in it. There's nothing gradual about it. When you get in, start swimming. Try not to splash, and don't talk. Almost anything could get the attention of the souls in there. It's named the River of Wailing for a reason. The sound will be painful and hard to listen to. Whatever you do, don't stop swimming. If one of them grabs you, it can get bad fast."

Alaria scowled. "They'll try to drag you down and force themselves into you. Brax, your anti-possession tattoos will stop that, but Rhad and I are both at risk, especially him since he doesn't have a soul to begin with. That makes it easier for them to wiggle inside."

Braxton lifted his eyebrows. "Is there a way to kill them? Or to stop them if we get grabbed?"

Rhad sighed. "Think of them like zombies. One isn't a problem to handle. Generally, they're non-corporeal. They have to take physical form in order to grab you, so as long as they're physical, they can be hurt the same way one of us can. Unfortunately, it's when they swarm you that you have problems, and if you make a lot of noise fending off the one, you're going to have all the others to deal with."

"What do we do if we get swarmed?"

Alaria laughed. "Let's not get swarmed. If we do, we're as good as dead. Or possessed, anyway."

Braxton was grim as he approached the foggy gray water. "All righty then. Let's get this show on the road."

One by one, they hopped into the water and paddled quietly, treading until they were all in. The liquid was cool and silky, though it was thicker than normal water. It clung to them, making it hard to lift either an arm or a leg from it. Fortunately, that also muffled the sound of their strokes as they swam.

Braxton looked from side to side almost constantly. His heart pounded in his chest, and he had to concentrate on breathing to make himself take and expel breaths. Every sound, from Alaria breathing to the water lapping against their bodies, worried him. Twice, he thought he felt something brush his leg and went absolutely still, turning onto his back and floating to make sure he was completely silent.

When Rhad spoke, his voice was a whisper. "We need to pace ourselves. We're going to be in this water for a few hours. You'll know it if they grab you. They won't just brush against you. That's the non-corporeal forms going by. When they're in that form, unless you're making noise, they aren't really aware of a lot."

Braxton slowly rolled onto his stomach and resumed kicking his legs. "I've never done this before. Everything I feel makes me nervous."

Alaria laughed softly. "We're doing just fine. Just keep swimming."

In unison, the three paddled through the water. Several times they went still as a corporeal soul popped to the surface and looked around the river with hollowed eye sockets and paper thin skin stretched over bones. Rhad had sent a bolt of fire flying, creating a loud splash close to ten yards away from them, drawing off their attention. The sound of a herd of souls swarming the spot where the flame hit was enough to make their blood freeze in their veins.

The minutes blended together as they swam. After two hours, Alaria's legs felt like lead, and her heart was pounding so loudly in her chest that it was all she could hear. Her stomach was clenched with fear as she took deep breaths to keep herself from gasping. Still she paddled, forcing her arms to move and her legs to kick.

"How much longer?" Braxton rolled back onto his back to float for a moment, allowing himself to catch his breath and rest his burning muscles.

Rhad treaded water and looked around. "We're halfway there." He glanced from side to side. "We're okay so far." He followed Braxton's lead and rolled over, letting the water support his weight. "I think I can transport us if we can keep going to about another thirty minutes. It'll be close to the edge of my ability, but I might be able to make it work. I would need time on the beach to rest before we continue the trip, but it would get us out of here sooner."

Alaria stopped paddling and joined the men floating. "I'll be honest, I don't know how much more swimming I've got in me. It took a lot of my strength to kill Cerberus, and we didn't take time to rest between, which I could have used, so I think a couple hours on the beach will do us all some good if we can swing it."

Rhad nodded. "Okay, then, let's put the pedal to the metal and get as close as we can in the next thirty minutes, and then I'll transport us out."

Before either could answer, two hands closed on Alaria's ankle and dragged her beneath the surface. She had time to scream once and suck in a breath before the thick liquid closed around her and she was underwater.

The soul had claws instead of fingers. They dug into Alaria's leg, breaking through skin and ripping through muscle. She felt the claws hit the bones in her ankle and continue to dig, breaking through the plate. Struggling and flailing, she kicked with her other foot, trying to break its hold.

When that failed, she bent, punching at the thing with both hands, her strikes weakened by the viscosity of the water. She fumbled for the knife in her belt and hacked at the bony arms that dragged her down. From all around her, she felt souls materialize and hands grabbed at her, ripping furrows in her arms and trying to force her mouth open to worm their way into her body.

Her lungs burned from being under for too long. Alaria tried to find any of her Devil abilities, but the pathetic beginnings of her fireball was almost immediately extinguished by the water.

Black spots swarmed in front of her eyes. She opened her mouth to scream and sucked in a lungful of water. Consciousness was beginning to wanes and she knew there were only moments left before she would slip away.

Hands burst through the water and seized her by the shoulders, ripping her from the grasp of the souls. Alaria exploded through the surface and into a battle. Braxton and Rhad were hacking their way through hundreds of souls. Panicking, she turned her head and gasped deeply when she saw Gabriel in the water. The Angel didn't say a word, merely reached out and grabbed Braxton, yanking him close before doing the same thing with Rhad. With a flash of light and a loud crack, they went from the middle of the river to the rocky beach on the other side.

Alaria hit the ground on her knees, gasping and coughing until she gagged and threw up river water. Braxton was at her side within seconds, scraping her hair back from her face and hugging her tightly, his heart pounding so hard she could feel it thumping against her chest.

Gabriel sat on the sand, leaning against a boulder, his face pale and drawn. Rhad was lying flat on his back with his arms spread out wide, kneading sand in his hands. Alaria looked around, her eyes still glazed with fear.

Making eye contact with Gabriel, she managed to force sound from her burning throat. "How are you here? What happened? How did they know we were there? We were being quiet!"

Gabriel took a deep breath. "I told you I was keeping an eye on the baby. When you were drowning, the baby was drowning, too. It took almost every bit of my power to get down here to you, but the baby is destined, so God allowed me to interfere with your task." He raked his hands through his hair. "How did you become involved in this, Rhadamanthus? You haven't been heard from in centuries."

Rhad looked up. "I've been stuck here for those centuries. When they crossed into the Elysian Fields, we struck a deal that the witch wouls try to free me from Hades if I helped them get to Bub. As you can see, we had been doing quite well up until a few minutes before you popped in."

Gabriel laughed. "I'm surprised to see you got past Cerberus. Nicely done." He looked up at the sheer rock cliff in front of them. "I won't be continuing on with you, as I'm sure you understand. I will offer to take all three of you out of this place if you wish to terminate your suicide mission." He looked at Alaria sadly. "I can't be a part of what is a lost cause, and I don't know if I will have enough power to come back should you get into trouble yet again. You may be completely on your own if you continue."

Alaria closed her eyes and laid her head on Braxton's chest. "We'll be okay, Gabe." She smiled at him. "Thank you for saving me. I don't know how they heard me, but I was about to be a goner when you got there."

"I was hoping you would be strong enough to fight through them without my interference." Gabriel sighed deeply and stood, his suit somehow dry, despite having been submerged in the river less than five minutes previously. "Unfortunately, it seems as if my faith in humans and their ability to handle situations is almost always overly optimistic."

Alaria rolled her eyes. "Do you have to turn everything into an insult?"

He looked at her blankly. "What are you talking about?"

Braxton laughed and flopped onto the sand. "Never mind, Alaria. He'll never get it." He turned his head to look at the Angel. "We appreciate the help, but we're going to finish what we've started. We're way too close to finishing this to give up on it now."

Gabriel nodded curtly. "As you wish."

He disappeared with a crack and left the three alone on the beach. Rhad coughed and rolled onto his side. "Did we know that Angels could just get in here?" He lifted his head to stare at the other two.

"And what interest does he have in your baby?"

Alaria closed her eyes. "Angels can't just get in here. Gabriel has been given some additional leeway by Heaven given my situation."

Awareness dawned in Rhad's eyes, and he lay back down. "Braxton isn't the father. Gabriel is. Which means you're carrying a Cambion/Nephilim hybrid." He laughed. "Man, that is going to be one powerful kid."

Braxton groaned and dug through the bag for water. "They tell us she'll be the only one who can kill Lucifer."

Rhad sat up, moving in one motion. "Kill him? As in dead? Like, never to return dead?"

Alaria nodded. "That's the idea." She looked at him curiously. "Is that making you change your mind about working with us?

He shook his head. "Not for a second. If Lucifer was dead, we could all have our own existence and not have to worry about what the jackass says about it."

Braxton drained the bottle of water. "How long do you need before you can get us up that cliff?"

Rhad judged the distance with his eyes. "I'm going to need two hours, give or take."

Alaria sighed as sleep threatened to overcome her. "I think we could all use some sleep. Let's take four hours and all be in tip-top shape when we head up there."

Rhad had been able to get them up the mountain but barely. The farther he got from the Elysian Fields, the weaker his powers became. Alaria felt the drain, too, but staunchly ignored it. They had known coming to Beelzebub's territory was dangerous, and they had known there would be a drain on supernatural power.

Braxton crouched behind the rock line and looked across the plateau to the shining black castle. "What's the plan, guys? Storm the castle like Normandy? Or do either of you have something more subtle in mind?"

Alaria took a deep drink of water. "I don't think subtle is an option. You're forgetting he knows we're here. Unless he's going to try and trap us down here, he can't leave without this place closing up again. At least, I don't think he can, but that's neither here nor there. The point is, he knows we're here, so let's just head on in."

Rhad wiped his forehead with shaking hands. "Love, I don't know if I can. I'm so drained I don't think I could do any good as anything other than cannon fodder." He laughed. "I know it's very suspect timing and all, but I really believe I'd be doing more harm than good if I went with you in the state I'm in."

She studied him closely, taking in his pale, clammy skin and the dark blotches under his eyes. His hands shook whenever he moved them, and when he tried to stand up, he wobbled. She smiled softly and reached out to pull him back down.

"It's not suspicious timing. Without you we'd have never made it here on time. Brax and I can handle it from here. You stay here and rest up a bit. We'll come back for you before we leave."

Rhad looked up at her with eyes showing mixed emotions of hope and doubt. "Do you promise you won't just leave me here?"

Braxton nodded. "We promise. You're the only reason we've got a shot at this. I'm not going to forget it." He stood and chose a machete. "Let's go kill us a Devil bastard."

They climbed over the rocks and swiftly jogged across the field to the castle. Alaria ran her hands over the wall, trying to find the seam of a door. It took fifteen minutes, but on the second wall, her fingers ran into a divot halfway down. She followed the indention up and around, looking for anything that would release the door hinge and open it.

Finding nothing, she pressed hard against the door with both hands and stepped back. The door creaked in protest but swung open. Exchanging a nervous look at one another, they entered the castle. Alaria clenched her hand and conjured a whip in one hand and a sword in the other, exchanging army fatigues and a ratty ponytail for red and black leather and sleek locks. Her heels clicked on the floor as they crossed the massive entryway.

Braxton turned in a circle, taking it all in. When he spoke, his voice was a whisper. "Where do we go from here?"

Alaria looked from side to side, then shrugged and planted her feet, raising her voice so it filled the room. "Come out, come out, wherever you are!"

The only response they received was silence. Braxton and Alaria exchanged a worried look. Together, they systematically searched every inch of the first floor. Finding nothing, Alaria leaned against the wall and crossed her arms.

"The dungeons are the next logical place to look, then the upstairs, but the problem is, if we're playing a giant game of hide and seek, there's nothing to stop him from coming onto this floor and hiding."

Braxton knelt and unzipped the bag. "We still have a few cans of spray paint. We can paint wards on the doors. That way we'll know if they've been disturbed because the lines will be broken."

"Okay, you do that while I go check the dungeons. If I find him or anything of interest, I'll yell."

"Be careful."

She grinned and pushed through the door to the stairwell leading down. "I always am."

Slowly, Alaria descended the steps to the dungeon. Dust covered everything in a thick layer. A guillotine sat in one corner of the main room and a gallows directly across from it. Chains were bolted to the wall and there were several trays with an assortment of torture devices.

Methodically, she went through every inch of the dungeons. Not only did she not find Beelzebub, there was no sign anyone had entered the basement since Hades had been sealed shut centuries before. With a niggling feeling of dread in her gut, she set about painting traps on the floor and ceiling.

Braxton was pacing in front of the main staircase when Alaria came back up. "Anything?"

She shook her head. "Not a thing." She cast a glance up the steps. "Let's head on up."

There were six floors to the castle aside from the dungeons and the main floor. They combed through every inch of it, taking two hours to search for secret passages or rooms and looking for any sign of Beelzebub. While searching the top floor, the sound of a door slamming wafted up through the floors to them. Exchanging one look, they dashed back down the stairs to the main floor.

Rhad stood in the entryway, a ball of fire sitting in his palm. He lifted his eyebrows when he saw Alaria and Braxton coming down the stairs. "Is it over? Did you get him already?"

Alaria shook his head. "He's not here. We've looked everywhere."

The air crackled, and Beelzebub appeared, looking strangely transparent. He smiled at them and began speaking.

"I had hoped this would work well. If you're seeing this, you've triggered my message, which means I, once again, am smarter than you. By now you've been through Tartarus, seen my fun, and climbed that cliff. You must be exhausted. There's food in the kitchen and beds on the second floor. Enjoy your visit. I'm not here, in case you haven't noticed. When you triggered the silent alarm informing me someone had entered my castle, I left my real hiding spot—thank you Michael for creating that hut on the mountain—and I'm going after whomever stayed behind and the other Devils. You're not going to get my wings. Ta ta for now."

Alaria swore. "Motherfucker. It was a ploy. A fucking trap to split us up and get some of us down here so he could arrange an attack on us." She tipped her head back. "Aradia! Aradia, we need you now!"

Braxton waited thirty seconds, hoping against hope the redhead would appear before speaking. "We need to figure this out. We don't have time to go back to the Styx. It would still take us hours at best. Rhad, do you have anything useful to add?"

Rhad tapped one finger against his chin. "Come to think of it, I just might." He started climbing the steps. "Beelzebub has a trapdoor for him to bring his guests in. I know he didn't take me across the Styx when he brought me here—did he you, Alaria?"

Alaria shook her head. "No, he brought me straight to the castle. We came in onto the roof."

"Exactly. When he opened this back up, it would have had to have been through that since it was made just for him and would be the easiest thing for him to access. He'd have had to leave that way, too, which means it has to be accessible. If we can find it, we should be able to go out the same way."

Braxton put his hands on his hips. "How do we find it, and can we do so quickly?"

"Let's get up to the roof and find out." Rhad climbed the ladder that led to a door onto the roof. "Alaria, we should be able to see the fold in the sky where he came in. No offense, Braxton, love, but you don't exactly know what to look for, so try to be patient with us while we're finding it."

One by one, they climbed out onto the roof. Rhad and Alaria stared up at the sky, discussing the swirling black and purple. Braxton walked to the edge and looked down.

"Um, guys?"

Alaria looked over. "It'll take a few minutes, Brax. The swirling makes it harder for us to see what we're looking for here."

Braxton chuckled and shook his head. "I think I found it."

Rhad looked skeptical. "You don't even know what you're looking for. How could you have possibly found it?"

Amused, Braxton put his hands on his hips. "Oh, I don't know. Maybe because there's a portal about fifteen feet down this wall. If one of you would come look at it, you could tell me whether or not I'm right."

Alaria walked over to the edge and peered over the wall. She laughed and leaned over. "Beelzebub, you son of a bitch. I'd never have found it." She pointed. "Rhad, check this out."

Rhad joined them at the edge and looked down. "That's the portal, all right. Now the only question is where we're going to surface when we jump through." He glanced between Alaria and Braxton. "We should hold hands when we leap to make sure we all go to the same spot and time. That would be just like Beelzebub to have it pop open somewhere different each time someone goes through."

Braxton held out his hands. "Whoa, now. You're telling me we're just going to jump off the roof of this thing and into that without knowing what's going to happen? What's to say it isn't just an illusion and we're all going to go splat?"

Rhad pursed his lips. "Good point. May I see one of your water bottles?"

Braxton handed it over silently and watched as the Devil pitched it over the edge and into the portal. They all waited ten tense seconds and sighed in relief when nothing came out the other side and nothing hit the ground below.

"Well, then, I think that settles it." Alaria climbed onto the edge. "Let's get this over with." She held out her hands and waited until each man held one of them. "On three."

Braxton spoke first. "One." He tightened his grip. "Two." They all tensed in anticipation. "Three!"

With a leap, the three dove off the roof and into the swirling black of the portal out of Hades.

Aradia walked from one end of the room to the other, Michael's son nestled in her arms. She hummed softly, bouncing slightly to soothe the baby. The boy had arrived three days earlier, and Michael had barely let him out of his sight since. Aradia had finally convinced the Angel to let her take him for a few hours so he could get some rest.

Gage was sitting behind his desk, watching Aradia with the baby while he worked. He set aside his papers and leaned back in the chair. "You're a natural with him." He smiled and sipped from a snifter of whiskey. "You're going to be a great mother."

She looked over her shoulder, a soft smile on her face. "And you will be a great father. I have no doubt about that, even though I know you do."

He looked sad and averted his eyes. "I had my chance at fatherhood.

I lost any chance I had at being a good father the moment I rose as a vampire."

Aradia settled the infant in the bassinet under the window and walked to the desk, taking Gage's hand in both of hers and pressing it to her stomach. "This is your second chance. Our chance. I know it's hard for you, and I know you don't like to think about it, but I believe this is your chance to make up for what you did. You couldn't help it. You were a victim as much as they were. But this baby, this one we made, this is our chance for a family together. It's something we never thought we would get, and I intend to treasure every moment of it I can."

Gage smiled softly as he listened to the heartbeat of their child. "I love you, and I promise I will do whatever I can to be a good father." He looked up when Damon appeared at the door. "What's going on?"

Damon crossed his arms. "There's someone outside."

Gage concentrated. "I don't hear a heartbeat. Do you know who it is?"

"No. I was walking down to the kitchen to get Greer a glass of milk and crossed in front of the door. There's a man in a suit and tie standing at the end of the drive, just staring at the monastery."

Gage's eyes darkened. "That's impossible." He stalked out of the room he was using as an office and ran down the stairs. "Fuck. That's Beelzebub."

Panic dawned in Aradia's eyes. "If he's here, that means that Alaria and Braxton didn't get his wings."

Gage looked out the window in the hall. "Shit. We've got bigger problems than one Devil. There's a whole flood of vampires coming in." He pointed to the wood line. "See there, coming through the trees?"

Damon followed his gaze. "Fucking hell, there have to be fifty of them."

"At least." Gage looked around. "Okay, we can handle this." He took the baby from Aradia and handed him to Damon. "Get him to Greer and get her a sniper rifle. She can keep the baby in the tower and pick people off from up there. Aradia, go with him and ward the door to the tower to keep anything out while the rest of us go fight. You're going to have to take on Beelzebub. Damon and I will take off after the vamps and anything else they've brought with them."

Damon took the infant and cradled him against his body. "Sniping vampires isn't going to be easy. She has to hit the heart, which is a smaller target than the head."

"I know. Just make sure she has a wide assortment of ammo. We can see the vampires, but I can hear the Hell Hounds coming up. We're going to have those to deal with sooner rather than later, and I'd be willing to bet there are some demons hiding out here somewhere waiting for the right time, too." Gage looked up at the ceiling. "Michael! Michael, get down here now!"

Michael appeared in a flash of light. "What's wrong? Is it the child? I knew I shouldn't have left."

Gage shook his head. "The baby is fine. Greer has him. We're under attack. Beelzebub is outside, and an army is amassing to back him up. No clue why he's here, but it can't be anything good."

Michael's eyebrows drew together. "Alaria and Braxton went after Beelzebub in Hades. Are they back?"

"No, which is what I need you to do. We can hold it down here, though a couple Angels as backup would not be turned away. I have no idea where Alaria and Braxton are, and we need to figure it out. I know you can't go to Hades on a normal day, but it would be nice if you could figure out if they're even still alive." Gage strode into the room where they kept weapons and threw it open. "I'd ask Aradia, but she's going to be doing battle with Beelzebub. Problem with that being Alaria and Braxton have the knife we need to use to carve his wings out, so we could really use them back here about now."

Michael nodded. "Swear to me Greer will keep my son safe."

Gage looked at him levelly. "Greer would lay down her life for your son. Any of us would. He'll be as safe here as we can make him, and there isn't one of us who would hesitate to die, the same as you would for one of us." He studied his selection of weapons and chose a double-edged axe. "I really never learned to like guns. I prefer weapons that don't run out of ammo."

Michael smiled. "We have that in common. I'll see what I can find out about Alaria and Braxton. I'll ask Gabriel to come down here and help. I can't make any promises on his willingness to do so, but I will ask."

Gage hefted the weight of the axe and twirled it in his hand. Michael disappeared the same way he'd arrived, and Gage strode down the stairs toward the front gate. By the time he opened the door, Aradia was on one side of him and Damon on the other. Together, they left the safety of the monastery and its protections and headed into battle.

Beelzebub stood at the end of the driveway. He smiled widely when they came toward him. "I was hoping you'd all be here. I've come for Azazel and Lilith. Abalam and Abaddon, too, if you have them."

Gage lifted his shoulder in a careless shrug. "Abaddon is dead, and Abalam is still in Purgatory. I'll let you get them on your own. As for the others, I'll make you a deal. Give us the wings, and we'll cut them loose, free and clear."

Beelzebub pretended to consider the offer. "I don't think so, but thanks for asking. Be a good little vampire and scurry in there and cut them free before I'm forced to kill all of you."

Aradia stepped forward, her hair whipping around her face as she let her magic rise up within her. "Where are Alaria and Braxton?"

"I imagine they're still in Hades, fighting their way through Tartarus trying to get to me." Beelzebub grinned at Gage. "Did you really think I didn't know you had the contact? I opened Hades up and made you think that was where I was, all the while staying on Earth and planning this little party. If you won't hand over my brother and sister, I will rip your head off your shoulders and burn this building to the ground."

"Then you won't get them, will you, if you burn them to death?" Damon laid his hand on the handle of the short sword strapped to his waist. "Let's just get this show on the road. We're not turning them over and you're not going to give us the wings. That means we're going to have to see who is still standing at the end. We think it'll be us, you think it'll be you, and there's only one way to see." He raised his voice. "Bring it on, boys and girls."

Aradia closed her eyes for a moment, opening the door to the black magic she rarely channeled and funneling it through the prism of her citrine pendant. When she opened her eyes, they were black. She held out one hand and flicked her wrist, sending Beelzebub flying into a tree. The trunk cracked and shook at the force of the collision. Damon and Gage rushed to stave off the flood of vampires running through the yard, and Greer's first shots rang out through the night.

Beelzebub dusted himself off and lobbed a fireball at Aradia. She dodged it and sent back one of her own, nearly striking him in the chest. He moved at the last second, and the only damage done was to his suit.

"You're a strong witch, I'll give you that." He circled with Aradia, working up his own power.

The sky was turning red, which Aradia knew was nature's way of objecting to the amount of power being put on display. She tapped into her anger, using it to augment her own power. She was taking in more than she ever had before, knowing Beelzebub was at least as strong, if not stronger than Garrick had been.

"I'm going to rip those roots from your back, Devil." Aradia's voice was deep and gravelly as she worked her magic into a tidal wave.

"You'll have to get the knife from Hades before you can do that, and I doubt Alaria and Braxton ever find their way out of there. Even if they make it back through, Charon won't ferry anyone back across. Hades is going to become their Hell."

"We'll see about that."

The two clashed over and over again, their power colliding and neither giving ground. Aradia knew she couldn't last against him forever, while Beelzebub had an unlimited amount of Devil abilities. She could feel herself weakening and opened the door wider to the black, cringing when it was too much for her to filter and her white magic turned gray.

Blood trickled from her nose and eyes, and she stumbled when one of Beelzebub's fireballs caught her in the side. Her skin singed and bubbled, and she clutched one hand to the wound, using the other to dodge a second projectile.

Desperate, she sent out one stream of magic, forcing Beelzebub to use his own to match it. He wasn't a warlock, though he had access to black magic through his Devil powers. His stream was black, while Aradia's was red.

She chanted under her breath, doing everything she knew how to do to borrow a little more time, trying to give Gage and Damon time to fight off the vampires. She knew she wasn't going to be able to beat him. The black magic was taking its toll on her body. Blood dripped off her chin and onto the ground, and her mind clouded with pain from the wound in her side.

"Give it up, witch. I'm going to kill you. I'll rip your baby right out of your gut and eat it while I watch you die."

Aradia opened the door more, taking in as much black magic as she could hold and forcing it through her citrine. The stone cracked and a prism of magic formed, sending out streams from all around her. It was getting out of control.

Beelzebub cackled with glee as he watched what was happening. If she took more, she risked destroying herself. If she didn't, Beelzebub would win. The Devil began forming the streams of magic into a wall of flame. It rose up and spread out, shielding him from her and using her magic to feed it. Aradia was too far into the magic to stop it. She struggled to draw back and close the door, but found she couldn't.

Vaguely, from far away, she could hear Gage screaming her name, but it didn't quite penetrate the fog. She heard footsteps and Beelzebub laughing. Then Beelzebub used the wall of fire to engulf her. Aradia tensed and prepared to die.

It was a death that never happened. Instead, a hard body collided with hers, shielding her and driving her to the ground. The hold the magic had on her was jostled loose by the impact and her vision cleared.

Gage was on top of her, his back smoking from where the fire had singed him. His hair had been burned and the skin on one side of his face was scorched and blistered. She looked past him in shock to where Beelzebub lay on the ground, unconscious and similarly burned.

"What happened?"

Gage rolled onto his back. "He couldn't control it either. When he tried to use that fucking wall of fucking fire to kill you, it got him, too. I got to you just in time. Another ten seconds and you'd have been dead."

Aradia laughed. "I'd resigned myself to being dead. I was just trying to make sure he went with me." She stared at Gage and lifted her hand to the side of his face. "Gage."

He looked at her blankly. "What?"

"You came through fire. The prophecy."

Gage's eyes widened briefly. "Don't get your hopes up. We don't know this will do it." He climbed to his feet slowly. "We can hope, but don't convince yourself it's going to happen." He glanced back at Damon, who was limping toward them. "Let's get the bastard inside and let Greer fix us up. As soon as Michael gets back with the other two, we'll get the wings carved out and start making plans for how we intend to defeat Lucifer."

Alaria paddled dejectedly. "Gabriel, you rat bastard, get your fucking ass down here right this instant!"

Braxton, who was floating on his back, laughed. "Alaria, you've been screaming for him for the last hour. I think it's safe to say Gabriel doesn't think we're in enough danger to warrant him coming to our rescue."

Rhad stared up at the sky as he also floated. "I don't understand why you won't let me teleport us somewhere."

Alaria glared at him. "Because you haven't been on earth in ten thousand years and there's no telling where you'll take us to. We could end up in a volcano or in the Amazon River. Both of which are worse options than being here. At least here we're safe. You might drop us into a lion's den or something."

Braxton sighed. "Can't you describe to him where we need to go and see if he can get us there?"

"Again—volcano, alligator, lion. No." She flopped onto her back to float with the other two. "It would all be done and over with if Gabe would just come get us."

Rhad turned his head to look at Alaria. "You will get desperate enough you will let me try. You understand that, right?"

"That time is not yet here. Though if you want to zap out and see where you land and then come back for us, then by all means, go right ahead."

"I have no guarantees I could get back to you, and then you'd be in a worse state of affairs than you are now. At least you have my sparkling personality to keep you occupied while we wait for the sharks to come."

"The sharks aren't going to eat us." Alaria sighed deeply. "The odds of even running into a shark are astronomically small."

"As are the odds of my transporting us to a volcano, alligator, or lion. The odds are fairly good we will land somewhere on dry land."

Braxton closed his eyes. "Just let it go. She's made up her mind, and there's not a damn thing you can do to change it. She'll keep yelling, and eventually Gabriel will come down here and see what she wants. He can't help himself."

Michael appeared in a crack and hovered above the water, staring down at them drolly. "I've been searching for you two for hours, and I find you enjoying a swim? Really, Braxton, I expected better from you."

Braxton laughed and righted himself. "It's about damn time. We've been floating here for a few hours. The damn portal made us come out straight into the ocean. Alaria has been screeching for Gabriel ever since."

Michael scowled. "My brother does not believe the life of the child is in danger, therefore he is uninterested in the current goings on." He reached down and touched each of them. "Do you have the knife?"

Alaria patted her belt. "It's safe and sound. Don't worry."

"Good. You'll need it. Beelzebub showed up at the Choosing Place, and there was one hell of a fight, from what I understand. I, unfortunately enough, had to spend the skirmish searching the globe for your sorry asses." He snapped his fingers, and they found themselves standing outside the Choosing Place. Michael looked at Rhad appraisingly. "I can't let you continue on with us, and I'm sure you understand. Given that your help has been, from what Gabriel told me, invaluable, I can, however, guarantee you will have the chance to eke out whatever existence you wish for yourself. No one will pursue you, and as long as you do not join in the fight on the other side, you will be off limits to ours."

Rhad dipped his head. "No offense, but I wouldn't go with you even if you wanted me to. Helping down there was my only way out. I don't want to be involved in a war on either side. Been there, done that, have the t-shirt." He grinned. "I am going to get laid until my dick won't stand up anymore. Ten thousand years of forced celibacy is more than any man should have to endure." He winked at Alaria and Braxton.

"Loves, it's been a blast, but alas, I must say adieu."

With a blast of smoke and fire, Rhad disappeared. Alaria tugged at her wet clothes and scraped her hair back from her face. "Is it true you knocked Lilith up?"

Michael couldn't help but smile at the mention of his son. "It would seem Gabriel is not the only Angel who has fathered a child with a Devil."

"What's his name?"

"Deacon is what he has been called. I see no reason to change it. According to Gage, Lilith gave the child over to a human caretaker as soon as he was born, and the human named him. Her memory has been removed and all evidence of the child erased."

Braxton yanked open the door and slogged inside. "I don't know about the two of you, but I could use a shower and some dry clothes before we meet up with the others."

Michael held out his hand. "The knife, please. We'll take care of the removal of Beelzebub's wings and securing him while you bathe. Afterward, I will transport you all back to Gage's and then return here to stand guard over the Devils until we have a plan set for calling forth Lucifer."

Alaria looked over at Braxton. "I don't have any clothes here. They're all back at Gage's."

Michael sighed and reached out. "I'll send you both back. Try not to get in too much trouble until the others return."

Alaria opened her mouth to speak and found herself standing in the kitchen in Gage's manor. Shaking her head in disgust, she kicked off her soggy boots and hopped on each foot in turn to tug off her socks.

"I don't think a shower will ever have felt so good. Do you realize by real time it's been two weeks since we've showered?"

Braxton shuddered. "Two weeks since we've had sex." He wiggled his eyebrows at her. "We have to get naked to get clean. Might as well take advantage of the situation."

Alaria chortled and climbed the stairs, yanking her shirt over her head as she did. "Are you channeling Damon or something?"

"Damon has been known to have a good idea or two in his time." He followed her up the stairs and into the room they shared.

Together, they walked into the bathroom. Braxton turned on the water while Alaria fetched towels from the cabinet while Alaria stripped off her clothes and stepped into the hot spray. She turned her face up into it and moaned from the sheer pleasure that was hot water.

"I feel like this is the first time I'm experiencing a shower." She grinned and let it sluice over her body. "I never knew water could feel so fucking good."

Braxton stepped into the shower and reached up, adjusting the spray so it was hitting him too and picked up a bar of soap, rubbing it between his hands to create a thick lather. He reached out and ran it over her body, skimming over her shoulders and neck then down her sides and over her stomach. Working in ever increasing circles, he covered the expanse of her stomach and up to the lush curves of her breasts, skating the bar over the hardened points of her nipples.

Alaria sucked in a deep breath and closed her eyes, enjoying the feel of his hands on her body. He gently brushed her nipples with his fingers under the guise of washing her and slid the bar down her body, running his hand between her legs and sending a bolt of electricity through her entire body.

"Only you would want to come straight home and have sex instead of food or sleep."

Braxton leaned forward and nibbled her shoulder. "Oh, I want both food and sleep, but I want sex more. Once I have the one, I'll be able to concentrate on the other two." He massaged her breasts gently, lifting them in his hands and rubbing his thumbs across the sensitive tips. "Are you opposed to sex?"

She reached down and cupped his hardening length in her hand, rubbing gently and sliding her fingers up and down. "When have I ever been opposed to sex?" She ran one finger down his chest and smiled saucily. "Though sex in the shower is a little too acrobatic for my taste. Let's get clean and take this to the bed."

Hurriedly, they scrubbed their bodies and dried off. Braxton bent and lifted Alaria in his arms, carrying her swiftly to the bed. He put her on it and lay next to her, dipping his head to suck on one nipple while one of his hands nudged her legs apart.

She was warm and damp, and he flicked his fingers against her, trying to ready her for him. Her thighs fell open and her chest flushed with color. Enjoying the feel of his fingers and mouth on her, she tangled her fingers in his hair and held him to her.

Braxton slid one finger past the folds of her entrance and into her body, using the pad of his thumb to apply pressure to her clit while be penetrated her. She tightened and released around his finger rhythmically, her body pulsing from the pleasure he gave. Alaria's hand gripped his, guiding his movements and showing him precisely what she wanted. Taking her lead, he slid the digit in and out, using the heel of his hand to give friction.

She tugged sharply on his hair. "I don't want to come like this. I want you inside me when it happens."

Braxton released her nipple with a pop and looked up at her through heavy lidded eyes. "What makes you think you're only going to get off once?"

Alaria giggled and moved her hips against his hand. "Come on." She groaned when he flicked his finger against her clit. "This is just mean."

He slid down her body and buried his face between her thighs, licking her and slipping his tongue inside, taking in her flavor and moving his mouth to bring her pleasure. Alaria's legs came up and wrapped around his shoulders, holding his head to her. She tangled her fingers in his hair and tugged sharply, urging him to continue.

"Oh my God, that's good." She sighed in bliss at the bolts of pleasure rocketing through her. "A little more." She shifted her hips slightly and moaned. "Right there."

Braxton rolled his tongue slowly, sliding it into her over and over again, each time bringing her closer and closer to the edge. He read the signals her body gave off and adjusted his ministrations accordingly. When she was thrashing on the pillow and teetering on the verge of climax, he lifted his head.

Sliding up her body, he reverently held her hips in his hands and positioned himself between her legs, holding her thighs open and sliding heavily into her. Alaria, already on the edge, toppled off it when he entered her and she came, yelping from the force of the climax.

With a satisfied laugh, Braxton planted one hand on either side of her head and rocked his hips into hers, riding her through her climax until she was wet and hot around him. He glided out and back in again, enjoying the feel of her body enveloping him.

He captured her mouth in a deep kiss, stroking his tongue against hers at the same pace he stroked his dick into her body. Her thighs hugged his hips tightly, and she moved her hips to meet him thrust for thrust.

Slow and easy, he made love to her until they were both panting and desperate for orgasm. Alaria lifted her hands and rubbed her palms over her nipples, rolling them in her fingers and tugging gently to bring herself greater pleasure. Braxton's eyes darkened with heat as he watched her, and he balanced on one hand, using the other to cover hers, cupping her breast and kneading the soft, supple flesh in his hand. Close to climax, his cock twitched within her, and he fought back the orgasm viciously, determined to push her over the edge again before he took his own pleasure.

Alaria's eyes drifted closed, and her hand fell from her breast to fist in the sheet. Braxton shifted onto his knees and righted himself so he could stimulate both of her nipples while stroking into her over and over. He increased the pace of his thrusts until their skin slapped together and both of their bodies strained for release.

Bending to suck one of her nipples into his mouth, he gave her what she needed and sent her flying over the edge and into orgasm. With a ragged groan, he jerked his hips against hers and let himself go, emptying himself into her and sinking down on top of her with a low moan.

Her arms came up to hold him, and she cradled him gently against her. Alaria stroked her hands over the damp expanse of his back, and Braxton slowly rolled until they were facing one another, worried he would be too much weight for her to hold.

He reached up and ran one finger down the side of her face. "I think that gets better every time we do it."

She laughed and covered his hand with her own. "I'd only worry if it was getting worse. Better is good." She leaned over and pressed a kiss to his mouth. "Thank you."

Confused, Braxton lifted his eyebrow. "For what?"

"For not judging me just based on what I was. For choosing to be with me even though I'm a complete mess and for helping us finish this even though you had every right to tell us to go fuck ourselves."

He laughed and ran his hand over her hair. "I tried that once. You just kept cleaning the damn apartment anyway."

She smiled softly. "Regrets?"

Braxton shook his head. "Not a one. You?"

"None at all." Alaria rolled to the edge of the bed and stretched languidly. "I'm hungry."

"Me, too." He climbed to his feet and went to the dresser, donning sweats and a t-shirt. He tossed her a pair and watched as she tightened the strings to hold the pants on her hips. "You're starting to show a little."

Alaria looked down and ran a hand over the gentle slope of her belly. "It had to happen at some point. What are you going to think when it looks like I've got a beach ball strapped to my front?"

Braxton looked over his shoulder at her as he left the room. "I'll think you're just as beautiful as you are right now."

Alaria was making waffles and frying sausage links when the others came in through the front door. One side of Gage's face was pink and bore the mark of a healing scar. Aradia was pale and shaking and immediately sank into a chair at the table, laying her head on her arms. Damon and Greer looked better, and Greer was holding an infant with a diaper bag draped over one shoulder.

Braxton quirked an eyebrow as they came in and went to the fridge for more sausage and a carton of eggs. "I know we've been gone a while, but I didn't think it was long enough for you to have a baby."

Greer held out one hand, middle finger extended. "Bite me. This is Deacon, Michael's son. We've inherited him while his Daddy is Devil-sitting."

Alaria peered into the blanket. "Cute kid. Do we know if he's human?"

Gage shrugged and thrust a mug of blood into the microwave to heat. "He has a heartbeat and breathes, so as far as I can tell he is. Only time will tell, though."

Damon leaned over Alaria's shoulder and inhaled deeply. "That smells like heaven." He planted a smacking kiss on her cheek. "I'm glad you're still alive."

Alaria grinned and swatted Damon's bottom as he walked away. "You, too, even though you're like the annoying younger brother I never wanted."

Greer rolled her eyes and sat at the table. "Isn't he, though?" She reached out and patted her husband's arm. "It's a good thing you're great in the sack, or I'd trade you in for a more mature model."

Alaria laughed and smiled as everyone settled in around her talking, amazed that they were able to laugh and joke after all they'd been through. She looked from one face to another, watching the smiles and expressions and a warmth rose up in her. She felt a knot form deep in her gut and tears burned the back of her throat.

Braxton slipped his arms around her from behind and hugged her against him, leaning down to press his mouth to her ear. "What's wrong? You never cry."

She wiped her face and smiled at him. "Stupid pregnancy hormones. I was just looking around at all of them and thinking about how happy I am. For the first time in my whole existence, I feel like I'm part of something. All of you know who I am and what I did, and you're still here with me anyway. I feel like we've made ourselves a family here. Complete with stupid fights and babies and teasing. It's the most amazing thing I've ever experienced."

He pressed a kiss to her cheek and looked around the room. "It's all what you make it, babe. We've taken a horrible situation, and we've made ourselves a family. That's a miracle in and of itself."

CHAPTER TWENTY-NINE
SEPTEMBER 14, 2031 - SCOTLAND

ARADIA LOOKED up from scribbling when Michael walked into the library. She smiled and hurriedly cleared off a portion of the couch for him to sit. "I thought you were guarding the Devils."

Michael perched next to her. "Gabriel is giving me a break. I've been up with the baby for the past couple hours. He is very well taken care of, so thank you for that. Before I head back, I wanted to talk to you about hailing Lucifer and everything you need to know about it."

"Father Dooley sent a spell back with Alaria and Braxton. I've been working on tweaking it some to make it work better. It's a fine spell, but I think I can make it more powerful if I try hard enough."

"I think you're right about that, though you know more about spell casting, so I'll leave it up to you to decide. I know there is only a week left, and I wanted to check with you to see if there is anything you need before we try the ritual."

"Actually, I think we should move the Devils somewhere else. I'm afraid Lucifer might be able to draw from their powers to give him more, and that's the last thing we want or need. Worst case scenario, he couldn't and we move them for nothing, but I'd rather not take the risk. Is there somewhere else safe we could put them?"

Michael considered the problem for several moments. "I'll figure something out." He crossed one leg over the other. "I don't want you to worry. I'm not going to allow Gage to be cast out with the demons."

"I didn't want to pressure you since I wasn't sure whether or not you had any say in what happens to him. Gage is a good man. He might not even realize it sometimes, but he truly is. He deserves his humanity."

"If you succeed, I can give that to him. It is his gift for betraying his nature and following the path of God. He has spent centuries preparing for this and knowing he may eventually be asked to fight. We are not going to let him be sent to Hell where he would be tortured like no other has ever been. It will not happen. Even if you don't succeed, he has met half of the prophecy to earn his humanity. All he has to do is allow himself to love in a way no other vampire has ever loved, and his heart will begin beating. I want you to know there is still hope."

Aradia smiled sadly. "Even if there isn't, I would stay with him until I die. I would be an old woman and he would be a young man, but I would stay with him for as long as he would have me. I love him in a way I never thought was possible, and he is going to make a wonderful father to this child." She laid her hands on her stomach. "I made a choice to be with Gage, and I knew part of that choice likely meant no children. It was a sacrifice I made willingly for the opportunity to have him. Just getting to experience motherhood is a miracle in and of itself. Thank you for that. Thank you for letting us have this gift and for stepping in to protect Greer and me."

"It's my job to protect you. When you asked I take over for Gabriel, I took on all the responsibilities he had, which includes watching over all of you. I'm glad to be doing this for you all. I'm honored to fight alongside such brave people—human or not." Michael leaned back against the couch. "I wish I could tell you everything is going to be okay, but the truth is that I do not have that knowledge."

"I know. We all do." She closed the spell book and crossed her legs. "We're all terrified of what we have to do, but we're not going to back out on you. We knew when we agreed to do this there was no guarantee we would survive. We're all here with our eyes wide open. We know you're doing the best you can." She smiled and reached out to pat his knee. "I know we're human, and you're not, but I want you to know I really do consider you to be a friend. Truly I do, and I hope once all of this is over that you won't just disappear and never visit again."

Michael's face clouded with grief and strife. "I will never be allowed to go home. God will not let me back in. I have betrayed him. I'm lucky to still have my wings. I disobeyed a direct order and refused to submit to my Father. No, I imagine you'll see quite a lot of me. After all of you have passed, I will continue to look after your descendants." He stood and touched her shoulder gently. "I must return before Gabriel becomes too impatient. Thank you for talking with me."

Aradia smiled. "My pleasure." She glanced down at the books. "I think it's time to call it a night. Greer has had Deacon all day, and I suspect she's ready for a break."

Michael's expression softened at the mention of his son, and he smiled. "Call if you need me. I'm just a moment away."

Aradia waited until Michael disappeared before leaving the room. She passed through the den and dining room before entering the kitchen. Her face split into a grin when she found Alaria at the island, Deacon in a bouncy chair on the floor next to her, one of her feet bobbing on the edge to rock him.

"You're good at that."

Alaria looked up from her bowl of ice cream. "I've always been a good multitasker. Greer was tired and wanted to go to bed, so I offered to take over for a few hours. Braxton and Damon are watching some sports something or other on the television, and Gage is bent over his work like always. Something about stocks and a board meeting in between getting everything in order in case he doesn't survive. I swear the man thinks he has to update things every three weeks." She took a bite of ice cream and gestured to another chair with the spoon. "Grab a bowl and enjoy the indulgence. You're pregnant. Take advantage of it."

Aradia wrinkled her nose. "I never understood the concept of ice cream. It's flavored cream that's frozen. There's nothing special about it." She slid onto the stool and looked longingly at a bottle of wine on the counter. "Though merlot is another story entirely. I have missed wine since conceiving. In my time it was normal for a woman to consume wine while with child."

Alaria laughed. "That's because there wasn't anything else for you to have." She sighed and scraped the bottom of her bowl for the last bite. "Are you going to be ready for this?"

"I think so. I'm working on the spells now, and we're really just biding our time until the Solstice. I have a week to rest and to regain my strength after battling Beelzebub. I also have time to use herbs, candles, and symbols to help magnify my magic. Gage is getting me a new citrine to cleanse for my amplifier, so that will help, too. All in all I feel pretty good about where we are."

"What will you need from us?"

"I'm working on that. Writing spells is a hard thing, and I have to make sure it'll work. There will be a part for all of you, mainly because I think having you involved will strengthen the magic. There's magic in this circle we have, and I intend to use every bit of it I can."

"Good. You'll need to if we're going to have any chance at all to win this." Alaria took a drink from a bottle of water and slid off the stool to rinse her bowl. "What do you think you're going to do after this?"

"I don't know." Aradia's voice was small and her expression was sad. "Enjoy whatever time I have with Gage, I suppose. Raise my child the best I can and hope we win so he or she is born into a world worth living in instead of a world where she'll be nothing other than a soldier in a war we failed to win."

"This war has been going on as long as time has existed. The chance to end it forever is an incredible gift. If we lose, it will go back to how it has always been. A war that must always be fought and can never be won." Alaria looked down at the baby sleeping in the bouncy seat and smiled. "They'll fight admirably and carry their task as we have ours. This hasn't been all bad. We've had good moments and forged relationships that will last long beyond next week. Provided we survive, of course." She chuckled wryly. "We could always die, but the point is this: we never forgot to live. We didn't let this consume us. We dealt with it, and we fought as hard as we had to fight, but as long as people live, we are still fighting, and we are still winning. As long as we live, as long as we love, we have something that they never will."

"I just wish there was a way to know we'll be okay come next week. What we're trying to do is something that has never been done before." Aradia glanced down at the baby. "You can go on up to bed. I'll take him tonight. Gage doesn't need much sleep, and I haven't taken a night shift yet." She bent and gathered the infant in her arms, cradling him against her body and humming softly when he stirred. "Good night."

"Night." Alaria took the water bottle and headed for the stairs, smiling as she heard the sounds of the men watching television trickle to her from the living room.

She entered her room and flipped on the light, changing silently and brushing her hair until it shined in the harsh light from the ceiling fixture. Her heart missed a beat when she saw Braxton's stuff lying next to hers on the sink, and her chest tightened as emotion over took her. She laid a hand on her throat and cursed her pregnancy hormones for making her so emotional.

"I never thought I'd see the day a toothbrush made you tear up."

Alaria froze at the familiar voice and turned slowly, half-afraid to see what was behind her. Standing across the room, wearing a trim ivory suit and heels with her blonde hair floating around her shoulders in ringlets, was Griffin.

"You're dead."

Griffin sighed. "I know. I didn't think you of all people would need an explanation as to how I'm here. I still exist in Heaven, and apparently I get some added perks like being dragged out of my perfectly nice place and sent down here to deal with this crap I thought was put to bed."

Alaria lifted her eyebrows. "Why are you here? We're doing everything we can and everything we're supposed to."

"I'm supposed to come here and tell you to stop. God doesn't want this to continue. He thinks humans have made their choice and have chosen Hell. He believes they have taken affirmative steps toward Lucifer—and I mean, come on, it was humans who undid the Choosing, so He has a valid point—and they should be left to their own devices. Michael is an outcast. It's a minor miracle God hasn't taken his wings by now."

"You said you're supposed to tell me that. Does that mean there's something else you needed to tell me?"

Griffin sighed and looked around the room. "When I'm in Heaven, I have no sense of how long it's been since I've been here. How long has it been since I visited Brax?"

Alaria sat down on the edge of the bed. "About three months, give or take a few days."

"Have the two of you figured out your shit? Or do I need to have another chat with him about letting go of me?"

"We've basically got everything down."

Griffin looked pointedly at Alaria's stomach. "How is he handling that?"

"As well as he can. He's a good man. I'm the one holding back a bit on it. He tells me he'll be there for me and for the baby, and he'll do whatever I want him to do to make it easier for me, but it's so damn hard for me to let go and trust him to keep his word that I find myself fighting against it." Alaria ran her hand over her hair. "Though why in the hell I can tell you all of this when I have problems admitting it to myself is beyond me."

"It's because I'm dead. I can't tell anyone what you said and in ten minutes when I go back to Heaven, I'll forget all about the conversation until the next time they inevitably pull me out to be some sort of cosmic messenger. I think I must feel things like an Angel now, because I don't seem to have much in the way of emotions going on." Griffin pursed her lips and sat next to Alaria. "Do you want Braxton?"

"You're a little late to that party, sweetheart. I wanted him, I had him, and I intend to keep him."

Griffin laughed richly, her face lighting up with glee. "Oh, I'm so glad it's you. He needs someone to keep him on his toes and give him the fun I never could." She hugged Alaria tightly. "Thank you for taking care of him for me. I know your emotions are tied up in it too and you and Brax share something special, but if I had to pick one person I would want to stay with him after I died, you would have been it."

"Why the fuck would you want him with me? I was a screwed up evil mess."

"No, you were someone who risked her life going after what she wanted and who didn't back down even when the odds were against her. You're a fighter, and I knew if you decided you wanted Braxton you would fight for him. I'm glad it ended up that way." She leaned back until she was lying on the bed, staring up at the ceiling. "I'm not going to tell you to stop. I'll probably be in trouble when I get back, but I can't do it. I want you to make my death worth something. I want Lucifer to get what's coming to him, and I want for you and Braxton to be able to settle down after this and have little kids who will be way too fucking gorgeous for their own good." She ran her hands over her face. "I want you to go after those fuckers with everything you've got and make them pay for what they've done. To me, to Sam, to Allen and Miranda, everyone they've touched. Promise me you won't give up, no matter what."

Alaria flopped back to join Griffin. "You know I like a good fight." She sighed deeply. "It wouldn't matter if you had told us to stop. We aren't going to. We're going to try to finish this with everything we've got, and we won't stop until we're either dead or we've won."

Griffin smiled grimly and nodded. "Good. You're doing the right thing. I know it might not seem like it, but I promise you are. Even if

God doesn't see it." She sighed deeply. "Do you love him?"

Alaria closed her eyes. "I don't know." She groaned and tugged sharply at her hair. "I feel for him more intensely than I remember feeling. It's so different than with Gabe. With Gabriel, it was all consuming and intense, and it left me torn up inside when he left. With Brax, I feel comfortable and safe and warm, like I could stay there forever and be content to just be. Sorry if it upsets you, but the sex is fucking hot, and he's the best lover I've ever had. When I think about him with this baby, I get tingly, and I go blubbery seeing our stuff next to each other on the counter, so I don't know what I think or what I feel. I don't want to know what it's like to not be with him now that we're together. If that's love, then yeah, I feel it, but it's not like it was with Gabe."

"It shouldn't be. Braxton is a good, solid man who is there when it counts. He can be an absolute ass, and sometimes it's hard to make him see reason, but he has the best heart of anyone I've ever met, and he'll never leave you high and dry." Griffin sighed and climbed to her feet. "I can't stay any longer. I'm sure I'm going to get quite the lecture when I get back. Just remember what I told you. God wants you to stop. He isn't going to do anything to help you out here."

Alaria's eyebrows drew together, and she sat up slowly. "Are you trying to tell me God is going to let Lucifer out no matter what we do?"

Griffin shook her head. "No. I'm telling you He isn't going to do anything to help and that He believes you will fail. I want you to prove Him wrong."

"I'll do my best. We all will." She smiled when the other woman embraced her tightly. "I hope you're happy. You deserve to be."

"I am. I have been since the moment I died. Don't worry about me. I'm perfectly fine. No problems to report." She looked around as she started to fade. "That's my cue. Do me a favor and tell Braxton I'm proud of him and that I approve. And whatever you do, don't ever stop fighting. It's never hopeless. Even if you fail, the baby might not. Keep fighting."

Alaria smiled softly as Griffin faded. Alone in the room, her voice was a whisper. "I don't know how to do anything other than fight."

CHAPTER THIRTY
SEPTEMBER 20, 2031 - SCOTLAND

ALARIA HELD her breath and gripped one side of her jeans in either hand. She tugged on the unforgiving denim and tried to force the button into the hole. Frustrated, she flopped on the bed and attempted the maneuver again, struggling to make the clothes fasten. The button popped off the pants and flew across the room, landing with a click and rolling under the dresser.

With a ragged groan, she slammed her head against the mattress and closed her eyes tightly. She cringed when the door opened and Braxton entered the room.

"Are you okay? You've been getting ready for over an hour now." Braxton looked around the room and took in the piles of clothing on the floor. "Having a wardrobe crisis?"

Her face flaming, Alaria sat up. "Nothing fits! Stuff has been getting tighter for a few weeks, but I thought I still had some time before I would grow out of everything, but I guess I was wrong. I've grown out of most things in the last two weeks, and now my jeans—my last pair of jeans that fit—won't fasten." She threw herself back down on the bed. "They fit yesterday!"

Braxton bit down on his knuckle to keep from laughing. When he was sure he could speak normally, he cleared his throat. "Have you asked Aradia or Greer to lend you something?"

"No. Greer is smaller and shorter than I am, but I guess Aradia's stuff might fit. She's a little bit bigger than me, but not much."

Braxton stared at her. "It's not like you gained fifty pounds overnight. It's an inch or two." He opened the door and stuck his head out. "Aradia! Come up here a minute!"

Aradia climbed the steps quickly, coming down the hall within thirty seconds. "Is something wrong?"

"Alaria's pants don't fit."

Aradia bit her lip. "It's about time for that to happen." She stuck her head in the door and studied Alaria, who was even redder than she had been before. "It's okay, honey. We're all going to be there sooner rather than later. Let me get you something to wear. We're going to need to get you some maternity clothes soon."

Alaria grumbled deep in her throat. "I don't want to wear maternity clothes. I want to wear my jeans!"

Braxton leaned against the doorframe and grinned widely. "Well, hello there, hormones."

He barely had time to duck out of the room before the boot that was aimed for his head struck the doorframe directly where he had been standing. Aradia glared at him as she returned from Gage's quarters with several pairs of jeans stacked in her arms.

"Here we go. Problem solved. These are a size bigger than yours, I think, so it'll give you some extra room." Aradia looked fondly at Alaria's protruding belly. "That's one of our babies needing more room. It's a beautiful thing watching a woman grow a child."

Alaria scoffed as she wriggled into the jeans, which were still—to her consternation—snug. She fastened the garment and bent to tug on her boots, scooping her hair into a ponytail before she did so.

"Okay, I'm ready." She looked at Aradia. "Are you ready for this? It's just a few hours until midnight."

Aradia nodded. "Midnight is the most powerful hour of the Solstice because the power is the most concentrated. If I start at the stroke of midnight, I'll get the most power from nature and I should be able to use the residual power of the Choosing since Griffin did the ritual at midnight as well. Any little bit of power I can suck in is going to help." She followed Alaria down the stairs. "I'm ready for this. I promise. We're going to be fine."

Michael was waiting for them in the foyer, his wings folded against his body and his jacket tossed carelessly over the post, leaving him clad in a long-sleeved shirt and slacks. "Good, you're ready. I've moved the Devils to another secure location." He smiled grimly and surveyed the faces. "I thought Purgatory was a nice place for them. It puts them out of reach of Lucifer, and they'll be in there months figuring out how to escape, which will—if everything goes as planned—be well after all demons are securely back in Hell."

Gage carried in a box of supplies and placed it on the floor. "I think we have everything we need. Is the Choosing Place done?"

Aradia glared at him. "I've told you a dozen times that I finished with the amplification symbols last week. Either you're finally going senile, or you don't trust me to do this."

"I trust you, but I can't help but make sure we have everything we need to give us the best possible chance at coming through this alive." He glanced around worriedly. "We need to get going. It'll take a while to get set up."

Damon hefted the box and glanced up at Michael. "Do you have the cup?"

Michael held out his hand, and a small bronze goblet appeared in his palm. "I got it from Heaven once we knew we would need it and have been storing it along with the wing roots." He reached out and touched each of the six on the forehead. "Let's get this done."

Aradia worked diligently to prepare the room. Michael had cleared out all of the pews, giving her the room she needed to arrange it in a way most conducive to her magic. The floors, ceiling and walls were completely covered in symbols—some to trap Devils, others to keep them out, still others to ward away Angels, and some to amplify Aradia's power.

Clove and ambergris burned, perfuming the air. On the floor were six clusters of thirteen candles, forming a circle around the stain where Griffin had died. Aradia drew a circle of lead powder with a slightly larger ring of salt outside it. Inside, she placed three chunks of citrine in a triangle formation. Carefully, she placed a matching stone at each group of candles, setting it in the center.

Greer watched with curiosity. "Why do you do all of that?"

Aradia looked up. "Witchcraft is all about nature and finding the power in things. There are herbs that amplify certain things and formations of candles and stones that do the same thing. A lot of being a good witch is in knowing which materials you need to use. The clove and ambergris will strengthen our anger and wrath, making the spells stronger. The lead powder and salt will help contain Lucifer. The candles are placed equilaterally around the circle in six groupings of thirteen because those are important numbers in witchcraft. I don't normally use this stuff, but I figured in this situation anything we can use to our advantage, no matter how small, is good. The citrine will help me increase the black magic I can use by cleansing it, and the candles around it will protect it from being manipulated by Lucifer. The simple fact is we don't know how much power he has, so I am doing every single thing I know to do to help hold him."

Michael entered the room carrying a box. "Here are the wing roots. Once we start the spell, there is no going back, only forward. Once Lucifer is here, I will cut the roots out as soon as Aradia has him bound with the witch rope. We'll only have a few seconds before he's out of that, so I'm going to work fast. As soon as they're out, we have to start the spell to cast out the demons and rechain Lucifer. That makes three very intense spells. Are you sure you can do it?"

Aradia smiled. "That's the beauty about what I've done. The spell to hail him is what I need the others' help to do. I'm going to use their strength and add it to my own. I've got it handled. Don't worry."

He looked at her drolly. "The fate of the world is in our hands. I cannot help but worry." He flicked his wings in annoyance. "There are ninety minutes left until we must begin the ceremony. What is left to do?"

Aradia looked around. "Not much. The circle is set. I'll need you to be inside it before I start the ceremony or you won't be able to get in once I have. I will need everyone to be absolutely silent while I work and listen to me absolutely. If I tell you to move, you must listen immediately and leave the circle. If he starts to get loose, I can try to send him back to Hell and buy us some time, but I can't do that if you're near him."

Michael nodded. "I will do as told." He crossed his arms. "It is my understanding that we will have one hour from the time you begin until the end of the spells to take advantage of the most powerful period of time, is that correct?"

"Yes. I'll keep going, obviously, if I'm not done by one, but the power won't be as strong. I'm just trying to take advantage of every little thing I can."

Braxton strode into the room. "As well you should." He turned to address Michael. "Let's discuss weapons. What will work on Lucifer?"

"Nothing you have." Michael chuckled wryly. "There is no human weapon powerful enough to hurt him. Your bullets would bounce. Your blades would not pierce his skin. There is nothing I know of that can kill him. Believe me, if it existed, I would have tried to use it on him already. The knife used by Griffin can hurt him, but it cannot kill him. There is rumor that not even God can actually kill him or he would have by now. From my understanding, the only thing powerful enough to kill Lucifer is going to be the child you carry, Alaria. A cross of human, Devil, and Angel. Let's just hope we're successful tonight and we never have to find out if that part of the myth is true."

Alaria sighed deeply as she strode into the room and stood next to Braxton. "Wonderful part of the conversation to come in for." She put one hand on her hip. "Are we ready to go?"

Aradia ran her hands through her hair. "We've got about an hour before we start."

Braxton withdrew his gun from his waistband and checked the clip. "I'm going to do one last sweep of the premises before we get this underway. I want to be absolutely sure we're not going to be interrupted."

Michael laughed. "With all of the Devils in Purgatory and no one up here calling the shots, I think it's a safe bet there isn't a demon alive brave enough to come in here—or try to—and get in our way. They're likely all in their hidey holes holding their breath and praying to Lucifer that we fail."

"Regardless, it'll give me something to do other than sit here and talk about all the ways this can go wrong."

Alaria chuckled. "I think it sounds like a good idea. I'll go with you."

Together, they left the room and headed down the hallway. Alaria slowed when she passed what had been their war room in the days leading up to the Choosing and nudged the door open with her foot. A thick layer of dust covered everything. Nothing had been touched since they had painted it with traps. She made a humming noise in the back of her throat as her eyes drifted over the books and pieces of paper with battle strategies on them.

Braxton reached out and took her hand. "Brings back memories, doesn't it?"

"This whole place is one big memory." She squeezed his fingers.

"There isn't anywhere I can look in here that doesn't remind me of what happened. I know it has to be the same for you."

"It is, but it's better now than it used to be. Before, all I felt was pain when I thought about Griffin. Now at least I feel peace knowing she's okay. The couple visits she's paid us have helped."

"It freaked me out when she showed up the other night." She began walking again. "That room is where I banged Gabe for the first time."

Braxton made a face. "They really did screw up the filter installation when they made you human. Why would you tell me that?"

Alaria looked at him innocently. "It's not like you don't know that I had sex with him. Why does it shock you to know where?"

"I don't want the details. I don't give you the details of when I had sex with other women. There are just some things couples don't talk about."

She scoffed. "You're going to have to get over that. There's not much off limits with me." She smiled saccharinely. "Just don't ever ask me to share. I've never been into orgies, and I don't relish the idea of open relationships since I want to keep you all to myself, but other than that..." she trailed off as Braxton closed his eyes, seemingly in pain. "What?"

"You are too much,." He tucked her under his arm and led her down to the front door. "Sometimes I don't know what to do with you."

"Get us through this, and I'll let you do whatever you want to me." She grinned up at him. "For some reason, I'm a bit amped up by this. I think I'm starting to actually believe we might win this. We're so close now and there's just this one last thing, and when I look back at all we've done and then I think about what is still left to do, I really think we might just do it. Just the fact we're all still alive is a fucking miracle."

Braxton's eyes clouded with sadness. "We're not still all alive. A lot of people have made sacrifices for this to happen. Finn, Sam, my parents, Lex, Calder, Father Dooley, Griffin, her grandparents. There's a lot of blood covering this up. We're not home free even though the six of us have made it through."

"I didn't mean it that way." Her voice was soft and apologetic. She tightened her fingers on his. "I meant the six of us."

"I know. I'm sorry." He smiled with false brightness and held open the door for her. "What's the first thing you want to do when we get through this? Tan in Mexico for a month? Skinny dip in the Mediterranean? Name it and we'll go do it."

Alaria leaned her head on his shoulder as they walked, enjoying the warm night and the bright moon. "I don't think I should skinny dip when I'm huge, so if we're going to do that, it needs to be soon."

"We'll leave tomorrow. I'll use Finn's private jet to come get us. A getaway for two."

She laughed. "Let's get through tonight before we make plans."

Braxton shook his head. "No. We have to have plans. Even if we fail, we still have to go on living, provided, of course, we're still breathing. No matter what, we still have lives. We're going to have children to raise. We're going to have to live, regardless of whether we win or lose."

"If we lose, we're going to be fighting. It's going to be nothing but fighting. There won't be time for vacations or fun."

"Yes, there will be. Even when Griffin was in her last few months, we managed to go do some things she wanted. We saw the world together. It's the only way she made it through, and it'll be the only way we do if we lose tonight." He pressed a kiss to the top of her head. "Greer and Damon got married in the middle of all of this. It was the right thing to do, and it gave us all something to celebrate. New life is something to celebrate. We have to hold on to those things."

Alaria turned her face into his chest and inhaled deeply. "Okay." She shook her head and stared up at the sky. "Next thing is you're going to be asking me to marry you once this is all done and over with."

Braxton drew to a stop and looked down at her. "Is that something you want? We've never talked about it."

"And now is not the time, but no, I don't think that's something I want. I'm happy with the way we are, and I don't want to change it. We're not like the others. We're together because it makes sense, because we like each other and because we're friends. There's no need for big white dresses and wedding bands with the two of us. I trust you to tell me the truth when you tell me you're committed, and I know I'm telling you the truth. I don't need any piece of paper to prove that. There's nothing wrong with us." She nestled her head against his shoulder again, and they continued to walk. "I still don't think I love you."

"Me either." He tightened his grip on her slightly. "But I don't want to let you go. I care for you more than I ever thought I could care for anyone after Griffin."

"I'm not asking you to." She sighed. "We should head in. It's thirty minutes to go time and we need to be there with the others." She rose onto her tiptoes to press a light kiss to his mouth. "I'll make you a deal. I promise if I ever want to get married, I will tell you, and you promise to tell me if you want to, but unless that ever happens, we won't stress over it and we won't talk about it. I'm happy with how we are, and I see no reason to fuck with something that's working."

Braxton laughed and led her back into the house. "Deal." He freed her so they could walk up the stairs to the main floor. "You ready for this?"

"As ready as I'm going to get. There's no time to rethink it or change our minds now. Everything's ready, and for better or worse, tonight is the night we find out the fate of the whole world."

They entered the chapel together and went to the front where the others were standing. Damon quirked his eyebrows at them and grinned.

"Any threats to report?"

Braxton shook his head. "All appears quiet, at least for the moment. It's twenty minutes and counting. Do we need to start getting ready?"

Aradia nodded. "Yeah. It's time to start." She nodded to the circle. "Everyone get in their places."

Chapter Thirty-One

Aradia stood directly behind the candles at her station. "Every number has meaning. There are six groups because there are six of us, but also because six is a very powerful number. It stands for harmony and balance. It increases luck. It is the combination of male and female. There are thirteen candles to represent upheaval and breaking new ground. It is a very important Karmic number. By placing the two together, we are using our balance and love toward one another to increase the power of upheaval which will help us do what we need to do."

She pulled a slim blade from its sheath and held it up. Slowly, she dug the point into her palm, dragging the edge across her skin and slicing deeply. Wincing against the pain, she clenched her hand until the blood ran down her arm. Deliberately, she reached out toward Gage, who stood to her right and drew a line of blood between them.

"Blood is power. It contains life force. There is no more powerful substance than blood. By using our blood to form this circle, we bind our life force together so I can use the strength of six instead of one. Together, we live or die—succeed or fail. Each of you needs to cut your right palm and use your blood to connect you to the one to your right."

Aradia waited patiently while the five followed her directions. Gage to Damon. Damon to Greer. Greer to Alaria. Alaria to Braxton. Braxton to Aradia. When Braxton handed her the knife, she placed it between her feet and straightened.

"The first part of this is bringing Lucifer from Hell. Once he's out, we have to work fast. Whatever you do, do not break the circle. If the circle breaks, it will lessen my power and give him a better chance of escaping." She laughed nervously. "The only exception is if I yell at you to run. Then you run."

Aradia tipped her head back and held her hands out to her side, letting her power whip up inside her. She closed her eyes and focused on condensing all of the energy into one controllable beam. The energy from the other five was bright and hard to control, but it was malleable. Within moments, she braided them together and pushed them through the citrines in the candle groupings, forming yet another circle.

She lowered her head and opened her eyes, which were pitch black. When she spoke, her voice was deeper and stronger than normal.

"The time has come, the hour has struck. Tonight we fight, we test our luck. Power rise, magic flow. God on high, Lucifer below.

"Chains of God, doors of stone. Free Lucifer from his hell-fire home. Circle round, power strong. Hold him here, do no wrong. Power of mine, power of they. Hear my plea, do as I say. I call upon the Witching Hour, heed my magic, fear my power!

"Open the gates, unlock the door. Chained to Hell, he is no more. Conveyed to this circle, blood of my kin, Lucifer shall rise, covered in sin. Chains shall form, holding him tight. Mask his power, take his sight. Anchor him to this holy place. Heed my words, by God's Grace.

"Power of magic, power of word. Obey me now, let me be heard! Crack open the gates, unlock the chain. This is the end of Lucifer's reign! Hear my words, obey my plea. As I command it, so shall it be!"

An earthquake shook the building, making it hard for them to remain standing. Aradia sent a stream of magic into the lead and salt circles, and the bricks fell away, revealing a door. She repeated the incantation, continuing to blast the hatch with power. Michael stood ready with the dagger clutched in one hand and the Holy Grail in the other.

Rain and hail hit the windows as nature rebelled against the magic. The flames on the candles leaped up until there was a ring of fire extending to the ceiling. Doors opened and slammed shut; and the lights flickered and went out.

Inch by excruciating inch, the hatch peeled open. Black fire rose out of it, and a silvery smoke poured from the hole. There was a shuddering creak and a loud crack as it banged shut, and the smoke formed into a man.

He wore a white suit and had white blond hair slicked back from his handsome face. His jaw was smooth, and his eyes were bright blue. He wore a red belt and black shoes and stroked his hands down his sleeves lovingly as he surveyed the seven people in the room.

"Well, I never dreamed you'd actually get this far." He looked between them as the flames from the candles went back to normal height and addressed them each in turn. "Damon. Greer. Alaria. Braxton. Aradia. Gage. Nice to see you." He smiled brightly at Michael. "Hello, brother. I haven't seen you since you impermissibly trespassed on my property."

Michael sneered and rolled up his sleeves. "I am not your brother." He glanced to Aradia. "The witch rope, please."

Lucifer cocked one eyebrow at Michael. "Witch rope won't hold me. You know that." He looked at the circles surrounding him and the traps. "Nice job on the digs, though. This is some powerful mojo you've all got going on." He clapped his hands three times. "Aradia, my love, you are the most powerful human I have ever had the pleasure to lay eyes on. I'm so going to enjoy forcing you to work for me once I've shaken off these pesky chains."

Aradia flicked her wrist and bound Lucifer with the witch rope. Michael used the knife to slice away the suit jacket and shirt and ruthlessly carved into the alabaster skin on Lucifer's back.

Lucifer did not scream. He did not whimper. He stood stoically while Michael carved the roots of his wings from him. Unlike the silvery color of all the others, Lucifer's were pitch black. Michael held the cup and collected several drops of blood in the bottom.

"Should I come out of the circle now?"

Aradia nodded. "Yes. Come out of the salt, but do not cross over the candles. Make sure not to break the line. You're going to need to mix your blood in there and then stir it with the dagger you just used. Once you've done that, hand it to me."

Michael followed her directions quickly and handed over the cup. Aradia stared into the blood and began to chant, her voice filling up the room and echoing off the walls.

"Blood of Heaven, blood of Hell, blood of the pure. Come together in the cup of Christ. By the blood of Heaven, I bind thee. By the blood of the Chosen, I chain thee. By the blood of Hell, I command thee.

"Chains form, locks turn. Bind Lucifer tight, always to burn. Fate of sin, you've earned your fate. Eternally locked behind the gate. Blood boil, blood burn, form the chains and locks to turn.

"Rise up, blood of Michael and anchor Lucifer to Hell. Rise up, blood of Griffin and chain Lucifer to the Lake of Fire. Rise up, blood of Lucifer and do as I command.

"We the six have met the tasks. The purge has ceased, the doors are closed, the roots have been taken." She reached out and lifted her hand, causing the roots to lift from the box. They spun in a slow circle and then slammed together, melding into a pewter cord. "The price has been paid with blood and life, and I stand here tonight to command the power of God. By God we were born, through His Grace we have fought, and tonight we succeed! Lives laid down with dignity and grace. Blood poured out across time and space. Wars fought, battles won, lives lost. We have paid the price. We've met the cost.

"By the power of God, I command you to Hell, never to rise again. I command you to iniquity. Be gone, Satan, and languish in Hell for all time!"

The flames leaped again, spinning a web of red and black fire until it surrounded them, from floor to ceiling. Lucifer thrust his arms out and sent the witch rope flying. He laughed, the sound getting louder and louder until it blasted through the room at a painful volume.

"Nice try, witch. You're very talented." He bent down and drew his finger through the lines, breaking both of them. "I'll admit that I was curious to see if you could do it. That's some crafty spellwork you've done, but it's not strong enough. See, in order for you to succeed, your task had to be blessed by God. You lost that blessing when God declared this to be a lost cause. Because He said it, it became. That's the pathetic thing. If He'd continued to believe in you, you'd have won."

Aradia let power flow out of her hands, streaming into him and driving him back. "Don't break the circle! Whatever you do, don't break it!" She looked at Michael with panic. "I don't know how long I can hold him! Get whatever Angels you can! Get someone!"

Michael disappeared in a crack, his determination to win the war outweighing his concern for the six people he left. Aradia reached deep within herself and opened the door to the black, letting it in unchecked. She forced it through the citrines around the circle, forming a black wall of magic that rose up and engulfed Lucifer.

Blood bubbled out of her eyes, nose, mouth and ears. Aradia screamed as she felt it overtake her. Her eyes turned red, and she threw her arms out in a panic, sending the magic hurtling toward Lucifer. Knowing their task was lost, Aradia poured everything she had into containing Lucifer, not caring whether she lived or died.

It swarmed him, wrapping him in its fingers and attempting to strangle him. She chanted rapidly, trying to open the hatch to put him back in Hell. For a moment, she thought she'd won. Lucifer screamed, the sound strangled by the magic.

But then, he sucked in the magic, taking it from her and using it. He waved his hand and the magic dissipated. With a jerk of his head, the candles and citrine hit the walls, splattering into shards of crystal and puddles of melted wax.

Lucifer clenched his hands and struck out as if to punch, sending out a wave of power so strong that it sent all six flying. He slammed them against the wall, knocking them out. Chuckling, he stepped over the line of blood and out of the circles, shivering when he felt the tingle caused by breaking the barrier of the trap.

"Nice try, ladies and gents." He tipped his head back and extended both middle fingers toward the ceiling. "In case you missed the lesson in slang, Daddy dearest, that's a great big fuck you!" He rolled his shoulders and strode across the room. "I wonder what Earth looks like in the twenty-first century."

With a careless glance back at the six unconscious humans, he tucked his hands in his pockets and left the sanctuary, the sound of his humming echoing through the otherwise silent monastery.

Michael reappeared in the sanctuary with a half dozen Angels, all heavily armed. Smoke still lingered in the air. Blood smeared the walls and piles of debris littered the room. A feeling of horror rose in his throat as he looked at the six unconscious people. Aradia lay crumpled nearest him, blood dried on her face, her pulse weak and thready.

He looked at the Angels, who stood shocked and horrified. "Go! Return to Heaven and inform the Host that Lucifer is free! Ready yourselves for war! Now!"

The Angels disappeared in a flurry of wings. Michael rushed to Greer, dropping to his knees and pressing his fingers to her throat. Her pulse beat strongly beneath them. She stirred when he touched her, rolling and coughing. She blinked rapidly and stared up into Michael's face.

"What happened? Did we do it?" She looked around. "Where's everyone else?"

Michael helped her to her feet. "Aradia needs your help. She's been badly drained by the spell she wove. Heal her while I wake the others."

Greer rushed to the witch, pressing her hands to Aradia's chest and healing the damage done by the black magic. Michael worked his way around the room, waking Alaria first and then the three men one by one. When they were all sitting up and rubbing their heads, he cast a look at each of them in turn.

"Lucifer is loose. We've failed."

Aradia's eyes filled with tears, and she covered her face in shame. "I thought I could do it. I really believed I was powerful enough." She sobbed into her hands raggedly.

Gage wrapped his arms around her and pulled her head into his chest. "It's not your fault, baby. You did everything you could." He looked up at Michael, his eyes burning with anger. "She nearly died working on a lost cause! Did you know this would happen?"

Michael shook his head morosely. "I had no idea until Lucifer told us. If I had, I would never have asked you to risk your lives." He sighed deeply, his own eyes shining with sadness. "Gage is right. We knew we were taking a risk, and we knew there was a substantial risk we would not survive." He looked around the room solemnly. "You all fought bravely. You risked your lives, and you fought with everything you had. Each one of you did everything asked and more."

Braxton ran his hands through his hair and leaned against the wall, the hard set of his jaw and clenched fists belying his fury. "What the fuck do we do now?"

Alaria brushed tears from her cheeks, then laid her hands on her stomach. "We wait." She looked to Greer and then Aradia, her voice whisper-soft and filled with sadness when she spoke. "It's not our fight anymore. We failed, so our children have to pick up the fight. We go on, we have them, we raise them, and they fight."

Michael lifted his eyebrows. "There is much less screaming than I anticipated."

Alaria lifted her shoulders. "What point is there in yelling? Instead of fixing the world, we let Lucifer out of Hell all because God gave up on us. He let this happen, not us. We were doomed before we ever started." She shook her head grimly. "There's nothing to scream about. We were fighting a lost battle and didn't even know it."

Damon groaned as he climbed to his feet. "We can still fight. We'll try to stop him. There has to be a way to do it." He spread his arms and regarded the other six in the room. "Come on, guys! We can't just give up! We've had setbacks before. We'll figure out another way." He trailed off when no one else jumped up, the last part of his statement sounding more like a question. "There has to be a way."

Aradia rubbed at the smears of dried blood on her face. "There is. Alaria's baby." She glanced around nervously. "I think we should leave this place. It's not safe anymore. We need to get out of here and find a way to keep Lucifer out."

Alaria reached out and laid her hand on Michael's arm. "Take us home. We're going to have to watch the world burn."

"Push, Alaria." Aradia stood between Alaria's legs, her hair tied back in a ponytail and a smile on her face. "I can see the baby's head. A few more pushes and she'll be here."

Alaria leaned forward on the bed, straining to birth the child trying to force its way out of her body. Braxton stood at her side, holding her hand. He brushed damp hair away from her face and rubbed her back with his free hand.

"You can do it." He leaned over and pressed a kiss to her forehead. "We're so close, baby."

Alaria glared at him. "We are not so close. I am." She groaned as another contraction ripped through her body, and she bore down, pushing with all her strength and gritting her teeth as she strained to give new life.

She felt an intense pressure and then a release. The baby slipped from her body and into Aradia's hands. Aradia quickly clamped and cut the cord, placing the baby on Alaria's chest. Sobbing, overwhelmed, and not sure what to do, Alaria hesitantly reached out and patted the baby's back.

Almost immediately, the baby began crying—a loud, lusty cry that filled the room. Alaria fell back against the pillows and looked at Aradia helplessly.

"What the hell do I do now that it's out?"

Aradia laughed. "You didn't tear, so there's nothing for Greer to heal. You should nurse her. Your contractions will continue until the placenta is delivered, but that shouldn't be long, and there's no reason to wait on feeding the baby."

"But she's gross!"

Giggling, Aradia lifted the child and carried her to a bowl of warm water, using a cloth to wash the remnants of birth from her skin and hair, patting her dry with a towel before laying her back on Alaria's chest, arranging the infant's head near her mother's breast.

"Okay, she's clean. Now you should nurse."

"How do I do that?" Alaria's eyes widened in shock when the baby immediately latched on and began suckling. She sucked in a gulp of air and closed her eyes. "Jesus fucking Christ that feels weird."

Braxton reached down and stroked his hand over the baby's hair. "She's beautiful, Alaria." He ran one finger down the baby's silky soft cheek. "Absolutely gorgeous." He smiled at Alaria gently and brought her hand to his lips to kiss her knuckles. "Just like her mommy."

Aradia quickly cleaned up the remnants of birth and disposed of them. "I'm going to step out and call the others to let them know the baby is here." She looked at the infant, reaching out with her magic to weigh and measure her. "Six pounds, twelve ounce and nineteen inches long. Do you have a name picked out for her?"

Alaria nodded. "I do. I'm going to name her Amaya. Amaya Samantha Winslow." She looked up at Braxton, a thick sheen of tears in her eyes. "If we're going to do it, we do it all together. Okay?"

Overwhelmed and choked up, Braxton swallowed and nodded, pulling Alaria closer. "Together."

Aradia ran her hands over the mound of her stomach. "I wish we could all be together." She looked out the window at the dark sky. "I have to go soon. We can't be in the same place for very long without drawing attention. I'll be attending Greer's delivery if I can—provided I'm not laboring at the same time—but that will likely be the last time we see each other for years, if not decades." She brushed tears from her eyes. "I've missed you both so much these past few months. I hate needing to be apart, but we're in much more danger together than we are apart. This way makes it easier for us to hide from all the demons and Devils. The most important thing is keeping these babies hidden and safe. They're our only chance." Still teary, she gazed longingly at her friends. "Even so, I do miss you so much."

Braxton slipped away from Alaria and hugged Aradia tightly. "I know. We do, too, but with the way things are going, you're right. It's safest for us to stay far apart and concentrate on keeping these babies safe. They're our biggest concern now, and we still stay in contact via Michael and the mental links you helped us forge." He squeezed the witch's shoulders. "How is Gage handling being human?"

Aradia smiled at the mention of Gage before answering. "He hates that it happened. After we failed to re-chain Lucifer, he was praying he wouldn't ever turn human, at least not until the children come into their abilities and can protect themselves. He wanted humanity, but the lack of immortality when we don't know whether or not these children will be mortal or not concerns him. It does me, too. If they're immortal it could be centuries before they kill Lucifer. Even if they're not, it could be fifty years, and by then, we'll all either be dead or too old to help." She looked down at her belly, stroking her hands over the rounded bulge gently. "Who would have thought that an ultrasound would be enough to trigger the prophecy? He'd already fulfilled the fire part, so it was the love like no vampire has ever before experienced."

"No vampire has ever had a child." Braxton bent and kissed Aradia's cheeks, a subtle cue that their time was drawing to an end. "I know you need to go. We'll check in next week as planned, and you'll make sure to let us know when your child arrives."

Aradia smiled sadly. "I wish I could stay. She's so beautiful, and I'd love the chance to get to know her."

Alaria looked up from staring at her daughter. "One day you will. One day they're going to finish what we started. When they're old enough to understand, we'll bring them together. Someday, they're going to save the whole damn world."

Sirena N. Robinson is an author who lives and works in the foothills of the Appalachian Mountains. When she is not helping her characters defeat unspeakable evil, she spends her days working as a drug and alcohol counselor and as a court-appointed attorney in the local Juvenile Court. A firm believer in wearing many hats, she spends many weekend traveling the country with her husband, daughter and Bengal cats attending cat shows. On off weekends, she can be found with the rest of her family at a hunt-test or field trial helping shuttle dogs or holding down the fort at home, caring for the menagerie of dogs and cats living in her house.

Sirena writes in several genres, focusing primarily on novels with paranormal or supernatural elements. She has several other novels in various stages of planning, including a futuristic crime series. She writes both because she loves it and because she has no choice and is a self-proclaimed slave to her characters. She considers herself incredibly lucky to be the one chosen to tell their incredible stories. Keep in touch with Sirena via her blog at sirenanrobinson.blogspot.com or through her publisher Supposed Crimes, at supposedcrimes.com.